A Soldier's Desire

She lifted her fist to swing at him and he caught her hand in his. At that moment the moon came out from behind the clouds, flooding the cliff top—and the woman's face—with clear, silvery light.

Gabriel had had the breath knocked out of him a dozen times. Each time he'd thought he was dying.

He'd been kicked in the head by a horse once. It had scrambled his wits for a while.

And a couple of times in his life he'd been so drunk that he'd lost all sense of time and place.

Seeing her face in the moonlight was like all of those rolled into one. And more. Gabe's breathing stopped. He forgot how to speak. He was unable to think. He could only stare. And stare. And stare.

She had the sweetest face he'd ever seen, round and sweet and sad and somehow . . . right, framed by a cloud of dark, wavy hair. An angel come to earth. With the most kissable mouth in the world.

She gazed back at him. Her eyes were beautiful, he thought, eyes a man could happily drown in. He wondered what color they were.

"Release me this instant!" the angel snapped, and Gabriel's breath came back in a great whoosh of air. The angel was very, very human. And very, very frightened.

Praise for Anne Gracie

"Enchanting . . . Pure magic turning every page. If you haven't already discovered the romances of Anne Gracie, search for them. You'll be so glad you did. She's a treasure."
—*Fresh Fiction*

"Have you ever found an author who makes you happy? Puts a smile on your face as soon as you enter her story-world? Anne Gracie has done that for me ever since I read *Gallant Waif* and through every book thereafter."
—*Romance Reviews Today*

"One of the best romances I have read in a long time . . . *The Perfect Waltz* is the book to share with a friend who has never read a romance novel—consider adding it to your conversion kit."
—*All About Romance*

"One of those books that needs to be read from beginning to end in one sitting. Honestly, I couldn't put it down!"
—*Romance Reader at Heart*

The Stolen Princess

Anne Gracie

BERKLEY SENSATION, NEW YORK

THE BERKLEY PUBLISHING GROUP
Published by the Penguin Group
Penguin Group (USA) Inc.
375 Hudson Street, New York, New York 10014, USA
Penguin Group (Canada), 90 Eglinton Avenue East, Suite 700, Toronto, Ontario M4P 2Y3, Canada
(a division of Pearson Penguin Canada Inc.)
Penguin Books Ltd., 80 Strand, London WC2R 0RL, England
Penguin Group Ireland, 25 St. Stephen's Green, Dublin 2, Ireland (a division of Penguin Books Ltd.)
Penguin Group (Australia), 250 Camberwell Road, Camberwell, Victoria 3124, Australia
(a division of Pearson Australia Group Pty. Ltd.)
Penguin Books India Pvt. Ltd., 11 Community Centre, Panchsheel Park, New Delhi—110 017, India
Penguin Group (NZ), 67 Apollo Drive, Rosedale, North Shore 0632, New Zealand
(a division of Pearson New Zealand Ltd.)
Penguin Books (South Africa) (Pty.) Ltd., 24 Sturdee Avenue, Rosebank, Johannesburg 2196,
South Africa

Penguin Books Ltd., Registered Offices: 80 Strand, London WC2R 0RL, England

This is a work of fiction. Names, characters, places, and incidents either are the product of the author's imagination or are used fictitiously, and any resemblance to actual persons, living or dead, business establishments, events, or locales is entirely coincidental. The publisher does not have any control over and does not assume any responsibility for author or third-party websites or their content.

THE STOLEN PRINCESS

A Berkley Sensation Book / published by arrangement with the author

PRINTING HISTORY
Berkley Sensation mass-market edition / January 2008

Copyright © 2008 by Anne Gracie.
Cover art by Voth/Barrall.
Cover design by George Long.
Hand lettering by Ron Zinn.
Interior text design by Laura K. Corless.

ISBN: 978-0-425-21898-3

BERKLEY® SENSATION
Berkley Sensation Books are published by The Berkley Publishing Group,
a division of Penguin Group (USA) Inc.,
375 Hudson Street, New York, New York 10014.
BERKLEY SENSATION and the "B" design are trademarks belonging to Penguin Group (USA) Inc.

PRINTED IN THE UNITED STATES OF AMERICA

10   9   8   7   6   5   4   3   2   1

*For Anne McAllister and Marion Lennox,
wonderful writers and fabulous friends;
with my gratitude, my thanks, and my hope of
eventual forgiveness for the fate of Zouzou.*

Prologue

*T*he puppy was the final straw.

Nicky loved Zouzou with all his seven-year-old heart, so much so that on the second night he'd smuggled the puppy into his bed. Even if she hadn't heard excited puppy squeaks coming from beneath the bedclothes, Callie could have guessed by her son's look of extreme innocence that he'd broken the rules. But some rules were made to be bent a little.

She set the warm milk on the bedside table, kissed him good night, and left, hiding a smile.

Two hours later when the reception finally finished she looked in on Nicky again.

The puppy was dead.

Nicky was sitting up in bed, distraught, his face streaked with tears, the tiny puppy cradled stiff and lifeless in his arms. Dried yellow froth clung to its little muzzle.

"He wouldn't stop being sick. What did I do, Mama, what did I do?"

On the floor beside the bed was a half-drunk bowl of

milk and an empty cup, the same cup she'd given to her son.

"Did you drink any of the milk?" she asked, scarcely able to raise her voice from a whisper.

"It tasted funny," he said. "I didn't like it. So I gave it to Zouzou."

And then she knew. Had he not fed his milk to the puppy, Nicky's would be the small, cold body on the bed.

She understood then what she had to do. There was no longer a choice.

One

Dorset, England, 1816

"*B*est not take the cliff path home, Capt'n Renfrew. It's blowin' up a storm, and without the moon, that path is treacherous."

Gabriel Renfrew, late of the Fourteenth Light Dragoons, cast a cursory glance at the darkening sky and shrugged. "There's time enough before the storm hits. 'Evening, landlord." He let himself out of the small, snug tavern and made for the stables.

A buxom, blonde tavern maid followed him outside and slipped a friendly arm though his. "Why risk the cliff path, Captain, when I have a bed upstairs that's right snug and warm?"

Gabe smiled. "Thank you, Sally. 'Tis a generous offer but I need to go." He must be getting old, Gabe decided as he rode off. To choose riding a horse through the freezing darkness, home to an empty house, when he could be riding a curvaceous blonde in the cozy warmth of her bedchamber . . .

But though mindlessness was what he craved, mindless

coupling no longer appealed. And when the blue devils hit, as they had again tonight, neither drink nor women could help.

Nothing but darkness and speed and danger could scour his mind and heart clean.

Tonight the blue devils rode him worse than ever. Talk in the tavern had turned to the men who hadn't come home, to the families struggling on without them; Gabe's contemporaries, boys he'd grown up with, boys who'd followed him and Harry to war. "I'll take care of them," he'd said so blithely as they left . . .

But he hadn't.

Why had he, of all of them, returned? Those other lads were grieved for, mourned, desperately missed. They were needed by their families.

Not Gabe.

He galloped faster through the fleeting shadows. The narrow, moonlit path disappeared as the thickening clouds obscured the full moon. The waves pounded on the rocks below. Salt mist stung his skin and Gabriel rode the fine line between life and death, as he'd done so often before, giving fate a chance to change its mind.

Proving to himself yet again that, against all the odds, he was still alive. Even if he didn't know why.

The English Channel

"*N*o! This isn't right!" Callie, fugitive princess of Zindaria, was trying to force her dizzy head to steady. "I paid to be taken to Lulworth." She clutched the rail of the pitching boat and peered desperately out into the night. Shifting clouds blocked the moonlight and all she could see were white caps and looming dark cliffs. There was no sign of life, no building or habitation.

Was this even England? She had no way of knowing. It was the middle of the night and she'd been woken roughly from a fitful sleep. The seven hours before that she'd spent being violently ill.

"You and the lad are to go ashore here, ma'am. Captain's orders," a sailor told her.

"Nicky!" *Where was Nicky?* He'd been here just a moment ago. "Where's my son?"

"I'm here, Mama. I was just getting the bandbox." Her seven-year-old son stepped over a coil of rope and hurried to her side.

Callie put a hand on his shoulder. Nicky was the most important thing in her life, the reason she was here in the first place. "This is not where I paid to be brought," she told the sailor in a voice she hoped sounded firm. "Lulworth is a small town, on a sheltered cove—"

"Right, lads."

Without warning, Callie found herself seized by two burly seamen.

"What—? How dare you—!" What was happening? Surely they didn't mean to throw her overboard? Nicky . . . Terrified, trying desperately to reach Nicky, she fought like a wildcat, kicking, screaming, gasping in terror . . .

"The boy first," someone yelled. "She'll follow tame enough then."

She twisted frantically in time to see a seaman grab Nicky as if he weighed nothing. He hauled him to the ship's gunwale, lifted him, and dropped him over the edge.

"Nicky!"

The fight went out of her. She made no struggle as the men slung her, too, over the edge of the ship. *Nicky.*

She braced herself for the embrace of the sea. Death by drowning—dear God, don't say she'd brought Nicky this far just to have him die like this . . .

The sailors let go and she fell. And landed with a thud in a small, violently rocking dinghy. A sailor steadied her.

Nicky sat in the bow, his face pinched, pale, and fearful—but alive.

"Nicky, thank God!" She lurched across the wooden seats toward him.

The small boat rocked perilously.

"Sit down, miss! You'll have us all in the drink!" The sailor grasped her arm and wrenched her down to sit in the stern.

Furious, terrified, but realizing she had no choice, Callie sat, not taking her eyes off Nicky for a moment. The waves were getting larger and the dinghy pitched and tossed. She could swim a little; Nicky couldn't.

What was happening to them? She scanned the distant shoreline frantically. Thoughts of white slavers, wreckers, and worse flew through her mind. She knew it had been risky to pay an unknown captain of a shabby boat to take them across the Channel. It would have been riskier, though, to take the regular packet from Calais, for then they would have certainly been found. And returned.

"I demand you put us back aboard the ship this instant!" she stammered, trying desperately to make her voice work. "This is not Lulworth and I—"

There was a shout from above and her bandbox came flying down. The sailor caught it and passed it to Nicky. A moment later her portmanteau was dropped into the man's arms.

The sight of her possessions insensibly calmed her. Perhaps she and Nicky were not to be murdered for their belongings after all. But where was this place, this dark, unknown shore?

The sailor seized the oars and began to row.

"Where are you taking us?"

"Captain's orders to put you ashore here, ma'am. Storm's a-comin'."

"But there's safe harbor at Lulworth. It would give shelter from a storm."

"Preventives in Lulworth Cove, ma'am. Capt'n hates preventives."

"Preventives?" She was so bewildered she couldn't think. "But . . ."

"Orders, ma'am," he said indifferently and hauled on the oars.

She subsided. There was no point arguing. The sailor wasn't listening. All his effort was in rowing, and it took all her effort to hold on. The little boat was being tossed on the sea like a cork. She had her portmanteau under her feet. Nicky was wedging the bandbox under his, but they needed both hands to hold them steady.

"This is the breaker line, ma'am," the sailor said after a few minutes. The roll of the little boat was getting frantic. "I daren't take you further. You'll have to wade ashore from here."

"No. It's too deep and my son—"

Before Callie could stop him the sailor had hauled Nicky over the side and placed him in the sea.

"He can't swim!" Callie screamed. Without waiting for a response she scrambled into the water after Nicky, hauling herself along the boat's side until she reached him. The water was chest deep and freezing.

"Hold on tight to me, Nicky! Put your legs around my waist and your arms—yes, that's right."

Nicky clung to her, wrapping his arms and legs around her body like a small monkey. He was shivering.

"I-It's cold, Mama."

"Here's your stuff, ma'am." The sailor passed her the bandbox. As if she cared about the bandbox when her son was in the sea. But Nicky had made it his own personal responsibility during the journey and now he was reaching for it. Besides, it contained important papers and dry clothes for Nicky.

"Loop the strap around your wrist, Nicky," she told him. "It will float and the oilskin cover will keep it dry inside."

The dinghy washed closer. Maybe the sailor had more of a conscience than his captain—he was in real danger of capsizing but he seemed intent to see they had their luggage. He waited until he saw Nicky had hold of their bandbox.

"Your bag, ma'am." The sailor handed the portmanteau to her. Callie staggered as a wave broke over her. She clutched it in one hand, holding Nicky against her with the other.

"Godspeed, ma'am." The little dinghy moved swiftly away into the night.

"But where are we?" she shouted after him.

His voice floated back. "Go up the cliff path, then turn west to Lulworth."

"I don't even know which direction west is!" she yelled. But her words were lost on the wind. And in the darkness, she could no longer see the dinghy, let alone the ship they'd left France in.

"West is where the sun sets, Mama," Nicky told her.

Callie almost laughed. The sun had set a long time ago. But the waves were pushing them to shore. She shifted her grip on Nicky and waded toward the beach. The wind was getting stronger by the minute. It sliced through her saturated clothing. If she was freezing, Nicky would be even colder.

But he was alive, and that was more important than anything. And they were in England. And despite the fact that she was sodden and frozen and had no idea where she was, her spirits lifted a little. She'd succeeded.

Finally they reached the shallows and she put Nicky down. They stumbled, shivering, out of the water. The beach was studded with rocks and broken shells and was difficult to walk across in the dark. Callie's slippers had come off in the sea and she stubbed her toes painfully several times. She didn't care. The beach . . . Dry land . . . England.

"Come on, darling." Relief was making her feel dizzy. "Let's get you into some dry clothes and then we'll find that path. With any luck we'll be at Tibby's for breakfast."

"Will there be sausages, Mama?" he asked hopefully, through chattering teeth. "English sausages?"

Callie gave a choke of laughter. "Perhaps," she told him. "Now hurry!"

At the base of the cliff she opened the bandbox. Everything in it was dry, thanks to the oilskin cover. She took out a change of clothes for Nicky, a cashmere shawl, and her spare pair of slippers.

She swiftly stripped Nicky naked, dried him with her shawl and dressed him in clean, dry clothes. He'd been prone to all manner of ailments throughout his childhood and she didn't want him to catch a chill. She wrung out her skirts as best she could, dried her feet, and slipped on the shoes.

She glanced up at the cliff. She'd never get up the steep path with her skirts dragging and clinging around her legs. For two pins she'd remove her skirt and petticoat and climb in her drawers, only her petticoat, with its secret pockets, was currently her most valuable possession.

She knotted the skirt and her petticoat high on her legs, as she'd seen fisherwomen do. The icy wind bit into her wet skin. "Now, for the climb," she said and picked up the portmanteau.

Nicky stared up at the cliffs. "Do we really have to climb all the way up there?" No wonder he sounded daunted by the prospect. She could just make out the top by a faint lightening of the darkness—a change of texture, rather than shade.

"Yes, but the man said there was a path, remember?" Callie tried to keep fury out of her voice. The cliffs were enormous and very steep—dumping them there was more than outrageous, it was criminal, given Nicky's leg!

They scrambled upward, Nicky in front, so Callie could help him if he stumbled. The weight of the heavy portmanteau soon had her palms burning. Gusts of wind whipped at them.

"Stay away from the edge!" she called to Nicky every few minutes. The path was frighteningly narrow in places: in the darkness it was terrifying.

"I can see the top, Mama!" he called after what seemed like forever.

Callie paused for breath, cooling her burning palms against her wet skirt, and looked up. Almost there. Thank goodness! She heaved a huge sigh of relief. With any luck it would not be far to Lulworth.

Gabriel Renfrew rounded the bluff at a gallop. The narrow cliff path was barely visible yet Gabe didn't slow his pace. One misstep could send them over the edge but both rider and horse knew the path well. They'd ridden it almost every night for the past few weeks.

Cold salt air bit into his lungs. The storm was closing in, fast.

Trojan suddenly broke stride. Gabe looked up. "What the devil—"

A child stood directly in his path, staring and terrified. Horse and rider were almost upon him. There was no time to stop, no place to maneuver. On one side rocks rose steeply among scraggy bushes, on the other lay a plunge to certain death on the rocks below.

"Get off the path!" Gabriel shouted. He hauled on the reins, felt Trojan's muscles bunching in the effort to slow enough to stop before the child was trampled.

The little boy didn't move, was frozen with fear. There was no time to think, only react. "Get down!" Gabe yelled as he prepared to jump his horse over the child.

But as Trojan rose, leaping high in blind obedience to the command of his master's hands, a woman erupted from nowhere and with a scream flung herself at the child. It was too late—his horse was already in the air, clearing, Gabriel hoped, both woman and child. Did he feel a thud as he flew? It happened so fast he couldn't be sure.

He flung himself off his still-moving horse and ran back. He could hear something crashing down the cliff, sending stones and rocks rolling down. He hoped to God it wasn't the woman. The child, he was sure, had gone in the other direction, away from the edge.

In the darkness he could just make out a huddled female shape lying on the very edge of the cliff. Thank God it wasn't her he'd heard falling. But if she moved an inch . . .

He was three paces away when she started to stir. Before he could reach her she moved, tried to stand, and slipped toward the edge.

Gabe hurled himself forward, grabbed a handful of wet clothing, and dragged her back. *Wet* clothing? "Stay still," he barked. "Don't move."

"Where is—?" She batted his hands away and scrambled to her feet, looking around frantically. "Nicky! Nicky!" she screamed.

"Don't move!" he ordered sharply. "You're right on the very edge of the cliff."

She stared, horrified, at the edge. *"Nicky!"* She breathed. She swayed forward, peering over.

"He didn't fall," Gabe said firmly, easing her back again. "If Nicky is a small boy, he's all right."

"H-how do you know?" She was stuttering, almost past speech.

"I saw him run off that way." Gabe pointed further along the path.

"Run off? Oh God, he must have been terrified. What if he goes over the edge in the dark!" She started along the way he'd pointed. *"Niiicky!"*

"He's all right, I'm sure," he began in a soothing voice.

"Niiicky!" she screamed again.

"I'm here, Mama." The voice came out of the darkness. "The bandbox rolled away. I had to chase after it."

"Oh, Nicky! I was so worried." The woman pushed past Gabe and wrapped the child in a damp embrace.

"Mama, you're all wet!" said the boy, and with a laugh that sounded suspiciously like a sob she stepped back. She caressed the boy's hair gently.

"Are you all right, darling? That horrid horse didn't kick you, did it?"

"No, it jumped right over the top of me—like flying, like Pegasus. But you pushed me, Mama, and that's when I dropped this." The boy lifted the bandbox. "It rolled away. It nearly went over the edge, but I stopped it."

"How clever of you," she told him shakily, starting to recover from her fright. "I don't suppose you saw my slipper, too, did you? I dropped it somewhere." She was shivering quite badly, Gabe saw. Cold, or reaction, or both.

"I told you he was all right," Gabe said.

She turned on him in fury. "Don't speak to me! If you had hurt one hair of his head with your *criminally* irresponsible behavior, I would—I would—" Her voice cracked and she hugged her boy convulsively.

She took a deep, ragged breath and said shakily, "Are you drunk? I expect you are, to jump a horse over a child! The fact that my son is all right is no thanks to you and that creature!"

"I'm not drunk. Had I been, I could not have reacted with such split-second—" Gabe took a deep breath and harnessed his temper. He said in a deliberately calming voice, "Look, the boy is perfectly safe and—"

"Safe! You almost killed him!"

"Madam, I risked my horse and myself in order *not* to hurt him," he said with some asperity. "I don't normally use small boys and women for jumping practice. He suddenly appeared from nowhere and stood stock-still, right in my path—"

"With that horrid great beast thundering toward him, he was probably too terrified to move!"

"The sensible thing to do—"

"*Sensible?* You expect a child to think clearly when a man is riding straight at him? He's just a little boy!" She hugged the child again.

"I was not riding *at* him! He was in the middle of the path—and at a time when small boys ought to be in bed. And there was not enough time to stop—"

"Because *you* were riding like the devil!"

"Quite so. On my *own* land."

"I see." She took a deep breath, making a visible effort to gather her composure. "I . . . I see. I gather we are trespassing. In that case I shan't bother you any further. Good evening."

Gabriel frowned. The moon was still behind the clouds, but he could see her well enough to notice she was rubbing her shoulder. "You're hurt."

"A little bruised," she admitted.

"Are you sure it's not worse than that?"

"No, it's not serious. The shoulder was already sore from carrying the portmanteau."

Gabriel looked around. "What portmanteau?"

"It's . . . It must be here, somewhere. I lugged the wretched thing all the way up from the beach. It's as heavy as lead."

They all looked but there was no sign of a heavy-as-lead portmanteau.

"It must be here," she said. "It couldn't have rolled away like the bandbox."

"Ahh," said Gabriel. He had a sinking feeling where the portmanteau was. "I think it went over the edge when you, er, fell."

"Oh no!" she exclaimed. "Perhaps it didn't fall far." She started forward, but Gabe stopped her.

"I will look," he told her. "My nerves can't stand any

more of you perched on the edge of that drop." He stepped forward and peered down into the gloom.

"Perhaps it was further along," she prompted.

He moved along and his boot connected with something small. It fell, taking a light scatter of pebbles down with it. "Um, I think I found your slipper," he told her.

"Thank you. Hand it to me, if you please."

"I, er, just kicked it over the edge."

She sighed. "Of course you did."

"I shall retrieve the portmanteau for you in the morning," Gabe said stiffly. "The slipper may be more difficult to find."

"Pray do not bother about either," she said wearily. "The slipper was probably ruined anyway and I shall send someone to fetch my portmanteau in the morning."

"Fetched from where?" Gabriel asked. There was nothing for miles, only his house.

There was a short silence. "From where we are staying," she said warily.

"And where is that?"

"That's my business," she said firmly. "Thank you for your concern. Good-bye."

Gabriel admired her spirit. She'd dismissed him like a little duchess, and on his own land. "I'm not going anywhere, without you," he informed her. They were in dire straits and it was not in him to abandon any woman and child to their fate.

She edged away from him, clutching the boy to her. "Don't be ridiculous. You don't even know us. And we don't know you."

She took another step backward . . . Another . . .

He strode forward and grabbed her as she started to slip. Before she knew what he was about, he placed both hands around her waist and lifted her away from the brink.

"Let me g—Oh," she stammered, as he released her. She glanced behind her and saw. "Oh . . . Th-thank you."

"My pleasure. Gabriel Renfrew, at your service." He bowed. "And you are . . . ?"

She drew herself up straight, fighting desperately for dignity. "Appreciative of your . . . assistance. But my son and I shall do very well now, thank you, good-bye."

"It's my land," Gabe reminded her gently.

"Yes. Of course. We shall leave. Come, Nicky." She took the child's hand and took three lopsided steps away from him. Then she hesitated and said with a further heartbreaking attempt at dignity. "This is the path to Lulworth, I take it?"

"It is, but you're not going to Lulworth tonight."

"Indeed we are," she said as certainly as a female could whose teeth chattered like Spanish castanets.

Gabe ignored her. He took Trojan's reins and knotted them lightly on the horse's neck. He pulled out his caped overcoat from the saddlebag and took the bandbox from the boy.

"What are you doing? That's my bandbox," she said. "Give it back at once!"

Gabe tied the bandbox to the saddle, put on the overcoat and held out his hand to her. "Come on."

She pressed back against the rocks at the rear of the path. "I won't!" She gave a panic-stricken glance at the horse and in a different voice said, "I can't!"

He shrugged and swung the boy onto a ledge above the path.

"Let him go!" In desperation she swung a fist at Gabe, but he caught it easily.

She lifted her fist to swing at him and he caught her hand in his. At that moment the moon came out from behind the clouds, flooding the cliff top—and the woman's face—with clear, silvery light.

Gabriel had had the breath knocked out of him a dozen times. Each time he'd thought he was dying.

He'd been kicked in the head by a horse once. It had scrambled his wits for a while.

And a couple of times in his life he'd been so drunk that he'd lost all sense of time and place.

Seeing her face in the moonlight was like all of those rolled into one. And more. Gabe's breathing stopped. He forgot how to speak. He was unable to think. He could only stare. And stare. And stare.

She had the sweetest face he'd ever seen, round and sweet and sad and somehow . . . right, framed by a cloud of dark, wavy hair. An angel come to earth. With the most kissable mouth in the world.

He swallowed, drinking in the sight of her like a man facing a waterfall after a lifetime of thirst.

She gazed back at him. Her eyes were beautiful, he thought, eyes a man could happily drown in. He wondered what color they were.

"Release me this instant!" the angel snapped, and Gabriel's breath came back in a great whoosh of air. The angel was very, very human. And very, very frightened.

He held her clenched fist up, nearly at eye level. "This," Gabe shook her right fist a little, "would have hurt you more than it would have hurt me." He turned her fist palm up and explained. "See how your thumb is placed here? If you'd connected with my head, it would have been shockingly bruised, maybe even broken. I have a very hard head."

She frowned uncertainly. His tactics were confusing her. As he'd intended. Tension still vibrated in the small, rounded body, but she was listening.

"Next time you go to punch someone—anyone—some poor innocent fellow who accidentally rides his horse over you in the dark and keeps saving you from falling off a cliff, for instance—hold your fist like this." He showed her, rearranging her fingers. "And hit with the heel of your hand—not your knuckles—whack upward to the fellow's nose." He looked down at her and added, "Or his chin, if you're too short to reach the nose."

Her eyes narrowed. "I am not short."

"No, of course not," he assured her solemnly.

"Better still." He bent and picked up a stone and pressed it into her palm. "If you hit a man with that, it would really pack a punch. Make sure it is large enough that it fits in your palm and you can get a good grip, but not so small that your fingers can close right around it. Hit the man with the stone, not your hand. Next time you are in fear for your life, remember the stone." He released her hands and stepped back.

She clutched the stone tightly, staring at him in baffled suspicion.

Gabriel repressed a smile. The look on her face was priceless. Surprise tactics always had been his forte.

"You know I'm not going to hurt you or the boy. So just be sensible and get on my horse."

"I—I don't like horses. I prefer to walk."

"Don't be ridiculous, it's five miles and there's a storm brewing."

"I don't care. I've walked much farther than five miles before."

"Not in the dark and in a storm and with only one shoe," he reminded her. "Come, madam, I'll lift you up."

She fended him off, one-handed. "No, no, I can't!"

She was genuinely frightened, Gabe saw.

"It's all right, Trojan is a very gentle horse. There's really no need to be scared—"

"I'm not scared!"

"Of course you aren't," Gabriel agreed. She was terrified. "Don't worry, I'll hold on to you and you'll be safe as houses. I'll just lift you up—"

"You'll do nothing of the sort!"

"That's your last word?"

She gave him a stiff little nod. "It is."

"Excellent," said Gabriel and before she knew it, he lifted her by the waist and set her sideways onto the horse.

Trojan, bless him, stood steady as a rock. Almost in the same movement, Gabe swung up behind her and wrapped one arm firmly around her waist before she could jump off. She gave a small, stifled scream.

In her hand she still clutched the stone he'd given her. She raised her fist and waved it, fraught with indecision. Gabe waited.

Trojan stamped his hooves and moved restlessly.

She gasped and dropped the stone. Her free arm flailed desperately, touched Trojan's mane, recoiled, and then groped around for something to hang on to. She found Gabe's thigh. And gripped it tight.

He held out his hand to the boy, perched on the rocky ledge, watching unhappily. "Come on, Nicky, take my hand."

The child hesitated. Both of them were scared stiff of Trojan, Gabe saw.

"I promise you won't fall. Just take my hand and I'll swing you up behind me."

Again the boy shook his head.

"N-Nicky can't ride," she told him through clenched teeth.

Gabe said patiently, "I'm not asking him to. I'll do the riding. All he has to do is sit behind me and hang on."

"I can't ride, either." Her hand gripped him tightly.

"I know. I'm holding you safe, see?" He squeezed her waist gently. She was sitting so rigidly he could snap her in two. "I'll hold him safe, too."

She said in a voice that shook, "If one of your hands is holding me and the other is for Nicky, who will hold the horse?"

"I will. With my thighs."

"Your *what*?" Faint outrage showed through the terror.

He smiled to himself. She obviously had no idea it was his thigh she was hanging on to with all her might. "They're very strong thighs, and he's a very well-behaved horse. Now come on, Nicky, that rain is almost upon us. Get on."

As he spoke several large drops of rain pattered down. "Do it, Nicky," she said at last.

His misgivings obvious, the child hesitantly reached out and took hold of Gabe's arm.

"Good boy. Now put your left foot on my boot here and when I give you the word, jump and swing your right leg over the horse behind me. You're perfectly safe. I won't let you drop." The boy obeyed, closing his eyes and making a blind leap of faith. In a moment he was seated behind Gabe on Trojan.

"Now lift my coat over the top of you so that when the rain starts, you don't get wet. You can hold onto my belt or my waist, whichever you prefer," Gabe told him. He felt the coat lift, then two little arms wrapped around his waist in a convulsive grip.

Gabe nudged his horse and Trojan moved off as the rain started. The woman and boy clutched on to Gabe like grim death.

Icy needles of rain pelted down on Gabe's face and trickled down the inside of his coat. He was cold and wet and he should have been miserable.

Instead, he grinned, suddenly exhilarated. Until an hour ago his life had stretched out before him, an endless stretch of pointlessness and ease. A life sentence of tranquility.

Now, suddenly—blessedly!—he had a problem, a difficulty, trouble. And she was sitting rigid and unbending in his arms like a small, wet piece of wood, her eyes screwed tight shut, clutching his thigh as if she would never let go; his own little piece of trouble.

It suited Gabe perfectly.

Callie closed her eyes and clung on, enduring. If she'd thought this man threatened her son in any way, she would have fought him, but he'd been kind to Nicky, and to her, she admitted. Besides, she was all out of fight. She didn't know where he was taking her, but it couldn't be worse than trudging along a dark cliff top in freezing rain, not knowing where she was.

The worst thing was the horse.

She loathed horses. She hadn't been on one since she was six and Mama . . . She shivered, seeing it in her mind, as vividly as if it were yesterday, the horse's hoof smashing into Mama's head. And the blood . . .

Even Rupert hadn't been able to get her near a horse again.

But if it meant Nicky would be taken to warmth and safety sooner, well, she could put up with anything.

"Nicky, are you all right?" she called.

"Yes, Mama." She felt the flutter of small fingers against her waist and she clutched her son's hand thankfully. Her own personal lifeline.

"The coat has several capes," Gabriel Renfrew told her, his breath warm against her ear. "Nicky is warm and dry, so stop worrying about him. You, on the other hand, are frozen. Lean back against me and I'll button my coat closed. We'll all be warmer that way."

But Callie could not bring herself to move. If she did, she was sure she'd fall off.

"Don't worry, I have you safe," he said again. The deep rumble of his voice was soothing, but still she couldn't bring herself to change her posture one iota. She sat with a spine so straight she barely touched him, her eyes shut tight, her hand clinging to Nicky's fingers.

He sighed and pulled her right against his chest. "Now lean against me while I see to this."

Callie opened her eyes for a brief moment, then squeezed them shut, instantly. He was buttoning up the coat. With both hands. Nobody was holding the reins of the horse. She couldn't bear to look.

"It's all right to breathe, you know," he murmured in her ear. "There, that's better. Comfortable?"

Comfortable? On a *horse*? She shuddered.

"Pommel sticking into you, is it?" He adjusted her position so she sat across his lap, held firmly in a circle made up of his arm and his broad, warm chest, cocooned within his coat.

"This is kidnapping," she muttered.

"Yes, disgraceful, I know. But what could I do? You were all wet and cold."

"So are you, now," she pointed out.

"Ah, but a misery shared is a misery halved. Not that I'm the least bit miserable," he added.

Neither was Callie. She felt warm and, strangely, almost safe—despite the fact that she was on a horse. And forced into an intimate position with a man she'd never met.

It was most . . . unsettling, the feeling of his thigh under her bottom, shifting with each movement of the horse, hard and muscular. And the heat and hardness of his chest against her . . . breast. And his arms, bracketing her body, so warm and strong and intimate.

But his big, strong body threw out the warmth her body craved and she was cold, so very cold. Gradually, almost against her will, she pressed herself closer to him, her frozen body greedily soaking up the heat and the strength of him.

Her cheek rested against the fine linen of his shirt. He smelled of horse and cologne and leather and wood smoke . . . and the skin of a man . . .

She fancied she could hear his heart beating, a steady, soothing thump, thump, thump . . .

It was strange, she thought; Rupert had smelled of horse and cologne and leather, too, but it was very different.

Stop it! she told herself. This kind of stupid imagining, this stupid longing for something she knew she couldn't have, had made her miserable in the past. She was older and wiser now. She would make her own happiness, not depend on others—on men—for it.

She was in England and would be safe with Tibby very soon. This . . . *weakness* was just because she was cold and wet and tired. And because he was big and warm and strong.

That was the trouble. Because he was bigger and stronger, he'd got his own way. As men always did. Men never listened. Callie had had enough of it. Once she got to Tibby's she'd never have to take orders from a man again.

"Are you warmer, now?" he said. His voice was deep and the rumble of it reverberated in his chest, against her cheek.

"Yes," she said, and her conscience forced her to add, "Thank you."

"Nicky," he said in a louder voice, "We're going to go faster, so hold on tight."

Callie heard a muffled assent from Nicky. He didn't sound worried. But then the horse lengthened its strides and she closed her eyes and clung on tight, trying not to see the flashing hooves in her mind, concentrating on the man who held her so securely, even though the rest of the world was bouncing up and down . . .

"*W*e're here," the deep voice said in her ear sometime later. "Are you awake?"

Callie opened her eyes and stared up at him. "*Awake?*" she exclaimed incredulously. "Of course I'm awake!"

"Really?" She saw a flash of white teeth as he grinned. She turned her head to see where "here" was.

It was a substantial house, built of stone and rising to three stories, with dormer windows set into a slate roof. A single wisp of smoke curled lazily from one of many chimneys.

They rode under a decorative stone arch into a cobbled courtyard. A large black dog ran out barking but its barks turned to wriggles of silent pleasure as it recognized its master.

"Where are we?" she demanded, stiffening. "I thought . . . This isn't Lulworth."

"I didn't say I'd take you to Lulworth. It's too far on a night like this and even Trojan has his limits."

"Then where—"

"Welcome to my home," he said.

Two

H *is home.*

Whoever had built the house had liked light, Callie thought; the front of the house was almost all windows. As they rounded the side, heading for the stables, she saw a huge octagonal bay window rising almost the entire height of the wall. It would no doubt flood with sunshine during the day.

Now, the house was dark and still, except for a single lantern left burning around the back. Through the icy drizzle, the golden glimmer of light looked homey and welcoming, but they made straight for the arched entrance of the stables.

Her insides were hollow with apprehension. He'd brought them to his home. Why? All sorts of possibilities clamored in her brain. She couldn't think straight.

It was so difficult, deciding who she could trust and who she couldn't. Knowing her son's life depended on the judgments and choices she made. Her record so far of judging a man was woeful.

Once inside Gabriel Renfrew eased the horse to a halt. "Nicky, give me your hand and I'll swing you down."

Nicky dismounted and skittered away from the horse as quickly as he could, stumbling in his haste.

"He won't hurt you, I promise." He turned to Callie. "I'll dismount first and then I'll help you—"

She jumped down, and like her son, shot to a safe distance. Gabe began to unsaddle his horse.

"You're doing that yourself?" she exclaimed.

"There's nobody else to do it at the moment. Barrow, my groom, is spending a few days in Poole with Mrs. Barrow. I won't be a moment."

"I'll do that, Mr. Gabe," a voice said from behind. He turned. A middle-aged man hurried toward them, dressed in a nightshirt stuffed into a pair of trousers and a loosely laced pair of boots. His sparse hair stuck up around a red flannel nightcap.

"Barrow! I thought you were staying in Poole until the end of the week."

Barrow shook his head. "Changed me mind after a couple of days. Too much petticoat government! A man can't breathe. Four women in a small cottage and three of them widows!" He gave a hunted look as he took the reins from his hands. "Don't look at me like that, Mr. Gabe. Until you've experienced it, you don't know. My Bess is a fine woman, but the fuss her ma and sisters make!" He shuddered. "And every dratted bit of furniture, every chair, every table, even the sideboard, is covered with little crocheted . . . *things*!"

He shook his head. "No, we done what we went for, caught up with her ma and sisters and hired us some likely lads for the stable." He added with a grim smile, "I should warn you, Mr. Gabe, Mrs. B. has plans for some help in the house, too, now you're home. I'll be going back there come in a few days to fetch them all. Need a wagon, I will. You shoulda been there to keep her in check."

He glanced over at Callie and winked. "Not that any man can keep my Bessie in check, but Mr. Gabe—"

"Mr. Gabe wouldn't dream of attempting any such thing," Gabe interrupted him. "I have far too much respect for her."

Barrow chuckled. "Far too much respect for her cooking, you mean. And who do we have here? Guests is it? Nasty night to be caught out in." He beamed at the bedraggled pair.

"Yes, this lady and her son, Nicky," Gabe told him.

"Mrs. B. will be well pleased." He eyed Nicky, then—amazingly—winked at Callie. "You watch out for that boy, missy. My missus dearly loves to get her hands on a boy."

Callie put her arm protectively around Nicky. She wasn't going to let any strange woman get her hands on Nicky and she had never been winked at by anyone, let alone a groom!

Rupert would have had the man flogged.

She was very glad Rupert wasn't here. It made her ill when he had people flogged.

Barrow continued, "I'll see to Trojan, Mr. Gabe, while you take these two into the warmth. She looks worn to a thread, poor little lass."

The poor little lass closed her mouth. She was worn to a thread. And it was having a bad effect on her temper. She'd been ready to snap the nose of a kindly older man, only for being overly familiar. She used to be gracious and even-tempered. She would be gracious and even-tempered again, she resolved, as soon as she discovered who these people were and where they had taken her and her son. And as soon as she stopped shivering.

If she was behaving like a shrew, well, there had been provocation. Several provocations. Being dumped into the freezing sea, then being ridden over, kidnapped, and forced to ride a horse was not conducive to graciousness. Nor was constant fear.

"Yes, she's exhausted," the current provocation agreed. "She's had a trying time of it, I fear. Wet, cold, lost her luggage, and she's hurt herself into the bargain."

"*I* didn't hurt *myself*!" she said indignantly. "Your horse *kicked* me!"

"What, Trojan? Never!" Barrow exclaimed in amazement. "He's as gentle as a puppy, aren't you, my beauty?" he crooned to the horse.

"To be fair to the horse, you did fling yourself under his hooves," Mr. Gabe said.

"Oh, yes, by all means let us be fair to the horse!" To Barrow she explained, "He just happened to be jumping that dreadful creature over my son's head at the time. I took exception to it."

"Mr. Gabe? Jump his horse over a child?" Barrow exclaimed in horror. "I don't believe it."

Mr. Gabe said nothing. A small smile hovered around his lips and his eyes rested on Callie with a lazy appreciation.

Callie pushed back her hair and avoided his gaze. The knot had come undone and her hair draggled everywhere in damp strings. She knew she looked a sight.

"Mr. Gabe . . . you're smiling!" the groom exclaimed as if that was something amazing.

Callie's stomach chose that moment to rumble loudly. She coughed to cover the dreadful sound.

Barrow's smile broadened. "Take your young lady inside and feed her. What did you say your name was, Miss?"

"Prin—" Callie caught herself in time. "Pr—Prynne," she said, feeling her blush deepening and hoping they would notice nothing amiss. Her tiredness had made her forget for a moment who she was—or rather who she was pretending to be.

"I am Mrs. Prynne, and this is my son, Nicholas."

She glanced at Nicky, who'd squatted down to pat the dog. At her introduction he rose and gave a formal little bow. Callie bit her lip. She should not be teaching her son to lie and pretend with such facility, but she had no choice. They'd used several different names already in their journey. This was the first time she'd slipped and almost said Princess. She was so tired.

And that man had distracted her. She darted a glance to see if Mr. Gabe had noticed the pause or not and found he was watching Nicky with a faint frown. Perhaps he didn't like her son patting his dog.

"Nicky," she said quietly and gestured for him to leave the dog. Nicky moved to her side. His limp was worse than usual; the cliff climb on top of their long journey had worn him to a thread.

"How d'ye do, ma'am," Barrow said. "So, you're a widow, eh?"

She blinked. The habit of common people to ask direct, personal questions still shocked her a little. It was not polite to inquire so intimately of a stranger. But she had the response to this one off by heart—she'd learned by hard experience which answer served her and Nicky best.

"No, of course not. My husband was delayed on the road and is a short way behind us." Too late she realized she should have said he was delayed at sea. Or something. She darted another glance at Mr. Renfrew. He knew she'd come by boat. She bit her lip and tried to look indifferent.

He looked down at her, an odd look on his face. "I think, Mrs. Prynne, that you are quite at the end of your tether," he said softly. "And so is your son. Come on, let's get you both into the warmth."

Nicky took two ragged steps and without hesitation, Mr. Renfrew scooped him up and carried him from the stable.

She ran after him. "What are you doing?"

"He's hurt himself. Didn't you see he was limping? Badly, too." To Nicky he said, "Don't worry, lad, we'll see that foot seen to."

"But—" she began, then stopped. Nicky had made no

attempt to resist, which was unlike him. He must really be exhausted.

"Prynne," Gabriel Renfrew said as they crossed the courtyard. "Interesting name. A Quaker, are you?"

"No."

He carried Nicky into a large, open country kitchen. It was a cozy room, with copper pots gleaming in the lamplight and the smells of food and herbs. An enormous scrubbed wooden table stood in the center, with a dozen ladder-back chairs surrounding it.

A tall, plump middle-aged woman stood waiting for them, a dress thrown over her nightgown, a shawl knotted around her shoulders and an apron over them all. Mrs. Barrow, Callie presumed.

"'Tis a dreadful night!" she said. "Put the wee lad and the lady by the fire, Mr. Gabe. There's hot water on the stove. I'll go and make up a bed in the blue room."

Despite the size of the room and the stone-flagged floors, it was warm inside. The fire in the big cast-iron kitchen range glowed through the grill.

"Here you go." He set Nicky on his feet on a plaited rag rug in front of the kitchen range. "Sit down, both of you, and get yourselves warm."

"Thank you." She sat gratefully, soaking up the warmth, while Nicky sank onto the rug. The size, cleanliness, and homeyness of the room was reassuring. Too many people had lied to her for her to trust strangers easily, but a well-scrubbed kitchen was . . . different.

Villains could be clean and homey, too, she reminded herself. Probably. She might be exhausted—she could not recall when she'd last had a good night's sleep—but she needed to stay on her guard. Her journey was far from over.

Mr. Renfrew took off his wet overcoat and hung it on a nail at the back door. He removed his damp coat and waistcoat and hung them on the back of a chair. He rolled up his shirtsleeves, opened the stove door, and stirred the glowing coals.

She stared at his bare, tanned forearms and large, strong hands as he methodically fed small chips of wood into the coals, then larger pieces. He applied a pair of bellows and flames flickered up, gilding his profile, highlighting the bold nose and the hard angles and shadows of his face.

She gazed at the strong column of Mr. Renfrew's throat and the clean line of his jaw. His shirt was open at the neck. The flames leapt and crackled. His face was lit by fire. She shouldn't be staring, but she had to keep her eyes open to stop from falling asleep, and he was there, right in front of her.

He was not a pretty man, not handsome in the way of the young men Callie had admired as a girl, and yet he was . . . beautiful in a strange way. Hard and strong and ruthless-looking. A clean-limbed, sculpted warrior, pared down to the essentials. Formidable.

He'd ridden roughshod over her, ignoring her stated wishes completely, and yet, physically, he'd treated her and her son with surprising gentleness. She felt cared for, protected . . .

He straightened, and she couldn't help but look at him. He wore high boots and buckskin breeches, which were damp and clung to his long, hard, masculine frame. His legs were long and lean and hard-muscled. He'd told her his thighs were strong, she recalled. They looked . . . strong.

Rupert's thighs had been strong too. She supposed all horsemen's thighs were, but Rupert's had been somehow . . . meatier.

He finished stoking the fire and turned to Nicky. "Now, let's have a look at that leg."

Nicky pulled back, ashamed. "It's all right," he muttered.

"Don't be frightened. I'm not going to hurt you, but you

were limping quite badly before and it doesn't do to neglect an injury, take it from an old soldier."

Nicky looked away. "It's nothing."

"Nicky's leg was injured at birth," Callie said stiffly. "It's more noticeable when he's tired, that's all." Each time Nicky had to explain it, she felt the knife turn in her breast. It was her fault, she knew, that her son had to bear this burden. She braced herself for what would come next—the embarrassment, or the hearty reassurance, or the questions.

Mr. Renfrew surprised her. "That's all right then," he said in a matter-of-fact way to Nicky. "I was worried I'd hurt you, as well as your mother. In that case, how about you fetch me some clean towels from the linen press, Nick—that's the cupboard over there—and I'll fetch some hot water."

Nicky hurried off. Callie gave Gabriel Renfrew a silent look of gratitude. Very few men of her acquaintance made a small, crippled boy feel useful.

He took a paper spill from a small tin on the mantel over the fire, lit it, then stood to light the lantern that hung overhead. He had to reach to do it and she couldn't help but stare at the way his shirt pulled tight against his deep, powerful chest. There looked to be no softness in the man at all.

Her cheek had rested against that chest. She'd felt his heartbeat.

He'd treated her son with such sensitivity, respecting his small-boy dignity. And he'd brought them both in from the cold.

Soft golden lamplight poured out over the kitchen, and as she glanced up their gaze met.

"Green!" he said, sounding satisfied. He finished trimming the wick and stepped back.

She frowned. "I beg your pardon?"

"I've been wondering what color they were ever since I've met you."

"What color what were?"

"Your eyes. They're green."

She blinked and had no idea what to say.

Nicky came back with a huge pile of towels, and Mr. Renfrew filled a large bowl with hot water. He knelt and placed it at Callie's feet, then slipped off her remaining slipper.

"What are you doing?" she asked, startled.

"Your feet are a mess. They're all cut to ribbons; hadn't you noticed?"

Callie looked. Her toes were bruised and scraped and bloody, as well as muddy. They really were a mess. She'd hardly noticed. Her feet had been so cold, and though she was aware of some discomfort, other, more urgent things had occupied her attention.

"It must have happened when we were coming ashore. I do remember stubbing my toes a few times on the rocks." And now she thought of it, they did hurt.

"Here, put them in the water. Careful, it's hot and there's salt, which will sting, but it'll help the cuts to heal."

Gingerly she lowered her feet into the hot water. It burned at first; her feet were half frozen, and the cuts stung, but after a few moments it felt heavenly.

She sat back, soaking up the warmth and the comfort, rubbing her own and Nicky's hair dry with a towel.

"Better?" Gabriel Renfrew asked after a while.

"Yes, thank you. It's lovely," she said gratefully.

"Good." He smiled. His teeth were white and even. "Now, I'll just put some salve on those cuts. Mrs. Barrow makes an excellent salve for cuts and abrasions."

Callie's mouth dropped open as, in a matter-of-fact way, he began to dry her feet with a towel.

"I—I can do that," she stammered. It was rather unsettling feeling his big, warm hands caressing her feet so gently through the towel.

He smiled again. "I know, but I don't mind doing it.

Could you fetch me two more towels, please, Nicky." Her son ran off and a pair of guileless blue eyes met hers.

"I don't believe this is very proper," she muttered.

"Don't you like it?"

She gave him a troubled look. Yes, she liked it. Of course she liked it. And that was the point. She didn't even know him and he shouldn't be handling her feet so . . . so intimately. It made her . . . feel things, things she had no business feeling with a stranger.

As he dried the last toe, she said, "Thank you. You may now unhand my feet."

He took no notice. Scooping out a fingerful of aromatic salve, he proceeded to rub it into her feet with his hands, slowly, gently, and with a sensuous rhythm. Her toes curled in pleasure and she felt the tingles all the way up her legs.

She blinked, torn between pleasure and embarrassment. He was merely attending to her injuries, she reminded herself, but try as she might, she could not stop herself from reacting, even though she knew she should not.

"Please, that's enough," she said. "Did you not hear me, I asked you to unhand my feet!"

"Oh, *un*hand—I thought you said hand them," he explained, looking up at her with a twinkle. "Hand being a foreign term for massage."

Her jaw dropped. He *knew* what his touch was doing to her. He was *flirting*.

The realization astounded her. No man had flirted with her in . . . forever. She'd gone from being a child to being Rupert's wife. Nobody would dare flirt with Rupert's wife. She had no idea what to do.

She said feebly, "That's a barefaced l—nonsense!" She balked at calling the man a liar in his own house.

"Oh, massage isn't l—nonsense." His voice was serious, but the blue eyes danced. "It's very helpful. Helped many a soldier prevent frostbite, or chilblains. And it's wonderful for weary feet, don't you think?"

"I didn't mean—"

"And in English we don't say '*le nonsense,*' we just say 'nonsense.'" His eyes twinkled. He'd known very well what she'd been going to say.

It was so ridiculous she couldn't help but laugh. "I know perfectly well what we say in English. I was born here!"

"Were you? What a coincidence, so was I, so already we have something in common. And was Nicky also born here?"

"No," Nicky chimed in as he returned with the towels. "I was b—"

"No, Nicky wasn't born here!" She gave her son a warning glance. Nobody, even tall, unexpectedly kind men who flirted, should know who they were. "And, please, sir, my feet will do very well now, thank you."

"When the salve is absorbed." His deep voice was completely imperturbable. His long, strong fingers continued to knead and massage. He caressed each toe in turn, rubbing between them and sending tiny, invisible shivers thrilling up her limbs. It felt like her bones were turning to honey.

It was completely improper and utterly heavenly, and it was all Callie could do not to dissolve into a puddle of bliss.

She watched his face as he ministered to her, noting the quiet strength, the deep lines around his mouth, and the faint touch of bleakness that came to his eyes when he wasn't remembering to flirt. It was suddenly all too intimate.

Callie closed her eyes . . .

G abe fetched a pie from the pantry. Mrs. Barrow had cooked up a storm before she'd left to visit her mother.

"I'll wager you're hungry, eh, Nicky?" He cut a slice of pie and handed it to the boy. "Get that into you, lad. Cold pork pie; I can vouch for it."

Nicky hesitated and glanced at his mother. "Mama never eats pork," he said. "Papa says—said it's vulgar for ladies to eat pork."

"I see," Gabe murmured, noting the tense change. Papa sounded like a bit of an ass.

The boy glanced at his mother, who was three-quarters asleep. "Leave her be," Gabe said softly. "She's very tired. Just eat your pie and then we'll all get to bed."

Nicky looked dubiously at the wedge of pie. He made no move to touch it.

"Don't you like pork, either?" Gabe asked. "Well, then, if you don't want it." He took it and munched into it.

The boy watched him. "I didn't say I didn't want it," he said after Gabe had swallowed the last mouthful. "I'm very hungry."

"Right then, cut yourself another slice while I get you something warm to drink."

Nicky cut himself a small wedge and gave the pie a cautious nibble. His eyes widened. "It's very good."

"Told you it was," Gabe told him. He went back into the pantry and poured some milk into a pan. By the time he returned Nicky was finishing off his slice of pie with every evidence of satisfaction. Gabe heated the milk, poured some into a cup, stirred in some honey and handed it to the boy.

The boy stared at it as if the cup contained a live snake.

Gabe said in mild exasperation. "Is it some foreign custom of yours, to refuse what food and drink is first offered to you? Here, it's polite to accept the first time, so just drink the milk and don't make a fuss."

The little boy blanched. "Mama!" It came out in a thin, frightened wail.

His mother woke, saw him handing the cup of milk to the boy, leapt from her chair, and dashed it from Gabe's hands. Milk splashed over the stone floor. She thrust Nicky behind her, glanced around, saw the knife he'd used to cut the pie, and snatched it up.

"What on earth—" Gabe began.

"Don't touch him!" She was poised for action; a young lioness in defense of her cub. "Nicky, did you drink any of it?"

"No, Mama." She sagged with visible relief.

"It was only warm milk," Gabe said tightly. He bent and picked up the cup.

She waved the knife at him. "Stay back."

He ignored her and went to the door, opened it, and whistled. His dog, Juno, bounded in, her tail wagging joyfully. "Over there," he told her and pointed to the spilled milk and honey.

"No!" the boy gasped and moved to get between the milk and the dog.

She wagged her tail briefly—Juno liked boys—but food was always a priority, and she pushed past him and happily licked up the milk. The woman and the boy stared at Gabe as if he were a monster.

Gabe fetched another cup from the dresser and, from the small pot on the stove, poured hot milk into another cup. Two pairs of eyes watched him.

"He put something into it before," Nicky told his mother.

"From this pot, yes," Gabe affirmed and stirred a spoonful of viscous liquid into the mug. "It's honey. Warm milk and honey. Good for helping people sleep." He drank from the cup and then held it out toward Nicky.

There was a long moment of silence. Juno had licked every drop of milk from the floor and discovered a crumb or two of pie crust, and now was ready to renew her acquaintance with the boy. She nudged his elbow in a friendly fashion, demanding to be patted. He caressed her silky ears, felt her cold nose, and looked carefully into her eyes. Her tail thumped happily on the floor at this attention.

The boy and the woman looked from the dog to the man to the cup of milk and to the dog again. "Sometimes you just have to take people on trust," Gabe said quietly and set the cup on the table. "If I'd wanted to harm you, I could have tossed you both off that cliff and saved myself a lot of trouble."

For a long time nobody moved. Callie tried to read his eyes. They were steady and blue, very blue. But you couldn't decide a man was trustworthy just because he had eyes that were blue. But steady as well as blue . . .

She stared into his eyes and remembered how he'd pulled her from the cliff top. She thought about the way he'd held her on the horse, steady and warm, tucking his coat around her to shelter her from the rain.

Then, staring into the bluest blue eyes she'd ever seen, Callie picked up the cup of milk and took a mouthful. It tasted of warm milk and honey. Nothing else. Just as he'd said. She tasted it again, just to be sure.

The dog nudged Nicky's arm, her feathered tail waving gently, her brown eyes liquid and clear and trusting. And unharmed.

Slowly the tension flowed out of Callie. She nodded, passed the cup to Nicky, put the knife back on the table, and returned to her seat, feeling distinctly wobbly.

Nicky took a cautious sip of the milk. Meanwhile, the dog fetched a stick from the basket by the fire and placed it expectantly at Nicky's feet.

"No, Juno, no stick throwing inside," her master said. "Put it back." To Nicky's amazement, with tail drooping, the dog put the stick back in the basket, then returned to rub a mournful muzzle against Nicky's leg. Nicky swiftly drained the cup, sat on the rug, and began to pat the dog.

"Do you want some milk, too?" Mr. Renfrew asked her.

Callie shook her head. "No, thank you." She closed her eyes. She felt sick. The incident with the milk had brought it all back to her. She could never relax her vigilance.

"Mrs. Barrow has brought you some dry clothing," she heard Mr. Renfrew say a short time later. At least she thought it was a short time. Callie's eyes flew open. Where was Nicky? She couldn't have dozed off again, could she?

"He's asleep," said the man, reading her thoughts.

Her son was curled up on the rug with the big black-and-tan dog, sound asleep. His arms were wrapped around the dog, and the dog's muzzle rested on Nicky's shoulder.

Callie felt a lump in her throat, thinking of the puppy he'd lost.

"Worn to a frazzle, the poor little mite!" Mrs. Barrow said. "Take him up to bed, will you, Mr. Gabe, while I'll help missy change?"

Mr. Gabe bent and scooped Nicky into his arms. The dog scrambled to her feet, clearly intending to go with them.

Callie rose.

"No, don't come," he said. "He's sleeping like a babe and while I'm gone you can change into those dry clothes in front of the fire."

Callie looked at her sleeping son and swallowed. He looked so small and helpless in the tall man's arms. And so vulnerable. He didn't even stir as Mr. Renfrew pushed open the door with a shove of his boot.

Sudden suspicion shot through her. *Sleeping like a babe—or drugged?* Some poisons were tasteless. Was that why she'd fallen asleep? Oh God, how could she have trusted him, even for a moment, with her precious Nicky— just because of his eyes? She lurched forward to stop them.

"Nicky?"

Blessedly, he stirred and opened sleepy eyes.

"Mama." He smiled, yawned, and dozed off again, snuggling against the man's chest as if perfectly comfortable.

Callie examined him. He looked just as he did every night when she checked him. His breathing was deep and even, his skin slightly flushed in the way children's skin was in sleep. And his eyes just now had been clear, just sleepy. She cupped his cheek. Warm, neither too cool nor too hot.

She started to breathe again.

And then became aware that the man who held her child in his arms was staring down at her, silently absorbing the expressions on her face. She met his gaze. He looked thoughtful, the mobile mouth grim.

"I'm not Long Lankin, you know," he said quietly.

"Who?"

"A bogeyman in a song from my childhood. Long Lankin was a gentleman who drained the blood of innocent children."

She reddened. "I didn't think—"

"Yes, you did." There was an awkward pause, then he added in a gentler tone, "My guess is you have your reasons."

She looked at the face of her sleeping child and tried to swallow the lump in her throat. Yes, she had her reasons.

"Will you trust me to put him to bed?"

She hesitated. Nicky's hair was damp and spiky as a new-hatched chick. He looked small and pale and vulnerable in the tall man's arms, but his thin little body was relaxed. Tired beyond caring, or trustful? Sometimes it amounted to the same thing, thought Callie wearily.

"Mrs. Prynne?"

With an effort, Callie realized he was addressing her. "Yes?"

"Trust me," he said in that impossibly deep voice. The steady blue eyes never wavered.

Callie bit her lip, then nodded. She had no alternative. She leaned forward, kissed Nicky's forehead, and smoothed back his hair. "Sweet dreams, my darling," she whispered in his native tongue. She could feel the tall man's eyes boring into her, but he said nothing, just turned and carried her son from the room.

"Now, ma'am, time for you." Callie sat quietly while Mrs. Barrow fussed around her with towels and nightclothes. Swiftly the older lady stripped Callie of her clothes, tutting over the dampness of them and exclaiming over the weight of the petticoat. Callie hastily bundled it out of sight. Her future was in that petticoat.

Mrs. Barrow produced a large, bright pink flannel night-gown and dressed Callie in it, murmuring a stream of encouragement, as if Callie were a child. "That's the way, lift your arms. In you go. Now you just sit here by the fire and I'll fetch a blanket to make you all cozy and warm again."

Callie just let it flow. She was accustomed to maids dressing and undressing her, but none of them had ever called her lovie or bossed her around in such a warm, motherly tone.

It was quite inappropriate, of course, and if her father or Rupert had been there, they would have reprimanded the woman for her familiarity.

But Papa and Rupert were both dead, and nobody else was here to witness Callie's lapse of etiquette. And so she didn't have to hide how comforting she found it.

Mrs. Barrow reminded her of Nanny. She hardly remembered Nanny, there was just a vague memory of a large, soft woman, with a capacious bosom and a comforting lap, who'd muttered and crooned over her bossily, as Mrs. Barrow did now. Callie had forgotten how soothing it could be.

What had happened to Nanny? She didn't even know her real name. Papa had sent her away when Callie was six—not long after Mama had died. He'd found her sitting sleepily in Nanny's lap, listening to a story. She was far too old to be treated like a baby, Papa had said. And stories were just a waste of time . . . Filling girls' heads with nonsense.

She hadn't heard another story for years, not until Miss Tibthorpe came to be her governess. Dear Tibby, with her stern looks and rigid demeanor. Papa never even suspected Miss Tibthorpe was an avid reader of novels and romantic poetry. If he had, Tibby would have been sent packing.

"Ah, here's Barrow now." Mrs. Barrow said as she finished

draping a blanket around Callie's shoulders. "I'll be off now, lovie. Mr. Gabe will be down in a minute, he'll take you up to bed."

"Likes to see everyone safe, Mr. Gabe does," Barrow added, sliding an affectionate arm around his wife's waist. "Are you ready for bed, my bonny lass?" He bussed her on the cheek.

Mrs. Barrow blushed like a girl. "Get away with you, Barrow, what will the lady think? Good night, ma'am, sweet dreams." The middle-aged couple left, arm in arm.

Callie bid them good night, touched by their open affection. How marvelous to be so loving, so beloved after so many years.

She sighed wistfully. It was something she'd never know. Princesses married for reasons of state, or for blood or fortune, not for love. She'd learned that the hard way.

She glanced at the table. The pork pie sat on the table still. Mrs. Barrow had forgotten to put it away.

Her stomach rumbled . . .

G abe returned to the kitchen just in time to see Mrs. Prynne jump back guiltily from the table. He affected not to notice. She was swathed in bright pink flannel drapery; Mrs. Barrow was a woman of height and ample girth; Mrs. Prynne was small and almost lost in a sea of nightgown. It was buttoned to her chin and pooled in folds around her feet. On her feet she wore a pair of too-big slippers, also Mrs. Barrow's.

"He's all tucked up and sound asleep," he told her. "I see you have a nightgown—you look delightful in it. Now, are you sure you're not hungry?" He glanced at the pie, which had shrunk, and preserved a bland countenance.

She gave him an innocent look. "No, thank you."

"Then I shall put this away." Gabe put the leftover pie in the larder.

"Now, I think it's time for bed," he said and offered her his arm.

She eyed it warily, suddenly unsure of his motives. He smiled down at her and added, "You can thank me upstairs."

Her eyes widened. "But I am a respectable, married w-woman!"

"My favorite sort." He tucked her arm in his and led her upstairs, to a room with a big canopied bed hung with blue curtains. A fire was burning in the grate, with an ornate mesh screen in front of it.

"On a night like this you'll enjoy a hot brick in your bed," he murmured.

She stiffened. Was he really suggesting he warm her bed? "I warn you—"

"Hush, you'll wake Nicky," he whispered. "Juno is guarding him. I hope you don't mind sleeping with a dog in the room, but they seem to have taken to each other, and I thought it would make your boy feel happier about sleeping in a strange place."

Callie's eyes adjusted to the gloom. On one side of the bed the bedclothes had been folded back in readiness, on the other side lay a small, peaceful bump; her son, sound asleep. Beside him, on a mat on the floor, lay the dog. She looked up and her tail went thump, thump, thump, but she did not move.

"Oh," Callie said. He'd been teasing her.

He gave her a dry look and murmured in her ear. "Mrs. Prynne, were you having naughty un-Quakerish suspicions about my intentions? I'm shocked."

"No, you're not," she whispered back. "You, sir, are a rogue!"

"And you, Green Eyes, are very sweet." He stood for a moment, looking down at her. She could feel his eyes on her and closed her own in self-defense. She had no idea of what to say or do. She was too tired to think.

He gently touched a finger to her cheek. "Good night Green Eyes. Sleep well. You and your son are safe here with me."

Safe. The deep reassurance of his voice seeped into her bones like a drug. She heard him leave, heard the door shut quietly behind him.

"Thank you," she whispered belatedly.

She climbed into the bed and snuggled down, feeling . . . cherished.

Her feet touched something hard that radiated heat. Her toes explored it. Something square and hot, wrapped in what felt like flannel. A spurt of sleepy laughter bubbled inside her. There really was a hot brick in her bed.

And so, in a strange house and strange bed, and for the first time in weeks, Callie slipped into a deep, dreamless sleep.

Three

Despite his late night Gabe woke to the birds' dawn chorus. He smiled and stretched languorously. He felt alive and eager to meet the day, in a way he hadn't for years.

He slipped out of bed, padded to the window, and looked out. A chill, clear dawn greeted him, gray warming to palest gold. Wisps of mist hugged the ground. It held the promise of a beautiful day.

He dressed quickly. Her door was still shut as he passed. She'd sleep for several hours more, he thought. She and the boy had been exhausted.

Grabbing a couple of apples from the bowl on the kitchen sideboard, he bit into one with relish, pocketing the other. He'd break his fast properly and have a shave when he got back. He headed out, noting to his surprise that the kitchen door was unlocked. Barrow was up early. Surprising, after such a late night.

Opening the stable door, Gabe paused. Someone was talking in one of the stalls and it wasn't Barrow. He listened, but couldn't identify the speaker. He approached the stall, stepping softly . . .

"You do like them, don't you?" the light, high voice was saying.

He heard a deep whuffle, as Trojan responded. Gabe grinned. That horse was as close to human as a horse could be. Young Nicky was standing on a bale of hay, biting off chunks of apple and then tossing them over the open half door to his horse. Interesting, for a boy who was scared stiff of horses. Juno sat beside him, watching the passage of apple piece to horse with a jealous eye.

"Trojan is very fond of apples," Gabe said.

The boy jumped and whirled around, dropping a piece of apple. He clambered hastily off the stool, then to Gabe's amazement, stood rigidly to attention, like a small soldier awaiting punishment.

"I'm sorry, sir," the boy said stiffly. "I know I should not have come." He spoke English well, but with a faint trace of accent. His mother had no accent at all. Juno nudged the boy's leg, trying to snaffle the fallen apple piece. He stumbled, then straightened to attention again.

"Juno also likes the occasional piece of apple. As for coming in to the stables, as long as you didn't wake your mother, I don't mind," Gabe said easily. "I headed for the stables at every opportunity when I was your age. Come to think of it, I haven't changed much, have I?"

The child regarded him solemnly. His eyes were not quite as green as his mother's. After a moment he said, "At home I was not permitted in the stables without Papa or my guar—another man."

"I thought you didn't like horses, Nicky." Gabe finished his apple and held the core out to the boy. "Here, give him this. Only don't toss it in. I told you, Trojan won't bite."

Nicky shook his head, so Gabe cut the core in half and demonstrated. "Hold it on your palm, with your fingers flat, like you're serving it on a plate." He fed the morsel to his horse and Nicky watched, wide-eyed, as Trojan extended his nose and took the core delicately from Gabe's palm.

"It is because he is your horse," the boy said.

"No," Gabe said. "He'll be friends with anyone who brings him apples. Why don't you try?"

"Very well." His eyes alive with misgivings, the boy took the other half of the core and climbed back on the stool. With fingers held flat he extended his hand over the half door and waited, his face screwed up in anticipation of disaster.

Trojan leaned forward, lipped the core delicately, then lifted it from the boy's palm.

"He took it! He didn't bite me at all, not even a nip!" Nicky exclaimed. "Any one of Papa's horses would have had my hand off!"

"Fierce, are they?" Gabe pulled out his knife, cut a slice of the second apple, and handed it to the boy.

"Oh yes, they were bred for war, you know," Nicky said, as he fed it to the horse. "Papa's are the fiercest horses in all the land. I thought Trojan would be fierce, too, because of his name. And because he's so magnificent."

"I see." And Gabe thought he did. "Is that why you don't like horses?"

"I—I like them well enough, though I don't like to be bitten. It's just . . . I cannot ride." He said it as if confessing something shameful.

Gabe kept cutting slices and handing them to him. "How old are you?"

"I will be eight next month. His lips are so soft—like velvet!" He was feeding the big horse now with confidence.

"Plenty of time yet to learn to ride. Most people don't learn until they're much older."

Nicky shook his head. "In England perhaps," he said dismissively. "But not in Z—where I come from," he amended. "There we ride from the age of four or five." He looked away. "*They* ride," he muttered.

"Your mother can't ride."

"Yes, but she is a lady *and* English."

Gabe shrugged. "Lots of English ladies ride. I know ladies who can ride better than most men."

Nicky looked doubtful.

"Besides, what does it matter if she rides or not?"

"It matters in Z—where I come from. We are famous for horses and horsemen. Everybody rides—all the men and most of the women. Horses are my country's heritage."

Gabe nodded, understanding the implications. "Would you like me to teach you?"

The boy shook his head. "Papa tried many times. I just fall off—like a *baby*! Useless!" He thumped his crooked leg so hard it must have hurt. "This leg is no good. Not strong enough."

Gabe passed him the last slice of apple. "Many people with bad legs can still ride."

The boy shook his head. "Not me. Papa had me examined by the best physicians. My leg cannot be fixed. So I will never ride."

"Maybe," Gabe said. He entered the stall and slipped a bridle onto his horse. "My brother Harry's leg was hurt when he was tiny. He still limps, but he rides like a demon."

There was a silence. Gabe placed the saddle on Trojan's back and bent to tighten the cinch. "Harry will be here in a few days. He's bringing some horses." He glanced sideways at the boy's face. The boy made no sign he'd heard.

Gabe untied Trojan and led him out of the stall. Nicky hung back, still nervous of the big horse. When Trojan made a lunge toward him, he flattened himself against the wall. His fear faded when Trojan gently lipped at his shirt and nudged impatiently at his pocket.

"He wants more apples!" the boy exclaimed, laughing. He hesitantly stroked the horse's nose, then patted him with increasing confidence.

Gabe gave them a few minutes, then led the horse outside.

Nicky followed, his limp very much in evidence. "Where are you going?"

"I thought I'd see if I could retrieve your mother's portmanteau." He mounted and turned the horse toward the driveway. "If anyone wonders where I am, say I'll be back by bre—" He broke off. Turning unexpectedly, he'd caught on Nicky's face such a wistful expression he couldn't stand it. "Would you like to come with me, Nicky?"

"Me? Come with you?"

"You could ride with me. Trojan wouldn't mind. He likes you."

The boy hesitated, gave a longing look at the horse, and glanced back at the house.

"I'll have you back before your mother even wakes."

Still the boy agonized.

"You won't fall off, I promise," Gabe told him. "You can sit in front of me."

"Like a baby?"

"No, like Harry and I used to do when we were boys and only had one horse between us." There was a short silence. Gabe added, "Soldiers do it all the time, too—double up, when there's only one horse."

That was the clincher. The small boy drew himself up, gave Gabe a stiff bow and said solemnly, "I accept." Another boy might have jumped for joy, or clapped his hands or even just grinned with pleasure. Mrs. Prynne's child gave a correct, formal bow. Or was that Papa's child?

"Excellent. Now, grab onto my hands, and when I count to three, you jump and I'll do the rest. One, two, three!" He swung Nicky up in front of him. The child sat facing the front, his hands clutching Gabe's forearms tightly.

"Ready?"

"Yes."

Gabe nudged Trojan and his horse walked down the drive. The boy sat stiffly, holding on to Gabe's forearms in a death grip. Like mother, like son, he reflected.

Poor little lad, to have been forced onto horses only to keep falling off. Gabe remembered Harry falling off a great deal, but it had been Harry's choice to try and try again. Harry couldn't stay away from horses.

As they came to the open downs Gabe said, "We'll go a bit faster now, shall we?"

Nicky nodded. Gabe signaled Trojan to trot. Nicky held on tight, but soon caught the rhythm. "It'd be easier if you had a saddle that fits you," Gabe told him.

"I have never used a saddle," the boy said. "The only way to learn is bareback. That way one learns to master the horse. My father tried—" He broke off. "I'm not supposed to talk about Papa."

"It doesn't matter," Gabe said easily. He was starting to form a picture of the boy's father. "Shall we try a canter?"

"Yes," Nicky said firmly.

"Let me know if you want me to slow down."

Nicky said nothing. Trojan was a very smooth-gaited horse. They cantered until the sea came into sight, glittering in the brilliant morning sun. His horse's pace didn't alter, but he raised his head and snuffed the air eagerly. Trojan was itching for a gallop. So was Gabe.

"How about if we go a bit faster? You won't fall off, I promise."

The boy nodded, so Gabe allowed his horse to pick up speed. The boy made no objection so, after a moment, he gave Trojan his head. They thundered along, the horse's mane streaming back, his hooves cutting up the turf beneath. The boy made not a sound. His small hands clung to Gabe's forearms.

Soon they reached the narrow cliff path and Gabe reluctantly reined in his horse.

"How was that?" he asked the child. There was no response. Gabe leaned forward and turned the boy's face so he could see it. His eyes were shut tight, his pale little face blank of all expression.

Gabe winced. Why the devil had the child not said something if he was so frightened? He felt like a bully. He opened his mouth to apologize.

Nicky's eyes opened. He swallowed. "Again," he whispered. "Do it again."

It wasn't fear in the boy's eyes, Gabe suddenly realized. It was exhilaration.

"Again?"

Nicky nodded. "Yes, only faster!"

Gabe threw back his head and laughed. "You'll do, young Nicky! You'll do. But we can't go off gallivanting just yet—I need to get you back before your mother misses you. And first we have to fetch that portmanteau."

"And Mama's slipper?"

"Possibly." He added, "If I dismount and lead Trojan, can you sit up there by yourself?"

He looked uncertain, but nodded gamely. Gabe dismounted and left Nicky clutching the pommel. He led the horse along the narrow path, searching for signs of last night's activities.

"Ah, this is where it happened," he said at last. He lifted the boy down and tossed him the reins. "Tie Trojan to a bush, would you?" Nicky took the reins with an air of importance and led the big horse away.

Gabe peered over the edge of the cliff at the path leading up from the pebbly beach. A difficult climb for a woman and a child with a bad leg, especially in the dark, never mind the portmanteau. Why the devil had she landed here, of all places?

Nicky joined him and peered over. "It was very hard climbing up in the dark. We could not see and the path was very steep." He added, "But it was not so muddy as it is now."

"Yes, you are lucky you arrived before the rain came," Gabe said. It was going to be a slippery expedition; the slope contained several small mudslides. Gabe was glad he hadn't worn his good boots.

"Mama was very angry with the captain of the boat. She wanted him to take her to Lulworth Cove but *he took no notice*!"

Gabe repressed a grin. "Good heavens!"

"Papa would have had him flogged. Mama explained to me on the beach that they did not know who we—" He broke off with a guilty expression. "Oh."

"What was that?" Gabe said. "Sorry, I wasn't listening."

"Nothing." Nicky relaxed.

Gabe was intrigued. Who was she, that her son should be so astounded that the captain of a boat—even a smuggling boat—would refuse to obey an order from his mother?

"I can't see the portmanteau, but I think that's the trail it made when it fell—do you see?" He pointed to where some of the scrubby vegetation clinging to the rock had been recently broken and rocks disturbed. I'll climb down and have a look. I hope it hasn't been buried under mud."

"Look! That's Mama's slipper." Nicky pointed excitedly.

Sure enough there it was, a small scrap of blue, wedged against an outcrop of jagged rocks softened by a menacing froth of waves.

"That can stay there," Gabe decided.

"Oh, but they were Mama's favorite slippers."

"No, it's too dangerous. All that rain last night will have washed away some of the earth holding the rocks in place—that's what those mudslides are." Gabe enjoyed taking risks, but he didn't see the point of making such a perilous climb for a slipper.

He slipped over the edge and began the descent toward

the portmanteau. A small avalanche of pebbles behind him made him look back. Nicky was coming, too. "No, you stay there," Gabe ordered.

"I want to come."

"You can't, it's too dangerous."

"I can do it. And it's *my* portmanteau."

"Don't argue with me, boy! Stay there." It was a miracle the child had made it up the dangerous path. Climbing down again with such a bad leg—and after a night of rain had softened the dirt—was asking for trouble.

"I apologize. I just wanted to help," Nicky said in a small, stiff voice.

Oh God, he'd hurt the child's feelings. Too late, Gabe remembered his half brother's hatred of his weak leg, Harry's refusal to have it allowed for, his determination to do whatever any other boy did.

"You can help. You can—" He tried to think of a task. "You can mind Trojan."

Nicky looked mulish. "Trojan is tied up. And last night he was free but when you whistled, he came."

Gabe was not used to people questioning his orders. But he couldn't bark at a child of seven in the same way as he would a rebellious recruit. "Yes, but that was at night," he said. "In daylight there are more people around. He's a very valuable animal and I need you to guard him from, er, from horse thieves."

"Horse thieves?"

"Yes, horse thieves. Very dangerous men, horse thieves. Hordes of them roam the countryside, looking for valuable horses. They're not interested in boys," he added hastily, "only horses. So if you see any sinister-looking men coming this way, you must call down to me at once. As loudly as you can. Is that clear, Nicky?"

The boy clicked his heels in a military manner. "Yes, sir! I will guard the horse."

"Good lad!" Gabe recommenced his descent, slipping

and sliding in places where the rocks gave way to mud. It really was quite dangerous.

"Whatcher doin'?"

Nicky was so startled he nearly fell over the cliff. He'd been leaning out, watching. He raised a fist as he turned, but instead of a horde of sinister men, there was just one ragged boy a little older than himself, with a sharp face and bold, dark eyes. He was pulling a rickety two-wheeled handcart.

"Who are you?" He clutched Trojan's reins defensively.

The boy scowled. His face was remarkably dirty. Nicky doubted his hair had been brushed in weeks. His feet were bare, his trousers were tattered but he showed not a shred of shame. "I asked you first! And what're you doin' with Trojan?"

His tone stung Nicky, prompting him into responding to a boy of a class he knew was beneath him. "I'm guarding him," he answered in the crushing manner that Papa had taught him.

"From what?"

"From horse thieves."

"*Horse thieves?*" declared the boy scornfully. "As if anyone around here would be daft enough to nick Mr. Gabe's Trojan!"

"*Nick?*" Nicky didn't understand.

"Nick—doncha know what that means? Pinch, swipe, nab, steal—"

"Oh." Nicky thought for a moment. "So you don't think there's any horse thieves around here?"

The boy spat. "Nah. Never heard of any and I've lived here all me life. And even if there was one, he wouldn't get far. Everyone in these parts knows Mr. Gabe and Trojan."

Thoughtfully Nicky let go of the reins. It was as he had

thought at first: Mr. Renfrew had just wanted him out of the way. He, like Papa, thought Nicky was useless.

"So, what were you lookin' at?" the grubby boy demanded, still faintly hostile.

Nicky pointed. "That slipper, that blue thing down there."

The boy squinted down, then nodded. "A slipper, is it? That's all right then, you can have it. I was worried you was after me eggs and stuff."

"Eggs and stuff?"

The boy jerked his chin at the cliffs. "I get eggs from the nests there. Good eatin', those eggs."

"Oh." Eggs from wild seabirds? An English delicacy, no doubt, Nicky thought.

The boy looked down the cliff and wrinkled his nose. "What do you want with one slipper?"

"That is my business," Nicky said. He did not think it proper to reveal his mother's slipperless state to this strange and dirty boy.

"So you're goin' to fetch it, then?" The boy's tone was mildly skeptical.

"I might."

"Not in them boots ya won't."

Nicky looked down at his boots. "Why not?"

The boy spat again. " 'Cause you'll fall to your death, that's why not. Them fancy leather soles will slip on the rocks and mud. You won't be able to get a good grip at all."

"Oh."

"So take 'em off."

"You mean go down there with no shoes?"

"That's how I do it. You get a better grip with your toes. Never fallen yet. Ain't you never climbed a cliff before?"

"Never," Nicky admitted. He'd never walked outside in bare feet, either, but he wasn't going to admit that.

"Well take it from me—I know all about it," said the

boy. "Some folks call me Monkey on account of how good I can climb, but me real name's Jim."

"How do you do, Jim. I am called Nicky." He gave a slight bow.

"Coo, posh, aren't ya?" said Jim with a grin. He extended a filthy hand with black-rimmed nails, and Nicky gingerly shook it. "Pleased to meet you, Nicky. Well, go on, get them boots off."

Nicky sat down to pull off his boots. Jim watched curiously. "Gimpy leg, eh?"

Nicky didn't respond, but the shame crept back.

"Me da had a gimpy leg, too, sort of. Shark bit half his leg off. Didn't stop Da, but. Got himself a peg leg, didn't he?" Jim said cheerfully. "Well, you get on with fetching your slipper. I gotta get on. I made a real find this morning." He disappeared behind a scraggly bush and reappeared lugging a battered and muddy portmanteau.

Nicky had no trouble recognizing it. "That's our portmanteau!"

"It's mine. I saw it first. Rules of salvage." Jim said and heaved it onto the handcart.

"But it belongs to me."

Jim snorted rudely. "My arse it does! I found it on the beach this morning, and I hauled it all the way up here, so it's mine!"

"But it contains all the possessions Mama and I have!"

"Good try, but I wasn't born yesterday. Finders keepers. You get the slipper, I get this." He pulled out a piece of string to tie the portmanteau to the cart.

Nicky ran forward and tried to pull the portmanteau off him. "No! It's not yours. You can't have it!"

Jim shoved Nicky backward hard and stood over him with clenched fists. "Try and stop me."

"Very well." Nicky scrambled to his feet and put up his fists, ready to fight the bigger boy. He'd had lessons in the art of pugilism. He moved closer and jabbed at the boy. In return, Jim swung a punch, then followed it with a hard kick to Nicky's bad leg. With a cry of pain, Nicky went sprawling in the mud.

As he struggled to stand again, his fingers encountered a stone, and remembered Mr. Renfrew's advice to his mother. Seizing the stone, he ran at the boy, yelling at the top of his voice, and hit him hard on the nose.

There was a horrid sound, the boy's dirty face blossomed with blood and he fell to the ground. Nicky stared in horror, and dropped the stone. He had not meant to hurt the boy, just stop him from stealing the portmanteau.

"What the devil is going on!" Mr. Renfrew exclaimed from behind. "Who is that?

Nicky's lip trembled. "His name is Jim, and I think I have killed him!"

Four

*C*allie woke slowly, coming to consciousness as if gradually floating to the surface of a very deep lake. She awoke feeling safe . . . cared for.

Stupid. Dreaming foolish dreams again. Painful dreams. Dreams that made her ache inside. Dreams for *girls*, not a woman like Callie. She had done with such things. She knew better now.

She had the love of her son. That should be enough for anyone. And Tibby loved her, too, she knew. A son and a friend; more than many people had, she told herself.

She reached out to check Nicky as she did countless times in the night. These days she always slept with him in touching distance. She did not dare to let him sleep alone.

Her fingers only found sheets, cold and empty.

Nicky! Her eyes flew open and she sat up. Scarcely stopping to fling a rug around her shoulders for modesty's sake, she ran down the stairs in bare feet.

"Where's my son?" Callie burst into the kitchen. "What have you done with him?"

"Your boy?" Mrs. Barrow looked up from the pot she was stirring. "He'll be off in the stables or sommat, I expect." She smiled at Callie. "No need to ask you how you slept. Like death warmed through, you were last night and here you are, blooming and—"

"Where have they taken him?" Callie demanded.

"Who?" Mrs. Barrow frowned. "Nobody's taken your boy anywhere, don't you fret. He'll turn up when his stomach reminds him. Boys always do."

Callie searched the woman's broad, ruddy face for lies, but could see nothing but placid honesty. "Nicky isn't the sort of boy to run off."

"Well, I've been working down here since just after sunup." Mrs. Barrow nodded at a bowl of apples on the sideboard. "Someone took some apples. And the outside door was unbolted when I came down. He'll be in the stables. That's where boys usually go."

Callie shook her head. "Nicky never goes near the stables. He doesn't like horses. Someone must have taken him."

"Who? There's nobody here except us. The dog would have barked if there were strangers about."

"The dog!" Callie exclaimed. "Yes, the dog was with him last night. Where's the dog?"

Mrs. Barrow seized a folded pad of cloth and with much banging and clattering pulled two loaves of fresh-baked bread from the oven. "Outside, where dogs ought to be. Mr. Gabe will bring her in, but I don't like dogs in my kitchen!"

With a deft flick of her wrist she turned the loaves onto a wire rack. Steam rose from the toasty crusts and the room filled with the delicious fragrance. "There, that should fetch him in. Never knowed man or boy able to resist the smell of fresh-baked bread!"

But Callie wasn't reassured. "Where is Mr. Renfrew?"

"Gone out for 'is mornin' ride, Barrow reckons. Trojan and his saddle are gone."

"Aha! So he must have—"

"Master Gabe rides out every morning, rain or shine, he does. And sometimes at night. Helps chase away his demons, Barrow reckons. Not a good sleeper anymore, the young master. The war, you see. Hard on young men, it is. After nigh on eight years of war and living in tents in fur-rin parts, it's not easy for a man to settle down to a peace-able English life, Barrow reckons. Our Harry is the same. Restless. Always off and doing."

But Callie wasn't listening. Through the windows that looked away to the sea, she could see a rider coming fast toward the house, a rider on a big, black horse. A dirty bun-dle was bunched in front of the rider. A limp, child-sized bundle with dirty bare feet.

"Nicky!" She ran to the door and flung it open. Mrs. Bar-row followed, and Barrow ran from nearby outbuildings.

"Here, Barrow, you take him in! It might be a broken nose—"

"Broken nose!" Callie was horrified. She couldn't see Nicky's face for the blood-soaked white handkerchief cov-ering it.

"—or not, but there's rather a lot of blood." Mr. Ren-frew handed the bundle down to Barrow, then dismounted.

"Nicky! Nicky!" Callie tried to reach her child but Mr. Renfrew grabbed her by the arm.

"Nicky's perfectly all right," he told her.

"How can you say that? There's blood everywhere!" Callie struggled. "Let me go! I must go to him!"

"That boy is not Nicky!"

Callie froze, staring at him wide-eyed.

He said in a firm voice, "Nicky is perfectly all right."

She looked wildly around. "Then where is he?"

"He's back at the cliffs, minding your portmanteau."

"Minding my portmanteau?" she echoed stupidly.

"Yes, I had to leave him there with it." He brushed mud from his shirt and only succeeded in smearing it more.

"Otherwise the portmanteau could have been stolen. It's damp and looks rather the worse for wear after its fall down the cliff, and it's rather muddy. But otherwise intact."

She stared at him, unable to believe her ears. "You mean you left my child out in the middle of nowhere, on his own, *to guard a portmanteau?*"

"That's right." He gave her a reassuring smile. "I don't think it's in danger, but I didn't like to leave it."

"You don't think the portmanteau is in danger," she repeated faintly.

"No." Using the cast-iron boot scraper at the back door, he started to scrape the mud from his boots.

"But my son is alone."

He frowned. "Yes, but he's a sensible boy. He'll stay well away from the edge, I'm sure."

"Away from *the edge*? Of the cliffs? Where we were last night?"

"Yes, I took him for a ride there this morning. Don't you think you're being a bit overprotective?"

"Overprotective?" She looked at him and suddenly felt strangely calm. She scanned the nearby ground.

He watched her, puzzled. "What are you looking for? Dropped something?"

She gave him a limpid look. "I need a large stone."

"A large stone?"

"Yes, you said it would be better to hold a large stone in my fist the next time I punched someone."

"Ah," he said. "I see. You're upset. You're worried about the boy, but there's no need, I assure—"

Callie looked at him. She was not sure what kind of expression she had on her face, but it seemed to have a satisfactory effect. He backed away.

"I'll just nip back and fetch him, shall I?" Gabriel emitted a shrill whistle and his horse returned at a trot, his reins trailing. "Back in a trice," he said as he mounted with a lithe movement and galloped back the way he had come.

Callie watched until he disappeared from sight, then hastily ran upstairs to dress. She kept looking out of the window, fear and fury warring within her. Nicky was out there alone on a cliff top. Anything could happen.

"Ow, yer hurting me!" a young voice complained as Callie reentered the kitchen. Mrs. Barrow was struggling with the child, stripping him of his clothing while Barrow trudged back and forth with pails of water.

"I'll hurt you worse if you keep wrigglin' like that, me lad!" Mrs. Barrow snapped. "Look at the state of you! You're a disgrace!"

"He's not badly hurt, then?" she asked Mrs. Barrow.

"The nose isn't broken, just bloody. I don't think there's any other injury, but who can tell with such a filthy little beggar? What's your name lad?"

"Jim—ow!" The child, for Callie saw he was not much older than Nicky, tried to fend her off, but Mrs. Barrow was more than a match for him.

"Pour in the hot water, now, Barrow," she instructed over her shoulder. "It won't be as hot as I'd like, but it won't be cold, neither—keep still, you young devil!"

"Stop that! It ain't decent!" the child tried to snatch back the shirt she'd ruthlessly stripped from his skinny frame.

"The amount o' dirt on you is what's not decent, young Jimmy, me lad! I wouldn't be surprised if he's got potatoes growing in his pockets, ma'am!"

"I have not!" The boy looked at Callie. "I haven't, lady, truly I haven't! Make her let me go, please."

Callie gave him a helpless look. She was worried about her own son. This child's fate did not concern her; he was in good hands with Mrs. Barrow. This child was perfectly safe.

She glanced out of the window, knowing there hadn't

been enough time for him to return, but unable to quell the anxiety in her breast.

Mrs. Barrow continued, undaunted, "There's enough dirt on you to grow a dozen potatoes. You're havin' a bath, whether you like it or not." She yanked his ragged trousers off.

"Oyyy!" the boy yowled and desperately tried to cover his miniscule private parts. "I'm not getting in no bath! I'm not!"

"It's that or boil you in the copper with the sheets!" responded Mrs. Barrow fiercely.

"Boil me in the copper!" Jim's wide, shocked eyes stood out against the black grime of his face.

"With the sheets, that's right." Over the boy's head, Mrs. Barrow winked at Callie. "A good boiling in lye would kill all that nasty vermin you've got living on you! Fleas and nits and who knows what else? I'd do it, too, only Barrow said a bath would be kinder. But if you're going to argue . . ."

Amidst howls of protest Jim was dumped into the tin bath and scrubbed from head to toe, with no allowances for modesty. Each time he opened his mouth to protest, soap got in.

Callie was caught between the domestic comedy-drama unfolding before her and anxiety about her son. Nicky was scared of horses; why would he agree to go for a ride?

What if they had been followed? What if Count Anton's men found Nicky by the cliff top, alone and unprotected? Without witnesses.

Behind her, the water in the tin bathtub turned black.

Callie battled with a vision of a small broken body lying among jagged rocks and shuddered. He would be all right, he would. She prayed silently.

"Step onto the mat."

All resistance scrubbed out of him, Jim stood, like a drowned but extremely clean rat, his hair in wet spikes, as he was briskly dried and wrapped in a large towel.

"Now sit! And eat that—and don't argue!" Mrs. Barrow handed him a plate covered by a huge slab of pork pie. The pie disappeared in seconds.

Callie glanced out of the window for the twentieth time. Still no sign of a tall man and a small boy on a black horse. Anxiety gnawed at her.

Mrs. Barrow fetched a pair of scissors. "I'm going to cut your hair," she told Jim. "It's too knotted to comb out and besides, it's the only way for us to check for any cuts on your head."

He shrank back against the seat. "There ain't none! I'm all right, honest!"

"*Isn't any*, not *ain't none*," she corrected him. "And sit still or I'll end up chopping off your ears as well."

Jim sat very, very still. Hair fell in matted clumps around him.

"That's better, you look almost human now." Mrs. Barrow stood back and regarded him severely. "Now, let's have a look at this nose." Jim's hands came up protectively and she pushed them away. "Don't be silly. Do you think I'm going to hurt you?"

Barrow winked at Callie. "Aye, why would you fear Mrs. Barrow, lad?" he said in a deep rumble. "She's only scrubbed every inch of your body raw, threatened to boil you in lye and cut off your ears. Nothing to be worried about, there."

"Oh pshaw! The lad knows full well I wouldn't hurt him."

The boy gave her a wide-eyed look of amazement.

"Oh, don't give me that look—you knew! Now, sit still while I tend to that nose or I won't give you any fresh bread and jam. With clotted cream."

Jim worked out that threat and sat like a lamb while she cleaned and examined his nose. Barrow winked at Callie again.

She gave him a quick smile. Five-and-twenty years of rigid training slipping away, unregretted.

Papa would have pointed out that this is what came of such laxness—grooms winked at her in the most familiar way, and cooks cuddled her and called her lovie.

And the worst of it was, Callie quite liked it. Or she would if she weren't so worried.

"A nd you're sure that Jim is all right?" Nicky asked Gabe for the third time.

"Yes. It looked worse than it was. It's sore, that's all. The most important thing was to get it cleaned of all that mud. Wounds can fester if they're left dirty." Gabe finished strapping the portmanteau to Trojan's back. "You weren't worried about being left here?"

"No," Nicky said. "Here, I can see for miles. I can see the sea and the path and nobody could creep up to grab me. I saw you coming ages before you got here."

Gabe frowned at the boy. "Are you worried about people grabbing you?"

"Yes, of course." He spoke as if it was a perfectly normal fear.

"Has anyone ever tried to grab you before?"

"Yes."

"Really?" So Nicky's mother had grounds for her anxieties after all.

"How did you get that?" Nicky pointed at Gabe's ear.

Gabe automatically touched the thin, pale line that went along his jaw and ended with his severed earlobe. "A bayonet."

"If he'd got you a bit lower down you would have been killed," said Nicky with a child's blunt relish.

"Yes, or my ear cut right off," Gabe agreed. "I had a lucky escape."

"Mama has a cut like that in her ear, too."

"What?" Gabe stared at him. He hadn't noticed. Her hair had been loose over her ears. "How did that happen?"

"Someone ripped it."

"She was attacked?"

The boy nodded, frowning. "I'm not sure if I'm supposed to talk about it in England." He bit his lip. "I prob'ly shouldn't have told you about the bad men, either. The thing is, I'm not perfectly sure what I'm supposed to say and what I'm not."

"I won't tell a soul." Gabe checked the saddle, feigning indifference.

Nicky thought for a moment, then, apparently deciding he could talk about it after all, said, "Mama told me later it was just some thieves after her earrings . . . One earring did get ripped out. It bled everywhere. Mama said it didn't hurt a bit."

Mama had lied, Gabe thought to himself, and wondered where Papa had been at the time.

"But I think she was just saying that so I wouldn't worry. Mama does that sometimes."

Gabe's brows rose. A perceptive lad for one so young.

Nicky fiddled with the reins that he was holding. He darted Gabe a solemn, fugitive look. "I don't think the men were thieves, either."

"You don't?"

The boy shook his head. "They were after me. Only Mama stopped them."

"Has that happened before?" Gabe asked him.

"Yes, I was kidnapped once, for three days, but they got me back. I don't really remember; I was little then." He shrugged. "Men are always after me."

"Are men after you now?" Gabe said quietly. It certainly explained a lot of things that had puzzled him.

The boy hunched his thin shoulders. "We don't know. Mama hopes not. That's why—" He bit his lip.

"Why you came to England," Gabe finished for him. And why she had been so mistrustful of him last night, he thought. "Well, I don't know who these men are, Nicky, but

I promise you this—if they do come after you or your mama, I'll do my very best to stop them." He added, "I'm pretty good at dealing with bad men, you know. I've been a soldier at war for the last eight years."

The child gave him a long, considering look, then nodded, as if satisfied.

Gabe mounted and swung Nicky up in front of him. "Time to go back," he said. "Your mother is worried about you."

"Yes, and I must see how Jim is."

They moved off at a walk. The cliff-top path was too slippery with mud to go much faster.

Nicky frowned. "I did the wrong thing, didn't I? Hitting him with the stone."

"Yes," Gabe confirmed. "Why did you do it?"

"Well, he did not fight as gentlemen do in my country, and he was beating me and I remembered how you told Mama to hold a stone and to go for the nose, and you are a gentleman, so I thought that was how it was done in England," Nicky concluded.

"It isn't," Gabe said ruefully. "I told your mother to do that because a lady should never have to fight, and she is smaller and weaker than most men, therefore not subject to the rules a gentleman is."

"So I should not have hit Jim?"

"Not with the stone, no. But it was not wrong to fight to defend your mother's possessions. And if he was fighting with gutter tactics, your move was understandable. You should not blame him for it, either; he has not been trained as a gentleman has."

Nicky considered that. "I am not sure what I should do—whether I should apologize to him or not."

"What do you want to do?"

"Papa used to say one should never apologize to an inferior. And Jim is a peasant, is he not?"

"We don't speak of peasants in England anymore," Gabe told him. "But Jim is probably a poor fisherman's son."

"So Papa would say I should not apologize." The boy sighed. "But Mama says if I do the wrong thing, I should always apologize, no matter who the person is. But then Mama is a lady and ladies are different."

"They are indeed," Gabe agreed.

"Of course I always *obeyed* Papa, but sometimes it did not *feel* good, here." He touched his chest.

"I see," Gabe said. "This matter has nothing to do with Mama or Papa, has it? So what do *you* think you should do?"

Nicky thought for a while. "I feel bad that I hit Jim and broke his nose, and that I did not fight him as a gentleman should."

Gabe nodded.

"I would like to talk to Jim again. He may be a peas—a poor fisher boy, but he is an interesting boy." Nicky gave Gabe an upward glance. "I don't want him to stay angry with me."

"So you would apologize so you can be friends?"

Nicky thought about that. "No, I will apologize because I did the wrong thing," he decided.

"And if you didn't like him? Would you still apologize?"

He considered the question. "I *think* I would still apologize but it would not be easy, for if he was my enemy, he would feel superior."

Gabe nodded. "Which is more important, what an enemy thinks of you, or what you think of yourself?"

"That is a good question," Nicky said thoughtfully. "My enemy's opinion is nothing to me. You are right, sir."

They rode on for a little. "Sir, this has been a very good conversation. Thank you," the small boy said solemnly.

Gabe ruffled his hair. "I've enjoyed it, too. You're a good lad, Nicky. No wonder your mother is proud of you. Now, shall we ride a little faster?"

"Yes, and gallop like the wind, please," said Nicky firmly.

They galloped like the wind, Nicky clutching Gabe's forearms, and urging Gabe to go faster, faster, *faster*!

Finally Gabe judged that Trojan had had enough, and slowed to a canter.

"That was splendid!" Nicky exclaimed. "I never understood before that riding could be like flying!" The boy held himself much more loosely now, responding to the movement of the horse instinctively. With a proper saddle, and a few adaptations for his weak leg, Gabe was sure the boy could ride.

"It is indeed. You said your father was an excellent rider."

"Yes, the finest rider in all of Z—my country."

Gabe drew a bow at random. "And he died in a riding accident. Was it jumping a fence?"

"No, he was shot. They said it was an accident, but it wasn't true, though."

So he *was* dead, Gabe thought. "Wasn't it?"

"No. They were after him and they got him. Now they're after me," the boy said in a matter-of-fact tone.

"I see. And how long ago was this?"

Nicky thought for a moment. "More than a year. Papa was killed a month before my birthday. I wasn't even seven, then."

"I see." Gabe was silent for a while. The child was in genuine danger then. He owed her an apology.

"And does Mama have a name other than Mama?"

Nicky laughed. "Of course. Papa called her Caroline, but Grandpapa always called her Callie."

Gabe rode the next few miles without thinking, his thoughts miles away.

Her name was Callie. And she was a widow. Of more than a year.

They came to the arch into the courtyard and Gabe slowed Trojan to a walk.

"Can't we do it again?" Nicky begged. "Gallop like the wind?"

Gabe grinned. "Not right now, you young fiend. Your mother would throttl—whoops, here she comes!"

The kitchen door crashed open and Nicky's mother came flying across the courtyard, fully dressed and wearing shoes.

"I'll take you out again later." He lifted the boy to the ground.

Nicky clung to his arms. "Promise?"

"I promise."

"Nicky, you're all right! Oh, thank God, thank God!" His mother hugged him fiercely. Gabe dismounted in a leisurely manner and unstrapped the portmanteau.

Nicky suffered his mother's embrace for a moment, then wriggled free. His face split with a grin, he gabbled, "Mama, I had the most splendid time! Mr. Renfrew took me out on Trojan—that's his horse's name—he's a magnificent animal, don't you think? As good as any of Papa's horses, and it was utterly splendid and I never fell off, not once, and we went fast, so fast it was like riding the wind and I never even got scared because Mr. Renfrew held me in front of him and he's very strong and an excellent horseman, and oh, we galloped across the moor so fast, Mama, and—"

She hugged him again, half laughing, half crying. "So you've had a wonderful time, you horrid boy, and to think I've been so worried. And look at you! You're covered in *mud*!"

"Yes, I know!" The boy's eyes sparkled in his dirty face, as if the dirt had been as much of a treat as the ride, Gabe thought. And perhaps it was. Nicky had been kept on a very tight leash. For good reason, he supposed, but still, it was hard on a boy, not to be allowed to be a boy.

"And I hear you've been fighting with that boy in there!"

Nicky looked suddenly guilty, "Yes, I know, Mama, but Mr. Renfrew said it wasn't wrong to fight to protect our portmanteau—"

"As if I care about the portmant—"

"Mama, I must go and see how he is. Mr. Renfrew said he was all right, but I must see him for myself. I owe him an apology. I know he's a poor peasant boy and very dirty, but—" He looked down almost proudly at his filthy state and grinned again. "So am I—dirty, that is! And I don't care if anyone forbids it—he's my *friend*, Mama."

And with that, he ran off with his ungainly, lopsided run toward the kitchen door, leaving his mother standing in the middle of the courtyard, staring after him with such a look of astonishment on her face it made Gabe laugh out loud.

At the sound she turned. *"You!"* she declared, her magnificent green eyes sparking with anger. "How dare you laugh? Do you have *any* idea how I felt? *Any* idea of what I went through when I found him missing?"

Gabe gave an apologetic shrug. "I was actually bent on fetching your portmanteau for you," he said mildly, backing slowly toward the stables. As he'd intended, she followed.

"You should have asked!"

"Would you have given me permission to take him?"

"Of course not! Why would I entrust my child to a perfect stranger?"

The stables were quiet; Barrow had unsaddled Trojan and put him in his stall. Gabe gave him a subtle signal to him to disappear. He went, quietly shutting the stable door behind him.

"And you *know* he is terrified of horses—"

"He's not. He's terrified of falling off, which I gather

he's done a lot of in the past. Once he was assured he would not fall off, he had a whale of a time."

She stared at him, nettled.

"So you think I'm perfect, do you?" he said as he opened a stall door.

She looked bewildered. "How could you possibly think that?"

"You just told me I was."

"I did not!"

"You said I was a perfect strang—"

She narrowed her eyes at him. "I meant a *complete* stranger," she corrected him. "A wholly unknown person, and certainly not a person to be trusted with my son. And do not be flippant when I am reprimanding you!"

"No, ma'am." Gabe murmured. "You're very pretty when you're cross, you know."

Her nostrils flared enchantingly as she gave a scornful snort.

"I'll wager you've been fretting yourself to flinders with all sorts of horrid imaginings and now that you've seen Nicky is perfectly all right and apparently as happy as Larry, you're feeling all cross and out of sorts. So you blame me."

"I do blame you, yes! Because it *was* your fault. If you hadn't taken him—"

"Yes, yes, mea culpa. Do you know, I have the perfect solution for the way you're feeling," Gabe told her.

"Oh, do you? And what might that be?"

"This." And before she could even guess what he intended, he took a step forward. Which brought her hard against him, breast to chest.

She gasped. The most kissable mouth in the world formed a perfect *O* of surprise and Gabriel did what he'd been planning to do since he'd first clapped eyes on her.

He kissed her.

Five

*H*is lips were warm and firm and his action so unexpected that at first Callie was too surprised to move. Or resist.

She was being kissed in the stable like a maidservant.

She ought to scream. She ought to resist.

But the way he kissed . . . resistance was futile.

He tasted of salt and apples and of man. It was just a kiss, she told herself, and yet it felt so . . . intimate. He kissed her with his whole mouth, not just his lips, possessive and sure, and she felt herself melting against him.

After a moment he released her. She stood staring at his mouth, dazed.

"That was wrong," she murmured. "I'm a respectable wi—woman. Let me go, please." He didn't move, but his gaze dropped to her hands and his mouth curved into a slow grin. She followed his gaze and saw her own hands clutching his coat lapels in a convulsive grip. She hastily released them.

"If it was wrong, we'll get it right this time," he murmured. "This will be a *very* respectable kiss."

She pressed her hands against his chest, meaning to hold him off, but somehow, it changed. His mouth closed over hers again, and again she felt those swirling, heady sensations. She could feel his heartbeat under her fingers. He cupped her face in his hands as if he were holding something precious and the kiss went on forever.

Her hands slipped up over his chest, along his strong, rough jawline, and her fingers tangled in his hair. His tongue caressed hers and flames licked along her nerve endings, pooling in her core.

By the time he stopped Callie could barely stand, let alone speak.

Her legs felt strange and rubbery and for a moment she thought she was going to sink into the hay on the floor. She locked her knees as stiffly as she could until they were back in working order and tried to look serene. And dignified. A princess, not a maidservant.

"I don't kiss strange men," she managed feebly after a moment. Had she really run her hands through his hair? It wasn't like her. And yet, his hair was undeniably messy.

He smiled down at her in a way that made her blush and feel strangely unsettled. "I'm glad to hear it. Though I'm not so very strange, am I? I always thought I was a fairly ordinary fellow."

He was far from ordinary. "I meant I don't *know* you!" she said, desperately trying to compose herself. She could not believe that she'd allowed herself to kiss him back. She knew where this sort of thing led.

Straight to heartbreak.

He gave her a tragic look. "You've forgotten me, so soon? But I'm the fellow who took you up to bed last night. You were dressed most delightfully in an enormous pink nightgown. Ring a bell?"

She blushed. "You know what I mean."

"Never mind, since you've apparently forgotten me, I'll introduce myself: Gabriel Renfrew, at your service." He gave her that wicked, glinting smile. "At your very exclusive, very personal service. How do you do? Redundant question, really. You do beautifully, don't you? You certainly taste delicious—like wild honey."

He leaned forward to kiss her again, but this time Callie managed to step back out of reach. "No! Stop. It's impossible."

"I'm hoping you'll decide I'm very possible. You have to admit we're progressing. Last night you called me a snake, remember? But you must concede now that I'm very warm-blooded. You can feel that about me, can't you? My warm blood?"

Callie's blush deepened. She didn't know what to say or where to look. Under no circumstances was she admitting that she could feel anything warm about him. Not his mouth, not his big, warm body, not anything. He was far too warm-blooded for any virtuous woman's comfort.

He smiled. "Well, if you're finished having your way with me, we'd better not stay here dillydallying the day away." She gave a gasp of indignation, but he continued, "We have to unpack that portmanteau of yours. I fear it's rather sea-damaged and some of your things could be ruined." He held out his hand to her. "And then there's the question of breakfast."

She turned toward the door. He followed her, saying, "Next time we'll find somewhere more comfortable."

She turned back. "Next time? There will be no next time. I told you before, I'm a respectable, married la—"

"Widow," he said, trying to keep his pleasure from showing. "Of more than a year, Nicky seemed to think."

"Did you grill a seven-year—"

"I didn't precisely grill him, just . . . put things together. He spoke of his father in the past tense. You do, too, as a matter of fact." He smiled. "And you're a widow."

"Yes, but I'm not *that* sort of widow!"

"What sort do you mean?" He sauntered toward her.

She took several steps back. "I am a widow, but I have no desire to change that state! I know what marriage entails and I want nothing to do with it ever again!"

"Who said anything about marriage?"

Her eyes widened. "I have principles!"

He shrugged and took another step forward. "Principles won't keep you warm at night."

Her eyes lit with a sudden gleam. "No, but thanks to you I know exactly what will."

His smile widened. "Excellent, so—"

"A hot brick," she said triumphantly and swept toward the kitchen door.

Her son was sitting in a tin bath, being ruthlessly scrubbed by Mrs. Barrow, while the urchin, Jim, watched gleefully. "'Orrible, ain't it?" he was saying, but Nicky knew better than to open his mouth while there was soap in Mrs. Barrow's hand.

"Wait till she cuts all your hair off."

Callie opened her mouth to forbid it, but Mrs. Barrow got in first. "I won't be needing to cut this boy's hair—*his* hair has been brushed in the last six months, unlike others I could name! And if you keep sitting there making foolish remarks, you won't be wanting any breakfast."

Jim shut his mouth.

Callie hurried to help Mrs. Barrow rinse the suds from Nicky's body. It had been years since she'd bathed her son. When Rupert had discovered how she bathed her baby herself, he'd forbidden it. The palace nursemaids did that sort of thing, not his son's mother. Such a menial chore was improper for a princess.

Callie poured warm water through her son's hair, smoothing it, enjoying the clean squeak of it, smiling at his screwed-up face, knowing perfectly well that Nicky was acting for the sake of the boy, Jim.

These moments of closeness with her son had been an unexpected consequence of this journey.

Nicky stepped from the bath to be dried. He stood stiffly, knowing his bad leg was visible to all in the room, making no sign that he cared.

Callie moved to shield him. She rubbed the small frame with rough towels, feeling defensive and angry, even though nobody had said a word. Just let them dare, that was all!

"Here y'are, lovie, he can wear these." Mrs. Barrow passed her a set of clothes from a small tin trunk.

Gabriel eyed the trunk. "Does that contain what I think it does?"

Mrs. Barrow didn't meet his eyes. "Just a few of Harry's old clothes."

"You've got a trunk full of Harry's old clothes? Small enough to fit these boys? How long have you been keeping them?"

"They were too good to throw out!" she said defensively.

"You could have given them away." He explained to Callie, "Harry's as tall as me."

"Well, I'm giving them away now," Mrs. Barrow retorted. "Now that our Harry's back, safe from the war—and if you want your coffee good and hot, you won't be saying another word, Mr. Gabe!"

"Not a word," he promised hastily.

Callie repressed a smile. It seemed Mrs. Barrow's threats worked as well on grown men as they did on small boys.

"Oh, but our portmanteau is here now. I don't know yet how much seawater got in—Nicky may have dry clothes of his own." She looked around, but could not see the portmanteau.

"Barrow has taken it up to your bedchamber," Mrs. Barrow told her. "Why not use Harry's clothes for the moment?" She scooped up the muddy pile of clothes from the floor and headed for the scullery.

Callie nodded and dressed her son in the clean, worn

clothes of another boy. Never in his life had Nicky worn such shabby clothes, but he seemed quite happy about it, and beggars could not be choosers.

"Lady, everything in that bag is wet," the boy, Jim, said.

"How do you know?" she said, as she slipped a shirt over Nicky's head.

"Jim, er, rescued the portmanteau for us, Mama," Nicky said. His eyes met Jim's. "He brought it all the way up from the beach. It was a very difficult and dangerous thing to do. The rain made mud slides over the path."

"Thank you, Jim," she said.

Jim scuffed his bare toes in embarrassment. "I didn't exactly rescue—"

Nicky interrupted, with a fierce look at Jim. "He did, Mama. He's very strong and clever."

Callie finished dressing Nicky and gave him a kiss on the forehead. She had a very good idea what a boy like Jim would be doing with her portmanteau, but Nicky's eyes were pleading with her to accept his new friend. He'd never had a friend. He had no relations his own age and his father hadn't thought it proper for him to play with common children. Callie knew what that was like. She'd grown up lonely, too.

"Thank you, Jim." On impulse she gave the fisher boy a kiss on the forehead as well. The boy squirmed and the tips of his sticking-out ears went red, but he tried not to grin. In Callie's head Papa and Rupert roared with outrage. Callie smiled. She was her own woman now, subject to nobody's rules.

There was a short silence, then the sound of a throat being noisily cleared from the doorway, where Gabriel had been lounging against the doorjamb, observing. "Don't I get a kiss, too?" he said.

She raised her brows.

"I fetched the portmanteau from the cliffs," he reminded her and puckered his lips suggestively.

"Thank you, Mr. Renfrew, but a good deed is its own reward," she said sweetly. To Mrs. Barrow she said, "I shall go upstairs and discover the condition of the things in my portmanteau."

"Won't you be wanting any breakfast, ma'am?"

"Oh, yes, a cup of tea and some toast would be lovely, thank you."

"And what about a nice bit o' bacon, ma'am?"

Callie hesitated. Bacon. How long had it been since she'd eaten bacon? Rupert had forbidden it to her.

"Very well then, some bacon, thank you." She paused. "Where shall I take it?"

"I'm having mine right here." Gabriel crossed the room and swung a long leg over one of the chairs that surrounded the long kitchen table.

Callie stared. The master of the house eating in the kitchen? She'd never heard of such a thing. He must have read her mind, for he said, "I've been breaking my fast in Mrs. Barrow's kitchen since I was Nicky's age and younger. Best place in the world, I thought it was when I was his age, apart from the stables." He glanced across at Jim. "I'll wager Jim thinks so, too, now he's tasted Mrs. Barrow's cooking, eh, Jim?" The boy nodded fervently.

"I shall take my breakfast in the . . ." Callie wasn't sure where. She only knew she wasn't going to eat bacon in the kitchen with that man watching her. And with the taste of his kisses still on her mouth.

"The breakfast room, ma'am?" suggested Mrs. Barrow. "In about fifteen minutes?"

"Yes, if you will just tell me where it is," Callie agreed gratefully.

Chair legs scraped on the stone-flagged floor. "I'll escort you." Gabriel held out his arm.

Unable to refuse, Callie took his arm and allowed him to lead her to the breakfast room. Sunshine streamed through long French windows. They opened on to a terrace that overlooked the garden at the side of the house. Small enough to be cozy without being poky, the room was decorated in pale green and white with rose upholstery and curtains. It was almost as if the garden had crept into the room.

"Oh, what a pretty room," she exclaimed, forgetting she'd planned to crush him with dignified silence.

"I believe my great-aunt was fond of it. I never use it," he said indifferently, pulling out a chair for her at an oval mahogany table.

She walked to the French windows and stepped out onto the terrace. "I never had a great-aunt," she said. "Were you fond of yours?"

He followed her outside. "Yes. She was a terrifying old lady, but with a very kind heart. She used to give me a daily grilling on my lessons." He quirked a rueful smile. "Boys were a variety of humanity she believed were in dire need of civilizing—which came in the form of discipline, exercise, and rewards."

He saw her expression and laughed. "Great-aunt Gert was passionate about the training and breeding of dogs. She treated boys much the same way—not the breeding, of course. But don't get the idea she was some mad old recluse—she also adored the social whirl and went up to London every season—to terrify the ton, Harry and I always thought. She always returned much refreshed."

Callie smiled and strolled a few steps along the path. "She didn't have any children of her own?"

"Lord, no! I doubt there was a man in England brave enough to marry her."

"That's sad," Callie said. It was warm in the morning sun. Bees were already out and buzzing around the sweet Alice and the lavender. The pathway led to a circular bed containing a sundial. She walked toward it.

He followed her. "With sentiments like that, I'm surprised you don't plan to marry again."

"No, I won't remarry," Callie told him. "Not ever. Not to anyone. I want nothing further to do with men."

He heaved a sigh. "That's my hopes and dreams dashed forever, then."

They walked on. It had been a good thing to set him straight, Callie thought. Best to get it clear and out in the open. No misunderstandings. He'd stop bothering her now. He'd leave her alone, and that would be a good thing.

She didn't need to be . . . bothered.

He was a very . . . bothersome man.

She darted him a sidelong glance. He'd been silent for several moments now. She hoped he wasn't too crushed by her announcement. Not that he should be—they'd only just met, for heaven's sake.

He caught her looking. "So," he said. "You're absolutely sure. No plans to marry again?"

She gave a firm nod. "None."

"You wouldn't consider becoming my mistress?"

She stopped short, scandalized. She'd told him she had principles. She whirled to face him. His eyes were laughing at her. He was teasing her, she realized.

The way he laughed with his eyes, laughing and seeming to . . . caress . . . at the same time . . . it was most disconcerting.

"You are joking," she told him.

"Am I indeed?"

"Yes, for you know perfectly well I am a respectable widow—"

"Oh, we needn't *tell* anyone, if that's what you're worried about—"

She gave him a severe look. "I told you, I have no desire to put myself under the thumb of any man, ever again."

"But it wasn't my *thumb* I was thinking of." He said it with such a wicked, laughing look she was hard put to know what to say. So she turned on her heel and walked off.

It took her several minutes of marching along as fast as

her legs could carry her before she was able to think at all, let alone think of an appropriately crushing, yet dignified response. His words, along with that laughing smile in his eyes, were a pure invitation to sin. She snorted, remembering the session in the stables.

Nothing *pure* about it!

She could hear him coming up behind her on the path. She quickened her pace. His didn't seem to alter, and yet he still gained on her. It wasn't fair that he should have such long, strong legs and hers should be short and rounded. The only way to escape him would be to run, but she wouldn't put it past him to run after her. The wretch probably would enjoy chasing her.

A small voice inside her suggested timidly that she might find it exciting, too. She ruthlessly squashed it.

She deliberately slowed her pace and stopped to stare earnestly at a flower. She had no idea what it was; she'd never been any good at botany, but he needn't know that.

He stopped beside her and waited. She felt the warm wash of his gaze flow over her. And ignored it. She stared hard at the flower. He bent and peered at it over her shoulder.

"Fascinating," she murmured, trying not to be aware of the proximity of his big, masculine body.

"Utterly," he agreed fervently. "Something special, do you think?"

She frowned thoughtfully over the small, blue-flowered plant. "It could well be," she said, hoping he was no botanist.

"It definitely could be," he agreed. "If only creeping charley was not regarded as a weed in England." He paused a moment, then added, "Shall I get someone to pull it out before it spreads, or would you rather paint it or press it in your Weeds of England scrapbook?"

She continued the walk in dignified silence. He strolled along beside her.

"This is nice, isn't it?" he said chattily.

She didn't respond.

"Getting to know each other like this," he continued unabashed. "Breathing the morning air. Learning about your fascination with English weeds . . . and your fear of thumbs."

"You know perfectly well what I meant by not wanting to be under the thumb. My entire life has been spent under the rule of two extremely autocratic men—first my father and then my husband. Now, I have had my first ever taste of freedom, and nothing—no man—could ever taste sweeter than that."

"Is that a challenge?" he said softly.

"No! Do not be so frivolous."

"I wasn't," he said in a meek voice, but his eyes were dancing.

It was the color, she thought irrelevantly. She'd never seen such blue, blue eyes. Like sunlight sparkling on the sea. Another thing that wasn't fair. Men shouldn't be allowed to have eyes like that.

They walked on and, as they turned a corner, the house came into view again. Thank goodness, Callie thought. She might have been walking on a firm graveled path, but it had felt as though she'd been negotiating a marsh, full of traps for the unwary.

He was a very dangerous man! She glanced at him and found him watching her.

"I'm so relieved," he told her.

Callie could not imagine what he was talking about. "Relieved?"

"That you don't dislike my thumbs. I think they're quite nice thumbs—for thumbs, that is. Don't you think?" He spread his hands out for her to inspect, and though it was clearly ridiculous, she couldn't help glancing at his hands.

"What do you think?" he asked.

She gave them a second critical look and sniffed. "All I

can see is that your thumbs are rather large," she said in a quelling voice.

He gave her a slow smile. "Exactly."

Callie had no idea why she should blush, but she did. "I think our breakfast will be ready now," she said and marched briskly back to the breakfast room.

He strolled along beside her. "Yes, I'm ravenous." The way he said it, he didn't just mean for food.

Callie walked faster. She reentered the breakfast parlor. "Did your great-aunt live to a great age?" She was determined to stick to safe subjects.

"Yes, I believe she was eighty or more—she never would let on how old she was. Harry and I thought her a hundred, at least, when we were young. She died just after I left for the war, and for some reason, she left this house to me. I have no idea why. I certainly hadn't expected it."

Callie knew from Mrs. Barrow that Gabriel had spent almost eight years at war, yet the curtains looked new and the paintwork of the room seemed fresh, as if done quite recently. "So you kept her color scheme in memory of her. That's lovely."

"No, it isn't. I had no say in the color scheme. When I sold out of the army, my eldest brother had this place cleaned up for me. I doubt he gave any orders about colors or fabric, so everything was simply renewed."

"That was nice of him," she offered.

"Hmm." He made a noncommittal noise. "I expect he was relieved to have somewhere to put me."

"Put you?" He didn't seem like the sort of man anyone *put* anywhere.

"I'm the youngest of three sons—legitimate ones, that is," he explained. "Surplus to requirements, therefore. My older brother is the earl of Alverleigh, my second brother is in the diplomatic service, and I entered the army. But now that Boney is finally defeated I'm surplus to requirements there also. Ah, here is our breakfast."

Mrs. Barrow entered, carrying a teapot, a coffeepot, and a jug, probably of milk, on a tray. She was followed by two small, ferociously clean boys, each one carefully carrying a tray containing silver chafing dishes. Callie stared. Her son had never carried a tray in his life.

The crown prince of Zindaria waiting at table. Papa and Rupert would have been utterly appalled.

Her Serene Highness, Princess Caroline of Zindaria, wanted to giggle.

The prince grinned at her, clearly enjoying himself, the mischief in his eyes conveying that he'd had much the same thought.

"That reminds me, Mr. Gabe," Mrs. Barrow said, "I hired a few servants while I was visiting my mother."

She set her tray down on the sideboard with a thump and fixed him with a contentious look. "You won't have any objection to that, I'm sure. They'll start tomorrow. Give us time to set everything to rights. Harry will be arriving any day now with Lord knows how many grooms and ostlers, and I'll be run off me feet with just the cooking. Yes, Jim, put the hot dishes on those cork mats, otherwise they'll ruin the varnish; careful now, don't burn yourself. Good lad. Now off you go and start toasting that bread."

She turned back to Gabriel, hands on hips and said, "There's bacon and scrambled eggs and I did you some deviled kidneys, Mr. Gabe, knowing as you're partial to them, so eat them while they're hot. I got three maidservants for the cleaning, and two footmen, and a scullery maid, so the next time breakfast is served in here it'll be by a footman or a maid. And Barrow reckons young Jim's pa has been missing for some weeks, now, so I thought we could take him in and train him up for something. Can't leave a boy to starve. Enjoy your breakfast, ma'am. I'll send one o' them lads back in with toast in a trice." And she swept out of the room.

Callie slipped Gabriel a sideways glance to see how

he'd taken this high-handed exceeding of her duties. Rupert would have exploded with rage. Even Papa would have dismissed the woman instantly.

He was convulsed . . . with silent laughter.

He saw her shocked look. "I know, I know," he said. "But you see, she's had me naked in the bath more times than I can remember."

Her eyes widened and Gabriel burst out laughing again at her expression. "Not for twenty years or so, I hasten to add. The last time I was about Nicky's age and scrubbed just as ruthlessly."

"Oh! I see."

He gave a furtive look around and added, "I know I ought to reprove her, but, well—" He sighed. "I'm frightened of women."

"Hah! Frightened as a cat fears mice."

"Fond of cats, are you? Me, too. Contrary, sensuous creatures. Like women." He grinned. "No, Mrs. Barrow more or less raised me, and I won't reprimand her for her plain speaking, particularly since she's right. I've been taking advantage of her good nature, and my brother Harry will be here next week and who knows who else." He strolled to the array of dishes set out on the sideboard, picking up lids and peering at the contents.

"Can I offer you some of this excellent bacon? And eggs? And kidneys? Mrs. Barrow's deviled kidneys cannot be beaten."

"Just a little bacon, please," she told him. She ought to have only tea and dry toast—she was cursed with a curvaceous figure and was very self-conscious of it. But the bacon smelled so delicious and it had been such a long time . . .

He filled two plates and set one in front of her. Hers contained a mound of bacon and some scrambled eggs. His plate contained even more, with deviled kidneys besides.

"Thank you." There was far too much, of course, but she

would just have a little. She inhaled the scent of bacon blissfully.

He drew out a chair on the adjacent corner to hers and sat down.

"I thought you were eating in the kitchen."

"And leave you to dine here all alone?" He shook his head. "Besides, it will give us a chance to get to know each other better." He gave her a look that brought back all the sensations she'd experienced in the stables.

"I don't wish to get to know you better." Realizing how rude that sounded, she added, "I shall be leaving here as soon as possible."

"Really? Let's discuss it later. Eat your breakfast while it's hot," he recommended.

She said a quiet grace and began to eat, very conscious of him seated only a few feet from her, those blue, blue eyes seeming to be on her each time she glanced his way. She was always self-conscious about eating in front of others.

Papa's voice echoed in her head, as it did at most mealtimes. *A lady does not eat like a horse, Callie, but picks at her food daintily, like a little bird.*

With Papa's critical eye on her, Callie never did enjoy a meal. No matter how delicately she picked at her food, no matter how often she came away from the table hungry, Papa's gimlet eye was on her, and she always *felt* like a horse.

She cut herself a sliver of bacon, just a tiny, delicate morsel, then paused. She thought of that scene in the stable, not the one where he'd—she darted a look across the table—where he'd kissed her. What had happened just before that. When she'd lost her temper with him.

Papa would have said, *A princess does not raise her voice, Callie. A princess is not a fishwife. A princess remains serene and dignified at all times.*

Callie *had* lost her temper. She *had* raised her voice. For all she knew she'd even screeched like a fishwife—she'd certainly poked him in the chest like one. She had been neither serene, nor dignified.

And it had felt wonderful.

Callie stared at the bird-portion sliver of bacon on her fork.

All forms of pork are anathema to any female of taste. Rupert's voice echoed in her head.

"Is something wrong with your bacon?" A deep voice interrupted her thoughts. "Mine is delicious."

Callie blinked at the man sitting across from her. "No. No," she said thoughtfully. "There's nothing wrong with it at all." She stabbed her fork into the pile of bacon and cut herself a proper mouthful. She chewed it slowly, savoring it.

Heavenly.

She could feel his disturbing blue gaze and decided she didn't care a rap for it. She ate another piece of bacon and another. She ate some of the scrambled eggs. They were creamy and delicious. She ate some more bacon.

He grinned at her. "Told you the bacon is good, didn't I? I can't tell you how I missed the smell of bacon—good, home-cured English bacon. There's nothing like it."

She looked down at her plate and blinked. She'd eaten the entire mound of bacon. And the eggs. And she felt wonderful. She'd been so hungry.

"I like to see a woman with a good, healthy appetite."

She gave him a narrow look, not sure how to take his words. He was probably hinting that she'd eaten like a horse, but Callie didn't care. It was none of his business—besides, he was supposed to like horses, so there.

Not that she cared what anyone thought of her anymore. She owed no obedience to anyone anymore. She was free, she told herself incredulously. Free to say what she liked, do what she liked, eat what she liked.

It was a heady sensation.

The door opened and Jim came in with a pile of toast followed by Nicky with honey, marmalade, and butter.

"Shall I butter your toast while it's still hot?" Gabriel asked as the two boys bounced from the room.

"No, thank you." She took a sip of tea: weak, black, and unsweetened.

He spread butter on the toast with a lavish hand. "Marmalade? Mrs. Barrow's finest."

Callie looked at the toast, melting with butter. She'd indulged herself with the bacon and eggs. Eating like a horse was one thing: like a pig was quite another. "No, thank you."

"Honey then. Good choice. You'll find it interesting as well as delicious. Our bees forage for nectar among the seaside plants and it gives the honey a unique flavor." He drizzled honey on a slice of toast and passed it to her. She should not. She really should not.

Weakly she accepted it. She bit into the warm, crunchy toast and closed her eyes in bliss, feeling the honey and melting butter slide down her throat.

"Told you it was delicious," he said, his voice oozing with satisfaction. "Nearly as delicious-tasting as you."

Her eyes flew open. "You, sir, are a shocking flirt. One should be free of such things at breakfast!"

She blinked. She'd just reprimanded a man at his own table. She glanced at him from under her lashes.

He seemed amused. "Anything and everything is on the menu here at the Grange. Kisses before breakfast, flirtation as an appetizer."

She wondered what he'd offer for the main course. And then was shocked with the direction of her thoughts.

"Careful, you're dripping honey down your wrist."

She snatched up her linen napkin and wiped the honey that had dripped onto her hand.

"I could always lick it clean for you—"

She gave him a warning look.

"Like a cat, I meant," he said with mock innocence.

"You like cats, remember? Lovely sensuous creatures, cats."

Callie decided it was more prudent to become interested in the pattern of the curtains. She hoped she wasn't blushing. She felt a little hot.

He certainly was a bothersome man.

He poured himself some more coffee and crunched through a pile of toast. She waited politely until he had finished, and the moment he had, she said, "Thank you so much for your hospitality and care, but we really should be leaving."

"Stay a few more days."

"Thank you, but it's not possible."

"It's perfectly possible. Stay and rest. There are lilac shadows under those lovely eyes."

Callie tried not to blush. "My shadows are none of your business," she said with quiet dignity.

"While you are on my land and under my roof, they are."

"I am leaving your land and your roof," she reminded him.

He frowned. "And where are you planning to go? Last night you were bent on getting to Lulworth."

She nodded. "Yes. The boat was supposed to take us right into Lulworth Cove, which is, I understand, an excellent safe harbor, but when it came to the point the captain simply refused!"

He shrugged. "Not surprising, if you travel with smugglers."

"They weren't smugglers. I would never risk my son to smugglers!"

He raised his eyebrows. "No, of course not, that's why they dropped you at Brandy Bay." He saw she didn't understand and added, "So named for all the smuggled French brandy landed there over the years. A landing place known well to men of the smuggling trade."

"Perhaps, but they weren't smuggling anything."

"Except you and your son."

She frowned, not liking to think of herself and Nicky as smuggled goods. "You may think what you like. One of the sailors explained to me the real reason they couldn't enter Lulworth Cove. It was because there were too many *preventives* in the harbor."

He gave a shout of laughter. "And what might *preventives* be, my pretty innocent?"

"Don't call me that," she told him. "I admit that I don't precisely know what a preventive is, but I imagine it causes some sort of obstacle, perhaps a large and dangerous creature—"

He grinned. "Indeed it is. A preventive is an officer of the law, employed to prevent smuggling."

"Oh."

"Yes, oh. So, don't you think it's time to tell me what sort of trouble you're in? Respectable, married ladies, or even young widows of a year's duration do not commonly hire smugglers."

Callie bit her lip. "No, I'm sorry, but it's better for you— safer, I mean—if you don't know anything about me."

He gave her a long look. "I don't know what country you've come from, but you've got things confused about how it is here. Things have come to a pretty pass when a woman and child must see to the protection of a grown man."

He folded his napkin and put it to one side. "So, who's the friend at Lulworth?"

Callie gave him a troubled look. "I'm not sure if I should tell you."

He frowned. "So, it's a man."

She gave him an indignant look. "No, it certainly is not! Tibby, Miss Tibthorpe, is my old governess."

"In that case you're definitely not going."

Callie's jaw dropped at the high-handedness of it. "Indeed I am! Where I go has nothing to do with you."

"You're a fugitive and believe yourself and Nicky to be in danger. An elderly governess cannot protect you. I can. You'll remain here."

His calm assumption of authority irked her. All her life she'd been ordered around, her wishes and feelings ignored.

She put her own napkin aside. "Thank you, but no," she said crisply. "I have made my plans and Tibby is expecting me. Nobody knows I am going to Tibby."

"Except Tibby, presumably. I suppose you arranged this visit by letter?"

She knew what he was implying, but she was not as naive as he supposed. "Yes, but the letters were sent secretly through an intermediary."

He looked skeptical. "Napoleon got some of his best information from letters sent secretly through an intermediary."

"I know it was a risk, but sometimes one has no choi—"

"Exactly! You have no choice. You must stay here." He stood up. "I will have a message sent to Miss Tibthorpe—"

"No, you won't." Callie was getting annoyed. "It is my life and my son, and I need to do what I think is best. You have been very kind, but it is not for you to tell me what I may or may not do. I never met you before last night; you are neither my father nor my husband. You have no authority over me. It would be utterly scandalous of me to take up residence in the house of an unmarried man unrelated to me, and I won't do it."

He sat back in his chair and folded his arms, clearly displeased with this summation. "Nonsense! You forget Mrs. Barrow. She would lend the situation respectability."

"A cook, however kind and respectable, is not sufficient."

"Yes, but she's also filling the place with maidservants." He tucked his chair back under the table and moved to assist her to rise. "It is the most sensible alternative. Nicky will be happy playing with Jim, Mrs. Barrow is in seventh heaven with two young boys to feed and nag. You will re-main here."

"No, I—"

"You are safe here," he added. "You and Nicky. Nobody else knows you are here. And if they do, I can and will pro-tect you."

She swallowed. "No, you don't know—"

"I don't care who or what the danger is. I am—I was—a soldier and I can call on my friends to help, if necessary." His voice deepened. "I promise you I can and will stand between whatever or whoever has made you and Nicky so frightened. You are not alone."

She blinked as her eyes swelled with sudden tears. Such kindness from a stranger . . . Who was he, this man? One minute outrageous flirt and the next, masterful protector. And he didn't even know who she was.

That was the trouble. She couldn't tell him, for if he knew, he would be in danger, and so would everyone in this house. People had died already for the sake of Callie and her son. She could not bear the guilt of any more.

It had been against her better judgment to go to Tibby, but Tibby had written that she knew the risks and would never forgive Callie if she didn't come. Tibby had known and loved her since she was a child, the closest thing Callie now had to family.

And Tibby needed her. Tibby was lonely, too. And for Callie to feel needed . . . she couldn't remember when any-one apart from Nicky had needed her for anything.

"Of course," he added in a different tone of voice. "I should expect you to protect me in return."

"What?" Callie's jaw dropped. "Protect you from what?"

"From the wrath of Mrs. Barrow when she finds out I have been feeding my dog deviled kidneys under the table."

She could not help but smile. "No, you are very kind, and I am grateful, but I could not possibly trespass any longer on your hospitality. Nobody will know I am in Lulworth, and

Tibby is expecting me. Nicky and I will depart as soon as is convenient."

He set his jaw. "I could force you to stay."

She met his gaze squarely. "But you won't."

"No," he growled. "Though it is against my better judgment. I will escort you to this Tibby, but you haven't seen the last of me, I warn you!"

"Is that a threat?" she said coolly.

His eyes suddenly warmed. "No, a promise."

Six

Callie came down the stairs, buttoning her gloves. In the hallway sat her salt-stained portmanteau, much lighter than before. As she'd feared, the seawater had ruined many of her clothes, shrinking some garments and causing the dye to run on a red spencer, which had stained everything it touched.

"Nicky," she called back up the stairs. "Hurry up. Mr. Renfrew will be waiting."

As she spoke Gabriel stepped into the hallway. He looked up. She froze, immediately feeling self-conscious. Ridiculous, she scolded herself silently. As if she hadn't come down a staircase hundreds of times—with hundreds of people watching her. She was used to people watching her every move, critically assessing her. Usually finding her wanting.

That was the trouble. He wasn't watching her critically at all, even though she was wearing his late great-aunt's old traveling cloak, hastily tacked up at the hem. Mrs. Barrow had pressed it on her. She'd also given Callie one of the old lady's hats, a black felt one with a bunch of purple flowers, just right for a widow.

She forced herself to move, pretending to button her gloves again so she didn't have to meet his eyes and see the warmth there.

"Nicky!" she called again.

"He's down here already," Gabriel said. "In the kitchen, saying good-bye to the Barrows and Jim. And eating jam tarts, I'll be bound. Mrs. Barrow has made a fresh batch."

Callie nodded. That deep voice. Even when he uttered the most mundane things, it made her quiver inside. She'd found his offer to protect her very . . . appealing. Had her situation been different, she might have been tempted to risk it.

He stepped forward and held out his hand as if to assist her down the last few steps, as if she were fragile. She wasn't, not a bit, but she allowed him to tuck her gloved hand into the crook of his arm. At the same time Nicky and his friend, Jim, came into the hall, followed by the Barrows.

"Here, lad, you come back here," Mrs. Barrow said, and with a swift hand she seized Nicky by the collar and drew him back. "I'll not have any boy leaving my kitchen looking like he'd come from a sty!" With a damp cloth she rubbed jam stains from his face, while Jim, watching his immediate future with foreboding, hurriedly scrubbed at his own mouth with his sleeve.

Nicky submitted to the washcloth with a bemused glance at his mother. He'd never been so summarily manhandled in his life, but from the look of him, he didn't mind at all. Perhaps he enjoyed being treated like an ordinary boy, instead of a prince.

She liked these people. They'd been very good to her and Nicky, but she could not tell them the truth. If they had any idea who she and Nicky were, it would be bound to leak out, and any talk would bring the wrong people to their doorstep.

Callie would never forgive herself if any of them were hurt—or worse—just for giving her and her son succor.

They said their good-byes and Callie reiterated her thanks for their help. But just as they turned toward the front door, there was a loud commotion outside—hoofbeats, dozens of them—as if a small army had arrived.

Count Anton! Callie grabbed Nicky.

"That'll be Harry. He's early," said Gabriel and before Callie could warn him, he threw open the front door. To her amazement, instead of Count Anton's liveried cutthroats, nearly a dozen horses passed through the front gates and milled around near the front door.

There were three grooms, each leading two or three riderless horses. A dark-haired, swarthy man mounted on a powerful-looking roan horse seemed to be in charge. Was that Harry? she wondered.

"Good day to you, Captain Renfrew, sir, and where would you have me put these beauties?" he called out in a broad Irish brogue.

"Good God, it's Sergeant Delaney!" Gabriel exclaimed. "Through the archway, Delaney," he called. "You'll find the stables with no trouble."

"I'll go and see to it, Mr. Gabe," Barrow said. "What a fine collection of horses! Good day to you, Ethan," he called to Delaney.

The dark man's face split with a grin. "Barrow, is it? I didn't know you'd be here. Old home week it is to be sure! You'll take good care of these lovelies, I know." Delaney dismounted and tossed his reins to one of the grooms. "Right, boys, take 'em round and get 'em settled—Mr. Barrow is in charge. I'll have a word with the captain here."

The herd of young horses, mainly mares, streamed around the side of the house and disappeared through the arch into the courtyard. At the same time Barrow shot back through the kitchen, the shortcut to the courtyard, followed by Nicky and Jim.

Mr. Ethan Delaney came up the steps, and the two men shook hands. A man of no more than medium height, the Irishman was thickset and powerful. He walked with a roll that was only too familiar to Callie: the walk of a man who'd been practically born on a horse. His tough-looking face and pugilist's build contrasted oddly with his attire, for though he was in riding dress, he was very neatly and stylishly turned out, with shining black boots, an elegant neck cloth, and a well-cut coat of dark blue superfine.

"Where did you spring from, Delaney?" Gabriel exclaimed. "The last time I saw you was at Salamanca, bleeding all over your beautiful uniform like a stuck pig."

"Your brother ran into me, hanging around Tattersalls." He shook his head. "I've not exactly been havin' a run o' luck, sir. No London gentlemen wants to take an ageing Irishman on; old soldiers are a penny a dozen. But your brother seemed to think I might be useful for this new scheme of yours, so he's appointed me his head trainer."

"So I should hope!" Gabe clapped him on the shoulder. "Once they see what a wizard you are with horses, they'll be trying to steal you from Harry."

"Well, mebbe they'll be findin' I'm not such an easy man to steal," Delaney said. "Now, do you want to take a look at those horses, Captain?"

Gabe glanced at Callie. "Delaney, this is Mrs. Prynne, who, with her son, have been my guests. I'm about to escort Mrs. Prynne to her friend's house near Lulworth, so I won't have time to look at the horses until after my return."

"Lulworth is it?" Delaney said after they'd exchanged greetings. "Would you mind if I came with you, then? I picked up a whisper of a stallion near Lulworth that might be for sale, and the sooner we get on to it, the better." To Gabe he added, "A fellow called Blaxland, a devil for the tables he is and havin' to sell up. The whisper is that he'd sell Thunderbolt for the right sum—"

"Thunderbolt! The derby winner?"

Delaney grinned. "Aye, the very one. Harry and I mean to make Blaxland an offer."

Gabriel's brows rose. "Harry and you?"

The Irishman nodded. "I've some savings put by, a nest egg. I've been looking for an investment in my future to keep me in my old age." He shifted awkwardly. "I'd not be just the head trainer but a junior partner—that's if you're amenable, sir." He eyed the younger man uncertainly. There was a difference in station as well as age here, Callie could see.

Gabriel shrugged. "It's Harry's dream and Harry's scheme, so it's for Harry to say. But if it were up to me, I'd say welcome, Delaney. A man of your talents is a valuable acquisition. You're no shirker and an honest man. We'll work well together."

The Irishman's face lit up. "That's grand, sir. Harry said you'd not mind, but I wasn't sure. I mean, you're a lord's son, and I'm just a poor bog Irishman—"

"—who's a genius with horses," Gabriel finished. "Now, I'd rather not keep Mrs. Prynne standing about any longer, so—"

"I am very well able to stand about a little longer," Callie interposed. "Certainly long enough for Mr. Delaney to refresh himself after his journey. And I can see you're itching to see those horses he's brought, so shall we delay my departure for an hour or two?"

"That's very considerate of you, ma'am," Delaney said. "Thank you kindly. I'll be off and see the mares are settled and then I'll have a quick wash and brush up. And mebbe a quick cup of tea." He bowed and hurried off.

Gabriel took Callie's gloved hand. "Thank you," he said

in a low voice, and he raised her hand and kissed it. "We depart for Lulworth in an hour then."

She blushed as she watched him run down the stairs, two at a time. Even through the glove, she could still feel his kiss.

"*T*hat's West Lulworth, down there, and over there is Lulworth Cove." Gabriel gestured with the handle of his whip. They were traveling in his curricle, a sporty vehicle painted in dark gray with cherry-red trimmings and pulled by two gray horses.

"What a lovely view," Callie exclaimed, looking at the perfect horseshoe-shaped stretch of water beyond the straggle of thatched cottages that comprised the village. Lulworth Cove shone a dazzling blue in the sunshine. It was dotted with a few small fishing boats and a large, sleek white yacht.

"Where exactly does your friend live?" Gabriel asked.

"A house called Rose Cottage. It's half a mile to the west of the village. There's a kind of map here." Callie drew a letter from her reticule and gave it to him.

Ethan Delaney rode alongside the curricle, on his big, ugly roan horse. It suited him, Callie thought. Mr. Delaney had the look of a man who'd lived a hard life. He had a large nose that had been broken more than once, a number of scars on his face and hands, a chipped tooth, and an ear that appeared to have been chewed at some stage. His hair was thick and dark, beginning to go gray at the temples, and cut brutally short—to hide the fact that it was curly, she suspected. Yet his waistcoat was splendid, if a trifle loud, and his boots gleamed with polish.

"A grand job you're doing there, young Nicky," Delaney called out. "It's never your first time with the ribbons!" Nicky straightened his back and gave a quick, shy nod of acknowledgment.

Callie warmed at once to the man. For all his rough looks, Mr. Delaney had a kind heart. Nearly as kind as Gabriel's.

Gabriel had decided to pass the journey showing Nicky how to drive a pair, demonstrating and explaining in a quiet, deep voice. Then, on this open stretch of road he'd handed Nicky the reins, showing him how to hold them and letting him get the feel for himself. No stream of advice to make the boy nervous, no anxiety. He'd simply sat back, trusting Nicky with his precious matched grays.

"Yes, he's a natural," Gabriel agreed, perusing the letter. "Handles the ribbons with a nice light touch."

Callie saw her son dart a sideways glance at the big man beside him, trying to gauge if the compliment was genuine or not. He almost visibly swelled with pride as he turned his gaze back to the road, frowning with fierce concentration.

Callie bit her lip. Why could his father not have offered such casual advice and praise? Callie could not remember a single instance when Rupert had told his only son he'd done something well. In his father's eyes, Nicky could never measure up: he was a cripple, therefore an unworthy heir.

Ironic that here, among strangers, her son should begin to blossom. Both of these very different men had shown Nicky casual acceptance and the sort of undemonstrative kindness that only men who were very sure of themselves could show a shy, needy boy.

After a brief perusal of Tibby's letter, Gabriel took the ribbons back from Nicky and turned up a narrow, rutted roadway. After a few minutes, they came to a rose-covered cottage. It stood at the end of a muddy track, too narrow for the curricle to pass. The front door was not visible, but in a window, a curtain twitched.

"Someone's home there," Gabriel observed.

"I'll nip down and ask," said Ethan Delaney, and rode his horse down the track. The garden was as neat and well-ordered as a picture, Ethan thought. His footsteps crunched

as he walked down the cinder path that led around the side
to the entrance.

The front door had a well-polished brass knocker. Ethan
rapped a smart tattoo. He was aware of being observed.

There was a short delay before the door opened a crack.
A small, pale, severe-looking woman of about thirty-five
stood there, looking . . . angry?

"Can I help you?" she said. Her tone was in direct con-
tradiction to her expression. She fixed him with an intense
stare and, in a furtive manner, produced a piece of paper
from her sleeve and showed it to him.

Ethan glanced at the paper. It meant nothing to him.
"Good day to you, ma'am, I'm wondering if this would
be—?"

She shook her head, staring at him so hard he thought
her eyes would pop, and thrust the paper at him. Bemused,
he took it. "And what would you like me to do with—"

To his astonishment, she reached up and pressed firm
fingers over his mouth. "I'm sorry," she said in a clear
voice, "but the place you want is on quite the other side of
the village. You have wasted a trip. You must turn around
and go the other way." She pushed urgently at him with her
hand, glared at him, and rolled her eyes backward, first
right and then left.

Ethan frowned as it dawned on him. She was in trouble.
And she was trying to send him away.

In an easy, carrying voice he said, "Well, drat the fellow
and his poor directions. Sorry to have bothered you, ma'am.
See, we're looking to inspect a stallion—Thunderbolt—
perhaps you've heard of him, ma'am? A champion he was,
now owned by Mr. Blaxland, of Rose Bay Farm. I'll be off
now, and thank you for your assistance." He gave her a nod
and ambled back down the path, whistling in his teeth. He
heard the door close behind him.

Mr. Delaney mounted his horse and trotted back to the
waiting curricle.

"It wasn't Tibby's house then?" Callie said.

Ethan shook his head slightly and waved vaguely up ahead. He walked his horse away.

"Mr. Delaney?" Callie prompted him.

He did not answer her until they had gone over the hill. Then he stopped and turned to her. After a moment he said, "Your Tibby, now—would she be about thirty-five, little, neat, with brown hair and brown eyes and a way of looking at a man as if he was lower than a worm?"

"Yes!" she exclaimed. "That's my dear Tibby exactly. Why are we leaving, then, if she is back there?"

"Because your dear Tibby is in trouble," Ethan Delaney told her. "She did her damnedest to get rid of me just now. She gave me this." He passed her the scrap of paper.

Callie read the note. "Oh my God. It's my fault." She crushed it in nerveless fingers.

She'd gone quite white, Gabe saw. "What does it say?" he asked, but she was beyond hearing.

Gently he freed the paper from her fingers and read the note aloud. *"Help. I am being held prisoner by evil foreigners. Please inform the authorities. Miss J. Tibthorpe. Rose Cottage."*

Gabe looked at Callie. "And you know which evil foreigners, don't you?"

She shivered and nodded. "Count Anton and his men. He's my husband's cousin." She gave him a bleak look and said in a lowered tone. "He—he wants Nicky dead. Me, too, I suppose."

"Well, he won't succeed," Gabe told her calmly, "So stop looking so miserable. Now, tell me, how many men is he likely to have?"

She shook her head helplessly. "I don't know."

"My guess is there are three or four in that cottage," Ethan said. "Don't worry, ma'am," he added. "The captain will have a plan."

She turned to Gabriel. "Have you?"

"I have," Gabe said with a faint smile. "Don't worry, we'll get your friend safely out of there."

He spoke with a calm confidence that worried Callie. Count Anton was a ruthless, evil man, and here, where nobody knew him, he didn't even need to pretend to be otherwise.

There was an intersection up ahead and Gabriel used the extra space to turn the curricle around. "Nicky, I hope you remember what I taught you because I need you to drive back the way we came—"

"I can drive," Callie told him. "I don't enjoy it but Rupert—my husband—made me learn."

"Excellent, in that case, you shall drive. But first, put this on." He pulled off his driving coat and thrust it at her. "My hat, too. I don't want the men in the cottage to see you're a woman." He reached for her hat and helped her to remove it, then helped her into his coat. It was far too big. He folded the sleeves back for her and buttoned her into it, then placed his hat on her head.

"I feel ridiculous," she muttered.

He smiled. "You look delightful. Tuck this rug over your skirts—good, that's it. Now, drive the curricle home—to the Grange. Tell Harry what has happened and he'll take care of everything."

"What about Nicky?" she asked. "They will be looking for him, too." She glanced back at the dog box on the back and asked him a silent question with her eyes.

He caught her drift. There was a box built onto the back of the curricle to hold hunting dogs. It would certainly hold a small boy and hide him from sight, Gabe thought. An excellent idea.

Turning to Nicky, he began, "Nicky, I want you to—" He broke off. Nicky's face was stark, with huge green eyes, a miniature version of his mother. The boy's lips were trembling but the small, thin body was held ramrod straight, his little chin clenched firm. Nicky was ready to face his fate.

No power on earth could have made Gabriel tell this brave little boy to hide in a box—a coffin—like a scared rabbit.

He gave the boy's mother a warning look and said to the boy, "I want you to take care of your mother."

She frowned at him and opened her mouth to argue. He gave his head a tiny shake.

"Yes, sir!" Nicky replied like a little soldier and Gabe saw her look at her son and bite her lip.

"Your mother will drive the horses and won't be able to take her eyes off the road. You are to be her eyes and ears. You will keep a lookout for any strangers on the road."

"Yes, sir."

"If you see anyone, you are to tell her, and if she thinks there is any danger, she will pass the reins to you—you can manage that, I'm certain. You did very well before. I trust you to keep a cool head."

Nicky swallowed, but his chest swelled. "Yes, sir."

Gabe helped her to climb into the driver's seat, then from a secret compartment beside the driver's seat, he drew out two pistols, which he checked.

Callie's eyes widened. "But if you shoot at Count Anton's men, Tibby might—"

"I'm not doing any shooting. These are for you."

"*Me?* But—"

"If you are accosted, all you need to do is point the barrel and squeeze the trigger. They're primed and ready." He placed them on the seat beside Callie.

"It doesn't matter if you don't hit them. We will hear and know you are in trouble, and we will come."

"But I know how—"

"Keep the lid of this compartment open. They are designed to keep the pistols ready to hand in case of highwaymen or footpads. All you need to do is pass the reins to Nicky and take the pistols out."

"But the men in Tibby's cottage will be armed—"

"And so am I, ma'am," Ethan Delaney said and, with a subtle movement, produced a wicked-looking blade, apparently from thin air.

She looked at Mr. Renfrew in distress. "Don't worry about us," he told her. "We're soldiers, remember?"

"But you don't know how many—"

He gave a faint smile. "It doesn't matter."

She looked from one to the other. "But—"

He patted her on the hand. "Don't worry about us. Ethan and I can look after ourselves. Just you concentrate on getting yourself and Nicky—and my grays—back to the Grange in one piece. And tell Barrow. We'll do the rest. Now, let me see you hold the reins."

She gave him a troubled look, but wrapped the reins around her hands in the correct manner and he nodded.

He leaned forward and before she realized what he was doing, he kissed her on the mouth, a hard, brief, possessive kiss. "Take care. Now go."

He sprang down and gave the near-side gray a slap on the rump. The horses moved off rapidly. He watched her until she'd turned left and was heading up the hill back toward the Grange, away from the village of West Lulworth. Not a soul followed.

He waited until the curricle was out of sight, then turned to Ethan. "How many are we talking about?"

"There's at least two of them in there with her, mebbe more. I heard several voices."

Gabe nodded. "Good. Then here's the plan," he said and explained to the Irishman exactly what he wanted him to do.

Ethan whistled. "Audacious, sir, not to mention risky to your good self."

Gabe grimaced. "Just do as I tell you and I'll worry about my good self." He grinned. "To tell you the truth, I'm rather looking forward to it."

"Bored with the peaceful life, eh, sir?"

"A little," he admitted. Before she arrived.

Ethan grinned. "Then let's get on with it."

Gabe climbed over the dry stone wall and stealthily circled around behind the cottage. He signaled to Ethan, who trotted back down the road, whistling loudly, then turned in again down Tibby's lane way. He looped the reins lightly around a bush and strode noisily down the cinder path, still whistling and rapped on the door.

After a short murmured debate, the door opened a crack and Tibby looked out. When she saw Ethan, her eyes widened.

He grinned at her and gave her a wink.

Color surged into her pale cheeks. She was not blushing, Ethan saw. She was angry.

"I'm sorry to bother you again, ma'am," he said in a loud voice, making his accent thicker than usual and sounding as if he'd had a few drinks. "But I forgot that I had a map on me, so to avoid gettin' any more contrary directions to Rose Bay Farm—where that stallion is—you know the one I told you about, the champion. So I thought I'd show you this map and see if you could give me get some good, commonsense directions."

There was a pause and then the door cracked open wider.

"Show me the map," she said through thin, irritated lips. She put half her body in the gap. Only one of her arms was free and Ethan could see that her skirt was awry, as if someone was holding onto it.

Ethan pulled out the note she had given him and showed it to her. She gave him an incredulous look and irritation gave way to thoughtfulness. He winked at her again.

He said loudly, "Now here is Rose Bay Farm, ma'am, if you could just show me where we are now." He made the paper crackle and took her free hand in his. She went to resist in an automatic movement, then stopped.

"You are here," she told him, "and this is where you need to go to find the farm you want."

Ethan gave her hand an approving squeeze and said, "Ohh, so that's it. And, ma'am, can you just show me the turnoff. Point it out to me—I'm not so good with paper maps."

"Yes, of course." She gave a little tug and, after a moment, whoever had been holding her other arm released it. Her skirt was pulled tighter than ever. But most of her body was in the gap between the door and the jamb.

Ethan gave her a meaningful look, then silently counted, one, two, three. On three, he pulled her out of the doorway and hard against him. There was a ripping sound but Ethan didn't stop to look. He gave a piercing whistle and immediately a loud crash sounded at the back of the cottage.

In the same moment Ethan scooped Tibby into his arms. She squeaked and gave a halfhearted struggle. He took no notice. He raced down the path and tossed her onto his waiting horse.

She almost fell off again, but managed to straighten herself and stay on. "What on earth—"

"Hush!" He swung up behind her and, with an arm around her waist, galloped away. Behind them, the cottage rang with shouts and crashes.

Seven

"**M**y house! My cat! What—who—!" Tibby gasped when she'd got her breath back. "I need to warn—"

"Don't worry, miss. It's all in hand and you're safe now." He urged his horse on.

"Safe. Y-yes." She clung to the saddle. She'd never traveled so fast in her life. She tried to look back, trying to see over his shoulder. "But what was that crash? And who are you?"

"Ethan Delaney, at your service, miss."

Tibby belatedly remembered her manners. "Thank you, Mr. Delaney," she managed shakily. She could hardly believe she'd actually escaped from those vile men, safe and in one piece. Sort of.

Bouncing along on top of a horse galloping ventre à terre, having been kidnapped by a strange Irishman, was not exactly safe.

"Did the swine hurt you at all?"

"N-no. Thank you." Tibby winced at the tightness of his arm around her. She tried to look back. What was happening? She'd expected to see them rush into the road after them, but she couldn't see anyone.

"I can't see anyone following us," she said.

"Are they armed? With guns, I mean."

"No. I think the leader had a gun, but he left."

"How many of them are there?"

"Four. They just appeared," she said shakily, remembering. She'd opened the back door to let Kitty-cat out and seven large foreign men had burst in on her. "There were seven this morning, but their leader and two men left after they'd tied me up." She rubbed her wrists.

He lifted her wrist and glanced at it. It was chafed and raw-looking. "The devils!" he muttered.

She stared at his big, rough-looking paw. Scarred and nicked, bearing testament to a rough life, it was not a gentleman's hand.

She couldn't see his other hand, but she could feel it. Holding her tight.

"They untied me to cook for them!" she told him. "And to answer the door."

"They didn't . . . hurt you in any way?"

Tibby knew what he was asking. "No," she told him. "Plain spinsters are not to their taste, thank God."

He gave her an odd look. "But they made you cook for them?"

"Yes. They've eaten every scrap of food in the house." She added angrily, "And they poked through my things in the most insolent way. And they smoked! And one kicked my poor little Kitty-cat and the others laughed in the most callous fashion." She was badly shaken, but now that she was free, the anger that had been simmering inside her all day was growing.

"Thank you for rescuing me. It was very brave of you to involve yourself in someone else's troubles."

"Oh, I'm right at home in trouble, miss. You did well to warn me the way you did."

He meant her note. She'd hoped he would help her, but she'd imagined nothing like this. So bold! So audacious— to simply snatch her from the grasp of those despicable villains and ride off with her like . . . like Young Lochinvar.

The lines rang in her mind, to the beat of his horse's hooves.

One touch to her hand and one word in her ear,
When they reach'd the hall-door, and the charger stood
*   near;*
So light to the croupe the fair lady he swung,
So light to the saddle before her he sprung!

She was no fair Ellen from a poem. Nor anyone's bride. Her note had told him to fetch the authorities, not gallop away with her.

It was such a foolhardy thing to do. Brave. But he hadn't hesitated.

"What was all that noise I heard when we—er, left?"

"That'd be Captain Renfrew, makin' a little distraction while I snatched you."

"It didn't sound very little. I hope my cottage is all right." She had no idea how to ride a horse, but strangely, she had no fear of falling. His arm was like a steel band around her; his chest felt like a warm, hard rock. And his steed thundered along, ventre à terre.

"What was he doing?" she asked, turning her head again.

White teeth flashed briefly in a crooked grin. "Keepin' them busy."

She stared at that smile, a slash of white in a darkly tanned face. She could see the texture of his skin, finely lined and darkened with the faint roughness of bristles. The smile widened slowly and she realized she was staring.

"Shouldn't we go back?"

"What for?"

"To help your friend fight them. They are four to his one."

"Aye, but I've seen him handle worse odds. My orders were to get you to safety first."

"I shall do very well here. I insist you put me down and go back and help him!"

He shook his head. "Captain's orders were to take you to safety. Don't worry about him. Just sit tight. It's over now, Miss Tibby," he murmured.

It wasn't over, Tibby knew. She had to warn Callie somehow. "We must notify the authori—" She broke off. He'd called her by her name! She stiffened. Ethan Delaney had called her Miss *Tibby*. She'd thought him a passing stranger, but if he knew her name, he wasn't. *So who was he?*

They came to the main road and instead of turning right, to the village, he turned left.

"You're going the wrong way, Mr. Delaney," she told him, her suspicions deepening.

"No, we're going to the Grange."

"The Grange? Why? I don't know anyone at the Grange." She nerved herself to jump off the horse.

His arm tightened. "Your friend, Mrs. Prynne, is there."

"I don't know any Mrs. Prynne," she said in a tight voice.

He tipped his head sideways. She could feel him looking at her. "She knows you, Miss Tibby. She and her son were coming to stay with you."

"You mean—?" Tibby caught herself in time. This could be yet another one of Count Anton's stratagems. She pressed her lips together, determined not to give anything away.

"Mebbe I have your name wrong," he said easily. "I thought she called you Tibby. Said she'd not seen you since she was a young girl. She's a little, plump lass with dark hair and pretty green eyes."

She relaxed. "I am Miss Tibthorpe." Only a few of her dearest pupils had ever been permitted to call her Tibby.

"Frantic she was, on your behalf," Ethan Delaney continued. "If she hadn't been in desperate fear for her son, I think she would have stormed the cottage herself. Seemed to think it was her fault you were in trouble."

"Oh, but she shouldn't blame herself."

"Never mind, me dear, it'll all work out," he said and gave her waist a squeeze. Tibby should have reprimanded him, but for some reason she could not bring herself to do so. No doubt because she owed him her rescue.

And because the Young Lochinvars of this world knew no better.

"She is won! we are gone, over bank, bush, and scaur;
They'll have fleet steeds that follow!" quoth young
*   Lochinvar.*

His large body was very warm. His heat soaked though the bodice of her dress.

Tibby stared ahead. Her hair streamed out behind her, catching in his face. Once or twice she felt him brush it aside, and she burned with embarrassment and tried to tuck it into her collar. She couldn't think of the last time she'd been out of doors with her hair uncovered, let alone unbound. It felt so . . . so shameless.

The horse was tiring. They slowed to a canter. A smart gray curricle came around the corner up ahead and his arm tightened around Tibby, almost squeezing the breath from her.

"What the devil—" he exclaimed. "She's goin' the wrong way! And where's the lad?"

Tibby gasped something and he looked down. "Sorry," he said, and the steel band loosened. "Don't know me own strength sometimes. Are you all right?"

Tibby nodded, gasping in great quantities of air, then realized that the curricle coming toward them was being driven by none other than Callie in a man's coat and hat.

"Tibby!" Callie called out as soon as she was close enough. "Oh, my dear Tibby! Thank God you're all right!"

The moment the curricle stopped, Ethan came aside and dropped Tibby into it, cutting across the ecstatic feminine reunion with, "I don't know what you're doing here, ma'am, or what you've done with your boy—"

"He's safe, of course! I wouldn't be here, otherwise!"

"The captain's not going to like this, ma'am. He expects his orders to be followed to the letter."

"Well, I'm not one of his soldiers. It's my fault Tibby and you and he were endangered and I am not going to run off with the only weapons."

"Not the only weapons, ma'am. With respect, you haven't seen the captain fight. His bare hands are weapons. Now, I'm heading back to help him—and no, you're not going," he said as she picked up the reins, looking all set to follow.

"But—"

"Ma'am, you can't fight: fighting is men's business. The captain and I have been in more fights than you've had hot dinners—"

"But—" She looked mutinous.

"You'll only get in the way. The best you two can do is go back to the Grange. You take Miss Tibby back there and give her a nice cup of tea. Tell Barrow what's going on. I'll get back and help the captain!" He wheeled his horse and prepared to gallop back.

"Take the guns!" Callie shrieked.

He hesitated, then said, "No. Captain's orders were that you have 'em to protect you. We'll do as we are, never you fear." He urged his horse back the way he'd come off.

Both women watched him. "Men are so thickheaded," Callie fumed. "Going off to do battle and leaving me with the guns!"

Tibby was equally cross. "Nice cup of tea indeed!" She looked at Callie. "Where's Nicky?"

"Safe," she said. "I left him with the Barrows. Tibby, how many men were in your cottage?"

"Four," Tibby told her.

"*Four against one!* And Mr. Renfrew with no weapon and Mr. Delaney a knife!" Callie swallowed and looked at her friend. "Tibby, would you mind very much if we went back to your cottage? I won't be packed off tamely, not when I have guns, and when he is outnumbered four to one! Particularly since I am the cause of all this trouble."

"It's not your fault and I don't mind in the least," Tibby said instantly. "I wanted to go back and help, only Mr. Delaney wouldn't allow it." She snorted. "I'll give him a *nice cup of tea!*"

The grays moved off at a smart clip. "The pistols are in that case there," Callie said. She snapped the reins and the grays picked up speed.

Tibby opened the case and examined one of the pistols out with great care. The curricle bounced and swayed and she put the gun back hastily in case it went off. "It looks quite straightforward," she said briskly.

"Have you ever shot a gun?" Callie asked.

"No. I thought you were terrified of horses."

"I am."

The two women exchanged glances and burst out laughing. "Tibby darling, you haven't changed a bit! I will hug you properly after this is all over, but oh! How glad I am you are here!"

"My dear, you have turned into a splendid woman—as I always said you would!"

"I'm so sorry to have dragged you into th—"

"Nonsense! I dragged myself," Tibby declared stoutly. "I urged you to come to me, remember? I knew the risks."

A little of Callie's guilt faded. "I felt sick when I heard they were holding you—but you're all right, truly?"

"Yes, perfectly. Mr. Delaney snatched me away in the

most audacious way." She added after a while, "I felt quite like fair Ellen for a moment."

The reference surprised another laugh out of Callie. "Young Lochinvar"? Tibby's favorite poem.

They raced on. It took all of Callie's concentration to drive.

"Count Anton himself is here," Tibby said suddenly.

"Where?" Callie looked around in alarm.

"I meant in England. He came to the cottage. I am sure it was him. The others called him 'Excellency'—a slender, pretty man with golden hair and a smooth, nasty way of talking."

"That's him." Callie felt sick.

"He knew all our arrangements. They came straight to my cottage. He knew I was expecting you and Nicky."

"Then he must have read our letters," Callie said. "But how? There was no sign of tampering . . ."

The cottage came into sight and they fell silent.

"We need a plan," Tibby said.

"Yes. Have you ever shot a gun?"

Tibby shook her head. "Never."

"Then I will take them. I know how to shoot. Rupert had me taught." Her face hardened. "And if it's Count Anton or one of his thugs, my aim will not waver. You must make some sort of loud, shocking noise the moment we enter the cottage. It will get their attention." Callie took a deep breath. "I will do the rest."

Gabe was two men down and two to go when Ethan arrived; he seized a heavy brass vase and smashed it over the fourth man's head. He dropped like a stone. Gabe threw a final mighty punch at the last man standing, and the cottage was suddenly silent.

The two men grinned at each other. "A fine fight, by the looks of it, Capt'n," Ethan said.

Gabe heaved a satisfied sigh. "It was indeed." He flexed his knuckles gingerly. "Though it's some time since I've fought with just my hands."

"If you'd borrowed me knife—" Ethan gave the vase a rub on his sleeve and replaced it on the mantel. He turned it so the dent wouldn't show.

"No. As I said before, killing anyone would complicate things too much and draw unwanted attention to Mrs. Prynne and her son. We'll hand these fellows over to the law for attempted burglary or false imprisonment or something. They will hardly admit their true purpose—"

Just then, one of the fallen men groaned and started to move. Ethan grabbed the brass vase again and thumped the man unconscious. The vase was now dented on both sides. He set it back on the mantel. It listed sadly.

"Let's get this lot tied up," Gabe ordered.

There was no rope to be found in the small, feminine cottage, but they found a pile of folded sheets in a cupboard and ripped the top one into long strips that they used to tie up the villains.

"I'll inform the magistr—" Gabe began, when *crash*! A large clay pot containing a geranium came smashing through the side window and shattered on the floor, sending glass, earth, and bits of geranium everywhere.

At the same time the front door flew open. "Nobody move!" a feminine voice bellowed. "I have a gun!"

"Two guns!" an equally strident feminine voice behind her added. "And I have a spade!"

Gabe sighed. He understood now why the army contained no women. Women didn't understand about orders. They confused them with advice.

He watched as his small avenging angel sprang into the room, her pistols—his pistols, actually—cocked and ready. She looked flushed and tense and beautiful. Her hair was starting to slip out of the knot he so disliked, and the most kissable mouth in the world was pushed forward in a belligerent pout he found enchanting. And infuriating. One long, silky tendril drifted down over her nose. She blew it aside and glared fiercely around the room.

"Aim for the heart," he told her and strolled forward. She met his gaze and the pistols wavered. She glanced around the room again and her hands dropped to her sides.

"Oh," she said. "You managed without us." She sounded almost disappointed.

"Yes, as you see, I managed without you." He removed the pistols from her far-too-lax-for-his-comfort grasp and laid them aside. "Where is Nicky?"

"With the Barrows. He'll be safe back at the Grange by now."

"As you should be," he ground out. All he could think about was what if he hadn't managed. She would have walked in here to a room full of thugs. Pistols or not, she wouldn't have stood a chance.

"Pooh," she said. "I had the pistols and you were unarmed and outnumbered."

He wanted to throttle her.

He wanted to kiss her.

He stepped back, forcing himself to take several deep breaths. She became aware of his expression and bit her lower lip in sudden doubt. Gabe stared at her mouth. It was red and soft and luscious and he hadn't been able to get the taste of her out of his mind all day.

He still wanted to throttle her.

He wanted more than ever to kiss her.

Most of all, he wanted to bed her.

He dragged his gaze off her. Behind her stood a small, thin woman brandishing a spade over her head. She, too looked around the room, and the spade fell, along with her face. "My house!" she cried. "All my things!"

Everybody looked. For the first time Gabe took in the

wreckage of the room. Furniture overturned, china smashed
and scattered across the floor, pictures askew, some dam-
aged beyond repair . . .

Her gaze fell on the tightly trussed men and sharpened.
"I suppose you had to use my new sheets for that."

"Oops," Ethan murmured. "It's not as bad as it looks,"
he began. "Why don't I—"

She shot him a glance that would have felled a lesser
man. "Oh, just make yourself *a nice cup of tea*," she snapped,
and began to straighten the room with brisk movements.

"You don't have time for that," Ethan said. He turned to
Gabe. "She says there were seven men originally, so there
are at least three others out there."

"Then they could return at any moment," Gabe said.
"Miss Tibthorpe, you have three minutes to pack a bag,
then you two ladies will leave this place. It is not safe for
you."

"I would prefer to stay here and defend my home," Miss
Tibthorpe told him in a crisp voice. "Forewarned is forearmed."

"Yes and I will help." Callie stepped forward.

"No, you won't," Gabe informed her. "Miss Tibthorpe is
too sensible a woman not to realize the danger she would
be putting you in. She wouldn't want that, I'm sure."

"But I'm the reason there is danger in the first place.
Those men are after me."

"Exactly," Gabe said. "Which is why both of you must
disappear from this place immediately!"

Tibby considered his words then looked at her friend.
"He's right," she said. "Your safety is more important than
my things." She hurried upstairs.

Gabe turned to his green-eyed thorn. "You will go
straight to the Grange, you will not return for any reason
whatsoever, and you will take the pistols with you. That is
an order, understand?"

"Yes, but—" She opened the adorable mouth and Gabe

could think of only one way to shut it. And it was neither the time nor the place.

"Do not argue with me, woman," he roared. "It is an *order*!"

"Yes, but I am not in your army, and I take orders from no man," she said sweetly. But before he had time to say anything she added, "I will do it, because it seems to me the most sensible thing to do, but what I wanted to say is—"

"Say nothing if you value your life," he growled.

She gave him a speculative look and opened her mouth to speak.

"Or your reputation," he added and fixed his gaze on her mouth.

It shut. With something of a snap. And remained pursed in a disapproving line.

That mouth would be the death of him, Gabe thought.

Without a word she turned and walked upstairs, head held high, queen dismissing peasant. Her deliciously rounded backside swayed enticingly with every step.

Once she'd disappeared, Gabe turned back, to find Ethan watching him with a broad, knowing grin.

"Well, don't just stand around looking witless," Gabe snapped. "Let's get this place cleared up a bit."

Ethan nodded. He started picking up overturned furniture. "Gone to a lot of trouble, she has, to make it nice. And keep an eye out for her kitty-cat. She's worried about it." He shuddered. "Can't stand cats, meself. Make me sneeze."

Gabe looked around the room and realized Ethan was right. Under the smashed china, the scattered earth and geranium and spatters of gore, the woodwork and floors had been freshly polished and were fragrant with beeswax. Everywhere were small, fussy feminine touches of curtains, ornaments, hand-hooked rugs, framed watercolor pictures, all knocked awry or ruined.

Gabe hadn't noticed; Ethan had. Interesting.

They set to, cleaning up as best they could. First they carried the prisoners and slung them out the back. Three of them had regained consciousness and struggled, spitting abuse in some language he didn't recognize. One spat at Ethan.

"That does it," he muttered, seized a dented brass vase from a shelf, and used it to biff each of them unconscious again.

Gabe looked at the vase and snorted. "She probably loved that vase, Ethan."

Ethan shrugged. "It was ruined anyway."

They picked up everything that had been dropped and swept up everything that had been smashed.

Gabe glanced at the ceiling. "What the devil are those women doing? How long does it take to pack a bag?"

Ethan shrugged. "They're women." He picked a book up and sniffed it. "Leather. Beautiful embossing." His fingers traced the decoration before setting the book carefully on the shelf. He looked through a few of them, then noticed Gabe watching and closed them with a snap. "No pictures." He quickly shoved all the books back on the shelves, then went in search of a broom.

Gabe was righting the upside-down books when the two ladies came downstairs.

"About tim—er, all set?" He hurried forward. Miss Tibthorpe was carrying a faded carpet bag, and an umbrella and Callie was carrying a large, covered box.

Gabriel relieved her of it. "Good God," he exclaimed. "What's in this? It weighs a ton."

"Tibby's things," she said in a voice that indicated she thought the question impertinent.

Gabe grinned. A few minutes in her governess's company and his avenging angel was turning back into a snippy little duchess. Gabe didn't mind. He liked her either way. He noticed the pistols and placed them carefully in his pocket.

"I've packed enough for a few days," Miss Tibthorpe said, "but I'm worried about my dear little Kitty-cat. I can't find him anywhere." She went to the back door and called, "Kitty-kitty-kitty!" No cat came forward.

"You get along to the Grange, we'll find your cat," Gabe told her. "We'll finish tidying up here—"

"Oh, but I can do that later." Miss Tibthorpe glanced doubtfully from him to Ethan, who'd been pushing the mop around the floor a bit, leaving smeary marks. He looked like a big ox in the feminine little cottage.

"Madam, we made the mess, we will clean it up—or rather, I will. Ethan will escort you two ladies back to the Grange and I will bring these villains before the local magistrate."

"No, you mustn't!" Callie gasped. "I don't want them reported."

Gabe frowned. He didn't like it. "The crime should be reported. Any other action is to invite anarchy."

"If you report that foreigners broke into Tibby's house and held her prisoner, there will be a huge fuss. Count Anton must be staying somewhere nearby. The local constable is bound to speak to him, Count Anton will find out who reported it and where you live—he will know where I am."

He stared into her eyes. He read in them fear and determination. "Very well. It goes against all of my instincts, but I won't report it," he said, comforting himself with the reflection that no red-blooded man could resist the appeal in those green eyes. "Now come along, let's get moving. I'll finish up here and follow shortly."

"What about my cat? Kitty-cat doesn't like men," Miss Tibthorpe said, looking as though she and Kitty-cat shared the same views. "He will be even more mistrustful now, since that horrid beast kicked him!"

"I'll find the blas—I'll find the cat." Gabe told her, trying to mask his impatience. He looked out the front and checked to make sure the coast was clear. "Cats like me, don't worry. But I can do everything much better once I know you are both safe."

"And out of the way," Callie said in a voice only Gabe could hear.

"Exactly." He gave her the sort of smile one gave to a clever pupil.

She glowered at him.

"You can glower at me even better from the curricle," he said. "It's higher up." Slipping his free arm around her waist he propelled her toward the door.

"I can walk perfectly well by myself," she muttered.

"Yes, but will you? That's the question." Gabe compelled her onward. "Ethan, escort Miss Tibthorpe, if you please," he ordered over his shoulder. "Now move!"

"There is no need to shove," his duchess said snippily.

"There is every need. Think of it not as shoving, but an affectionate nudge." He marched her out of the cottage, dumped the box in the back, and lifted her bodily into the curricle. Ethan did the same with the governess, then climbed up, squashing in beside the governess. Gabe handed him the pistols. "You know what to do."

"So do we," said Callie with pursed lips.

"Hah! I've heard that before," Gabe said and slapped the grays on the rump.

He watched until the curricle was out of sight. Nobody followed. Gabe started to breathe normally again. He'd fought four men this afternoon and was still standing, but she'd delivered him a blow that had knocked him endways.

The way she'd come back and burst in the door, pistols waving. To help him. *Him.* Risking herself to save a man who was more than capable of looking after himself. He'd survived eight years of warfare.

Crazy female. She had no idea of how it was supposed to be between men and women. He was the one who protected her, not the other way around.

Gabe checked the men at the back door. They were still unconscious. He was tempted to hand the cowardly swine over to the authorities, but he'd given her his word he wouldn't. The first time in his life he'd been swayed from doing what he considered to be the right thing.

He checked the cottage. There was damage to the doors and windows. He'd send a man down tomorrow to effect any repairs needed. He straightened a couple of rugs and some pictures.

He couldn't get it out of his head; no woman, ever, had tried to protect him.

He had no idea how to handle it.

She had known him a day—less than a day.

He heard a sound behind him and whirled. Nothing. Then he glimpsed a movement under the kitchen dresser. He crouched down and saw a big, old, ugly, battle-scarred ginger tomcat peering warily back at him from one good eye.

"You can't possibly be her dear little Kitty-cat," Gabe told it. "You ought to be called Cyclops, or Ulysses."

The cat glared at him in silence. A bitten-off, sorry-looking excuse for a tail twitched angrily. But the cat, though angry, was very much at home.

"Come on then, Kitty-cat, you old reprobate." Gabe reached under the dresser to take the cat and the cat lashed out. Gabe swore and sucked his well-scratched hand. He wrapped a handkerchief around his hand and, uttering soothing noises, he tried again. The handkerchief got shredded and Gabe acquired some more scratches. "Look, you ugly old devil, I'm not going to hurt you, I'm just bringing that poor deluded woman her sweet little Kitty-cat."

"Where's ze princess?" a voice from above him said, and Gabe's head exploded with pain.

"Princess? What princess?" he said, groggily. A boot kicked him hard in the groin and Gabe doubled up, groaning and cursing his own stupidity. At least three of them stood over him. He'd been half under the dresser, caught unawares like any wet-behind-the-ears novice.

The leader, in shiny black riding boots with silver spurs, snarled, "Don't waste my time, peasant! I want ze princess and her son!"

"Don't know what you're talking about. Don't know any princess." Gabe tried to push free, but the heel of another boot stamped down on his hand. The pain was excruciating.

"Tell us where she is. She and ze prince."

"Never seen any princes or princesses," he ground out. "Saw the king once, afore he went mad." He tried to look up at the speaker and found a boot planted on his head. He was pinned down and helpless.

The boot pushed down. "The princess and the boy are all we want."

Gabe was a soldier and a realist. There was only one thing he could do. So he swore at the man, insulting him in the worst ways he could think of. Years in the army had given him an excellent vocabulary.

It had the desired effect; they stopped questioning him and started beating him up, instead.

The last thing Gabe saw was the cat streaking between a forest of black boots and out of the door . . .

"Capt'n, can you hear me, Capt'n?"

Cold water splashed onto Gabe's face. He tried to move and groaned. Every inch of his body ached. He managed to crack open one eye and saw Ethan, anxiously looking down at him.

"Are you hurt bad, Capt'n?"

Gabe shook his head and winced. His head felt like it was about to split. "No, just battered. Are they gone?"

"Aye. Can you move?"

"Of course." Gabe moved and swore again. He examined

the inside of his mouth with his tongue, checking to see he still had all his teeth. He did.

"Drink this." Ethan put a flask of brandy to his lips. Gabe swallowed, then waved him back, coughing, as the fiery liquid burned its way down.

"What the devil—?" he gasped.

Ethan grinned. "A little drop of Irish mountain dew, sir—what we call poteen. Good for what ails ye."

"If it doesn't kill you first!" Gabe spluttered.

Ethan gave him a few seconds to recover, then helped Gabe to stand. "I have the curricle outside. When you didn't turn up, I got worried. Left the ladies at the Grange and came back. So, what happened?"

Gabe pulled a wry face. "The blackguards got the jump on me."

Ethan's jaw dropped. "You, Capt'n?"

"Me," Gabe admitted ruefully. "Own stupid fault. Worse than the greenest new recruit. They caught me half under that dresser, chasing that blasted cat."

He staggered to the front door and looked at the cinder path, at the end of which waited his curricle. "Any more of that blasted Irish firewater?"

Eight

The first thing Gabe saw when he and Ethan entered the house was the battered portmanteau and band-box sitting neatly, side by side, in the entrance hall.

Callie appeared at the end of the corridor. "Oh no, what happened?" she exclaimed and ran to meet them. She was still wearing his great-aunt's cloak.

Gabe staggered and clutched Ethan's arm, forcing Ethan to look at him in surprise.

"Are you all right? Can I help?" she asked, her brow furrowed with concern.

Gabriel immediately put an arm around her shoulders and gave Ethan a little push. "You may see to the horse, Ethan," he said, guiding Callie's other arm around his waist. "I shall do very well with Mrs. Prynne's help, thank you."

The Irishman shot him an amused glance. "Oh, I can see that fine," he murmured.

She struggled to wedge her shoulder more firmly under his arm. Gabe found the sensation of her squirming and thrusting against him quite delightful. He moaned softly and let his knees sag and his arm curl around her waist. Her arm tightened around his midriff and her other hand came up and pressed firmly against his chest.

"Ouch!" he said involuntarily. She'd pressed right where that swine's boot had landed.

"Oh dear, I am so sorry! Does it hurt very much?" she said. "What happened? I thought you were just tidying up. Did the men get free?"

"No. Why are you still wearing that cloak?"

She shot him an indignant look. "I was waiting for you, of course. Oh, your poor face." She examined his face anxiously. He wasn't a pretty sight, Gabe surmised ruefully. One eye was swollen shut. It would make a devil of a shiner. And from the way the rest of his body ached and stung, he was a mass of cuts and bruises.

She, on the other hand, looked so beautiful it made him ache, and not from any bruises. Her lovely green eyes scanned him.

"What's the verdict?" he asked softly.

She bit her lip. "You look, you look . . ."

"Heroic?" he said hopefully. "Intrepid? Valiant?"

"Dreadful!"

"Oh," he said, dampened. "So why do you need to wait for me in a cloak?"

"You didn't think I'd leave without thanking you, do you?"

Gabe frowned and tightened his grip on her. "Leave? Leave for where? You're not going anywhere."

She tried to shake off his hand. "Of course I am. Count Anton—my enemy—is here. Those were his men at Tibby's cottage. I have to leave before they discover me."

"Nonsense! Stay here. I will protect you."

She gave him an incredulous look. "You?" From the look on her face Gabe gathered he was a less than reassuring sight.

"These," he gestured to his injuries, "are just superficial."

She gave him a look that said she didn't believe him, but was too polite to say so. "Thank you for your offer, but really, it is imperative I leave as soon as possible."

She was utterly determined to go, he could see. "Very well, wait until I can get cleaned up. It won't take long."

She jerked her head back and stared at him. Her face was just inches away. "Wait? Why wait, when I can thank you and take my leave of you just as well now?"

"Because I'm not traveling all bloodied and in a mess, that's why." At her look of confusion he added, "You don't imagine I'm letting you and that boy travel on alone when there is a pack of vicious thugs after you, do you?"

She stared at him for a moment, then shook her head. "No, thank you. It is very kind of you, but it's not necessary. I could not ask you—"

"You're not asking me, I'm telling you." His arm tightened around her.

Her green eyes narrowed. "Mr. Renfrew, as I've pointed out before, you have no authority over me. It's kind of you to be concerned, but it really isn't your business what I do or where I go. I don't wish to quarrel with you, so—"

"Good. Then you will wait."

"No. I am my own woman and—"

He turned his head. "Ethan, are you still here? Good. Take that luggage and lock it in the cupboard down the hall. Lock everything in there—that hat, too—and give the key to me."

"You will do no such thing, Mr. Delaney," she said instantly. "It is my luggage and I intend to depart as soon as practicable."

"Ethan, go."

Ethan grinned. "Yes, sir, Capt'n Renfrew." He picked up the valise, tucked the bandbox under his arm, and picked up the hat.

"Unhand those items at once!" With some difficulty she

untangled herself from Gabe and ran to wrest her things from Ethan.

Gabe grabbed her cloak and when she pulled up short, he twirled her around, snatched her hand, and tucked it into the crook of his. "Let us discuss this," he said and propelled her toward the sitting room.

She resisted. "There is nothing to dis—" she began, then noticed with amazement his sudden ability to walk unaided. "You fraud! You can stand perfectly well without me!"

Immediately Gabe had a relapse, one that necessitated his arm clamping hers to her side, while he held tightly onto her other hand.

"I am not the least bit deceived by that," she told him. "How dare you confiscate my luggage!"

"Oh dear, I think I'm going to swoon," Gabe murmured and clutched her as feebly as he could manage while restraining her from running after Ethan.

"Are you indeed?" said a caustic voice from behind. "That'll be a first, then." He turned and saw Mrs. Barrow, hands on hips, observing the whole scene. Behind her stood Miss Tibthorpe, and the two boys watching with wide eyes, his dog, Juno, peering between them.

Mrs. Barrow took one look at him and sniffed. "You'd better bring him in to the kitchen, ma'am. He needs cleaning up." She darted him a look and added, "In more ways than one."

Ethan returned and tossed him the key. Gabe caught it. He looked down at his stubborn, angry princess and said softly, "Just give me an hour. If you don't, I will come like this."

She opened her mouth to argue and he added in a firm voice, "I am not taking no for an answer. I go with you bloodied or I go with you clean, but you won't leave this house alone and unprotected."

She scowled at him a moment, then her face cleared and she nodded, as if capitulating. "Very well, I'll wait. Give me that key and while you're getting cleaned up I'll get my luggage ready." She held out her hand.

For answer, he slipped the key into his breeches pocket. "After we've talked this through rationally."

Callie glared at him. "Don't you trust me?"

He gave a faint smile. "I told you, those eyes of yours give your every thought away. If you had your luggage, you would leave the moment my back was turned. Shall we go?" He held out his hand as if to usher her to the kitchen.

She gave him an icy look, then, with her little nose held high, she glided past him, the very picture of a royal princess: gracious, dignified—and fuming.

It was all Gabe could do not to snatch her back and kiss the starch out of her. But in her current mood she'd probably box his ears. And quite rightly. He'd been atrociously high-handed. But he couldn't let her leave. Not without him.

In the kitchen Mrs. Barrow said to the two boys, "Jim, you'll know where the best pool for leeches is—the one in the hollow behind the copse. You and Nicky take this jar and fetch me some nice big ones. And take that dratted dog with you—you know she's not supposed to be in the kitchen."

"Leeches?" Callie exclaimed in repugnance.

"Best thing for black eyes and bruises." Mrs. Barrow turned back to Jim. "You know how to catch them, don't you?"

Jim nodded.

"Good lad. Off you go then, boys, and don't fall in!"

"Nicky can't go," Callie said quickly. "He—he cannot swim."

Nicky's face fell. "I would be very careful, Mama," he said in his polite, little-old-man way. "I have never before fished for leeches. It sounds very interesting." His green eyes beseeched her.

She hesitated. Gabe understood why. He found it almost impossible to resist her when she looked at him with her version of those eyes.

But the events at the cottage had obviously given her a bad fright and she was clearly reluctant to let her son out of her sight.

She chewed on her lip indecisively. Gabe watched. She had no idea how erotic he found it. Even battered and aching, and in a room full of people, his body stirred at her action.

"I would dearly love to experience a leech hunt," the boy added in a wistful voice. His hands unconsciously fondled Juno's ears.

"Then you shall go," Gabe told him. He needed to talk to her in private, about things she wouldn't want to discuss in front of her son. "Take Miss Tibthorpe with you. She will find it, er, scientifically interesting."

Miss Tibthorpe looked surprised and faintly indignant, but before she could say anything, Gabe noticed Ethan lounging in the doorway and added, "And Mr. Delaney will go, too, which will set Nicky's mother's mind at rest."

"Indeed it will," Ethan agreed. "Where am I goin' again? A leech hunt, is it?" He gave a rueful glance down at his immaculate outfit and gleaming boots. "That'll be . . . grand." With gloomy resignation, Ethan offered his arm to Miss Tibthorpe. She hesitated, then took it, and in seconds the kitchen was deserted.

The princess stamped her foot. "How dare you take over like that! You have no right! It is for me to decide if my son stays or goes."

"I know, but we have things to discuss. And he'll be perfectly safe. The pool is just a few minutes away; they'll be half an hour at most. Let Nicky have his fun. From the sounds of things he hasn't had much fun in his life. You do keep him wrapped in cotton wool."

Her eyes glittered. "That's not fair. I do what I must for Nicky's own good."

"I know, to keep him safe. But you can't keep running."

She made a frustrated gesture. "What else can I do? I can't fight Count Anton myself. And nobody else believes me."

"I believe you. And you can't fight him, but I can."

"How?" she demanded. "You are but one man. Count Anton has practically an army."

"A battle is not always won on brute strength alone."

"You might be more convincing if you looked less like something the cat spat out, Mr. Gabe, so let's get you cleaned up," Mrs. Barrow interrupted. She'd brought hot water, clean cloths, and a daunting array of medicinal-looking pots.

Callie stood back to let Mrs. Barrow at him.

"How do you imagine you can defeat Count Anton?" she asked Gabe as Mrs. Barrow stripped off his coat, waistcoat, and shirt, leaving only his breeches. Gabe placed a hand on his waistband to make sure they stayed that way.

Callie stared. Angry marks were all over his body, where he'd been kicked and punched. There was even the imprint of a boot heel on the back of his left hand.

It was her fault he was hurt. He'd got like this defending Tibby from Count Anton's men. Her anger faded and guilt replaced it.

"Don't do that," he told her.

"Do what?"

"Chew your lips like that. They're a work of art, those lips, and should not to be chomped on or mangled. Nibbled on tenderly, perhaps. I'll show you how, later."

Callie stared at him, unable to think of a single thing to say. *A work of art?* And then she realized he'd just offered to *nibble on her lips.* She fought a blush.

"That's enough of your mischief, Mr. Gabe. The lass has been beside herself with worry for you," Mrs. Barrow said. "And you, ma'am, don't give this another thought."

She indicated the battered masculine torso. "I've been patching up him and Harry since they were knee-high to a grasshopper. As long as the devilment is still in this one, he's all right."

Callie took comfort in the woman's words. She could see the devilment dancing in the one blue eye that could open. So while Mrs. Barrow dabbed at the cuts and abrasions with a mix of vinegar and hot saltwater, he explained what had happened.

He'd been caught half under the dresser trying to catch the cat. A high-booted thug with a thin golden mustache had demanded he produce a princess. "As if I had hidden one under the dresser!" he scoffed.

"That was Count Anton," Callie confessed, "I am the princess he was after."

"I knew that. Princess Caroline of Zindaria."

Her eyes widened. "How did you know?"

He shrugged. "The Zindari horsemen and their fabled savage horses have been an interest of my brother Harry's for years, so I'd already worked out where you came from based on Nicky's talk. And you being a princess? Well, since Nicky's father was one of the top men, it wasn't much of a stretch."

Mrs. Barrow's jaw dropped open. After a stunned moment she slapped the wet cloth across his chest. "If you knew she was a princess, you should've warned me," she scolded. "I've been calling her *lovie*! And *you* shouldn't be sitting here half naked in front of her."

"I don't mind," Callie said, meaning she hadn't minded being called lovie.

His lips quirked. He winked and Callie blushed, realizing her words could also mean she didn't mind his semi-clothed state. And though she hadn't meant that at all, it was not untrue.

Even beaten up and covered in scrapes, his body fascinated her.

Mrs. Barrow poked him. "You don't wink at princesses. I'm sorry, Your Highness, but he wasn't brought up to be so rag-mannered. It's all that time he spent in foreign parts. Lift up and I'll check for broken ribs," she ordered him. He lifted his arms for her, and she poked carefully along the line of each rib.

Callie watched anxiously.

Mrs. Barrow noticed. "Don't you worry, Your Highness," she assured Callie. "There's nothing broken. It looks worse than it is."

"But—"

"He's been much worse and survived, Your Highness. Like a cat, he is. Besides, never happier than when he's in trouble, Mr. Gabe. Fretting himself to flinders, he was, Your Highness, before you arrived. Bored to death and miserable with it. Blaming hisself for things that weren't his fault. Turn."

He turned. "I never believed your name was Prynne," he told Callie. "You're a terrible liar."

"Then why didn't you say anything?"

"You were so determined to pretend, I didn't have the heart."

She made an impatient gesture. "No, not to me—to Count Anton."

His eyebrows shot up. "You mean why didn't I tell him where you were?"

She nodded. "It would have saved you . . . that." Her eyes ran over his bruised and battered body.

He stared at her a long moment. "Yes, why didn't I think of that? What's the safety of a woman and child, after all, when I could have saved myself a couple of bruises. I'll remember that next time."

"I hope there won't be a next time," she muttered, dropping her eyes to evade the look in his. There was a short silence.

"You know there's going to have to be a confrontation," he told her.

She shook her head. "I've already brought enough trouble on Tibby, and now you. I have to leave."

"And do what?"

"Hide."

"Again? And when he finds you again—for if he's been able to trace you across Europe from Zindaria, he's not going to give up here! So then what—flee and hide again? And again? And again? And is that the way you want young Nicky to live?"

There was a short silence. Mrs. Barrow glanced at Callie. She said nothing, but Callie knew she agreed with Gabriel. So did Callie, for that matter, but what else could she do?

"At least he would be alive. If I'd stayed in Zindaria, Nicky would be dead by now!"

He nodded. "Yes, the poison."

She was shocked. "How did you know about that?"

"The way you both reacted to the hot milk last night."

Callie glanced at the door. The boys were still down at the pond. "There have been several attempts to kill Nicky in the last couple of months," she told him. It was a relief to talk about it to someone who seemed to take her seriously. "I am certain my husband's death was no accident, too, though I have no proof."

He nodded.

"The puppy was the last straw. I'd given Nicky a puppy—his first." She glanced up at Gabe. "He loves dogs, but his father never let him have one, not until he could—well, that doesn't matter."

Rupert had promised Nicky a puppy when he learned to ride bareback. Only Nicky couldn't, not with his bad leg. Rupert would put the little boy on one of his great, savage horses, hand Nicky the reins, and slap the horse on the rump.

The horse would move away and Nicky would try to ride it, but his leg didn't have the strength, and after some bouncing around he would fall off. His father would pick him up and put him back on the horse, and again Nicky would fall, and his father would pick him up, and he would fall, over and over until his small body was covered with bruises and he could hardly walk.

Nothing she could say to Rupert had the slightest effect. Callie had begged and pleaded with him, then stormed and railed, but it had made no difference. She was just a silly, fearful woman and he was the prince: his word was law.

It had gone on for years, until Nicky was terrified of horses, knowing he would be hurt. But he never refused; he tried his little heart out every time, and though he was hurt, he never once cried.

His father hadn't relented, hadn't even praised Nicky's courage. A prince of Zindaria must never fail.

Nicky had stopped asking for a puppy. There was no point; he would never ride bareback.

So, a year after his father's death, she'd given him a puppy.

"Of course he took it to his bedroom." She gave a rueful smile. "You saw how he was with your dog. Love at first sight."

He nodded. "Even more so with a puppy, especially if it was his first."

"I always brought him hot milk before bed. That night, instead of drinking the milk himself, he gave it to the puppy." She tried to remain calm as she said, "It died. Horribly. In my little boy's arms." Her face crumpled, remembering Nicky's desperate grief, and how he'd blamed himself for the puppy's death.

She pulled out a handkerchief and blew her nose. She wasn't going to cry about it, she wasn't. She was angry.

"Who prepared the milk?" he asked when she had mastered herself.

She gave him a bleak look. "Me. I heated it myself, and took it up to him. Not one other person touched it, or touched the cup after I washed it."

He frowned. "So how did they do it?"

"He'd poisoned the entire jug of milk. One of the servants put some in her tea. She was very sick, but she'd used just a few drops of milk, not a whole cup." She shuddered and wrapped her arms around her body. "He didn't care how many people he killed, as long as Nicky died, too."

"Count Anton?"

"Yes, he is next in line for the throne after Nicky."

Mrs. Barrow clicked her tongue. "Such wanton wickedness!"

Callie nodded. "He is truly evil."

"So that's when you ran."

"Yes, I'd thought of escaping for some time, but when that happened, I knew I had to act."

"You didn't try to have Count Anton arrested?" Gabe asked.

She threw up her hands. "Of course I did. I told Count Zabor—Uncle Otto—he is uncle to both my husband and Count Anton, and currently the regent, ruling on Nicky's behalf until Nicky turns eighteen."

She threw up her hands in frustration. "Uncle Otto thinks I am just a silly woman. He thinks I mollycoddle Nicky too much, and 'worry my little head over nothing.'" She mimicked his voice. "It makes me so angry the way they all think they know better."

"Who do you mean by 'they'?"

She bared her teeth at him. "Men, of course."

"Of course. I suppose you showed them the poisoned milk."

"No, because when the kitchen maid got sick, the other servants threw the bad milk out. I couldn't prove anything. And though I knew it was Count Anton, he wasn't even in the palace at the time. Besides, poison is such an unlikely

weapon for him to use. He's known and feared for his un-
governable temper . . ."

She shrugged and mimicked, " 'Milk goes off sometimes, and people get sick, Princess. And young pups taken
too soon from their mother can die. That is sad, Princess,
but it's life.' "

She looked at him and added fiercely, "But the puppy
was *not* too young to leave its mother. And the milk *was*
poisoned. So, yes, I will run and run and run, if it will keep
my son alive. What other choice do I have?"

"You can't keep running. Count Anton must be stopped."

She nodded. "Yes, I know I should shoot him, but I
don't think I *can* kill a man in cold blood. If he was attack-
ing Nicky, I could, of course, but—"

His lips twitched. "That's not what I meant."

"You mean I could pay someone to kill him? I know, but
that would make me just as wicked as Count Anton. And I
don't want my son to have a murderess for a mother." She
frowned and looked at him indignantly. "Besides, I don't
want to *be* a murderess."

"I'm very glad to hear it," he said, amused. "And don't
look at me like that, I didn't suggest you should murder
anyone."

"Then what did you mean?"

He gave her a long look. "I have a plan," he began.

"And we've got *dozens* of leeches!" the crown prince of
Zindaria announced from the door. "And some of them are
still on me!" A wide grin split his face. Mud and water
dripped from him. He was utterly filthy, and as happy as
she'd seen him for . . . ever.

"Nicky, look at you!" Callie exclaimed. "I thought
Tibby—"

Tibby stepped into the doorway. Mud and water dripped
from her. She, too, was utterly filthy. "I tried to stop him
falling in, I truly did. But I slipped." She met Callie's eye
and started giggling. "I've never been so dirty in my life."

Ethan stepped in. He was also covered in mud. "Me new coat, too," he said, looking dolefully down at the mud-caked garment. "Miss Tibby fell in tryin' to save Nicky and I fell in tryin' to save her."

"I didn't fall in at all," Jim announced proudly. "I just picked the leeches off 'em. The ones I could see, anyway. Here y'are." He handed over a jar containing a black mess of writhing leeches. Callie felt squeamish looking at them.

"What do you mean, the ones you could see," Tibby said suddenly. "Do you mean I could still have some of those horrid creatures on me?"

"Bound to," Jim said cheerfully. "You did a lot of splashing around and they like that. And you wouldn't let me look on your legs, remember?"

"She wouldn't let me look, either," Ethan murmured.

Tibby gave him a severe look. "I should think not." She turned to Callie. "I must go upstairs immediately. Could you help me, please?"

Pick those dreadful, slimy things off someone? Someone on whose flesh they'd attached themselves, whose blood they were drinking? She felt her gorge rise at the thought.

But someone had to help poor Tibby. There was only herself or Mrs. Barrow. She looked at Mrs. Barrow, who was attending to Gabriel's injuries.

She could face any amount of blood without turning a hair, but those ghastly wriggling, black, slimy things . . . She felt queasy just thinking about it.

She turned to Mrs. Barrow and in her most gracious, princessly manner she said, "Mrs. Barrow, would you mind assisting Miss Tibthorpe? I will attend to Mr. Renfrew's injuries."

"Yes, of course I will, lovi—Your Highness," Mrs. Barrow said. "You've gone quite green, haven't you? Miss Tibby, you get along upstairs and get those wet things off you. Take this salve." She took the small pot from Jim and handed it to Tibby. "Leeches hate the smell of that; one touch and they'll drop right off you, no harm done to you or them. I'll see to Mr. Gabe here, then I'll come up and check you over for any in places you can't see."

She turned to the boys. "You boys go upstairs with Mr. Delaney. Change into clean clothes and ensure no leech remains on any of you." She handed Ethan another little pot and gave them a look that had all three exiting meekly.

"If Mrs. Barrow had been a general, I would not have been at war for eight years," Gabe said to no one in particular.

"Right, let's see to you," Mrs. Barrow said. She reached into the jar and fished out several leeches. They looked like dark, slimy worms.

Callie's stomach lurched as Mrs. Barrow placed the creatures against the swollen and discolored flesh under his injured eye. The creatures instantly attached themselves to the tender flesh.

Callie shuddered and turned away. "Doesn't it hurt?"

"Not a bit. Can't feel a thing, as a matter of fact," he told her cheerily.

After a few minutes Mrs. Barrow said, "That's that. Now, Mr. Gabe, you know what to do—you can see Her Highness can't stand the things—they take some people like that, I know. When they've finished, put 'em in the jar again. There's a market for good leeches and young Jim could earn a few pennies for 'em. I'll go and see how those others are doing and then I'll be back to do the rest."

"I am perfectly capable of tending injuries," said Callie feeling ashamed of her weak stomach. "Tell me what needs to be done after those creatures are finished."

"If you really don't mind, Your Highness." Mrs. Barrow passed her a jar. "Rub this salve into the cuts and bruises on his back. He can do the front himself, but he can't reach the back."

"Of course I don't mind. It's my fault he was injured in the first place," Callie said.

"Rub it in well. It's my own special mix. It'll help loosen up the tightness and help him to heal faster. But it has to go on after all the leeches are finished—they can't abide the smell." The elderly woman hurried out and they were left alone.

"I don't mind blood, you know," Callie said defensively, even though he hadn't said a word and she had her back to him so she couldn't see his face. But she was sure he must be laughing at her.

"Really?"

"I've tended some quite serious injuries and not turned a hair. And vomit—I have cleaned that up before. I didn't mind." Much.

"Dear me."

"And pus. I've dealt with pus and I wasn't the least bit sick." Not true. She had felt quite ill when that pus had come gushing out of Papa's swollen leg that time, but she wouldn't have Gabriel thinking she was some sort of weakling who felt ill at the sight of a small black leech.

"Even pus, eh? Well, well, well."

He was laughing at her, she could tell by the way his voice quivered. She turned to glare at him, but was forced to turn her back again, quickly.

The wormlike creatures fastened under his eye had thickened, like slugs, engorged with his blood. The creatures dotted his torso, clinging to every major bruise, feeding off his body.

"I don't know why it works," he told her, "but it does and it's painless. And see? The salve works—one sniff and they drop off."

"I'll take your word for it."

Silence fell.

"So," he said after a moment or two, "while we're sitting here waiting for these things to finish their picnic, how about you tell me how a girl born in England came to be a princess of Zindaria?"

"My father was English, but Mama was a princess. Papa was ambitious. He'd inherited a substantial fortune, but his birth was merely genteel, so he found and married a princess—"

"Just like that, eh? How did he manage it?" Gabe inquired. "I have a friend who'd like to marry an heiress."

"Oh, Mama wasn't an heiress, only royal. She was the youngest daughter of the house of Blenstein, hereditary rulers of the tiny and very poor Principality of Blenstein before it was absorbed by the Austrian Empire, but she was a princess, and that was all that mattered to Papa."

"And you were born here."

"Yes, in Kent."

"So how did you end up married to the prince of Zindaria?" he asked, adding, "Those leeches have finished now; they drop off when they're full. You can turn around."

Callie turned cautiously. "Good heavens." The swollen eye was no longer so swollen. He could see out of it almost normally and the darkening color had faded considerably. There were two small bloody marks where the leeches had been.

"It's amazing, isn't it," he agreed. "All the bad blood is inside them," he said, holding out his hand. In his palm lay two bloated black leeches, now the size of giant slugs.

"Eeyech." Callie averted her eyes and waited until he'd dropped the leeches back into the jar.

"There really is no need for you to accompany me," she told him. "If we leave here quickly, Count Anton will be none the wiser. Nicky and I will do very well by ourselves. I did get him across Europe without assistance, you know."

"I know, and I'm impressed. Nevertheless I shall escort you. You can't pretend you wouldn't welcome an extra source of protection for your son."

She couldn't. She'd be happy to have some protection. She just didn't want it to be him. He unsettled her, the way he looked at her, teased her, treated her as something fragile and precious when she knew she wasn't at all fragile. And nobody had ever thought of her as precious.

It was very seductive to be treated like that, and she had no wish to be seduced in *any* sense of the word.

She'd fallen into that trap before. Fool me once, shame on you; fool me twice, shame on me.

The kisses in the stable had been difficult enough to resist, but if she lived to be a hundred, she wouldn't forget that kiss he'd given her as he went off to rescue Tibby.

Hard. Possessive. Passionate.

She didn't want to be squashed into a carriage for hours on end with a man who thought nothing of kissing a woman he barely knew, and whose kisses made her forget all her resolutions and go weak at the knees.

Besides he was bossy. Really bossy. All her life she'd been ordered around by men, her wishes ignored, her opinions spurned. Finally she was free: as a widow she owed obedience to no man.

And no man was ever going to take that freedom from her. Not even a blue-eyed devil who kissed like a dream.

But there was her son to think of. Gabriel had offered to protect Nicky as well. She knew he'd protect her and her son or die trying. One couldn't ask for more.

But it was a lot to ask of a man, especially when you offered him nothing in return.

"You can't risk your son's safety merely because you're cross with me," he said quietly.

She looked at him, astonished. Was the man some kind of mind-reading warlock? But he was right. Despite her reservations about him, he was a strong, honorable, protective man and she would be criminally foolish to turn down his offer of protection.

"I will accept your escort, thank you," she told him.

Gabriel would protect her son from Count Anton.

And she would protect herself from Gabriel.

"Excellent. Now, for the salve." He picked up a clean

cloth and dabbed at the small bloody leech bites. The bruised red marks all over his body were less red and angry-looking. He saw her watching and said, "Shall we go into the sitting room? It gets the afternoon sun and I believe Barrow has lit a fire in there, so it will be nice and warm, and you can put the salve on me there in private."

Callie wondered briefly what he suddenly wanted privacy for—after all, he'd sat, unashamed and unembarrassed, naked to the waist in front of Tibby and her, but he'd already picked up the salve and a large green tin and headed out, so she followed.

The green tin proved to contain jam tarts and Gabriel stood in the sunlight that streamed through the big bay window munching them. His body was powerful, though not in the thick-muscled way that Rupert was powerful.

Gabriel's body was lithe, sleek, and hard . . . He was like a Greek statue in the sunlight, only warm and made of muscle and bone.

She glanced up, to discover he'd been observing her examination of his naked torso. She felt the heat rising in her cheeks. "Just checking where I need to put that stuff," she muttered. "Turn around."

"You'll need this," he said softly and held out the pot of salve. She took it and he turned his back to her.

She'd never really looked at a man's back before—not naked and not up this close. Rupert was the only man she'd ever seen even partially unclothed. Rupert had been a man of physical modesty; he'd kept his nightshirt on at all times.

This was . . . extraordinary. Broad and powerful, with smooth, golden skin, as if he took his shirt off in the sunlight often.

The recent scrapes and bruises overlaid other older scars: the mark of a blade here, the round puckered scar of a bullet, perhaps, there. Testament of battles fought and survived. A hardened, experienced warrior.

I will protect you, he'd said.

She uncorked the pot of salve and sniffed it cautiously. It was pungent, but pleasant, too. A thick muddy green in color, she could smell camphor, marigolds, mint, and the bitterness of pennyroyal perhaps, as well as other herbs. She sniffed again. Maybe myrrh, too. "What's in this, do you know?"

He shrugged. "I'm not completely sure, but I expect it will contain goldenseal, plantain, and Saint-John's-wort, as well as comfrey root. Mrs. Barrow used to send us to collect the herbs when I was a boy. The knowledge came in very useful when we were at war.

Carefully, gently, she smoothed salve into the abraded flesh. The cool ointment warmed under her palm, absorbing the warmth of his body and flowing over the planes and hollows of his back.

"Tell me about Tibby," he said after a while. "You have, I think, a closer relationship with her than most women do with their old governess."

"Yes, Tibby is a darling. She was, in many respects, like a mother to me. My father was very . . . particular about my education. He had plans for a brilliant marriage for me."

"And he succeeded."

"Yes." Callie dipped into the pot and scooped out another fingerful of salve. She refused to think about her successful, brilliant marriage. She took an odd comfort from kneading and massaging the firm, warm flesh beneath her hands.

"How did it come about?"

"Papa's original plan was for me to marry the prince regent, but he married Princess Caroline of Brunswick when I was just a little girl, so Papa was forced to look to European courts for a suitable husband for me. He went off on a tour of the various European courts, leaving me in England with Tibby, to grow up and become educated."

"He left you behind? Why? And how did you feel about it?"

Callie thought about it as she rubbed salve up and down the strong ridge of muscle that enclosed his spine. "I think he thought he could arrange a better marriage for me sight unseen." The way she'd turned out had been a crushing blow to Papa. He'd made no secret of his frustration that she'd taken after his side of the family in looks, instead of the tall, cool blondes of her mother's family. Had Callie been a beauty, she could have married into one of the great royal families, instead of a small obscure principality.

"I didn't mind being left behind," she said. "In a way, it was a relief."

"Good God, why?"

"I never could do anything to Papa's satisfaction. I was a thorn in his side, really—not a drop of royal blood visible in me. I'm too short, too plump, my face is too round and with an undistinguished snub nose. And I have a great many character faults as well."

"Such as?"

"Oh, I'm argumentative, stubborn—"

"I've noticed that."

She slapped a glop of cold ointment on him. He chuckled. "I know, I asked for that."

"And I cannot seem to be interested in the *important* things."

"And what were the important things?"

"Oh, you know, etiquette, diplomacy, female accomplishments—I mean, what is the *point* of embroidery?" She rolled her eyes. "The palace was full of the most hideous, perfectly executed pieces of embroidery—cushions, hangings, screens—you name it, so there was no need for any more. But no, I must embroider."

"So, you hate sewing."

"No, I quite like sewing, but I like it to be useful. But a princess should do nothing useful. Or interesting." She laughed wryly, thinking about it. "I don't know who was more frustrated by me, Papa or Rupert."

The happiest time of her life was when she'd lived with Tibby, she thought—apart from when Nicky was born. Tibby never expected her to be someone else. Tibby liked her the way she was. And Tibby was interested in all kinds of different, unsuitable things and had encouraged Callie to be, too.

Saving Nicky was the reason she'd fled Zindaria, but it was for both their sakes that she'd fled to Tibby. She'd planned to make a new life for herself as well as Nicky, where both of them could live without the constant criticism.

Tibby had always wanted a child. Callie knew that. Just as she used to pretend in her heart of hearts that Tibby was her mother, Tibby pretended that Callie was her daughter.

Now Count Anton had ruined that dream, as well. She could never go back to living with Tibby now Count Anton knew where she lived. She rubbed harder.

Gabe arched his back into the sensuous rubbing he was receiving and thought about what she'd told him. "So while Napoleon was doing his best to gobble up Europe, your father was doing the grand tour and interviewing potential royal sons-in-law. Didn't Boney cramp his style at all?"

"Oh, indeed yes," she told him. "Napoleon kept taking over the royal houses of Europe and making his own relatives into kings and queens. Papa was utterly furious about it. Napoleon came from very common stock, you know. Not at all good ton. And his conquests ruined some quite good chances for me, so Papa was forced to look further afield. He found it all terribly inconvenient."

Gabe spluttered at this novel view of the conquest of Europe. He was almost sorry he hadn't met Papa.

"Papa was quite relieved when he got Prince Rupert to accept me. Rupert didn't care about looks or fortune—just blood. Mama's family was poor, but enormously distinguished. Rupert took bloodlines very seriously—well, he would, being a horse breeder."

Gabe gave a spurt of laughter. "A romantic fellow, I perceive."

There was a sudden cessation of movement. "No. No, he wasn't," she said in a quiet voice. After a moment she started rubbing in salve again.

He'd obviously touched a nerve. Gabe turned to look at her. She kept her head down, smearing cold ointment onto him and continuing to massage it in without meeting his eyes.

He didn't know many young girls, but for all he knew marrying a mysterious foreign prince was the summit of her girlish dreams.

Something made him ask, "How old were you when you married him?"

She shrugged and avoided his eyes. "Nearly sixteen."

He frowned. "That seems rather young."

She shrugged and slapped on more ointment, almost angrily. "Rupert thought a young bride would be more fertile. I was his second wife, you see. The first one was barren." She rubbed hard at Gabe's skin.

"After years away, Papa arrived out of the blue and told me we were going to Zindaria and that I was going to be married to a prince." She rubbed at the marks on his skin as if they were stains to be got out. Gabe didn't flinch or make a sound.

So much for girlish dreams, he thought. If he hadn't thought the man a complete ass before, he would now. A complete royal jackass.

How could any man not see what a treasure she was?

He looked down at the little, round-faced, snub-nosed, dusky-haired princess, scowling fiercely as she rubbed enough unguent into him to waterproof a boat.

Deep in the past, she stared blindly at his chest and rubbed unguent into his nipples.

Pain he could withstand in silence. This he could not. A soft moan escaped him. She took no notice and kept rubbing, circling the nipples with intense concentration, a faraway expression on her face. He moaned again and arched involuntarily.

She blinked and recalled herself. "I am so sorry you had to suffer in this way—"

"Hush." Gabe put a finger over her mouth, pressing her soft, satiny lips together. "There is no need to fret. Mrs. Barrow was right. I do enjoy a good fight."

She looked at the marks on his skin, now glistening with unguent. "How could you enjoy it? How could anyone?"

"It's a—a form of release." He could see she didn't understand, so he added, "A bit like, er, congress."

"Congress?" She gave him a puzzled look. "Like the Congress of Vienna?"

"No, marital congress. In the bedchamber."

"Oh." She dropped her eyes. "That. Yes I see."

They fell silent for a moment. She stared at the mess of bruises on his chest and stroked the softened ointment carefully over and around them, long, delicate sweeps and soft butterfly touches. The sensations were both seductive and agonizing.

Gabe watched the emotions flitting across her face and realized she didn't have a clue.

She didn't know how seductive her touch was to him, that he was fighting for control, that the tension in the body under her fingertips was because he was fighting arousal, not pain.

It was obvious to him that she was a deeply sensual creature; the intensity with which she concentrated on massaging the pungent ointment into his flesh, her eyes dark and slumbrous, her lips full and pouting in concentration, the dark, silken brows knotted in thought—he'd wager of a place and time far from here.

She was becoming aroused, he was sure. Her soft breaths were coming shorter and faster, and she kept licking her lips, all unconscious. The moist dampness of her lips made him want to groan. If he just bent his head a few inches he could taste them, taste her. And she would taste him.

Deeply sensual.

He recalled the half-embarrassed, half-defiant relish with which she'd savored the bacon this morning, her way she'd fought against pleasure when he dried her feet, and then abandoned herself to it.

And yet she seemed ignorant of the sensual pleasures between a man and a woman.

Gabe stared at her luscious mouth in disbelief. Nine years of marriage and she couldn't imagine how a good fight could give the same sort of release to pent-up feelings as . . . what did she call it? *That.*

Sensual but straitlaced. If she had any understanding of what her touch was doing to him, she'd be on the other side of the room.

"You have no idea, do you? Was your husband a monk?"

"Of course not," she said. "I told you, he was a prince. And what do you mean, no idea? No idea of what?"

"Of this," he said and pulled her into his arms.

Nine

He'd caught her off balance and unawares. She
gasped and tried to pull back but his arms locked
around her. Her hands pressed against his chest. She could
feel the rhythm of his heart beating, faster than before.

One of his arms circled her waist, the other slid slowly
up her spine, bringing slow shivers of heat with it. It
stopped finally at the nape of her neck. He stroked the tender nape with one finger, lightly, rhythmically, causing
prickles of sensation to flow up and down her spine.

"Wh—what are you doing?" she managed to say.

"Showing you." His voice was deep and soft and sure.

"Showing me what?"

He didn't respond, not in words, but she felt him shift his
position and suddenly she could feel his hard, strong thighs
bracketing hers. The warmth of his body seeped through her
thin dress. The blended scents of the unguent on his skin in-
tensified. It was bound to stain her dress, she thought, but
somehow she couldn't bring herself to move.

This close she could see that his eyes were not simply

blue, but blue with tiny gold flecks, and ringed with a darker blue. The flecks were what made them dance, she thought. They weren't dancing now. His irises were dark and large, and seemed to draw her ever closer, like the eye of a whirlpool.

Under her fingertips his heart thudded in an insistent beat. It echoed in her mind, in her body. She could feel the rhythm of the beat through his thighs, his chest, in the muscles of the arms locked about her, in the heat of him pressed against her stomach.

She stared into his eyes, mesmerized. The way he was gazing at her made her nervous and oddly weak. She could hardly breathe. Her breath was coming in shallow gasps.

Her lips were dry. She moistened them with her tongue and his gaze dropped to her mouth.

And with agonizing, unbearable slowness he bent his head and lightly, shockingly, licked her on the mouth. Barely a touch, it shuddered right through her, coming to pool, achingly, somewhere deep inside her.

"Your lips are so soft, so silky," he murmured and began to feather all around her mouth with tiny, tantalizing kisses. "Amazing, considering what you do to them."

"I don't do anything to them," she managed, shivering deliciously as he planted kisses along her jawline.

"Oh, but you do," he breathed, and she could feel the warm breath of him on her moist lips, like an echo of a kiss, moonlight after sunlight. "You're always chewing or biting them."

She couldn't think of a thing to say. It was all she could do to stand. She clutched his shoulders for support. Broad, smooth, and rock hard. Her hand slipped on the sticky remains of the unguent.

"And if you must bite them," he went on, his deep voice vibrating against her skin. "This is how you should do it." He nibbled at her lips until they parted, then he took her lower lip very gently between his teeth and bit down on it softly, over and over, laving and sucking between each bite.

With each tiny bite, sensations coursed through her body, arrowing in wave after wave, straight to the core of her. Her knees buckled and she felt herself jerk and shudder helplessly in his arms, as if she'd been taken over by something. Or someone.

The moment he released her lips she pulled back, shocked at herself. She shoved at his chest and he let her go. She staggered back, there was something wrong with her knees. She found a chair and sat down with a thump, gasping for breath, for some vestige of control.

He gave a soft groan.

She stared at him. "Did I hurt you?"

"Yes." His chest was heaving, his voice ragged. His eyes bored into hers, a dark, midnight blue.

She scanned his body. Who knows what she had done to him? She'd been completely out of control. "What did I do?"

"You stopped."

She didn't understand. "How could that hurt?" Her emotions were in turmoil. What had just happened?

He stroked a finger down her cheek. "He wasn't a very good husband to you, was he?"

She blinked at the abrupt change of subject and jerked her head away from his hand. Even the stroke of one finger sent shivers through her. "Rupert? Yes, he was. He gave me Nicky. And he protected us." She took deep breaths and gathered the shreds of her composure together.

"But you weren't happy."

"Of course I was. I was the crown princess, the highest lady in the land. Every girl wants that." She was much calmer now that she was back on familiar territory. As long as she didn't look at him. Or touch him. Or smell that unguent. She wiped her hands on her skirt. It was ruined anyway.

"Not you. You don't care a snap of your fingers for that."

"How would you know?" She wished he would stop looking at her. Even though she had her head turned away, she could feel the warmth of his gaze.

"A girl who cared for position wouldn't let someone like Mrs. Barrow call her lovie. Wouldn't let her precious son make friends with a scruffy little fisher boy. Wouldn't leave it all behind her without a thought."

She said nothing. She was calm and back to herself, she thought. She must never let him do that to her again.

"Being the princess didn't make you happy, and I don't believe he did, either."

"You're wrong," she flashed. "I was happy. And I did love my husband, I did." She'd promised to on her wedding day and she had, she really had. With all her foolish sixteen-year-old heart.

"I see, so it was love's young dream?"

Her mouth wobbled and she jerked her back to him. She marched to the fire, seized a poker, and jabbed the fire savagely with it. Smoke gushed into the room.

After a few minutes she put the poker down. "We will leave in the morning," she announced.

He sighed.

She frowned. "What?"

He shook his head. "Nothing. It is just that I had hoped to be here when Harry arrived. The day after tomorrow." He slanted a look at her.

Callie stared at him, unable to believe the effrontery of the man. No doubt that's why he'd kissed her like that, to soften her up. "Let me get this clear," she said. "First you lock my luggage away to force me to delay my departure, then you foist your company on me—unwanted!—for the journey, and now you have the gall to suggest I wait another two days?"

He nodded, his blue eyes dancing. "That's it, in a nutshell."

"Because you want to meet your brother."

"Yes."

She glared at him.

After a moment he added, "He's a very nice brother. I'm fond of him." He seemed not the least bit abashed.

"I'm not surprised you survived the war," she said at last.

His mouth twitched. "And why is that?"

"Because you were clearly born to be hanged," she told him. "Or throttled. It does amaze me that nobody has throttled you. That you've escaped hanging doesn't altogether surprise me—government authorities are so rarely efficient, I find. You can wait for your brother as long as you like. Nicky and I will leave first thing in the morning."

Gabe watched her sweep from the room, his mouth drying at the sway of her hips. His body was aching and aroused and he felt simultaneously frustrated and exhilarated.

He shrugged on a shirt, then sat down at the writing desk in the corner, pulled out a quill, and began to sharpen it with a small pearl-handled knife. His mind kept reliving that kiss, but he forced it instead to consider what he'd learned about her.

He hadn't meant to distress her, hadn't meant to stir up painful memories. But his questions had produced such revealing answers he could not regret asking them.

Most fascinating was her answer to the question he hadn't asked. She'd answered it with such vehemence, too. *I did love my husband, I did.*

Was it the truth? Or, to paraphrase the Bard, had she protested too much?

And did it matter anyway? After all the man was dead.

It was bizarre, Gabe reflected. He'd known her such a short time and knew so little about her, yet, somehow, she had become so important to him. And it wasn't just lust, though he was beset with lust the entire time he was with her. That mouth of hers would be the death of him yet.

He groaned just thinking of how she'd tasted, her sweet, frantic response. She'd almost dissolved right there in his arms. Had they not been standing, she might have been his yet.

But he'd been in lust many a time before, and it had never caused him to panic at the thought of the woman leaving. He'd never panicked in his life, let alone over a woman. But the feeling in his chest when she'd declared she was leaving, he was pretty sure that had been something akin to panic.

The soldier in him had reacted immediately to secure his position; he'd taken her luggage prisoner. Held it hostage until she gave her parole. Not one of his more glorious military moments.

It was only afterward that he'd analyzed his actions. It had shocked him to realize it, but there it was, as large as life in his consciousness.

After so short an acquaintance he had no business thinking the thoughts he was thinking, or making the plans he was making. But he seemed to be making them anyway. He couldn't seem to help it.

All unknowing, like a sniper in the dark, she'd taken him neatly in the heart.

He'd had no idea it could happen like that. He'd never had plans to settle down, had never once considered marriage.

Marriage? Surely he wasn't. He couldn't be.

Marriage was for family men, for eldest sons who needed to get heirs, for men in need of an heiress, or for fools who fell in love.

Gabe was about as far from being a family man as he could imagine; he'd never met his father, never once been to the family home. He'd met his two older brothers twice in his life that he recalled. It might be three times. Those occasions had been stiff and uncomfortable, and none of them had made a push to see each other since they'd become adults.

His father had died while he was away at war and his brothers hadn't even thought to inform him. He had been informed of his mother's death a short time later—not that he'd seen her since he was a child. Great-aunt Gert's death had affected him the most; the degree of grief he'd felt for the stern old woman had shocked him with its intensity. His most distant relative, she'd been his closest family member, apart from Harry. So no, he was no family man.

He had no need of an heir, either. As the third son he was surplus to requirements, so any potential heirs of his body were even more so.

He didn't need to marry an heiress, or earn his living. Great-aunt Gert had left him the Grange and most of her fortune, with a list of stipulations, bless the tyrannical old dear. None of the stipulations had included his marriage.

As for being one of those poor fools who fell in love, he'd never imagined it could happen to him. Had planned never to allow it. People in love could do terrible things to each other, and innocents suffered when they did. He and Harry had both experienced that firsthand, though in different ways. Bad enough to ruin each others' lives, but children became pawns when things went wrong in a marriage . . .

Gabe pulled out several sheets of writing paper, slightly yellowed, untouched since Great-aunt Gert's day. He had watched love happen to others time and time again and thought himself immune. He wasn't even sure it had happened to him now.

All he knew was that every time he looked at her he wanted to touch her, taste her, hold her. And every instinct he had was screaming at him not to let her go.

He shook up a pot of ink. Those instincts had kept him alive throughout eight years of war. He wasn't going to start ignoring them now.

The last of the sun's rays touched the octagonal bow window and slid away. It would soon be dark. She had not yet conceded defeat, but she'd given him a reprieve. He had one night. He needed at least two more. It would take the others that long to get here.

Once she was on the road, she was that much more vulnerable. He hadn't wanted to alarm her any further, but if he'd been Count Anton and his quarry had slipped though his fingers, he would put men on each of the main roads leading away from Lulworth and at several of the main coaching inns on the London road. A lone woman and a small boy with a limp would be easily traced.

When she finally left for London, Gabe decided, she'd be accompanied by four of the best—the Duke's Angels or, as some had called them, the Devil Riders: Rafe, Harry, and Luke. And, of course, himself.

Harry was already on his way, bringing horses.

Rafe was at a house party at Aldershot, trying to nerve himself to do what his family expected—nay, urged him to do, no matter how much the idea of it stuck in Rafe's throat—marry an heiress.

As for Luke, he was in London, but the Lord knew what he would be doing—anything that could blot out memories of the Convent of the Angels. Poor Luke. Of all of them, he was the most haunted by the past. If he didn't learn to master it, Gabe feared he would go mad. It would be good for Luke to have a real problem to worry about, something in the here and now, a woman, a child he *could* protect.

Gabe dipped the quill in the ink and began writing.

*D*inner that evening was served in the small breakfast room and once again, Mrs. Barrow used the boys as waiters, only this time she sought Callie's permission.

She'd feed the boys in the kitchen first, she explained. "Young Jim's manners not being fit for company, Your Highness. Your Nicky now, he's that correct a little gentleman that it practically hurts to watch him, so I reckon Jim'll soon pick up the way to behave."

Callie was not surprised by what Mrs. Barrow had said. Nicky was painfully correct, it was more noticeable here, where everything was more relaxed.

At home, whenever they'd dined en famille, Rupert had directed a nonstop barrage of instruction and criticism aimed at his son—at his manners, his bearing, the way he broke his bread, his attempts to respond to the conversational gambits his father shot at him.

Rupert had been a good enough man, she thought sadly, but he'd been determined to forge his son into a prince worthy of the name. His methods were crushing to a small, sensitive boy.

It was something she needed to redress.

Perhaps being the kitchen role model in manners for Jim might give Nicky a little of the confidence he lacked.

"Very well," she agreed, knowing how much Nicky had enjoyed waiting on table this morning. "But after dinner, send him to join me in the drawing room, please." It had been a big day, and she wanted to talk to her son, to hear his thoughts, and to reassure him if necessary.

She was also a little worried about the way he'd taken her announcement earlier that they were leaving. He'd said nothing—he was invariably obedient and well behaved—but his face had fallen with utter dismay.

It was hard for him, she knew. He'd taken to this place like a duck to water, and even seemed to relish Mrs. Barrow's brusque bossiness. He'd hunted leeches, had his first-ever fight, and made a firm friend from it—males were strange creatures.

He'd even had his first ride on a horse that hadn't ended up with him sprawled painfully on the ground to laughter or, more humiliatingly, embarrassed silence.

If she lived to be a hundred, she would never forget the way he'd greeted her this morning, all covered in mud, grinning at her from the back of a giant horse in front of Gabriel, breathless with exhilaration and triumph. And burgeoning confidence.

He was happy here, happier than she'd ever seen him, and it pained her to tear him away. But it was his happiness or his safety. Count Anton had not pursued them this far to give up and tamely go home.

*S*he'd had in mind an intimate after-dinner conversation with her son, but Nicky brought his friend Jim with him, and then the men had surprised her by not lingering over their port, and joining her, Tibby, and the boys.

"Do you play chess, boys?" Mr. Delaney had asked and produced a small wooden box that opened up to become a chessboard. "A grand game to while away a chilly night."

Jim was eager to learn, so Nicky hovered, observing quietly. Tibby wandered over to watch, too. Callie smiled. Even Papa had deemed Tibby a worthy opponent.

Gabe pulled a chair up next to her. He said nothing for a while, just divided his time between watching her pretend to sew and watching the chess lesson.

"Your son already knows how to play chess," he commented.

She glanced at him in surprise. "How did you know?"

He shrugged. "He's watching the interaction between the players, rather than trying to learn the mechanics of the game. And since he strikes me as the kind of boy who likes to know things, I assume he already knows the moves."

She gave a little nod. "Yes. My father and my husband were keen chess players."

"Took it very seriously, too, I'll wager."

She nodded.

"It's like watching myself and Harry all over again," he said after a time. "Harry was just such a wild child as young Jim, and I was probably just as needy as Nicky."

Needy? Gabe caught himself up on the word. He'd never thought of himself as ever being needy.

But watching the young boy's reserved, intelligent face, his quick, shy responses to Ethan and Jim's noisy repartee, Gabe suddenly remembered what it felt like to sit on the outer, yearning to be accepted, to truly belong. Grateful for any crumb of approval.

He'd forgotten he'd ever felt like that.

He glanced at her face. His words had annoyed her.

"He's a fine, spirited boy. He'll grow out of it," Gabe told her soothingly. Gabe had grown out of it.

"My son is not needy, and I doubt you even know the meaning of the word," she told him.

It was meant to be a reprimand, but she'd unwittingly offered Gabe an opening he couldn't resist.

"Oh, I assure you, I understand what needy means, especially after this afternoon," he murmured, his voice deepening. His gaze dropped to her mouth and he sighed suggestively. And even though he was only teasing her, the memory of their earlier kiss rose up and he had to battle with his body.

The color in her cheeks rose. "If you were any sort of gentleman, you would not refer to that incident."

His gaze dropped to her mouth and stayed there. "It was a particularly sweet incident. As are your lips."

"You will not flirt with me here!" she ordered in an undertone.

"Won't I?" He gave her a look of faux-innocent surprise. "Where shall we go to flirt then?"

She narrowed those glorious eyes at him. "We shan't go anywhere."

"You don't want to go somewhere?"

"No, I am not budging from this place."

"Excellent, I thought you were leaving in the morning," he said instantly. He raised his voice. "Listen, everyone, the princess says she's not leaving after all. She has decided to stay on here."

Her jaw dropped but before she had time to refute his outrageous misinterpretation of her words, her son came flying across the room and flung his arms around her.

"Oh, Mama, thank you, thank you! I did want so much to stay, and Jim has told me of a place where we could go fishing and could we go tomorrow please? I have never been fishing and perhaps I could catch you a fish for your supper. Mama, you know how much you like fish!"

Over her son's head she glared at Gabe, who hoped he was not looking as smug as he felt. She'd walked so neatly into his trap, and he was rewarded with another day, at least. More if he could persuade her. His letters were speeding on their way.

"It will be perfectly safe," he reminded her. "Nobody knows you are here and there is nothing to connect this place with Miss Tibthorpe."

He saw her consider his words, biting her lip thoughtfully. He watched, reliving the sensations that had coursed through him as he'd nibbled on that very lip. He could still taste the wild, dark honey taste of her. His body throbbed with remembrance. And need.

She remembered, too, he could tell by the way she abruptly stopped biting her lip and flickered a self-conscious glance his way. She saw he was watching and flushed even deeper.

He could also see she was quietly furious about the way he'd tricked her, yet she told her son that very well, they would stay another day, and that yes, if Mr. Renfrew would escort them fishing and guarantee their safety, she would allow it.

"I'd be delighted," Gabe said.

Nicky straightened. "Thank you, Mama, sir." Scarcely able to contain his excitement, he still managed a creditable bow and ran back to the chess game.

She gave Gabe a wry glance. "I do hope you enjoy your fishing."

He laughed. "No, you don't."

"You're very rude," she told him. "How would you know what I think?"

"I told you, your face gives your thoughts away."

"Nonsense!" she retorted. "Nobody else has ever indicated anything of the sort."

"I know exactly what you're thinking," he murmured.

Her eyebrows formed a skeptical arch. "Oh? Pray tell."

He leaned forward, rather too close for her peace of mind, for she swayed back warily. He scrutinized her face. Then he grinned. "Right now you're hoping I fall into some very cold, very muddy water—with leeches."

She gave him a cool look. "And lots of slimy weeds." She glanced around the room in search of a new topic of conversation. Something innocuous and dull. Without hidden shoals. There were several paintings; some landscapes, rather dark and gloomy, and a few portraits, years out of date.

A portrait that intrigued her hung over the mantelpiece. It was of a woman in middle age, sharp-featured and severe-looking. Bright blue eyes glared down at the occupants of the room, along a great beak of a nose.

Poor woman, to be afflicted with a nose like that. It made her grateful for her own undistinguished snub nose.

"My great-aunt Gert," he said, making her jump.

"She raised Harry and me and left me this house." He rose to his feet. "Now, since you won't let me flirt with you, I'll salvage my pride, take myself off, and offer your son a game. He's looking a little bored and there's another chess set in the cabinet there. Would you care to join us?"

"No, thank you, I have my sewing to do," she said politely. She watched him cross the room and invite her son to join him in a game. He might have been asking another adult to play.

She glanced at the portrait of the harsh-featured woman over the fireplace and wondered how an elderly great-aunt had come to raise the two younger sons of an earl, but not the two older ones. And why Harry was a half brother. And a wild child.

*T*he next morning after breakfast, true to his word, Gabriel took Jim and Nicky fishing. It was a simple breakfast: four maidservants had arrived to start work that morning and Mrs. Barrow was busy directing a joyful frenzy of housework.

Callie and Tibby took refuge in the octagonal room, taking some sewing with them. Nicky needed new shirts and Callie needed more underclothes, so the two women sat in the warm, sunny room sewing and catching up on the important minutiae of the years they'd spent apart, talking and making plans.

Around eleven o'clock, Mr. Delaney poked his head around the sitting room door. "Miss Tibthorpe, I was wonderin' . . . I'm planning to drive over to Rose Bay Farm to see that stallion and, since your cottage is on the way, I thought mebbe you might want to stop off and see if you can find that cat of yours. As long as you don't mind waiting while I inspect the stallion, that is."

"Mind waiting? Indeed no." Tibby set down the shirt for Nicky she was sewing and jumped up. "Thank you, Mr. Delaney, it's very thoughtful of you. I've been so worried about Kitty-cat. He's such a sweet little creature and he's had such a hard life." She turned to Callie. "You don't mind, do you, Callie?"

Callie smiled. "No of course not, Tibby dear. Go. I hope you find your Kitty-cat."

Tibby had hurried off, leaving Callie alone.

She continued her sewing. To tell the truth, she was rather enjoying the peace—for the past eighteen days she'd been traveling, rarely stopping, barely sleeping. It was wonderful to be able to just sit and not have to worry or be alert; her whereabouts were unknown and Nicky was safe.

He really was safe, she knew, with Gabriel. He was a man she could rely on—in matters of protection, at least. She'd been lucky to have fallen under his protection when she did, to be given this respite before continuing on her way.

But that's all it could be—a respite. She hadn't gone to all this trouble to break out of one sort of prison only to exchange it for another. And it would be a prison, she could see the warning signs. A safe and comfortable one, perhaps, but a prison, all the same. A prison of her own making.

She had a tendency to want to run her head into the noose.

It had been the first true lesson of her marriage. Even after so many years, it had the power to fill her with remembered humiliation. What a fool she'd made of herself with Rupert. What a public fool.

She thought she was over all that, but that kiss in the octagonal room, that amazing, mind-scrambling, sublime, and dreadful kiss had given off warning signs ten feet tall.

Never again would she place her happiness in the hands of a man. She was older and wiser now.

She would leave. Protect Nicky, protect herself.

She took advantage of the privacy to unpick some of the jewels she had sewn into her thick petticoat—not the most valuable ones, just a ruby pin and some pearl earrings—small and easily sold items that would give her ready money for traveling.

The question was whether to go to some other rural location and live there quietly, or to disappear in London.

You can't keep running. Count Anton must be stopped.

He was right, she knew, but how could she stop Count Anton? The only thing that would stop him was death, and she wasn't sure she had it in her to kill someone. She tried to list her options, but it kept coming back to just two: Run or kill Count Anton . . . run or kill Count Anton.

If Nicky could abdicate . . . but he couldn't, not until he was eighteen. And she didn't want him to, anyway. To be the prince of Zindaria was his birthright.

Plans and possibilities swirled in her brain. The sun streamed in through the octagonal window. The warmth was heavenly. She folded her sewing on her lap and closed her eyes, just to enjoy it for a moment.

"Mama, I have had the most splendid time!" Nicky burst into the room chattering nineteen to the dozen. "We caught lots of fish, and we lit a fire on the beach and cooked them and ate them—with our fingers, Mama! And they were the most delicious fish I have ever eaten in my life. And little shells we dug out of the sand and we boiled them and ate them, too. And we met two other boys that Jim knew and they are splendid fellows and I fell in and got wet, but I am dry now because one of the other boys lived in the oddest little hut near the beach and he lent me some clothes while mine got dry. Oh, Mama, you should have been there!"

By the time he stopped to draw breath Callie was laughing helplessly. "And did you think to save a fish for me, my brave fisherman?"

"Yes, of course, Mama. I promised I would."

"Of course you did, darling. Thank you." She looked at the tall man who was lounging in the doorway, watching them with a faint smile.

"Thank you, Mr. Renfrew." She smiled up at him. "I have not seen Nicky this happy in . . . oh, forever. It makes everything worthwhile."

"Even the delay I foisted on you?"

"Yes, even that, though . . ." She scanned his long, lean body. "I don't suppose you fell in, too, did you?" she asked hopefully.

He laughed. "Nope."

"No fingers or toes nipped by a lobster or a crab?"

"Nope."

She produced a mock sigh. "Oh well, one cannot have everything, I suppose. We must be content with Nicky's splendid time." She tried not to smile, but it broke out anyway.

She ran her fingers affectionately though Nicky's hair. And saw something. She frowned, and peered closer. "What? It's a, it's a—"

"A nit. A louse," said Gabriel, looking over her shoulder. "In fact, several lice. See there's another one."

"Lice?" she exclaimed. "My son has lice?"

He seemed to find her horror amusing. "Don't worry, they don't eat much."

She stared at him in speechless indignation.

"You're not very good with things that wriggle and crawl, are you?" he commented. "Leeches, lice . . ."

"No, I'm not!" she snapped, annoyed by his amusement. Lice were horrid, dirty things. Her son had never in his life been exposed to such creatures. "Nicky, how did you—" She broke off. It would have happened when he swapped clothes with that other boy. She looked at Gabriel. "How could you let this happen?"

He shrugged indifferently. "Nits won't kill him. You said yourself he had a splendid day. Besides it might even do him good."

"Do him good?" She shuddered.

"Nicky will one day be crown prince of Zindaria. Tell

me, who will make the better ruler—the man who has no idea of the daily life and hardships of the ordinary folk, or the man who as a boy, rubbed shoulders—or heads—with the sons of the poor?"

She closed her eyes. "All right, I suppose I can see your point."

"So don't worry about lice and bangs or scrapes or mud or fleas—"

She opened her eyes. "*Fleas?*" she said faintly.

His blue eyes twinkled. "Bound to be fleas. Mrs. Barrow is well used to dealing with boys and the livestock they can bring home. She'll whisk Nicky and Jim into a bath, go over them with a fine-toothed comb and rub her special nit cream into their hair—it's stinky, but efficacious, I promise you. And she'll boil their clothes in the copper."

"How do you know so much about . . ." She glanced at the lice in her son's hair and shuddered.

"I've had lice before. They're a constant nuisance in the army—yes, even the officers get 'em. And when I was a boy Harry and I picked up our share of bodily livestock. We ran wild with the local lads, too."

Callie gave her son a little push. "Go on, Nicky, go and show Mrs. Barrow what else you caught today beside the fish."

Nicky stood. "I have had leeches and now I have lice!" he exclaimed.

Both Callie and Gabriel laughed at his apparent pride in his achievement.

"Indeed, Nicky, and the experience will make you a better prince, someday," Gabriel said, ruffling his hair as he passed.

Callie watched him and smiled.

"I'm glad to see you've accepted it," he said after Nicky had left.

"Far be it from me to stand in the way of Nicky's princely development." She glanced at Gabriel. "I don't suppose you've picked up any livestock, too."

"No. Your luck is quite out today."

"I'm not so sure," she said, trying not to smile. "You ruffled my son's hair just then. And for the past few minutes, you've been scratching. Perhaps you'd better see Mrs. Barrow, too."

Ten

Callie was bored. She'd spent the whole morning sewing, and now she wanted a change. The books in the library didn't appeal—it seemed Great-aunt Gert had disdained frivolous reading matter of the sort Callie and Tibby adored, for there was not one single novel—she had no letters to write and nobody to talk to.

She'd even offered to help Mrs. Barrow organizing the maidservants, an offer that had been received with horror. A princess, keeping a bunch of useless scatty girls applied to their work? Heaven forfend! And Mrs. Barrow had bustled off.

The princess, feeling a certain kinship with the useless, scatty girls, dolefully returned to her sewing.

A shout and the clatter of hooves in the courtyard outside caused her to jump up and run to the window. In the courtyard two horses were walking around in a rough circle, their hooves clip-clopping on the stones. Gabriel stood in the middle, observing, giving instructions.

Jim clung to the back of the first horse like a little monkey, his face alive with excitement.

Her son sat on the back of the second horse, pale and straight-backed, his face stiff with anxiety, his hands in the correct position.

Callie pressed her hand to her mouth. How many times had she watched this scene before, the prelude to the moment when Nicky went crashing on the ground, to lie crumpled and shamed, a failure yet again.

Gabriel called out something and she saw Nicky stiffen and rein his animal to a halt. His face frozen, he waited as the tall man strode across the courtyard, a frown on his face.

If he dared to yell at her son . . . Callie stood poised, ready to fly to Nicky's defense.

He stood on the other side of the horse, fiddling with something, and suddenly she realized he was adjusting the stirrup. Callie blinked. She hadn't even noticed there was a saddle. Every other time her son had been put on a horse it had been bareback.

Gabriel said something and stepped back. Nicky gave him a startled look, then grinned. He made a movement and the horse moved off.

Callie watched.

As the horses moved around the courtyard, Nicky's stiffness faded. His face lost that frozen look, and he even began to call out remarks to Jim. Callie wished she could hear what they were saying, but she was glued to the octagonal window.

Gabriel said something else, and the boys kicked their horses into a trot. For a breathless moment, Nicky bounced unsteadily, clinging on, his face white with the expectation of falling, but Gabriel called out advice and suddenly Nicky was rising and falling with the rhythm of the horse.

She was biting on her knuckles, she realized. Even from here she could read the pride in his bearing.

He was riding. Not bareback, not fast, but alone and un-aided.

He glanced at the window and saw her watching. His eyes lit up. With great daring, he raised a hand and quickly waved to her, his small face incandescent with joy.

Callie waved back, hoping he could not see the tears in her eyes. Nicky returned to his lesson with renewed determination.

Callie's gaze drifted to the tall man in the center of the courtyard. He was watching her, an enigmatic expression on his face.

She mouthed the words "thank you" and he gave her a slow smile, before turning back to the boys.

She stood watching with a lump in her throat and a hard knot in the middle of her chest. It was going to be harder to protect herself from him than she thought.

He had a way of sneaking under her defenses.

Suddenly there was a flurry of noise and movement as the curricle, driven by Ethan Delaney, came shooting under the arch and into the courtyard. The horses shied and the two boys clutched their manes, all instruction forgotten, but thankfully nobody fell.

Gabriel strode forward, lifted first Nicky, then Jim down, handed the boys their horses' reins and ordered them to the stables. Callie could see why.

Ethan had a face like a thundercloud. Tibby sat on the seat beside him, stiff and bolt upright, her face pinched and colorless.

Something was horribly wrong. Callie ran from the room.

Her initial fear—that Mr. Delaney had done something dreadful to Tibby—faded as she saw the gentle way he lifted Tibby down from the high-slung curricle, as if she were a child, or an invalid.

Tibby's face was ashen, but she showed no self-consciousness about the Irishman's big hands spanning her waist. She murmured an automatic thanks to him and stood, looking blankly in front of her.

"Tibby, what's wrong?" Callie asked as she hurried toward her friend.

Tibby tried to speak and failed. She swallowed, then tried again. "My cottage," she croaked. "It's all burned. Burned to the ground. There's nothing left, just charcoal and ashes." And then she burst into tears. Callie ushered her inside.

"Is there truly nothing left?" Gabe asked Ethan after the two women had gone into the house.

"Nothing at all."

Which as they both knew, was most unlikely, even with a thatched cottage. "So, it was deliberate?"

"I'd say so," Ethan said, his face grim. "I checked that house before we left. There was nothin' left alight. Not so much as a spark in the fireplace—all swept out clean, it was."

"Those bastards! Revenge, do you think? They wanted the princess and she'd eluded them, so they burned down her friend's house."

Ethan nodded. "Probably. And mebbe they were hopin' to smoke her out as well. Hopin' she'd lead them back to the princess. Nothin' more natural if you hear your house is burned than to come and look. I had the devil's own job stoppin' Miss Tibby from jumpin' out of the curricle as it was. Frettin' about her poor little cat and her books, she was." From Ethan's tone he didn't understand why anyone would worry about either.

"That 'poor little cat' is the ugliest thing you've ever seen," Gabe told him. "A battle-scarred old ginger tom, with a broken tail and"—he glanced at Ethan—"ears a bit like yours."

Ethan began to saddle a fresh horse.

"Where are you going?" Gabe asked.

"I'm goin' back to check."

"Check what?"

Ethan gave him an opaque look. "Something." He mounted his horse and rode back the way he'd come.

An hour later Callie came downstairs. "She's resting now," she told him. "Poor Tibby. She's lost everything." She hung her head. "I should never have written to her, never have come here."

"It's not your fault," Gabe told her firmly.

"It is. I knew what Count Anton was like." Guilt mixed with anger flickered across her face. "It's not the first time he's burned someone's house. He has a terrible temper and cannot endure to be crossed. But I promise you I never imagined for one moment he'd do something like that here in England, where he isn't even a member of the ruling family." Her voice choked on a sob. "It's my fault this happened to her."

"It's no such thing."

She looked away. An errant tear slipped down her cheek. She dashed it angrily away.

Gabe gripped her by the chin. "Look at me. This is not your fault."

"I am responsible. And Tibby is my friend. She is now destitute because she tried to help me. You cannot imagine I would simply leave and let her fend for herself."

No, Gabe didn't imagine that. Not for one minute. His Callie . . . his Callie was a woman in a million.

He pulled her into his arms and held her for a long moment. Then he gently tipped her tear-stained face up and kissed her. He kissed the tears from her cheeks and the distress from her lips. It wasn't like their last kiss; this was comfort. And reassurance. Tender.

O n Ethan's return he entered the house by the kitchen. "Do you know where Miss Tibby might be?" he asked Mrs. Barrow.

She nodded. "Poor little soul, like a wrung-out rag she

is. She's in the conservatory, though why anyone should want to sit in that gloomy old place, I don't know."

"Right," Ethan said and headed for the conservatory.

"But she said she wanted to be alone," Mrs. Barrow called after him. He took no notice.

The conservatory was built on to the back of the house. The walls were mostly windows. It must have been put in by whoever had built the octagonal bay window, Ethan thought, for it had something of the same style, and looked the same age, but it had been left too long neglected. The windows were crusted with sea salt and the few plants inside were long dead.

He could understand why Miss Tibby had chosen to come here to sit. It was a good place to be miserable. He spotted her sitting quietly on a bench between a dead potted palm and a large brown fern. "Miss Tibby," he said and sneezed.

She jumped and turned. "Oh, Mr. Delaney, you startled me."

"Do you mind if I join you?"

"No, of course not," she said miserably. "I'm afraid though that I'm not very good company."

"That's understandable," he said as he threaded his way between the pots of dead plants. When he reached her seat he just stood there in front of her.

Her eyes were red-rimmed and swollen. She glanced up at him, then dropped her gaze. She knew what she must look like, he thought, and was beyond caring.

As her gaze dropped, her mouth dropped open in surprise. "Mr. Delaney, your hands! They're all scratched and bloody."

Ethan grimaced. "I know." He sneezed again.

"But how—" Her eyes sharpened, riveted to his overcoat, which bulged oddly, and then moved.

"I've got something for you," Ethan said and cautiously unbuttoned his overcoat. His waistcoat heaved and a yowl came from within. He gingerly unbuttoned his waistcoat, reached in, swore, and withdrew his hand on which were fresh scratches, reached in again and drew out a spitting, snarling cat.

"Kitty-cat!" she cried joyfully and lifted the animal out of his hands.

"Be careful it's a vicious, savage wildca . . ." His voice trailed off. The vicious beast that had scratched his hands to bits was snuggled against Miss Tibby's chest, purring like a coffee grinder and butting her chin with its big, ugly head. Its single yellow eye winked with evil smugness at Ethan as its mistress crooned over it like a baby.

"Oh, Mr. Delaney, thank you so much! I thought he was lost forever." Tears sparkled on the ends of her lashes, but they were happy tears. Her cheeks were flushed and not the ghost pale they had been. She kissed the cat's head repeatedly, nuzzling his fur, stroking and caressing the ugly beast as if she thought it the most beautiful creature in the world.

Women were strange, he thought, not for the first time. "I knew you were worried about him, so . . ."

"I was, and I can't tell you how grateful I am. But how did you find him? He doesn't usually come to men."

He hadn't come to Ethan, either. Ethan had coaxed him into a shed with a trail of ham pieces he'd bought at a farmhouse, then he'd trapped him in the corner and flung his coat over him. The cat had put up a mighty struggle, but Ethan had prevailed, at the cost of his hands, a half-shredded shirt, a ruined waistcoat, and a stained coat.

"Oh, I have a way with animals," Ethan said modestly. It wasn't a lie, he thought. He did have a way with most animals—just not fiends from hell.

They sat there for a while, in silence, her crooning over the cat and him watching, bemused. She was such a lady, so small and neat and finicky-looking. He could understand her owning a cat, yes—a small, fluffy creature, with dainty ways and neat habits. But this overgrown, ugly, scarred old bruiser, now that was a mystery.

After a while he realized she'd gone quiet. Too quiet. He couldn't see her face; it was hidden by the cat. He ducked his head forward and snatched a look. Tears were rolling down her cheeks.

He wanted to say something comforting, but could think of nothing. A sniffle escaped her. Ethan pulled out a handkerchief and handed it to her. She put the cat down and took the handkerchief with a muffled thanks. She mopped her cheeks with it then blew into it with a fierce feminine blast. The cat sat kneading her thighs with paws and claws.

"I'm sorry," she muttered. "You saved Kitty-cat and he's the most important thing in the world to me. I know I'm lucky and I'm trying to be stoic. That's why I came out here. I don't want Callie to see me like this. She blames herself, I know."

"She didn't set fire to the cottage."

"I know. But she knows who it was and . . . She takes the weight of the world on her shoulders, that girl. She always did take everything to heart. It's her strength, but also her weakness."

"Seems to me you're takin' a deal on your shoulders, yourself. It's not her you should be worryin' about. You're the one who's lost everything."

"I haven't lost everything. I'm just back to where I started after Papa died. Except then I had—had my books." Her words brought on a fresh battle with choked-back tears.

Her determination not to make a fuss touched him unexpectedly. Feeling out of his depth, Ethan patted her on the shoulder. He was more familiar with the sort of females who made their emotions very clear. Dolores, his last mistress, had thrown things and wept loudly and dramatically. Ethan understood that.

After a few minutes she regained control of herself and blew another fierce blast into the handkerchief. "I'm sorry. It's the books I mind losing most."

"Books?" Ethan asked cautiously. She'd lost her home, with all its pretty bits and pieces, so neat and shining and obviously loved, and she was grieving over *books*?

"Oh yes, my books are—were very precious to me. Some of them belonged to dear Papa. He was a fine scholar, you know, and his books were rare and irreplaceable. And others . . . some of my books were like friends, they gave me such comfort."

"Ah," Ethan made a sympathetic sound. He had no idea what she was talking about. Books like friends? Giving comfort?

The only book that had ever given comfort to Ethan was one he and a couple of others had burned one freezing night in the mountains of Spain. One of the others had found it in a looted house. It was a big book. It had kept them warm for an hour or two.

He didn't understand, didn't know what to say to comfort her. Apart from horses, he owned very little, just his clothes and a few bits and pieces. Nothing that couldn't be tossed in a valise.

He looked out of the salt-covered windows. It was almost dark outside. "Cottages can always be rebuilt," he said.

"I can't afford it. I had a small sum of money put by, but only enough to eke out a frugal living, supplemented by my chickens and my garden. The cottage was my sole asset. It was what allowed me to be independent, that and the small amount of income I earn from giving music lessons."

"So what will you do?"

She sighed. "I suppose I will have to go back to being a governess."

"Did you not like that, ma'am?"

She didn't answer. She picked up the cat again and buried her face in its fur.

Ethan knew what her silences meant now. He patted her on the shoulder again. She felt like a brittle little bird under his great clumsy paw.

The cat gave him a baleful look. Ethan sneezed.

After supper Callie kissed Nicky good night and came downstairs. What a day it had been. According to Nicky, it had been the best day of his life.

She had no doubt that for Tibby it was the worst.

She joined the others in the drawing room. Tibby was sitting by the fire, her cat in her lap, talking to Gabriel. Mr. Delaney was seated at a nearby table playing a solo card game.

"I've been explaining to Mr. Renfrew and Mr. Delaney that I have decided to return to my former profession as a governess," Tibby said. "If you don't mind, Callie, I have asked Mr. Renfrew if I could come with you to London. I will need to purchase some new clothes and London would be the best place to secure myself a post."

"There is no need to look for a post," Callie said instantly. "I will employ you as Nicky's governess."

Tibby shook her head. "No, my dear. It's very kind of you, but I am not nearly well educated enough for Nicky's needs. I am well enough schooled in female accomplishments, and I have a little mathematics but as for Greek, Latin, and the rest, no."

"Then I shall employ you as my companion."

Tibby gave her a straight look and said in a firm voice, "Princess Caroline, you are not responsible for the destruction of my cottage, and I will not be your pensioner."

Callie gave her an unhappy look. She was responsible for the burning of the cottage. If she hadn't fled to Tibby, it wouldn't have happened. But Tibby had her pride.

Gabriel leaned forward. "Would you consent to employment with me, Miss Tibthorpe?"

Tibby frowned. "In what capacity?"

"As a governess. I need someone to teach young Jim to read and write."

"What?" Ethan Delaney exclaimed. Gabriel gave him a cool look, and he returned to his card playing.

"It seems most unlikely that Jim's father will return, and as Mrs. Barrow is hell-bent on importing the imp to my house, I have no choice but to educate him."

Callie was delighted with the solution, but also puzzled, and more than a little wary. To take in an orphaned fisher boy and pay someone to educate him was highly irregular.

Tibby frowned, no doubt having the sort of doubts Callie was. But she was homeless and in need of an income. And while she would not take charity from her old pupil, it would be foolish to turn down a legitimate offer of employment.

"If you are sure, Mr. Renfrew, then of course I accept your offer, gratefully. I will instruct Jim until he reaches a standard sufficient to take his place in the village school along with boys of his own age. After that, I could not possibly trespass on your generosity any further."

"I thought this might be an appropriate remuneration." He handed her a slip of paper on which a figure was written.

Tibby glanced at it and flushed. "It's far too generous," she said lamely.

"Nonsense, that boy will be a handful, I'm sure. Sharp as a knife, but rough around the edges. He's run wild all his life, I'd say."

Tibby smiled. "Oh, I don't mind that. I like Jim and his rough edges. He has a bold and curious spirit. For the time being, I'll instruct the two boys together. Coming from such very different backgrounds, there is much they can learn from each other."

Ethan looked up from his cards. "What would a crown

prince have to learn from a lad like Jim, a lad who can't even write his own name?"

Tibby turned to him and said composedly, "Just because Jim's never had the opportunity to learn does not mean that he isn't an intelligent and valuable human being, Mr. Delaney. With a little education, who knows what Jim could make of his life? People may be born into poverty and ignorance, but they do not have to remain so." She folded the sewing she was doing and put it aside. "Perhaps I picked up a few radical notions from my father, but I believe people can learn much from walking in another's shoes."

Ethan stared at her.

"Besides," Tibby went on. "I expect most of Nicky's learning will have come from books. Jim, on the other hand, though wholly untutored, has a vast store of knowledge of the natural world. And excels in the practical application of it."

"Miss Tibthorpe, it's a shame you never met my great-aunt Gert," Gabriel said. "I believe you would have had a great deal in common." He nodded toward the painting of the severe-looking woman.

Tibby suddenly frowned as if she'd just thought of something. "How can I teach Nicky with Jim when you are taking him up to London tomorrow?"

Gabriel looked surprised. "You will come with us, of course. You said you needed to do some shopping."

"Yes, I suppose so . . . but what about Jim?"

"He will come, too. I expect he would love a trip to London. And Nicky will have a companion for the long journey."

"But do we know his father has indeed passed on? We cannot just pick a child up like a stray puppy and transport him out of the parish."

He looked thoughtful. "You are right. I shall investigate the matter more fully."

He turned to Callie. "Princess, can I interest you in a game of cards? And Ethan, perhaps Miss Tibthorpe would offer you a game of chess. I noticed last night she seemed more than a little acquainted with the game."

A few moments later Callie found herself frowning over a hand of cards, trying to recall the rules of bezique. With no apparent effort he had everyone sorted: Tibby's employment, Callie's future, her son's education, Jim's, too, and their entertainment for the evening.

"Why would you concern yourself with the education of a chance-met orphaned fisher boy?" she asked him, playing a card at random.

He glanced at the portrait of his great-aunt. "It's Great-aunt Gert's legacy. She was a great one for taking in stray, unwanted boys. I suppose that's how Mrs. Barrow ended up working for her—they were kindred spirits from opposite ends of the social scale. Great-aunt Gert took me in and Mrs. Barrow took in Harry." He played a card. "Great-aunt Gert shaped our futures and Mrs. Barrow mothered us."

"But I thought Harry was your brother."

"My half brother," he corrected her. "Born on the wrong side of the blanket. We had the same father, but Harry's mother was a maidservant. When she found herself increasing, my father paid the village smith to marry her."

"Oh," she said, then didn't know what to say, because she could hardly ask him whether he was born on the wrong side of the blanket, too. She put another card down.

"My mother was married to my father," he told her. "But they'd been having tremendous rows at the time, and both of them had been unfaithful, so when she told him I was not his true son, he believed her."

"But that's dreadful!" she exclaimed. "How could she do that to him? And to you?"

He shrugged. "I believe their marriage was famously tempestuous. Or should that be infamously?"

"What do you mean, you believe? Didn't you know?"

"No, they reconciled when I was three, and again when I was six, but my father would never allow my mother to bring me home on any of these occasions. I was kept in London. He refused to tolerate the sight of me, even though she insisted I really was his son." He shrugged. "He never believed her."

"But that's terrible."

"Not really. He had no reason to trust her word; her infidelities were almost as legendary as his."

Callie frowned. "Then how—" she began, then stopped. She'd been about to ask the most impertinent question. She bit her lip.

"How do I know I really am my father's son?" he supplied. "And I warned you about that lip-biting—you're doing it all wrong. D'you want me to show you again?"

Callie felt her face flame. "Stop that!" she hissed. "Not in front of other people!"

He heaved a sigh. "You are hard on a man, you know. Now where were we? Oh yes, you were wondering how I know I wasn't really a by-blow," he reminded her, and before she could inform him she was wondering no such ill-bred thing, he continued, "Harry and I are a few months apart in age, but the resemblance between us is noticeable. Does that explain it?"

It did. Obviously, with two different mothers, the resemblance must come from his father.

But it didn't explain why he and Harry had grown up together, and why Great-aunt Gert had raised him, and why Harry had been a wild child. She had no difficulty understanding why he'd described himself as a needy child. Any child would, in such an appalling situation. "You said you and Harry had grown up together."

"Yes, Great-aunt Gert took us both under her wing." He jerked his head toward the severe woman in the painting.

"My father's spinster aunt, a bold tartar of a woman who most people were frightened to death of."

Looking at that portrait, Callie could well imagine it.

"She descended on my mother's London residence one day, marched up to the nursery, and simply confiscated me. Told my mother she wasn't fit to raise any child, let alone a Renfrew boy, and that she, Great-aunt Gert, would do it from now on. She picked me up—literally, I was about seven, I think—handed me to her footman like a parcel, and swept us off in her carriage."

Callie was shocked. "But didn't your mother fight her?"

He shook his head slightly. "Mama didn't say a word. It was probably a relief to her to have me out of the way."

Callie couldn't believe the lighthearted way he spoke of it. "I would kill anyone who tried to take my son from me."

He smiled. "I can believe it. But Great-aunt Gert was not a woman to be gainsaid. Most people were terrified of her."

"And no wonder, if that's how she behaved. Poor little boy. You must have been terrified."

He trumped her card. "I was at first, but it wasn't long before I learned that under that Attila-the-Hen exterior, Great-aunt Gert had a heart of the purest gold. She was, quite simply, a darling." He glanced at the portrait and raised his brandy glass in a toast. "To Great-aunt Gert, who made me the man I am today." He drank.

Callie watched the movement of the strong column of his throat as he drank. Great-aunt Gert had much to be proud of.

"And Harry the wild child?" she asked, after a moment.

He set his glass aside. "Harry was a lot like Jim when I first met him—a wild little ragamuffin. But Great-aunt Gert had him educated—educated both of us together and sent us to our father's school, much to Father's fury. He had us removed in the end, so Great-aunt Gert sent us to Harrow instead, which angered him nearly as much."

He grinned reminiscently. "Great-aunt Gert was a radical with no opinion of the airs and graces of the aristocracy. She was also a crushing snob who considered a Renfrew—even a bastard Renfrew—superior to any other being. She left me her fortune, but she left a legacy for Harry, too, and my share has a dozen stipulations. Miss Tibthorpe's employment will fulfill one of them. It would have delighted her to have a fisher child educated with a royal prince. And she would have liked your boy a lot. Great-aunt Gert admired courage above all else."

*T*hey were to leave for London immediately after breakfast. Callie and Tibby had packed their meager belongings and their cases were waiting in the hall. Kitty-cat yowled angrily from a strong wicker basket, one ginger paw swiping furiously at anyone rash enough to pass close enough. Juno sat nearby, sniffing occasionally at the basket and watching interestedly as the ginger paw swatted at her in vain.

Breakfast was a quiet affair. Mrs. Barrow had done them proud, with mounds of bacon, eggs, deviled kidneys, and smoked kippers, lashings of toast, and hot, fragrant coffee, but nobody seemed to have much of an appetite except for Gabriel.

"Mr. Gabe!" Mrs. Barrow burst into the room. "Sir Walter Tinknell is coming down the front drive with a couple of his men, and there's other soldiers with them—half a dozen—foreigners, I reckon, and all on horseback."

They all hurried to the window to look. Sure enough, a small cavalcade was coming down the driveway. Two men rode at the head. One was red-faced, elderly, and fat, dressed in a tight blue coat with large gold buttons and riding a smart bay hunter. The other was beautiful, blond, and elegant: a picture of masculine perfection. Slender, lithe, yet with a sleek power, he rode a magnificent black stallion as if born on horseback. A thin golden mustache lined his upper lip. His uniform set off his fair good looks, being black and heavily frogged in gold. He wore a bell-topped shako with a gold coat of arms and a curled feather.

Callie felt her insides freeze. "It's Count Anton!"

Eleven

"*I* haven't seen so much gold braid since the last time the prince regent inspected the troops," Gabe murmured. "And what a magnificent horse!"

"I wish he'd fall off and break his neck! Nicky!" Callie looked around. "Where is Nicky? He's not outside, is he? If Count Anton sees—"

"He and Jim are in the kitchen, having breakfast," Mrs. Barrow assured her.

"Fetch him here to me at once! We must leave, immediately!"

Gabe held her by the arm. "Callie, you can't run from him now. If you did, he would only ride you down on that big horse of his." He glanced at Mrs. Barrow. "But fetch both boys here."

Callie tried to pull out of his grip. "But if he finds us, he'll take us back and then he'll—"

"I won't let him take you anywhere," Gabe reassured her. She didn't look very reassured. He held her hands tightly, stroking them with his thumbs, and added, "He can hardly kidnap you when the local magistrate is looking on."

She frowned. "Why has he brought a magistrate? He must think it gives him some advantage." She looked at him with misgiving. "I don't like it."

"Neither do I." He glanced out of the window. "A magistrate implies some legal maneuver."

"Nicky! He wants legal custody of Nicky."

Gabe wasn't convinced. "How could he gain legal custody of your son before you?"

"Because Zindarian law is Gothic, that's why. A female has no status in law. If the male heir is a child, the oldest adult male becomes the head of the family until the child becomes an adult. Currently the head of the family is Uncle Otto, but if he died—and he is an old man—Count Anton would become the head of the family until Nicky turns eighteen."

She clutched his forearms. "What if Uncle Otto is dead? Anton will have free rein."

Gabe stared at her somberly. "It's a bluff. He must *suspect* you are here, but he cannot *know* it. Take Nicky upstairs and hide there. I'll get rid of Count Anton and his magistrate."

"Give me a gun, just in case. Those dueling pistols."

He squeezed her hand. "No time, they're out in the curricle. Besides, what's needed here is strategy, not force."

Mrs. Barrow and the boys arrived, and swiftly Gabe explained their roles. They all looked stunned.

"It'll never work," Callie muttered.

"Trust me," he said softly. "I'll keep you and Nicky safe. Now go!" As he spoke, the front doorbell jangled imperiously. She glanced at it and fled with Nicky up the stairs.

Jim's eyes lit with excitement. "Are we foolin' the preventives, Mr. Gabe?"

"Something like that," Gabe told him.

Everyone disappeared to take their places. Mrs. Barrow eyed him. "They're never the preventives, Mr. Gabe."

"No, but the man with the magistrate is responsible for burning down Miss Tibthorpe's cottage. He's in pursuit of the princess and Nicky and he means them harm."

Mrs. Barrow bristled. "The villain. Will you have him arrested then, sir?"

Gabe shook his head. "We have no proof. And I have no doubt he has diplomatic papers to ensure he cannot be touched by English law."

The doorbell jangled again. "Shall I admit this cockroach, then?"

"Yes. Tell him I am unavailable." Gabe raced back up the stairs as Mrs. Barrow marched to the front door. He waited on the landing and listened as Mrs. Barrow answered the door and explained that the master of the house was unavailable.

"Unavailable! How extremely convenient," a smooth voice with a faint foreign accent said. Gabe recognized the voice. Last time he'd met it it had been attached to a pair of boots that were kicking him.

"I really must insist," the magistrate declared. "Count Anton, the prince regent of Zindaria, has laid very serious claims against Captain Renfrew."

Prince regent, Gabe thought. Uncle Otto must indeed be dead.

"Serious indeed to disturb the son of an English earl in His Own Home!" Mrs. Barrow countered in a belligerent manner.

The magistrate cleared his throat uncomfortably. "Count Anton claims that the young crown prince of his country has been kidnapped and, er—"

"What?"

"He claims the crown prince is being held here."

"Here?" Mrs. Barrow repeated in loud surprise. There

was a pause, then she raised her voice. "Oy, Barrow, the squire here reckons we've got a crown prince hidden away here somewhere. Have you seen one?"

"Nope, not in the kitchen," Barrow's voice floated back. Gabe grinned.

"Enough of this nonsense," Count Anton pushed his way past Mrs. Barrow. "We will search ze house!"

"You will do no such thing!' Mrs. Barrow told him. "Sir Walter, are you going to let this foreigner shove his way into an English gentleman's home? And you lot—get back!" she added to the entourage.

Gabe decided it was time to make his entrance. He sauntered down the stairs. "What the devil is all this commotion about?" he drawled. "Mrs. Barrow, I told you I did not wish to be disturbed."

Seeing the magistrate, he cut across her apologies, saying, "Ah, Sir Walter, excellent. Have you apprehended the culprits?"

Sir Walter looked surprised. "Culprits?" he repeated cautiously. "What culprits?"

"The ones who terrorized Miss Tibthorpe and burned down her cottage."

The squire's eyebrows flew up in surprise and Gabe nodded. "Appalling, isn't it? Whatever is the country coming to when a lone woman is terrorized by thugs and her cottage burned down." He glanced disdainfully at Count Anton and added, "Who is your friend, Sir Walter? I don't recognize the uniform. Not English, I hope. Surely not even Prinny would design such a ridicul—such a uniform."

The count regarded him with an expression of haughty contempt. He was indeed a handsome devil, thought Gabe, but it was a beauty that repelled. His eyes were strange, as if they had no color. They flickered and he gave Gabe a severe, military bow. "I, sir, am Count Anton, prince regent of Zindaria, and I demand you release ze princess of Zindaria and her son, Crown Prince Nikolai."

Gabe stared at him for a long moment and then turned to the squire. "Do you have *any* idea what he's talking about?"

The squire's ruddy face turned even redder. "Captain Renfrew, sir," he began in embarrassment. "The count insists these people are being held here. He carries letters of authority from his government—"

"I *am* the government of my country," Count Anton snapped. He stared narrowly at the marks of Gabe's injuries and glanced at the hand with the mark of his boot heel.

"Perhaps, but this is England. You have no authority here." Gabe gave him a cold smile.

The count's lips thinnned. "I demand you—"

"Your demands mean nothing here!" Gabe's voice cut across him like a whiplash. "And I don't take to posturing bullyboys marching into my house and issuing demands."

Sir Walter made placatory gestures. "Gentlemen, gentlemen, I am sure there is no need for this hostility. Count Anton, Captain Renfrew is a gentleman known to me, the son of the earl of Alverleigh and a fine officer, mentioned several times in dispatches. As I assured you earlier, he cannot possibly have anything to do with the kidnapping of your crown prince." He gave a look of appeal to Gabe. "Captain Renfrew, all this could be cleared up in a moment if you'd just allow us to search the house . . ."

Gabe fixed him with the sort of look that could make a troop of hardened soldiers hang their heads. *"Search my house?"*

The squire looked uncomfortable, but held his ground. "It's a grave accusation, sir, and one with government implications. I'm sure it's a mistake, but it would be better all round if we just cleared the air."

The man was embarrassed, Gabe saw. He was already half convinced he'd come on a fool's errand.

Gabe gave a curt nod. "Very well, explain." He folded his arms and waited.

"We're wasting time," the count began.

Gabe shot him a hard look. "I could always just throw you out on your arse."

"Captain Renfrew, Count, if you please," Sir Walter said. "The count has received reports that in the last two days you have had a strange woman and a small boy living here."

"He has, has he?" Gabe said. "What the devil business is it of his who I have here?"

"You have! Admit it!" the count snarled.

Gabe gave him a frigid stare.

"Captain Renfrew, please," the squire begged.

Gabe shrugged. "There is a lady and a boy staying here, Sir Walter, though if that boy is a crown prince of anywhere I'd be astonished. Still, I suppose he could have been stolen by gypsies at birth . . ."

"He was stolen by you!"

Gabe unfolded his arms. "You are becoming excessively tedious, my man. You need a good thrashing and a lesson in manners."

The squire stepped in between them. "Gentlemen, gentlemen, please. Captain Renfrew, if I could just meet this lady, all this could be sorted out."

Gabe considered it. "Very well, but you—" He stabbed a finger at the count. "—behave yourself. I would not have any lady exposed to your uncouth behavior."

He led them to the drawing room, opened the door, and said, "You see, Sir Walter? No stolen prince or princess."

Count Anton shoved past them. "Aha!" he exclaimed in triumph and pointed to the woman sitting in front of the fire with her back to them. "There she is!"

Tibby turned with raised eyebrows. "I beg your pardon," she said with frosty disapproval. She glanced from Gabe, to Sir Walter, to the count. "What is the meaning of this intrusion?"

Gabe turned to the squire. "This is Miss Tibthorpe,

whose house was burned down yesterday. I have offered her refuge here, indefinitely."

The squire bowed. "Miss Tibthorpe, may I offer my sincere condolences on your loss. It was a shocking thing—"

"A shocking thing indeed when one's house is burned under one." Tibby stared fiercely at the count. "My sole comfort is the sure and certain knowledge that the perpetrator will burn in hell!"

The count prowled toward her in a threatening manner. Gabe stepped in between them. "One more step . . ." he said in an icy voice.

Ethan moved in to stand beside Miss Tibthorpe. He said nothing, but his stance made it clear he'd heard the exchange.

The count snarled at Tibby, "Where is she? Where is ze princess?"

"Which princess do you mean?" Tibby said calmly. "I am acquainted with several."

The count gave a growl of frustration and glanced suspiciously around the room. Spotting a pair of small shoes behind a curtain he pounced. "Aha!" He dragged back the curtain and pulled out a small boy.

"Oy, watcher doin'? Lemme go, ya big ape!" Jim pulled free with a string of bad language that in normal circumstances would have had Mrs. Barrow reaching for a bar of soap to scrub out his mouth with. She beamed proudly at him from the doorway.

"The stolen crown prince, I believe," Gabe said to Sir Walter. "He learned that language from the gypsies, no doubt."

"Pah, he is nothing but a beggar boy!"

"Who are you callin' a beggar—" Jim began before he was hushed by Mrs. Barrow.

The count stabbed an accusing finger at Tibby. "This woman knows Princess Caroline!"

Sir Walter pulled out a handkerchief and wiped his brow. "Do you, madam?" he asked.

Tibby gave him a cool look. "Princess Caroline of

Zindaria? Yes, of course I know her. She was one of my most distinguished pupils. I also had the honor of instructing the current countess of Morey, and Lady Hunter-Stanley as well as the Honorable Mrs. Charles Sandford." She smiled graciously at Sir Walter.

"Then where is she?" The count ground out.

Tibby looked down her nose at him. "Princess Caroline left my care when she was fifteen years old."

"You have exchanged correspondence," the count alleged.

Tibby raised an eyebrow. "Naturally. I correspond regularly with all my girls."

The count snapped his whip against his boot. "She was coming here, to you! She said so in her letters."

Tibby raised both eyebrows. "Reading other people's letters? How very dishonorable."

"Pah! Do not evade ze question. She made arrangements to come here with the boy."

Tibby gave a faint smirk. "Did she? Really?"

Count Anton frowned. "What do you mean?"

Tibby smoothed her skirts placidly. The mouse teasing the tiger. Gabe bit his lip. She was enjoying this, he saw. Getting even for a little of what she had suffered at his hands. Count Anton snapped his whip against his boot, harder and harder, his temper mounting, his pale eyes boring into her.

Eventually she said, "What one writes and what one does are often quite different." She looked at the squire. "And if people who read letters not addressed to them go off on wild goose chases as a result, well . . ." She bared her teeth at the count in the pretext of a smile.

The count stared at her, goaded. His slender fingers flexed as if itching to throttle her. Ethan did not take his eyes off the count. He folded his arms and his jaw jutted pugnaciously.

Gabe stepped forward. "That's quite enough. If this princess was writing letters to arrange visits to her old friends, and you read them, why the devil are you telling everyone I kidnapped her? I've a good mind to have you up for slander! Sir Walter, you are my witness."

Sir Walter cleared his throat. "Now, Captain Renfrew, I'm sure there is no need for that. The count didn't mean anything by it, I'm certain. Did you, Count?"

There was a tense silence. The count knew he was on thin ice. After a moment he said stiffly, "Perhaps my informant made a mistake."

"Yes, yes, a mistake." The squire gratefully seized on the excuse. He turned to Gabe. "It was the horses, y'see. The count was told the princess was in a vehicle drawn by matched grays, and as everybody knows, the only grays of any quality in this area are yours. That was the error. Must have been some other grays passing through. Some other lady."

Gabe gave the count a hard look. "Indeed." The Zindarians were horsemen: of course they'd notice his grays.

The squire was grateful for an excuse to leave. "My apologies for the misunderstanding, Captain Renfrew, and Miss Tibthorpe, for the disturbance. After you, Count." He gestured toward the door.

The count hesitated, then stalked into the hallway, his face pale with anger and frustration.

Jim slipped ahead in the hallway and pulled open the front door. As the count, with very bad grace, stormed past, Jim said in a cheeky voice, "An' good riddance to bad rubbish, yer slimy yeller snake!"

Balked of his prey, the count slashed his whip hard across the boy's face. Jim screamed with pain as he crashed against the wall.

Callie sat on the bed upstairs with her arm around Nicky. She had been trying to stay calm, reassuring her son that there was nothing wrong, merely that Count

Anton was downstairs and she didn't wish to speak to him.

Nicky seemed to accept that, sitting quietly, docile and obedient.

To distract herself from what might be happening downstairs, she asked him about his riding lesson. But Nicky didn't respond. After a moment he said thoughtfully, "Count Anton wants to kill me, doesn't he, Mama? And become prince in my place."

She stared at him, shocked. She'd tried to keep it from him. How long had he known?

He added, "That's why we are hiding up here in your bedchamber. Mr. Renfrew and the others are going to save us, aren't they?"

"Yes, darling, they are."

"And we will wait here until it is safe to go down again." He was pale, she saw, and his eyes were troubled.

And suddenly Callie realized what she was doing. She was sitting up here, hiding like a frightened rabbit.

Teaching her son to hide like a frightened rabbit.

Sending other people to risk themselves for her sake.

Tibby's cottage had been burned to the ground. She had lost everything because of Callie, and yet Tibby was downstairs, facing the man who'd imprisoned her then burned her home.

Not hiding like a frightened rabbit.

In the last few days Nicky had started to glow with confidence; now he was pinched-looking and anxious again.

Callie was ashamed. She'd let her fear rule her. She looked down at her small son and recalled the conversation she'd had in the kitchen about the life she was giving him, a life of running and running and running.

She had escaped from Zindaria. She was now in a country where Count Anton's insidious influence was not so pervasive.

Here there was less chance of maidservants and grooms

being in his pay, owing him fealty, being terrorized. Here he was the stranger, the foreigner—not her.

Here, people believed her. Her fears had not been dismissed as female foolishness. She'd been taken seriously. And she had support.

So what was she doing hiding like a rabbit? Filling her son with fear and teaching him to be helpless in the face of it.

Here and now the running was going to stop.

"Mr. Renfrew said something interesting the other day," she told Nicky. "He said, 'A battle is not always won on brute strength alone.'"

Nicky tilted his head up at her and considered the words. "You mean we cannot beat Count Anton in a proper fight, but there are other ways to defeat him?"

She smiled. "When did you get to be so clever? Yes, my love, that is exactly what it means."

She stood and looked thoughtfully around the room. She had no weapon to defend herself and her son. In Zindaria she had owned a small pistol—Rupert had given it to her and taught her to use it after the attempt on Nicky's life where her earring had been torn out. But the pistol had disappeared after Rupert's death.

She might not be able to fight the count, but she could certainly bluff. And for bluffing, she had just the weapon.

She opened the bandbox and from beneath its false bottom took out a circular bundle.

"What do you want that for, Mama?" Nicky whispered.

"When you have nothing else to fall back on, my son," she told him, "remember who you are and where you have come from. The strength will come."

She unwrapped the bundle and took out her mother's diamond tiara. It was the only thing she had of her mother's, and she loved it dearly. She stood in front of the mirror and put it on her head. It looked ridiculous with her traveling clothes, nevertheless the feel of it gave Callie strength.

"I have this to fall back on," Nicky told her and showed her a long black cane with a silver handle. It was nearly as big as he was. "I found it in the wardrobe."

She smiled and tiptoed to the door, just to listen. She had no intention of showing herself unless she was forced to.

She was just in time to hear, "An' good riddance to bad rubbish, yer slimy yeller snake!" followed by a child's scream of pain.

Nicky leapt up. "That's Jim. He's hurt Jim!" And before Callie could stop him Nicky had dashed out of the room.

He ran toward the stairs, yelling at the top of his lungs in Zindarian, "Leave him alone, you bully! I *command* you to stand back!"

In one hand Nicky brandished—good God, Callie thought. It was a sword! Where on earth had he found a sword?

She raced after him. As Nicky pelted screaming down the stairs she saw the count turn. There was a feral light in his eye as he produced a long-bladed knife and turned it toward the small boy hurtling toward him.

"Nicky, nooo!" she screamed.

Gabriel turned at the sound of Nicky yelling. In a split-second reaction he reached out and caught Nicky in mid-flight just as he reached the foot of the stairs. In seconds he'd taken the sword from Nicky, passed him back to Ethan, and had the sword at Count Anton's throat. The knife in the count's hand wavered, then dropped to the floor.

Nicky was saved. Callie stumbled and almost fell. She clutched the banister and steadied herself. Her son was not yet out of danger. Gabriel had saved him from the knife, but there was still the law to be dealt with. Her knees wobbled. But it wasn't over yet.

The count snarled. "See, she is here after all! The missing princess of Zindaria, as I claimed all along. I demand you call off this rabid dog and hand her and the boy over to me." This rabid dog being Gabriel, whose only reaction was to press the tip of the sword a little harder against the count's throat.

Callie fixed her gaze on Count Anton, smoothed her dress with shaking hands, straightened her mother's tiara, and glided slowly down the remaining stairs. Nobody said a word. All eyes were on Callie.

She reached the bottom of the stairs and moved toward the count. She ignored the sword at his throat and addressed him in her most regal manner. "Count Anton, how dare you burst into this house, shouting and bullying children."

His lips moved in a soundless sneer and she poked him in the chest with her finger, hard. "You are a mannerless oaf and I am ashamed to acknowledge you as a son of Zindar. And how dare you inform others that I am missing. Do I look missing to you?"

"He told me Captain Renfrew had stolen you and your son away," Sir Walter said.

Callie didn't turn her head. "Did. He. Indeed?" she said, emphasizing each word with a poke of her finger. "Nobody stole me or my son. Things have come to a pretty pass in Zindaria when a woman cannot take her son to visit the country of her birth—I was born in England—" she added for the magistrate's benefit, "without an oaf like you telling the world I've been stolen." She narrowed her eyes at him. "And as for the way you treated my friend Miss Tibthorpe, and my son's friend, Jim—not to mention the way you turned a naked blade on your own crown prince—I've half a mind to ask Mr. Renfrew to lend me his blade so I can run you through here and now."

"Er, Your Highness, that's not allowed in England," the magistrate said nervously. "Summary executions are illegal—there must be due process, a properly conducted trial, and so on. Captain Renfrew, you know it."

"I am the princess's to command," Gabriel responded.

The count paled and jerked his head as Gabriel promptly passed the handle of the blade to Callie without removing it from his throat.

A trickle of blood ran down the count's throat. Callie watched fascinated. She hadn't moved at all, he'd done it to himself.

She stared down the long blade at her enemy. With one thrust she could stop the threat on her son forever. Her muscles tensed. She stared, mesmerized, along the gleaming silver blade. In the count's throat, a pulse throbbed.

It would be so easy. One thrust and her troubles would be over.

But she couldn't bring herself to do it. He was a man, a human being. He had Rupert's eyes. He was Rupert's cousin, her son's closest male relative. She would gladly see him dead, but she could not be the one to do it, not in cold blood.

He read it in her eyes and sneered. "You're a coward, like your weakling son."

"There's not a cowardly bone in either of them." Gabriel placed his hand over hers and took the sword back. "But she's no cold-blooded killer."

He paused, then added silkily, "I, on the other hand, after eight years at war, am."

"Princess, Captain Renfrew, don't do this," Sir Walter begged. "It would be murder, cold-blooded murder."

Mr. Renfrew looked at Callie. "For you, I'd do anything. Just say the word." His eyes were very blue and very steady.

Callie closed her eyes briefly, then reluctantly shook her head. "I can't," she whispered.

"By Jove, what's this? A reception committee?" A tall man wearing buckskins, an elegantly cut, though dusty coat and high, black boots strolled through the open door and tossed his curly-brimmed beaver hat on the hall table.

He raised a quizzing glass and inspected the collection of people standing in the hall. The glass hovered on Callie's tiara for a moment, then moved on.

Having finished his inspection, he smiled faintly and said, "If you're going to skewer that fellow, Gabe, get a move on. I've ridden all the way from Aldershot and I've got a devil of a thirst."

"Well said, Rafe." A second gentleman, better-looking but less elegant than the first, followed. Pulling off his leather gloves, he, too, glanced at the frozen tableau and said with a frown, "But not in front of the ladies and children, Gabe, there's a good fellow. Bad *ton* to murder people in front of ladies and children." He bowed gracefully to Callie and Tibby.

"Yes, a little consideration, brother mine," a third man declared. "Take the fellow outside to skewer him and save Mrs. Barrow's nice clean floor." He met Mrs. Barrow's eye and winked. This must be Harry, Callie thought dimly. He was the image of Gabriel, tall, dark, and broad-shouldered, only his hair was dark brown instead of almost black and his eyes were gray. He looked from his brother to Callie and back again. His eyes flickered to her tiara and one brow rose faintly.

"Go ahead, Mr. Gabe, don't mind me," called Mrs. Barrow. "I'd be delighted to mop up that villain's blood. And I wouldn't mind watching, neither. In fact I'd downright enjoy it!"

"Me, too," said Jim. "Bloody stinking—" Mrs. Barrow muffled him with her hand.

Gabriel looked at the count's stiff countenance and turned his head toward Callie. "Last chance."

She shook her head. "Let him go."

He lowered the sword and jerked his head. "Right, get out."

"I have the right to—"

"Just get out man! Don't make it any worse than you already have," the squire told the count, shoving him bodily toward the door.

"You haven't heard the last of this," Count Anton muttered. The squire grabbed him by the arm and pulled him outside, saying, "Bad enough to have clouted that ragamuffin brat, but to draw steel on a child, and that child your own crown prince! I'm shocked, Count, shocked! There's something devilish havey cavey about you and no mistake!"

Outside Callie saw the count's men waiting in an oddly still group.

Then she saw Barrow standing nearby, with a silver pistol in each hand trained on the waiting men. Callie recognized those pistols.

"I'll just see them off the premises," Gabriel told her, and he followed Sir Walter and the count outside.

"Shall we?" said the elegant man called Rafe, and without waiting he strolled outside, followed by his friends. Callie noticed they each had produced pistols as well.

Gabriel drew the magistrate aside and spoke to him for a minute or two. Sir Walter turned, stared at the count severely, then nodded.

As Callie watched the count and his men disappear from sight, her knees suddenly gave out and she plonked down on the stairs.

When Gabriel returned he said immediately, "Are you all right?"

Callie looked up at him. Was she all right? Yes, more than all right—she felt wonderful. Just a bit shaky, for some odd reason. She looked up at the man who'd offered to kill her enemy for her and asked him, "Do you have any brandy?"

"Yes."

"Then could I have a large glass, immediately."

"I'll have one, too," declared the man called Rafe.

"And me," said his friend.

Laughing, Gabriel held out a hand. "Come along then, I think we all deserve a drink."

Nicky took her other hand. "We showed Count Anton, Mama, didn't we?"

"We did, my darling. We all did." She could not get out of her mind the way Gabriel had looked at her when he'd said, *For you, I'd do anything. Just say the word.*

They retired to the octagonal room, where drinks were poured and everyone joined in relating the events of the morning for those who hadn't been present.

When Gabriel related the part about how Tibby had reprimanded the count for reading other people's letters, the room exploded with masculine laughter. Tibby, usually withdrawn and uncomfortable in the presence of men, laughed and blushed happily as Gabriel proposed a toast to the two heroines.

Callie could still not look at him. Something had happened there at the foot of the stairs that she wasn't quite sure of and didn't know how to deal with. She needed to think about it, and with his eyes on her she couldn't think at all.

"But tell me, Princess." Tall, elegant Rafe Ramsey turned to Callie. "Do you always wear that tiara?"

Callie's hands flew up to the tiara. She'd forgotten she was wearing it. She smiled sheepishly, feeling rather foolish. "No, I know it looks silly. It's just . . . It was my mother's . . . I wore it to make me feel brave."

She half expected them to laugh, but instead, Rafe Ramsey simply nodded. "I wondered if that was it."

"Like a uniform," Luke Ripton added. "Or a flag."

Their acceptance surprised her. They'd all been soldiers. She would have thought that soldiers would be scornful of such stratagems.

And then she remembered the sword. "Where did you get that sword?" she asked Nicky. She turned to the others and explained. "One minute he was clutching a black walking stick and the next he was charging down the stairs with a sword in his hand."

"The sword was in the stick," Nicky told her. "I twisted the handle and suddenly it came off in my hand and there was a sword inside the stick."

"Great-Aunt Gert's sword stick," Gabriel and Harry said at the same time.

Callie's jaw dropped. "Your great-aunt carried a *sword stick*?"

Gabriel gave a reminiscent smile. "Never went anywhere without it. She was a most redoubtable old lady. As far as I know she never actually used the blade on anyone, but the stick put paid to a highwayman, once. The fellow was a bit cocky, imagining he was dealing with a frail old lady, until the frail old lady whacked him hard over the head and knocked him cold."

Everyone laughed. He lifted his glass. "To Great-Aunt Gert and her trusty sword stick." They all drank.

"Are we still going to London, Mama?" Nicky asked as they drained their glasses.

Callie glanced quickly at Gabriel.

"Not today, Nicky," he said. "We'll wait and see if Count Anton has any more tricks up his sleeve. He has a habit of setting fire to places, so I'll post a watch and we'll see. I had a word to Sir Walter about the count's activities and he was going to question him. It seems the large white yacht we saw anchored in Lulworth Cove belongs to Count Anton."

"And if Count Anton doesn't come?" Nicky persisted.

Gabriel looked at Callie. "It's up to your mother. Whatever she wants."

She did not meet his eyes. *Whatever she wants.* It was what he'd said earlier, over the sword: *For you, I'd do anything. Just say the word.*

The way he said it sounded like a promise, an oath.

She didn't want to think about it. Refused to think about it. She was older now and wiser, and she knew better than to believe noble-sounding words. Or actions. But gallantry was second nature to the man. Some men were like that.

She couldn't stay here. She was, after all, an uninvited guest, even though he'd made her more than welcome. It was time she began her own new life. Running was only a short-term solution. She had to work out something more lasting, more durable.

In the meantime she would arrange protection for Nicky—indeed, Mr. Renfrew already had. What could be better protection than four tall former soldiers—five counting Mr. Delaney.

And London? She wasn't sure what she'd do with her life yet, but she had definite plans for London.

"Yes, Nicky, we shall go to London," she decided. "Tibby and I need to go shopping."

"All of us?" Nicky said. "Jim, too?"

Callie hesitated. Gabriel intervened. "I need to have a word with Jim in private, first. Jim?" He waved a hand toward the door, and with visible trepidation Jim went.

"Now, Jim, I don't think you've been completely honest with us," Gabe said once he had taken Jim into the library.

Jim sat on a chair opposite him looking small and skinny and scared. The livid mark of the count's whip bisected his swollen face. It gleamed with Mrs. Barrow's ointment. His head was hunched defensively into his shoulders. His ears stuck out, made larger-seeming by his severe haircut, and somehow adding to the look of vulnerability. He said nothing.

Gabe said gently, "You told us your father had only been gone for a week or two."

Jim nodded, then swallowed, the action painfully visible in his scrawny neck.

"Mrs. Barrow got Barrow to ask around," Gabe said. "Nobody has seen your father for at least six or eight weeks."

"You're not goin' to put me on the parish as an orphan, are ya, sir? Coz if you are, I won't go. I'll run away." Jim looked around the room desperately and tensed, as if preparing to flee.

"No, we won't put you on the parish," Gabe assured him.

Jim's eyes fixed on Gabe's. "You promise?"

"I promise. But you must tell me the truth."

Jim searched his face with painful intensity. He seemed to find reassurance in Gabe's expression, for the tension drained from his body. "Me dad's been gone more'n two months. I reckon he's dead. He ain't never left me for that long afore—never for longer'n a week." He sniffed and wiped his nose with his sleeve.

Gabe passed him a handkerchief. Jim thanked him, folded it, and put the handkerchief carefully in his pocket, untouched.

"I'll take care of you in the future, Jim, if you agree. But I will have the truth from you at all times."

The boy looked at him warily. "What would you want me to do?"

"I'm not sure," Gabe said. "For the moment, I want you to keep young Nicky company."

Jim frowned. "You mean look after him coz bastards like that slimy yeller count are after him?"

Gabe smiled. "Something of the sort. I want you to keep him company. You'll have to do lessons with Miss Tibby when Nicky does. And you'll have to do whatever Mrs. Barrow tells you. And when we all go to London in a day or two, we might take you with us. If you agree."

Jim's eyes bulged. "To London? You're not joking me are you, sir?"

"No joke, Jim."

The boy's eyes lit up. "I'll go to London, all right! And I'll look after Nicky and do lessons and I'll be as good as gold, sir, just you wait!"

Gabe laughed. "Good. Now, I think we should probably have a memorial service for your father, don't you?"

Jim frowned. "You mean like in a church?"

Gabe nodded. "Yes, that's right."

"Me dad hated churches and preachers, if you don't mind me sayin' so, sir. I don't want no church service for him." He looked at Gabe with an anguished expression. "If you want to change your mind about keepin' me, sir, I'll understand, but . . . I couldn't let me dad down on this. He was a good dad." He sniffed again, and again used his sleeve.

Gabe was touched. He ruffled Jim's spiky hair. "No, you're quite right to respect your father's wishes. But I think you should do something to say good-bye him. What do you think he'd like us to do?"

*T*hey all gathered at the beach next to Jim's cottage that evening at dusk. Mrs. Barrow had prepared a good spread of baked meats and funeral fare. Barrow had spread the word and about twenty of Jim's father's friends came. They seemed to know what Jim's father would wish.

They lit a fire on the beach. They carried beach stones to the top of the cliff and built a cairn looking out to sea. Then, down on the beach, they dragged out a battered dinghy, ancient and unseaworthy, with a large gash in its side. The fishermen repaired it roughly, hammering planks over the hole and plastering it with hot tar to make it temporarily seaworthy.

From the cottage, Jim brought out a number of items. He distributed his father's things among the fishermen; his clothes, his tools, various bits and pieces from a man's life.

There was pitifully little.

He gave something to everyone. To Callie he gave a beautiful stone, with a fern fossilized in it. To Tibby he gave one containing an exquisite shell.

Jim's father had been a carver of some talent, for there were some fine pieces of scrimshaw. He gave a whale's tooth with a sea monster carved on it to Nicky.

"Don't show this to Mrs. B.," Jim whispered to Barrow as he handed him a knife with a bone handle to Barrow. Barrow glanced at the knife and winked. The handle had a scandalous carving of a mermaid on it.

To Mrs. Barrow Jim gave a lovely necklace of polished green sea glass. "It was me mum's," he mumbled and quickly turned away. Mrs. Barrow wiped tears from her eyes.

To Gabe he presented another knife with a whalebone handle. Lastly he presented Ethan with a small wooden box. Ethan opened it and his eyes widened. It contained a fine whalebone chess set. "You should keep this, lad," he said.

Jim shook his head. "I can't play chess. I want you to have it."

Ethan touched the boy on the shoulder as he turned away. "I'll keep it for you until you can beat me at chess," he told Jim. Jim gave him a shy grin and went back to his duties.

After his father's main possessions had been given away, Jim placed the rest in the old boat. "Now fill it with driftwood," he ordered, and they all gathered wood until the boat was full. Under his orders, they pushed the old boat into the sea until it floated. Then Jim took a burning brand from the fire and turned to face the assembly.

"Me da never did hold wi' churches, as most o' you know," he said. "But he told me a story once about people called Vikings and how they done funerals. He told me he reckoned it would be a grand way to go. So, Da, this is for you."

He tossed the brand into the boat and the driftwood caught fire and blazed up.

"Push!" he ordered, and the burning boat floated out to sea. They watched in silence, then one of the fishermen produced a fiddle. He started to play a slow, haunting tune, and after a moment a woman started to sing:

> *Blow the wind southerly, southerly, southerly,*
> *Blow the wind south o'er the bonny blue sea;*
> *Blow the wind southerly, southerly, southerly,*
> *Blow bonny breeze, my lover to me.*
>
> *They told me last night there were ships in the offing,*
> *And I hurried down to the deep rolling sea;*
> *But my eye could not see it*
> *Wherever might be it,*
> *The bark that is bearing my lover to me.*

" 'Twas his mam's favorite song," Mrs. Barrow sobbed to Callie.

Rafe, Harry, and Luke stood to one side, watching.

"That boy will make a fine man one day," Rafe commented.

Harry turned to look at Jim. "He already is."

Twelve

Sir Walter sent word early the next morning that the count's yacht had sailed during the night, so a short time later they set off for London. They took two vehicles; Gabriel drove his curricle and Ethan drove a traveling chaise that had belonged to Great-aunt Gert. The other gentlemen rode.

Since no one was in a particular hurry, they took their own horses and completed the journey in a number of easy stages, stopping from time to time to stretch their legs and rest the horses. They also swapped around. From time to time Gabriel would take one of his friends up in the curricle, or they would drive and he would ride, or one of them would join Callie, Nicky, Jim, and Tibby in the chaise.

"It's rather fun, isn't it?" Callie commented to Tibby, "All this swapping around."

"Yes, and to have such dashing escorts," Tibby agreed. "Such a magnificent collection of men—it quite makes my heart flutter. They really are all extraordinarily handsome, don't you think?"

Callie smiled. "Yes, indeed." The chaise took a bend and she caught a glimpse of Nicky, sitting with Jim and Gabriel having a driving lesson.

Tibby followed the direction of her gaze. "He's kind, isn't he? The boys worship him."

"Mmm. I'm looking forward to our picnic in the New Forest," Callie said brightly. "I've never seen so much food." She didn't want to talk about Gabriel's kindness. Kindness was more dangerous than handsomeness.

Tibby looked at her. "I must say, Count Anton was not at all as I'd expected him to be."

"I know. That's the trouble. He seems too good-looking to be so evil. It makes people unwilling to believe the worst of him."

"Is there much family resemblance between him and your husband?"

Callie nodded. "Rupert's eyes were exactly the same as Count Anton's—that pale ice-gray color. Rupert's hair was darker golden in coloring and he was taller and broader: a big, handsome golden bull."

"Rupert sounds quite attractive." Tibby made it a gentle query.

"Yes, he was. Very."

"I was so worried about you. You were so young, so sheltered, and the prince so much older. It was the time I most regretted being poor; not able to afford to travel with you to be at your wedding. You must have felt so alone."

Callie stared out the window at the passing scenery. "You needn't have worried, Tibby. My wedding day was the happiest day of my life."

"Oh, my dear, I am so glad."

"I fell madly in love with Rupert, if not at first sight—as you said, I was very shy and naive—but in the weeks before the wedding. He courted me, showered me with jewels and expensive gifts." Most of them were now sewn into her petticoat. She could not regret them, at least. They would give her and Nicky a new life.

"Rupert was charming and attentive and gallant." She sighed, remembering. She'd been almost dizzy with the excitement of it all, the constant attention paid to her by such a magnificent golden creature. He was forty, but she hadn't thought of him as old, just glamorous and sophisticated. Godlike.

"It was like being Cinderella. Every day we'd go out driving in the streets of the city and he'd give me flowers and the people would wave and cheer and he would put his arm around me and kiss me, and oh, Tibby, it was like everything we'd ever talked about, everything I'd ever dreamed of. He was Galahad and Young Lochinvar and—well, you know what I mean—so romantic."

"My dear girl, I am happy to know it. You have no idea what torments I suffered when your father took you away. To be married to a man so much your elder, I felt sure it could not be a happy union."

Callie fell silent and looked out the window.

After several moments Tibby ventured, "It was, wasn't it? If he was everything you'd ever dreamed of . . ."

"No. It wasn't. I was playing make-believe."

"Oh."

"I learned later he didn't love me at all. He'd never loved me. He didn't even like me much. It was all for show, and because he was so handsome and charming and he was so experienced and I was just a stupid, dreamy, romantic, gullible child—" She broke off, the familiar, bitter taste of shame welling up in her throat.

Tibby placed her hand over Callie's. "I'm sorry, my dear, so sorry."

Callie shook her head and tried to smile. "It's all a long time ago now. I was another person then." She was relieved that Tibby hadn't asked how she'd come to discover that Rupert didn't love her. Not even to Tibby could she reveal that. It might be a long time ago, but some scars went deep. They could still cause pain.

"You are still young," Tibby began. "You could try again—"

"No! I couldn't bear it!" She took a steadying breath and said in a light tone, "I won't ever make the mistake of marrying again. You have no idea how much I'm looking forward to directing my own life, choosing what I do or wear or eat or read. I won't give up my independence for anything." She gave Tibby a bright smile.

Tibby, undeceived, said nothing, only squeezed Callie's hand.

Callie gazed out the window, forcing composure to return. She would not cry. She had wasted a lifetime of tears on Rupert.

Never again. Not on Rupert, not on any man.

Not even a kind one.

She caught a glimpse of the curricle up ahead. Rupert had been kind to animals and children, too. The way he treated Nicky was not a matter of unkindness—just insensitivity. He was hard on Nicky for Nicky's sake. He thought it the right thing to do.

The cruelty had lain in Rupert's inability to hide his disappointment in his son.

Not to mention his wife.

They entered the New Forest. It was quieter in the forest, the woods green and lush with new growth. The trees were less dense than she expected. There were even large patches of open space in which wild ponies grazed.

In Zindaria, the forest was darker, denser. Rupert's hunting lodge was deep in the forest. She'd only been there the once.

The worst mistake of her life.

He used to go to his hunting lodge often, almost every week. Sometimes for just a night or two, sometimes for longer. It depended, he'd said, on the game.

She'd thought he meant animals.

Women weren't allowed, he said. In those days she couldn't bear to be parted from him. She missed him with an ache that was almost physical.

He'd been gone a week and was expected to stay another week.

But at the beginning of the second week she'd been given some wonderful news. Her courses were normally as regular as clockwork and she was two weeks overdue. Her breasts were tender and a little swollen. And three mornings in a row she'd woken up feeling nauseous.

She thought she was ill, but her maid had become all excited when she'd been nauseous in the morning. She'd questioned Callie closely, then fetched the palace physician.

Callie remembered the joy she'd felt when she'd learned she was going to have a baby.

She was so excited she couldn't wait for Rupert to come home. He was desperate for a son, she knew. She'd ordered the carriage and had driven into the forest, to his hunting lodge.

She remembered every moment of that drive. It was spring, too, with new growth bursting all around her. There were snowy wee lambs with long, waggly tails, lanky, delicate foals hovering at their mother's side. In the forest she'd even caught a glimpse of a doe nuzzling a shy, leggy faun. The sight had brought her almost to tears.

She'd felt joyously at one with this new precious world, fertile, bounteous, successful: she was going to be a mother.

At the hunting lodge she hadn't let Rupert's servants announce her. She wanted to surprise him.

She did.

He was lying half naked on a thick fur rug in front of the fire. Sitting astride him was a naked woman, a voluptuous Valkyrie of a woman, with flowing golden locks spilling down her naked back and over her full breasts. She was bent over him, rubbing her breasts against his naked chest, saying in a breathy girlish voice, "Oh, Wupert, Wupert, I love you so much, my darling Wupert, I am so happy, so happy, so happy, my beloved ickle-wickle Wupert." She spoke in Zindarian, but Callie had no difficulty in recognizing the imitation of her own English accent, nor the subject of this cruel mimicry.

Herself.

Callie stood frozen, unable to move as the woman went on and on, talking in a ghastly baby-talk imitation of Callie.

She vaguely remembered thinking at the time that she never had called him Wupert, nor said anything like ickle-wickle, or used that horrid baby voice. The rest of it—the accent, the words, the sentiments—were horribly, shamingly, accurate. She had uttered those very phrases to Rupert—but only ever in private.

The only way the woman could have heard them was from Rupert himself. Callie's soul shriveled with pain and mortification.

The more the woman gushed in cloying imitation of Callie, the more Rupert had laughed, deep belly laughs of the sort she'd never heard from her husband before, until finally he ordered the woman to stop, saying he got enough of that sickening pap at home, and reminding the Valkyrie that the reason he came here was to get away from all that. He wanted a woman, not a dreary, love-besotted child.

The dreary, love-besotted child had managed to clear her throat, drawing their shocked attention. They had made no move to cover themselves, just stared at her from the fur rug.

Somehow—she had no idea how—she had managed to keep her composure. Some shred of ancestral pride had stiffened her sixteen-year-old spine. She would not make a scene. She would rather die than show her hurt and distress in front of them, in front of the husband who had betrayed her so cruelly, and in front of that naked, golden, shameless creature who had imitated her so horribly.

In a cold little voice, Callie managed to announce that she had come to inform Rupert that she was expecting his child and that having done so, she would now return to the palace.

They still hadn't moved when she turned and left.

She had walked straight out in that same distant, frozen state—she still had no idea how she had managed to find her way back to the carriage. And once safely inside, once the carriage was moving swiftly back through the forest, the tears came.

She'd sobbed all the way home, great choking sobs that scalded her throat and almost rent her chest in two, weeping until it made her almost sick.

Over and over she heard the woman's voice scornfully uttering the precious endearments Callie had whispered into her husband's ear. Her memory was seared with the sound of Rupert's belly laughs. *Sickening pap,* he'd called it.

She had wept and wept. The forest was dense and dark and ancient and it absorbed her pain, as it had absorbed pain for millennia, and by the time the carriage approached the palace, Callie had no tears left.

How many people in the palace knew Rupert did not love her? Everyone, she decided. She'd made no effort to disguise her feelings. She'd been overflowing with love and happiness and she'd stupidly imagined the whole world shared her joy.

She'd made a complete and utter fool of herself over him.

Never again, she vowed. *Never.*

And she'd kept her vow. By the time Rupert returned to the palace—two days later—and spoke to her, she had armored herself against him, against the shame deep within her that threatened to break out.

He'd made what he considered an apology: he told her that he was sorry she'd found him with his mistress, but that she had been informed that his hunting lodge was private. She should never have gone there. So that any distress or embarrassment she'd experienced was her own fault.

She had agreed. Calmly and quietly. Then she'd picked up her sewing in a clear dismissal.

He'd seemed relieved.

From then on she'd treated him with cool politeness. Two months after that vile day at the hunting lodge he'd congratulated her on finally growing up. He ascribed it to the maturity that came with pregnancy. Told her he was proud of her.

When Nicky was born, Callie poured all her love into her child.

Rupert hadn't come to her bed again until six months after Nicky was born. After all, her main purpose was to breed children. They'd coupled quickly, thoroughly, and more or less in silence, then he left. He came to her once a month, but she never fell pregnant again.

Later she'd heard that he'd told people that apart from her inability to provide him with more children, she'd become the perfect wife.

She stared out of the window at the New Forest. This was not the dark and silent forest of Zindaria, and she was no longer that miserable pregnant child, flayed by the folly of her own emotions. She was a widow, calm and mature, free to make the life she wanted for herself and her child.

And for her own peace of mind, it would not involve any man.

*T*hey stopped for a picnic on a sunny patch of grass beside a gurgling stream. Behind them the forest spread, sun-dappled and quiet.

Tibby and Callie spread rugs and a cloth and unpacked

the food, while the men and boys saw to the horses. Gabe handed Nicky the end of a halter and told him to lead the horse to water.

He glanced at Callie. The moment their eyes met, she looked away. She hadn't looked at him directly since he'd offered to kill the count for her.

Obviously he'd frightened her off. No doubt she'd taken his statement about him being a cold-blooded killer seriously. He resolved to do something about it fast.

"Mrs. Barrow has outdone herself," Gabe commented as he surveyed the spread.

"Yes, we'll never get though all this," Tibby agreed.

There were boiled eggs, sandwiches, a large egg-and-bacon pie, homemade Dorset sausage, and baked chicken. There were crispy red and green apples, jam tarts, a plum cake, heavy and rich with fruit, and to top it off, Mrs. Barrow's apple cake, Harry's favorite. There was also ale, ginger beer, wine, and cold, sweet tea in bottles. Mrs. Barrow had thought of everything.

Gabe laughed. "Don't you believe it, Miss Tibby. There are five men here who lived on army rations too long to waste anything, let alone Mrs. Barrow's cooking."

He sat down beside Callie and began to pour out drinks, as one by one the others arrived. She didn't move away, though she did inconspicuously lift her skirt away from where it touched his leg.

Experimentally, Gabe casually moved his leg so it touched hers again. Again, without so much as a glance his way, she moved. She was skittish, all right. More skittish than when he'd first met her.

Once Harry, Rafe, Luke, Ethan, and Nicky had joined them, Miss Tibby said grace and they all began to eat.

It was a very relaxed meal, and afterward, Miss Tibby told the boys about the New Forest, how it had been there forever, and how William the Conqueror had decided to make it a place for the protection of the deer he liked to hunt, so he drove many of the human inhabitants out, rating beasts above people.

"It brought him and his family bad luck," interposed Rafe. "His son, William Rufus, policed the laws most rigorously and horribly mutilated those who broke them. He was killed right here in the forest."

Luke added, "He was shot with an arrow, while out hunting with friends. His friends abandoned his body where it lay. A charcoal burner later found it and brought in on his cart."

"And the moral of that tale, young Nicky," finished Rafe, "is to ensure you make true friends in life." The men, as one, raised their cups and rank a toast to true friendship.

"Like you all are," Nicky said.

"Indeed we are," Gabe told him. "War forges the bonds of friendship. I asked Harry and Rafe and Luke for help, because you and your mother were in trouble, and they came, as I knew they would."

"Ethan told me in the army they called you the Devil Riders, because you all ride like the devil. And not even the devil could catch you."

Gabe shrugged. "People like to talk. We all love fast horses—which is why we're starting this horse-racing venture."

But Nicky wasn't to be diverted. "Ethan also said before that, they used to call you the Duke's Angels," Nicky said.

"Yes, the duke of Wellington made a comment once—he was using us for dispatches at the time—and the name stuck for a while. There were five of us then, but poor Michael was killed," Gabe told him. They each drank a silent toast to Michael.

"Why angels?" Nicky asked.

"Perhaps because of their names, Nicky," Miss Tibby suggested. "The named angels were Michael, Gabriel, Rafael, and . . ." She hesitated.

"Lucifer, who was a fallen angel," Luke explained. "I'm christened Lucian, which is close enough."

Nicky looked at Harry, disappointed. "So you weren't an angel, Mr. Morant?" Nicky was fast becoming one of Harry's staunchest admirers, thought Gabe. Harry could out-ride any of them, and he had a bad leg just like the little boy.

"Harry was one of the Duke's Angel's, all right," Rafe said. "Weren't you, Harold?"

Harry gave a wry grin. "I was."

Nicky looked puzzled. "Does England have an angel called Harold, then, for we don't have one in Zindaria."

Miss Tibby frowned. "No, we don't in England, either, Nicky." She turned to Rafe. "I've never heard of any angel called Harold."

Every one of the men produced a look of surprise, Gabe, too. It was an old joke.

Ethan leaned forward. "Sure you have, Miss Tibby. And don't you sing about him every Christmas?"

Tibby frowned. "I don't think so."

Ethan said, "Then do you not know the carol 'Hark the Harold Angels Sing'?"

Miss Tibby huffed with pretend disapproval and then joined in the general laughter.

Even Callie laughed, Gabe noted. It lit up her face briefly. He was determined to get her alone, find out what she was fretting about.

A fter the picnic, Gabe invited Callie to ride in the curricle with himself and Nicky.

"Oh yes, Mama," Nicky chimed in enthusiastically. "Come and watch me drive the horses. It is such fun."

She looked trapped. Her desire to please her son warred with her desire to avoid Gabe. Her son won, as he expected, and she moved toward his curricle feigning delight.

She held herself rigid when Gabe lifted her up into the curricle. He was about to lift Nicky in when right on cue Harry rode up, saying, "Nicky, would you like to ride with me for a while?"

Nicky's eyes widened. "Yes, please, sir," he responded eagerly, as Gabe had known he would, and before Nicky's mother could say a word, Gabe lifted the child up in front of his brother.

"He likes to go fast," he told Harry, who winked at him and moved off.

Gabe climbed nimbly into the curricle beside the princess and snapped the reins.

For a short distance she said nothing, then, "I suppose you're feeling pleased with yourself."

"Indeed I am," Gabe agreed, his eyes twinkling. "My stratagem worked perfectly. Your son is having the time of his life and I am alone with you. What could be more perfect?"

She didn't say anything.

"You expected me to deny it, didn't you?"

She laughed. "Nothing could have convinced me you did not arrange that beforehand with your brother. I have spent the last few minutes thinking up a good scold, and now you've taken the wind right out of my sails."

"Go ahead, scold away if it will make you happy," he invited. "I promise you, I will be suitably crushed."

She arched her brows skeptically. "Crushed enough to stop the curricle and let me return to the chaise?"

"No, not that crushed. Unfortunately I am quite resilient to scolds. Blame my military experience: people give thundering good scolds in the army. They quite ruined my ability to be crushed."

"I doubt you were ever particularly crushable."

He grinned at her. "See? I knew you would have liked Great-aunt Gert. She would have agreed with you there.

Mind you, she gave the best scolds in the world and came quite close to crushing me once or twice."

She laughed again.

"There, that's better," he said. "You climbed out of that chaise before looking so wan and dejected I was worried you were ill. But a good feed, some fresh air, and a little badinage has done you the world of good. The roses are blooming in your cheeks again. And see, Miss Tibby is doing the same."

They both looked to where Tibby sat up on the driver's seat next to Ethan. Gabe hoped Ethan knew what he was doing, fostering such an acquaintance. Ethan must have suggested the seating arrangement to Miss Tibby: a lady like Tibby would never have thought of riding up with the driver.

Gabe frowned. It was unlike Ethan to have much to do with respectable ladies. Socially, the two were poles apart.

Ethan had a certain rough charm, he knew. The ladies of Spain and Portugal had certainly appreciated him. But that was in wartime, and war made people act in ways they would not otherwise countenance.

Things were different now. He hoped Ethan remembered it.

They came to a clearing and he instantly reined in the horses. "Look," he said, pointing to where a small herd of deer grazed on the sweet grass by the forest's edge. As they watched the deer melted away into the trees.

"I expect they think we'll shoot at them," she said.

"I'm not really a cold-blooded killer," he said quietly.

She gave him a surprised look. "I didn't mean—"

"Not the deer; the other morning, with the count. You've hardly been able to look at me since."

Callie looked away, distressed. He thought she despised him for doing what he had done. He was so wrong. It was quite the contrary.

He went on, "Once a man starts burning women's houses and trying to murder children, he must be stopped. I would prefer the law to do it, I admit, but if it came to the crunch I would have no hesitation in killing him. And it would not bother me in the least." He paused and looked at her. "But I would never hurt you or Nicky, or any woman or child."

"Do you think I don't know that? Of course I know you wouldn't hurt us. You've been nothing but kind." If just one person in Zindaria had listened to her, believed her, as he had . . . but they hadn't. She'd had to travel across a continent and sail across the English Channel to find him, this one man who believed her, and without hesitation had declared himself her champion.

Sir Galahad indeed.

But how could she tell him that, and not reveal what was in her heart? What she thought might be in her heart, if only she dared to look. She didn't dare, she couldn't. She couldn't go through it all again.

He'd said it himself—he would protect *any* woman, *any* child. That is what a Galahad did.

"I'm sorry, I wasn't deliberately avoiding you," she lied. "It's just that I've had a lot on my mind."

"I know." He took her hand in his and squeezed it. "I was just worried that my actions that morning had given you a disgust of me."

"A disgust?" she exclaimed. "No, I thought you were a hero!"

"I wouldn't go that far," he said. "Just as long as you're not frightened of me."

It depended what the definition of being frightened was, she thought.

That morning had changed her life. Standing up to Count Anton had given her a small piece of pride back. She'd done something she'd never done before; she'd behaved like a ruling princess. And people had believed her. Even Count Anton had believed her.

It was a powerful thought.

And when Gabriel said he would kill Count Anton for her, he'd offered her the most powerful choice of all: the power of life and death. To protect her son.

She had no doubt he would have done it. And Gabriel would have taken the responsibility, the blame.

He knew what he was doing. How could he not—a soldier, an officer of eight years? And with the magistrate at his elbow, warning him of the consequences. A hanging offense.

At the very least he would have had to flee the country and live as an exile.

And he would have done it, for her, for Callie.

It threatened every carefully built wall she'd maintained around her heart since she'd walked out of that hunting lodge eight years ago.

To be that vulnerable to a man again?

Yes, she was frightened of him. He frightened her to death.

*T*hey stopped several nights on the road. The first night Ethan approached Tibby, and asked could he have a word in private with her. She agreed.

"Miss Tibby?" The room wasn't hot at all, but Ethan was sweating like a pig.

"Yes, Mr. Delaney?"

"I was wondering . . ."

"Yes?" She tilted her head inquiringly.

Ethan ran a finger around his collar. It was far too tight. He'd spent half an hour arranging his neck cloth just so, and now the damned thing was choking him. He cleared his throat.

"Miss Tibby, as you know, I'm plannin' to go into business with Mr. Morant. And Mr. Renfrew, of course," he added as an afterthought. Harry Morant was the driving force in this venture.

"Yes, I know. It sounds a most exciting venture."

"It is. The trouble is, Miss Tibby, there is . . . stuff . . . I need to learn. If I want to be a partner on the same terms as the others, that is. It's not just a matter of money. Or horse sense. Or work."

"Isn't it?"

"No." He wanted to rip his neck cloth off. He took a turn around the room.

"Miss Tibby, I want to hire your services."

"But Mr. Delaney, I don't know anything about horses or horse racing. Or business."

"No, not that." He pulled out a handkerchief and mopped his brow. "As a partner in the business there are things I need to know, to be able to do to be on the same footing as the people I'll be dealing with."

She looked puzzled, then her brow cleared. "Do you mean you want me to teach you how to go on in polite society?"

"No." He made a dismissive gesture. "I've been around enough officers to know how to ape the gentleman if I have to."

"Mr. Delaney," she said with brisk reproof. "You have no need to 'ape the gentleman,' as you put it. You are more truly a gentleman than many men in society. And believe me, I know."

"Thank you," he said after a moment. The unexpected compliment had thrown him—and he was already off balance. He returned to the main point. He was going to get this over with if it killed him. "To tell you the truth, Miss Tibby, I have no desire to be what I am not, but there are things I wish to learn. And I want to hire you to teach me."

"But, Mr. Delaney, what could I possibly teach you?"

Ethan took a deep breath. "Books," he croaked. There, it was out.

"Books? What books?"

"Any books. All of 'em."

"I don't understand."

Ethan drew himself up as if he were facing a firing squad and said, "I can't read, Miss Tibby. Or write."

She didn't say a word.

After a moment he looked at her. Her brown eyes were wide and steady on his face. "Mr. Delaney," she said softly, "I'd be honored to teach you how to read and write."

Thirteen

*L*ondon was bigger than she remembered. Bigger, noisier, dirtier, and more exciting. Callie started feeling a little apprehensive.

She'd quarreled with Gabriel at luncheon. He'd been quite unreasonable. She'd simply asked him to recommend a hotel, and he'd told her in no uncertain terms that she was not staying in any hotel, that she was staying with his aunt, Lady Gosforth, and no argument. He'd written ahead and Aunt Maude was expecting them.

Callie pointed out that she had no claim on his aunt or her hospitality. His aunt would be delighted, he said, and that was the end of it.

Callie didn't see how any aunt would be delighted to have complete strangers foisted on her. He'd made a rude noise and said he thought he knew his aunt better than she did.

The small cavalcade drew up in front of an imposing house on Mount Street. Gabriel handed her and Tibby down from the chaise and conducted them up the steps to the front door. It opened smoothly as they reached it.

"Afternoon, Sprotton, keeping well I hope?"

The very dignified butler bowed. "Good afternoon, Mr. Gabe, I hope your trip was pleasant and uneventful, and may I say how good it is to see you here, sir? Ladies." He bowed to Callie and Tibby. "Lady Gosforth asked me to conduct you all upstairs to Wash and Compose yourselves—"

"I did," a tall, elegant, Roman-nosed matron interrupted him. "But I've decided I can't wait to meet you." She swept forward holding out both her hands in a warm greeting, at odds with the severe cast of her countenance. "The height of inconsideration I know, my dears, to greet you when you are fresh from a long and tedious journey and I hope you will forgive me for it. How do you do? You are Prin—no, Mrs. Prynne of course—I know, Gabriel, but I am being very discreet—what glorious eyes you have my dear—and you are—?" She looked down her long nose at Tibby.

Callie jumped in, seeing a way of escape. "Miss Tibthorpe, my—my lady-in-waiting." She did not want anyone looking down on Tibby. "And my, er, equerry is waiting outside, with my . . . son's companion. I am sorry, indeed I had no intention of imposing on you but your nephew—"

"Nonsense, no imposition at all, my nephew was quite right to bring you to me. I presume your maids and footmen are following on. They're all welcome. I am delighted to have you, for the season so far has been utterly tedious and this house is far too empty."

She held out her hand to Tibby and said, "How do you do, Miss Tibthorpe, and you are, of course, Nicholas."

"Nikolai," he corrected her, then bowed very correctly and clicked his heels.

"What excellent manners, Nikolai. You will take note, Gabriel, this child has greeted me and you have not."

He bowed ironically and grinned. "I was waiting for you to draw breath, Aunt Maude."

"Nonsense, for you know perfectly well you would

never get a word in otherwise. Now, up you all go. Sprotton will conduct you to your bedchambers and arrange hot water. Did you say your maids are following?"

"No," Callie said awkwardly. No lady would travel without her maid.

"She lost her maid and footman and several grooms in a storm," Gabe told his aunt. "Washed overboard on the way to England. Terrible tragedy. When I met Mrs. Prynne she and her son had just waded out of the sea and were dripping wet."

Lady Gosforth stared. "How frightful, my dears. What a mercy you survived. I presume that's what happened to your clothes as well. Never mind, my maid shall attend you and tomorrow we shall procure new clothes. Tea in half an hour. Gabriel, where are you going?"

Gabriel, who had been heading back toward the front door, turned back. "I'll stay at my club—"

"Nonsense, you'll stay here with me, and so will that wretched brother of yours and don't try to tell me he is not with you for I looked out of the window and he is sitting outside on a rather good chestnut, looking handsome, brooding as usual, along with that lovely Ramsey boy and the other one—you know, what's his name?—the one the girls all sigh after. Divinely handsome with a fatally attractive air of tragedy."

"Luke Ripton," said Gabriel, trying not to smile.

"That's it, the Ripton boy. And the other man who looks like an elegant prizefighter, the one with the small boy sitting beside him—he's not a groom, is he? He doesn't look like a groom."

"No, that's Mrs. Prynne's, er, equerry and her son's companion."

"He looks interesting. Run outside and tell them they are all invited for tea and I won't take no for an answer. Cook's baked lemon curd cakes and gingerbread and some newfangled sugar wafers, which he fills with cream and are positively decadent. And you and Harry will *not* stay at your club." She gave him an imperious look down her long nose. "Well, run along, Gabriel. Take your horses around to the mews or they'll take a chill in this frightful wind."

Gabriel bowed ironically, then winked at Callie, who was trying not to giggle. "Now you know why I'm terrified of women."

Callie and Lady Gosforth both snorted in disbelief. Lady Gosforth turned to Callie with a smile. "My dear, I can see you're just what my nephew needs."

"But I'm not—" Callie began.

"Oh, and Gabriel," Lady Gosforth called. "Your brother Nash was here looking for you."

Gabe's face hardened. "Nothing to do with me."

Lady Gosforth rolled her eyes. "Well, it is to do with you—and your guests also." She nodded at Callie and Nicky and gave him a not-in-front-of-the-children sort of look. "Nash will dine with us tonight and explain." She peered beadily down her nose at him. "But first there will be tea—tell those other boys I expect them! Now hurry up and tend to your horses."

He gave her an ironic salute. "Yes, General Gosforth."

Nash Renfrew arrived an hour before dinner. "There is a fellow, a foreigner," he told Gabe when they were alone. "A count from some obscure little country who claims that a Mr. Renfrew, the son of an earl, is illegally holding his head of state. The Foreign Office thought he meant me, but that was clearly nonsense, so the finger got pointed at you, though personally I think he must have rats in his upper story. He says you have in your custody the crown prince of his country, Zan—Zendar—"

"Zindaria," Gabe corrected him.

Nash's eyes narrowed. "You mean you know what he's talking about?"

"I do. The lady currently staying in Aunt Gosforth's best spare bedroom is the crown prince's mother. I presume the fellow you've met is a dapper blond charmer called Count Anton."

"Good God. But this is appalling."

"He is an appalling fellow."

Nash made an impatient gesture. "This is serious, Gabriel. It's a matter of state. He's claiming the crown prince has been illegally removed from his country and must be returned."

Gabe shrugged. "His mother removed the crown prince from his country because people were trying to kill him. He's only seven, and being his mother she naturally took exception to it."

Nash frowned. "I wish you'd be serious. This is bidding fair to becoming an international incident."

"I'm deadly serious," Gabe told him. "The child's life really is in danger."

"This Count Anton is the regent. He'd take full responsibility for the boy's safety."

"He's the fellow trying to kill the boy. He's next in line to the throne after the boy."

"Ah, I see." Nash frowned. "It's a tricky situation."

"Nothing tricky about it—" Gabe began.

Nash shook his head. "It's very delicate. Count Anton has made an official complaint at the highest level, which means our government will be forced to act."

Gabe sat forward. "You can't mean to hand over that child to—"

"Not me, the government. I am but a minor official."

"The child belongs to his mother—"

"Not according to Zindarian law. As crown prince, he belongs to his country. And in any case, he is a Zindarian citizen."

"His mother is English."

Nash shook his head. "No. When she married the

prince, she became Zindarian. I have spent the last two days checking every aspect of the case."

"Even though you didn't believe it could be anything to do with me."

His brother gave him a withering look. "From the little I know of you, the very bizarre nature of the case seemed to fit with you perfectly."

Gabe gave a thin smile. "You know me better than I realized."

Nash leaned forward, his face suddenly earnest. "Gabriel, I wish we could heal this family rift. Surely, now that our parents are dead we can put their wretched folly behind us and finally behave like true brothers toward each other."

Gabe raised an eyebrow. "True brothers?" he said sarcastically. "When I am—what was it you and your brother called me? The legitimate bastard. And Harry was the illegitimate one. So clever you thought yourselves."

Nash shook his head. "I was eleven at the time, Gabriel, and Marcus was thirteen, and we were both just repeating what our father called you—foolishly and cruelly, I admit. And I've apologized for it before and will do so again, as many times as it'll take until you forgive me, for I bitterly repent it. If Father had ever seen you, he would have known that you are our true brother."

"And Harry?"

Nash said carefully. "I will acknowledge him as my illegitimate half brother."

Gabe snorted. "Big of you. I call him brother and I'll accept nothing less on his behalf. He's just as much a victim of my father's folly as I was. And Harry is the only family I have ever known: Harry, Great-aunt Gert, and since the latter part of my school days, Aunt Gosforth. Harry is my brother, my school friend, my comrade in arms. You and your brother are strangers to me."

"Don't say 'your brother' like that. Marcus is your brother, too."

Gabe folded his arms and changed the subject. "You were talking about the crown prince of Zindaria. You're not handing him over. I won't allow it."

Nash sat back with a thoughtful expression. "I won't give up on you, Gabriel. But, yes, to return to the subject of the crown prince, if the count wishes him ill, I agree, the boy must be protected. But how?"

"Boot the bastard out of England."

Nash gave Gabe a look that said he could throw the word "bastard" around all he liked, Nash would not react. "Unfortunately the government cannot," he said. "Zindaria, though small and obscure, is an ally of the Austrians and we cannot afford to provoke an international incident."

He steepled his fingers and stared at them thoughtfully. "What we need is a complication. Something for the Foreign Office to chew over, to debate, to delay. Delay can be a government's most useful weapon."

Gabe snorted. Delay had caused him many a problem in the army. Delay in funding, in provision of supplies. He had no patience with government delay. He looked at Nash. Except perhaps in this case.

Gabe sat forward as an idea came to him. "If the princess was married to an Englishman, would that make a difference?"

"Yes, that would certainly complicate things nicely, but she's not."

"She could be. To me."

Nash stared. "Are you mad? You hardly know her."

"That doesn't matter. What matters is that she would not only be married to an Englishman, it would be to an Englishman with excellent family connections. An aunt who is a leader of the *ton*, a brother with an inside track to government decision-making—"

"And another brother who sits in the House of Lords and would make a huge fuss if anyone tried to take his sister-in-law's son! And besides, you're a war hero." Nash sat back in his chair and gave his brother an admiring look. "It's brilliant. It will answer our purpose admirably—but are you sure you want to do this?"

Gabe nodded. "I'm certain."

"Beddable little filly, is she?"

Gabe gave his brother a hard stare. "No." He said the word like a whiplash.

"Not beddable?"

"Not your business, *brother*." The violence of his reaction shocked Gabe. The mere thought of his brother regarding Callie as "a beddable filly" had made him want to thrash Nash to a pulp. His brother hadn't even met her.

Nash gave him a cool look. "Point taken. She will be my sister-in-law, after all. But there will be a deal of talk."

"I'm counting on it," Gabe said. "The more people know about the wedding the harder it'll be to have her son whisked out of the country." *That's right,* Gabe told himself. *Keep reminding yourself that it's all about the child.*

Nothing to do with these primitive emotions surging up within him. The moment the idea had occurred to him he wanted it done, wanted her to be his wife. Now, without delay. His wife.

The woman who had sworn repeatedly that she would never marry again.

Nash nodded. "Yes, you're right. We'll get it organized at once."

Gabe frowned as a fairly large hole in the scheme occurred to him.

His brother noticed his expression and said, "You are having second thoughts, aren't you?"

"No, it's not that—"

"If it's the special license you're worried about, I will see to it. Aunt Gosforth will no doubt be happy to organize one of her 'small' receptions."

"Yes," Gabe said absently. "The more witnesses, the

more difficult it is for the government to act." And the more difficult for her to wriggle out of.

Nash nodded. "I'm glad you see the value of family, after all."

Gabe gave him a flat look. "For a good cause, yes. But don't get too excited about this scheme just yet."

"Why, what's the problem?"

Gabe said slowly, "There's just one small fly in the ointment."

"And what is that?"

"The bride."

"The bride? She's the fly? Do you think she might not like it?"

"That's putting it mildly."

"Don't worry, I'll talk to her," Nash said confidently. "I'm very good at explaining things and convincing people. It's my job, after all. Bring her in."

"*M*arry Gabriel Renfrew? Absolutely not!" Callie stared first at the man who'd been introduced as "the Honorable Nash Renfrew, something in government" and then at Gabriel. There was a strong family resemblance: the nose, the chin, and those intense blue eyes. Not to mention the shoulders, the height, and the infuriating assumption that he knew what was best for her.

"I won't do it!" she reiterated. "It's a ridiculous idea. There must be another way."

Nash shook his head. "We've given it a great deal of thought. It's the only way we can think of to prevent my government from handing your son back to the Zindarian government."

"Not the Zindarian government," she flashed, "Count Anton, the snake who has been plotting to murder him!"

Nash shrugged. "I know; Gabriel told me. It's unfortunate, but unless you have proof, which Gabriel assures me you don't, our government cannot concern itself with person-alities; the count has provided the appropriate paperwork."

"Paperwork!" she stormed. "What sort of people would put paperwork before a child's safety?"

Nash gave her a very Renfrew look. "Princess, to a gov-ernment paperwork is *everything.*"

She glared at him and took a few angry paces around the room. "Then I will take my son and flee."

He shrugged. "It will just delay the inevitable. They will track you down and bring you back, and then you will be in breach of the law and will be separated from your son."

"But I am *English*! I came back to my own country to be safe!"

Nash looked regretful. "Unfortunately, Princess, your nationality changed once you married. Which is why—"

"No! I won't even consider it! It's utterly ridiculous."

"It's not, you know," Gabe said. "It makes a great deal of sense. And I'm the perfect candidate."

She snorted.

"He is," Nash insisted. "You couldn't get anyone to suit your purpose better—not without wasting time, and time is of the essence here. With the Renfrew family connections—our elder brother is an earl, you know—we have the poten-tial to cause all sorts of scandal if anyone tried to separate you from your son, or you from your husband."

"Husband!" she declared with loathing. "I don't want a husband."

"Not even if it will save your son?"

She gave him an anguished look. "How would it work?"

"If you married Gabriel, you'd once again become an English citizen. And since he has excellent family connec-tions"—he gave his brother a direct look—"we'd use those connections to put pressure on the government to delay."

"Delay!" she exclaimed. "What good is delay? If I un-derstand you correctly, in the end, you will still have to hand my son over to a murderer!"

Nash gave her a shocked look. "Princess, I assure you, the English government may be riddled with imperfections, but in matters of creative delay we are unmatched."

She bit her lip and considered his statement. "How much of a delay do you think you could manage?"

"Until forever," Nash said with pride.

She gave him a doubtful look. "Forever?"

He made a careless gesture. "At least until your son is of age."

"Or until Count Anton dies?" Gabe asked.

Nash inclined his head. "Indeed." He narrowed his eyes at his brother. "But not if you murdered him, Gabriel. That would complicate things enormously."

She looked at Gabe anxiously. "I don't want you to commit murder."

"Then your only alternative is to commit matrimony," Gabe responded.

She flung him a resentful glance, cornered and desperate.

Gabe felt for her . . . almost. He was determined to convince her. Now that they were in London he wouldn't put it past her to simply disappear. Her notion of staying at a hotel had given him a jolt that had shocked him.

He had to get her to promise to marry him. A promise would hold her. "If it will save Nicky, is there really any choice?"

"I don't know. I can't think. I need time," she said unhappily.

Gabe looked deep into her eyes and saw she was terrified.

He wondered yet again what her husband had done to her to make her so fearful of marrying again. He had to reassure her. He wouldn't hurt her, he would treat her tenderly . . .

"It would be purely a matter of convenience," Nash said, and Gabe had the urge to strangle him again.

"If that was what you wanted," Gabe amended quickly with a hard look at his brother.

Nash's brows rose. He said coolly, "Don't think of it as a marriage; think of it purely as a legal maneuver, like a chess gambit. A marriage between you and my brother would block Count Anton's petition for custody of the boy and mire it in legal arguments, thus giving our government an excuse to delay." He waited a moment and added, "It's my considered opinion that it's the only way to keep your son with you."

He rose. "Gabriel, you were right about the fly in the ointment. I'll leave you two to discuss it in private. It seems to me that there are matters between you two that need to be settled before any agreement can be made. I'll see you at dinner, which is in—" He consulted his pocket watch. "—fifteen minutes."

"What did he mean about the fly in the ointment?" she demanded as soon as the door closed behind Nash.

"Nothing. Just a beautiful fly with lovely green eyes. And the most sweet-smelling ointment," Gabe said soothingly. "Do you remember the smell of the ointment? We have fond memories of ointment, you and I."

She gave him a flat stare.

"Or at least I do," he finished hastily. She was obviously not in the mood for seduction.

"You see, this is why I have such strong doubts about any agreement we might make," she told him. "You don't take women seriously."

"I do take women serio—"

"You take women like Mrs. Barrow seriously. You took your great-aunt Gert seriously, but not me. You never listen to me."

"I do—"

"You ignore my expressed wishes and ride roughshod over my decisions and I cannot and will not put up with it."

Gabriel was shocked. "But that's not how it is at all."

"It is. And when I object you tease me and play seductive games and pretend it hasn't happened. Like now. I have serious concerns—I told you repeatedly before any of this came up that I had no intention of remarrying—and then you talk to me of ointment! And call me a pretty fly! As if my concerns are foolish female nonsense. Well, back in Zindaria men told me my fears that someone was trying to kill my son were foolish female nonsense, and they were wrong and I was right and I won't put up with being treated like a ninny!" She stormed to the window and stood with her back to him. Her chest heaved and her spine was rigid with tension.

She was close to tears, he saw. And she was right. Gabe felt chastened and remorseful. He hadn't meant to belittle her, just coax her into a happier frame of mind.

Had he really been such an overbearing bully? He hadn't meant to be. He'd honestly done what he thought was right.

But he could see how it must look to her.

"It comes from years of being an officer," he said ruefully. "One is expected to decide what is best for everyone under your command. It becomes a habit."

He swallowed. "And the teasing, I don't mean to demean you at all. It is simply my way. What Great-aunt Gert used to call my 'lamentable and ill-timed tendency to levity.' It seems to have gotten worse." He took a deep breath and said resolutely, "But I am willing to change. I don't know if I can," he confessed. "But if you marry me, I promise you I'll try."

There was a long silence from the window embrasure. "I quite like your frivolity at times," she said eventually. "You make me laugh, and I know I'm too serious. But I think sometimes you use frivolity to hide something deeper." She turned and looked at him. "It's a way of dealing with the darker side of life, isn't it? Of showing gaiety in the face of darkness, or skimming over the surface instead of looking into the abyss."

He swallowed, feeling like an insect on a pin. Facing an abyss. "Perhaps. Sometimes. And sometimes it's just . . . I can't help myself. I'm sorry if it annoys you."

She gave him a searching look, then a faint smile. "Sometimes it makes me want to hit you!"

"Then hit me," he said at once. "I have a very thick head and—" He broke off and said ruefully, "I'm doing it again, aren't I?'

She smiled properly now. "Yes, but I don't mind. I don't care how frivolous you are as long as you listen. And you are listening, aren't you?"

"Yes." God, yes, he was listening.

She crossed the room and sat down again, smoothing her skirts and folding her hands in her lap before she began. "You've been honest with me, so I'll try to explain my position," she said. "I know I haven't always made the wisest choices, but deciding for myself is a new experience for me—a very new and precious experience.

"All my life Papa decided everything for me—what I did, what I wore, what I learned, ate, who I met—for every hour of every day. And then, when I was just sixteen, I married Prince Rupert of Zindaria, who ordered my life even more closely and rigidly than Papa.

"And then they they both died within two months of each other, and for a full year I remained trapped in that rigidly ordered life, until my son's life was threatened, and I didn't know who I could trust, so I had to decide for myself what to do because there wasn't another soul in the world I could rely on to protect me.

"So I made a decision—the first and probably the most important one of my life—not a very courageous decision, I admit, to flee, but it was my decision, and we did it—we ran.

"And every day of the next eighteen days I made decision after decision for myself and my son. And some were good and some were mistakes, but they were mine, too, and I learned from them."

She looked at him, "There hasn't been a lot in my life that is truly mine. But I learned something in that time: deciding for oneself can be terrifying. But it's also exhilarating. We got here, Gabriel. I got myself and my son, alone and unaided, across Europe. And I'm proud of it.

"So don't treat me as a foolish child. I was kept that way by my father and then my husband, but I vowed never to return to that state again. I planned never to marry, never to make vows of obedience and duty to any man." Her voice broke.

The speech had upset her again and she rose from her chair and took an agitated few steps around the room. Gabe watched, having no idea how to convince her. The only thing he could think of to do was to grab her and kiss her and not stop until she agreed to marry him.

But something told him she might not welcome that approach just now.

She said, "I understand why my marriage to an Englishman is necessary . . ."

Gabe held his breath.

She chewed her lip, gave him a troubled look, and said, "Perhaps I should ask your brother to find me another candidate."

"Another candidate?" Gabe was stunned. "What other candidate?"

She made an impatient gesture. "I don't know. Someone who won't care what I do, who won't try to order my life, who will let me go my own road. It doesn't really matter, does it? Not with a marriage of convenience. Your brother might even consider it. Marriage to a princess with connections to half the royal families of Europe could be quite an asset to a rising diplomat's career."

"You are *not* marrying my brother!" Gabe exploded.

"Well, no, he was just a case in point," she explained.

"You don't need any case in point—you've got me!"

She frowned. "But you said yourself, you have the habit of command."

He stared wildly at her. How could she even think of marrying someone else? "I'll change," he said.

"No, you won't."

He swallowed. "Probably not enough for your liking, but I promise you I'll try."

She frowned, puzzled and disturbed by his apparent determination to marry her. "It actually sounds like you want to marry me. Why?"

He gave her a blank stare. "Why?" he said in a strangled voice.

"Yes, why? You've known me less than ten days. Why would you want to make a convenient marriage with a woman you hardly know, who doesn't want to be married, and who won't promise to love you or obey you?

It was a good question. He ran a finger around his collar. He cleared his throat. His mind was completely blank. "Er—"

The dinner bell rang. "Dinner," he exclaimed gratefully and gestured toward the door. "Aunt Gosforth hates to be kept waiting."

She didn't move. "When you've answered my question."

Gabe searched for an answer that would satisfy her. The truth would frighten her off, make her run a mile. He knew because it had frightened him half to death.

Outside he could hear people coming down the stairs, gathering in response to the dinner bell.

"Gallantry," he said at last. "Pure, disinterested gallantry. I can't bear to see a woman and child in distress. And I have no plans to marry anyone else. If a convenient marriage is the price of your safety, it's a small price to pay."

She eyed him thoughtfully. "And you don't mind that I

will not promise to love or obey you? That for me it will just be a—a chess tactic?"

"No, I don't mind that at all," he lied with conviction.

She hesitated, then held out her hand. "Then let us shake on this agreement; we shall make a convenient marriage, a paper marriage, and we shall be completely honest with each other from the start."

"Absolutely, honesty from the start," Gabe agreed, uttering the lie with aplomb.

He had no intention of letting it remain as a paper marriage. He felt a slight pang of guilt at lying to her, but repressed it. It was almost the truth.

For some reason she was fearful of putting herself into the hands of a man. Obviously the fault of that clod Prince Rupert.

She needed to learn that with Gabe, she was safe.

Gabe's position was clear also; just not wholly and completely stated. He would try to change his autocratic ways—or at least to listen to her views. He would protect her and her child with his life. And he would marry her.

He could hardly repress the surge of fierce emotion at the thought: his wife.

He grasped her outstretched hand and shook it. "But that's not the way to settle a bargain such as this," he said. "I'm a traditionalist." And he drew her into his arms.

She stiffened warily and stretched her head back away from him. "What are you doing?"

"What do you think I'm doing? What's the expression: seal the bargain with a kiss."

"But we shook on it."

"Yes, and now we'll kiss." He could just take the kiss, he knew, but until now, all their previous kisses had been surprised out of her: stolen. Now, suddenly he wanted a simple, honest kiss from her, a kiss to make a bargain on, a kiss that bore a promise.

"We don't need to kiss," she insisted, her spine braced in resistance against the arm he'd slipped around her back.

He still held her right hand in his right hand, the handshake caught between them. His knuckles grazed her breast. He didn't think she'd noticed.

He noticed. A good part of his attention was on that faint teasing graze of skin against cotton, with warm, soft breast beneath.

He shifted his stance slightly and felt the back of his hand slide against one aroused, hardened nipple.

A shiver went through her at the touch and she glanced down at their linked hands. She'd finally noticed. Her eyes darkened and flickered back up to him. She moistened her lips.

His body instantly reacted. So did she.

She moved, trying to tug her hand free, but he didn't let go and all her movement did was drag his knuckle back across the thrusting nipple. She gasped.

"You're determined on this kiss, aren't you?" Her breathing made her bosom rise and fall.

"Yes." The slight, teasing movement of each breath against the back of his hand drove him wild. He fought to control his body.

"Why? You agreed this would be just a paper marriage."

"To the world, this has to look genuine," he reminded her. "If we want people to rally around to support us against Count Anton's legal petition, we'll need to gain their sympathy."

Her brow puckered as she considered his words.

"There's bound to be a lot of comment on the hurried nature of this wedding. Opinion will fall into two camps; either I have impregnated you and am making an honest woman of you, or we are so madly in love we cannot wait. Either way it will be regarded as a love match, and the world adores lovers."

Her body had softened unconsciously against him as

she accepted the truth of his interpretation. He continued, "However once the news of Count Anton's petition to have your son returned is out—and it will get out—the sharper minds among the *ton* will wonder about this sudden and convenient marriage. So we must convince them—all of them—I am talking about Aunt Maude, and my friends, and everyone—that this is real and that we are in love. Lovers under threat are even more romantic. Count Anton won't stand a chance."

"Your brother knows it's false."

"Nash is a diplomat. He can keep his mouth shut," Gabe said, hoping it was true. He barely knew his brother but he was generally a good judge of character. Despite their bitter history, Nash as an adult had surprised him.

She bit her lip and he tried not to groan. She said, "So we need to pretend to be in love?"

"I think it's a good idea," Gabe said in a dispassionate voice. His body was racked and aching with desire.

"And we start from this moment? With a kiss? To seal the bargain?"

"Yes, and to help us to get into the spirit of things," Gabe said, amazed at how disinterested his voice sounded. Now! his body was roaring silently. Take her now!

She swallowed. "Very well." She licked her lips and raised herself on tiptoe. Gabe lowered his head to meet her, but though it cost him every shred of control at his command, he didn't take her mouth; he wanted her to come to him.

She hesitated, her mouth a bare inch from his. He could feel her soft breath on his skin; she was panting gently. She gazed into his eyes, searching, wondering, uncertain. She was aroused, he could sense it, smell it, but she showed no awareness of it.

She pressed her lips lightly against his and pulled back, watching for his reaction. He didn't move, didn't release her, just waited. And tried to remember to breathe.

She touched her lips to his again, and this time she didn't

pull away. He felt the light touch of her tongue and he opened for her. She wasn't ready for anything more yet and didn't take up his silent invitation but she kissed him hard, pressing her lips openmouthed against his, mouth to mouth and breath to breath. And body to body.

It was enough. It was more than enough considering he couldn't take her here and now.

His knuckles were trapped between them, pressed against her breast. He kissed her back, forcing himself not to take control. His knuckle moved lightly back and forth against her rock-hard nipple and she shuddered and recoiled and pulled back.

He released her instantly. She staggered and he caught her by the waist and steadied her.

She stared at him wide-eyed. Looking shocked and on the verge of panic.

"So that's it," he said in his driest, dullest voice. "The bargain is settled. We will make a convenient marriage and do our best to fool the *ton* into believing we are lovers."

At his mundane response she calmed visibly. Yes, that's what frightened her, he thought. Passion. Prince Rupert must have been a clumsy oaf indeed to treat this treasure of a woman carelessly.

Gabe was not such a fool. He knew a priceless gift when he fished it off a cliff top. He would lavish care on her.

Once she was his, he would seduce her with every shred of power in him. He would do his damnedest to burn this paper marriage in the flames of passion and forge it into something precious and enduring.

He had to teach her to love him.

Because, God help him, he loved her.

Fourteen

"Come along, time to break the news to everyone." Gabriel offered his arm to lead her into the drawing room where everyone had gathered before dinner.

Callie felt as though the pit of her stomach had opened into a great hollow void. She should never have sealed the deal with a kiss. It was a mistake. A huge mistake.

She didn't want to break the news to anyone, didn't want to do anything to take this idea from the realms of fantastical nonsense into grim reality.

Betrothed! To be married. To Gabriel Renfrew.

Pretending to the world that they were in love. She couldn't. She wouldn't.

But she had to, she reminded herself. For Nicky.

And the first thing she had to do was to regain her normal calm mien. Forget the sensations that rocketed through her body when she'd kissed him. It shouldn't have been like that. It was supposed to be a businesslike kiss.

She couldn't face anyone like this, all shivery and hot and unsettled.

She needed a long, relaxing bath. A cold one.

But everyone was waiting to go into dinner. She delayed the moment, hovering in front of the mirror, checking that her hair had not slipped from its knot. For a one-minute arrangement, Lady Gosforth's maid had done an excellent job. It still seemed to be secure. And Lady Gosforth had given her an exquisite shawl of fine crimson cashmere, embroidered with gold thread, saying, "I adore crimson, my dear, but crimson, alas, does not adore me."

It was true, the color was too high for the middle-aged lady but it suited Callie perfectly. It looked so rich and elegant; the drab gray dress was a perfect foil for it.

Last-minute excuses whirled around in her brain. She squashed them.

The marriage would make Nicky safe. It was all that mattered.

She could do this. It was all just for show, an act. The problem last time was that she hadn't listened to all of Papa's talk about what a convenient marriage meant. She'd fallen for Rupert's handsome face and had allowed his attentiveness and gallant compliments to fool her into believing he returned her feelings. She'd convinced herself it was a love match.

She wouldn't do that again.

Forewarned was forearmed.

If she didn't fall in love, she couldn't be hurt. All she had to do was not to fall in love with Gabriel. She could do that.

Once bitten, twice shy.

It was amazing how many excellent mottoes there were to remind her. She'd stitched hundreds of the beastly things. Why hadn't she ever taken notice of them before now?

"What are you thinking?" her husband-to-be murmured.

"A stitch in t—" she began, then amended it hastily. "Just checking my hair."

"You look very beautiful."

Hah! Gallant compliment number one, she told herself.

She peered in the mirror again and saw a round face, undistinguished nose, tidy plain brown hair, and a flushed countenance. So much for very beautiful. She frowned at her rosy cheeks, thinking that perhaps the crimson shawl was the wrong choice after all.

"Come on, you can't spend the rest of your life hiding in here and hoping it will all go away. Dinner will be getting cold and I'm getting very hungry standing here watching you." His voice deepened as he added, "You look like a delicious bonbon wrapped in that red thingummy, so unless you want me to start nibbling on you—"

She whisked herself to the door. He tucked her hand into his arm and led her toward the drawing room. His arm felt warm and strong under her hand. He looked magnificent in his evening clothes.

Not that she cared what he looked like.

He smiled down at her, his eyes warm. She gave him a cool and gracious smile. Calm. Polite. Distant. That was the way to do it.

She wished she could have worn her mother's tiara, for courage and for luck, but it would be quite inappropriate for an informal family dinner. Callie held her head high as they entered the room, all eyes on them.

Mr. Harry Morant, Mr. Rafe Ramsey, Mr. Luke Ripton, and Mr. Nash Renfrew rose from their seats in unison. She blinked, not having seen them dressed formally before. Ethan Delaney would be upstairs, eating with the boys, she recalled. Gabriel had arranged for there always to be someone with Nicky.

"There you are, my dears." Lady Gosforth, who was wearing olive-green silk and diamonds, swept forward. "Take your breath away, don't they, dressed formally and en masse. You should have seen them in their regimentals. My dear, the palpitations! Every female from nineteen to ninety. Now come along, dinner awaits." Commandeering Nash as her escort, she led the way into the dining room.

"I know I should have imported a few females to make up the numbers," Lady Gosforth said as footmen came around the table, serving turtle soup from a silver tureen. She looked around the table with satisfaction. "But why dilute 'em, I say? Whets one's appetite with all this masculine beauty at table, don't you agree, Miss Tibthorpe?"

Tibby, who would never have thought of such a thing, but who, judging by her bright cheeks, was now considering the question, was spared an answer by Gabriel, who calmly changed the subject.

"It might interest you all to know that Princess Caroline and I will be getting married next Friday. Of course, you are all invited."

Callie who had just forced herself to take a mouthful of turtle soup, choked. Under cover of patting her back and offering her a sip of his wine, he murmured, "Did I not warn you about that? It must be soon. Time is of the essence."

Callie took a large gulp of wine and tried to recover her composure. "Yes, Friday," she said as brightly as she could manage. She was aware of Tibby staring at her with dropped jaw and flashed her a bright smile. Tibby jumped up and kissed her, but the faint pucker between her brows told Callie she was still concerned. Alone of all of them, Tibby knew her true feelings about marriage.

There was a chorus of congratulations. Each of the men rose from their seat and came to kiss her hand. Lady Gosforth was torn between excitement and horror: excitement at her nephew's approaching nuptials and horror at the timing.

She ordered the best champagne to be opened and in the same breath berated Gabriel soundly for "rushing the poor girl so that she has no time even to buy her bride clothes, let alone arrange any decent reception."

He smiled at Callie and lifted her hand to his lips, the picture of lover-like impatience. His lips were firm and warm. "It will be just a small, private wedding," he told his aunt.

Lady Gosforth's eyes bulged. "Small and private?" She looked at Callie and stated, "You cannot want a small and private wedding."

"Oh, but I do," Callie assured her, "for I know so few people in London and a small, private wedding would suit me perfectly." The smaller the better. She tried to ignore the way her hand tingled where he'd kissed her. She rubbed it surreptitiously on her napkin, as if she could remove it and somehow regain herself.

She was being stupid, she told herself. It was just a kiss.

"And a reception?" Lady Gosforth demanded.

Gabriel pursed his lips thoughtfully, then conceded, "Well, perhaps a *very* small reception."

Nash added, "With only one's intimate friends and nearest relations invited."

Lady Gosforth nodded. "Very well then, a small party on the following Tuesday, but with no notice at all, it will be positively meager, Gabriel, I'm warning you. It will, of course, be here."

"Meager will do nicely, Aunt, thank you," he said. Callie wondered why his eyes were dancing. As were Nash's. Even Harry who had said very little, looked faintly amused.

Some family joke, no doubt.

"And you are truly happy with a hole-in-the-corner affair?" Lady Gosforth asked Callie.

"Oh yes. Thank you." Callie smiled brightly. "Quite hap—very happy." She could see the pucker between Tibby's brow so she widened her smile, determined to convince her friend there was nothing at all to worry about. "I had a very big wedding once, when I married the prince of Zindaria," she reminded them. "I would like this one to be different."

Lady Gosforth sniffed. "It will certainly be different."

They drank several toasts to the bride and groom in champagne and then, thankfully, the next course was brought in. Callie ate nearly everything that was offered to her and tasted almost nothing. Gabriel was very attentive, passing her dishes and offering her tidbits.

Acting, she reminded herself. It's all acting.

Luckily no one seemed to expect her to make conversation. They all made plans. Plans for her wedding.

Lady Gosforth announced that she would take Callie and Tibby shopping in the morning. And "the boys" would entertain Callie's son and Jim.

And Callie remembered there was something she had to do, before she could go shopping. "Can I see you privately after dinner?" she whispered to Gabriel.

His eyes warmed. "Of course. You can see me wherever you want." He said it deep and low, as if arranging a lovers' tryst.

"Shall we say in the library after the gentlemen have finished their port and joined the ladies?" she suggested in a low but businesslike voice. There was no need to pretend when nobody else could hear.

He lifted her hand and kissed it again. "I shall look forward to it." His eyes caressed her. The place where his lips touched her skin seemed to throb. A shiver passed through her.

Gallant gesture number four, Callie reminded herself. Or was it five? Or six.

After the ladies withdrew to leave the gentlemen to their port and cigars or whatever it was gentlemen did after dinner, Callie found time for a quiet word with Tibby.

Lady Gosforth had swept off in a frenzy of happy planning, consulting with her butler, chef, housekeeper, and secretary. Callie had felt a little uncomfortable letting a relative stranger take on the burden of organizing her wedding and had suggested that she could arrange something suitable herself, but Lady Gosforth told her instantly she was not to think of such a thing.

It was soon borne home to her, most forcibly, that the planning of social events was the breath of life to Lady

Gosforth, and that the lady's only regret was that there was so little scope for her talents.

"Leave it to me, my dears. I know just what to do. All you have to do is be the radiant bride." And she'd swept out, leaving Callie and Tibby alone.

Be the radiant bride indeed, Callie thought and caught Tibby observing her. She gave Tibby a rueful smile. "I expect you're wondering what brought this on."

"I can't say I'm totally surprised," Tibby admitted. "I have noticed a certain intimacy developing between you and Mr. Renfrew."

"Intimacy?"

"Perhaps I should have said a closeness—I wasn't implying anything improper," Tibby corrected hastily.

"There is no intimacy. It is not a love match," Callie explained quickly, unable to bear any misunderstanding between her and Tibby. Bad enough that she had to play the radiant bride for Gabriel's friends and relations, she needed at least one person who knew the truth.

Two people, she amended. Three if you counted Mr. Nash Renfrew. The others might suspect that this hasty wedding had something to do with protecting her son from Count Anton, but Gabriel was pretending to be happy about it, so the least she could do was feign happiness as well. But not to Tibby.

"I do not want it widely known, for obvious reasons, but you are my oldest and dearest friend, so I want you to know. Count Anton has instituted a legal move with the English government to have Nicky returned to Zindaria under his authority as the regent."

"Oh, my dear!" Tibby clasped her hands in horror.

"Yes, so Mr. Nash Renfrew, he is some sort of diplomat in government, he says marrying Gabriel—Mr. Renfrew— will help me keep Nicky here with me. That is why it's to be so soon."

Tibby looked thoughtful. "I can see the logic behind it

all, and of course I understand you must do whatever it takes to protect Nicky . . . but have you thought about how this will affect you in the longer term?"

"What do you mean?"

"I mean . . . what we were talking about the other day, how things were between you and Prince Rupert."

"No. It's not the same at all." She was not going to let it be the same. "Tibby, dear, this wedding is nothing but a stratagem, a—a chess maneuver. It's all been very clear from the start."

Tibby's eyes were troubled. "You have a tender heart, my dear, and Mr. Renfrew is very handsome and can be enormously charming and persuasive."

"I know. And knowing how charming and persuasive he can be is what will prevent the same thing happening again. He is charming and persuasive to everyone—when he is not riding roughshod over their opinions, that is."

Tibby looked unconvinced.

Callie continued, "I am not the foolish girl I once was. I was married for nine years. Now I am a mature woman of five-and-twenty and I have put all that nonsense behind me."

"Do we ever put all that nonsense behind us?" Tibby wondered a little wistfully.

"I cannot speak for every woman, of course," Callie said with all the confidence she wished she had. "But I can for myself. Now I truly understand what a convenient marriage is and can avoid any pitfalls. And I can deal with Mr. Gabriel Renfrew."

Shortly after the gentlemen rejoined the ladies, Callie rose and excused herself. All the gentlemen rose and she felt ridiculously self-conscious, as though she was wearing a sign saying she was off to a secret tryst.

Tibby immediately jumped up, too, and said that if Lady Gosforth didn't mind, she had some lessons to prepare. Lady Gosforth said she quite understood and had lists to make.

It was a signal for the evening to break up. Gabriel's brother Nash and his other friends took their leave and Gabriel sauntered out into the street to farewell them.

Callie hurried upstairs to her bedchamber, grabbed the fabric bundle, and went back down to the library to wait. A few minutes later the door opened and Gabriel entered.

He seated them both on a chaise longue. "Now, what was it you wanted to discuss?"

"If we are to go shopping tomorrow, I will need money."

"Yes, of course." He reached into his pocket and pulled out a roll of notes.

She stared. "No, I didn't mean you should give me money. I wanted to ask you to get some for me. Papa left money in trust for me, but it'll take some time for the lawyers to release it. In the meantime I'll need money."

He looked rather taken aback. And intrigued. "How do you mean to do that?" He did not put his money away.

"I want you to sell some jewels for me." She took out the rolled fabric and showed him the jewels she had unpicked, hoping they would be enough.

He bent over the fabric, fascinated. "Is that what I think it is?"

"Which piece do you mean?"

"This." He seized the fabric and lifted it so it unrolled. She managed to catch the loose jewels before they fell to the floor.

"It is!" he exclaimed. "It's a petticoat!"

She snatched it out of his hands.

"So you were smuggling after all," he said. "I'm marrying a beautiful jewel smuggler."

"I was not smuggling," she snapped, bundling the petticoat up in embarrassment. "I carried them sewn into my petticoat for fear of thieves."

"Some people would call Customs and Excise officers

and the taxes they enforce a kind of thieving, but we won't quibble." He observed the remaining lumps and bumps still sewn into the petticoat. "Would these be one of the reasons Count Anton is pursuing you?"

"No! They are all my own jewels. None of them belong to the royal house of Zindaria—and you need not look at me like that, they don't."

"I was simply thinking how indignation makes your eyes sparkle brighter than any emeralds."

She decided to ignore that. He was a master of distraction.

"These are all jewels Papa or Rupert gave me: for my betrothal, for my wedding, for birthdays and other occasions. My husband was always very clear and specific about which things belonged to me personally, which were family jewels, and which belonged to the crown. I have brought only those which belong to me, personally. These pearls, for instance, Papa gave me for my sixteenth birthday. I wore them at my wedding."

"Then you are most certainly not going to sell them."

She looked at him in frustration. Only this afternoon he had promised not to ride roughshod over her decisions and now, here he was arguing with her. "They are mine to sell."

"And what if you have a daughter?"

She stared at him in surprise. "I won't." She'd had one child in nine years of marriage, and now she was entering a paper marriage. How did he imagine she would have another child?

He set his jaw stubbornly. "You might. But even if you don't, when Nicky takes a bride, wouldn't you like him to give her his mother's pearls to wear at her wedding? Or if one day he has a daughter going to her first grown-up party, wouldn't she feel special wearing her granny's pearls?"

She hesitated. She hadn't thought of Nicky wanting any of her jewels. She'd only thought of them as her funds to start a new life. "Why do you care?"

He shrugged and looked away. "It's just that I know that

women can be sentimental about things. Like that tiara of yours. It matters to you that it belonged to your mother."

"Yes, it does."

"So you wouldn't think of selling that."

She laughed. "No, I wouldn't, but not for the reason you imagine."

"Why not?"

"Because the diamonds in my mother's tiara are paste."

His jaw dropped.

"I told you my mother was from a very distinguished, very poor family—all the jewels were paste in the end. But they are very good quality paste and will fool all but an expert." She grinned. "As Mama used to say: 'We are, after all, royalty; if my jewels are to be paste they must be the finest paste in Europe.' "

He chuckled. "I like the sound of your mother."

"Yes, she was lovely," she said mistily.

"When did she die?"

"When I was a little girl. An accident with a horse. Papa married her because she was a princess, but I think they fell in love afterward. I always like to think so, anyway."

He didn't say anything, but she could feel his gaze on her.

"Papa always wanted to replace them with real diamonds, but I did not want him to, for then it would not be Mama's tiara anymore."

She took a deep breath and returned to the subject at hand. "But I must sell some of these jewels and I need your help to do so, as I don't know my way around London yet."

"Why do you need money?" he demanded.

She stared at him. "What a stupid question! Because I do. I'm going shopping tomorrow, for a start."

"You won't need money for that. Have them send their accounts to me at this address. And for any trinkets, here." He started to peel banknotes off.

"No, stop it," she told him. "That's not fair. Why should you be out of pocket for my clothes?"

He said through gritted teeth. "Because you are to become my wife and a man provides for his wife."

"I will be a paper wife only," she began, then said hastily as a speculative look suddenly lit his eyes, "and if you try to demonstrate that I am flesh and blood, Gabriel, I will smack you! I am being serious here and you promised me this afternoon that you would not ride roughshod over my opinions."

"I'm not," he said. "I'm listening."

She rolled her eyes.

"I am merely discussing options with you," he explained.

"Well, listen to this: I owe you enough as it is, without owing you the very clothes on my back. I have my pride, just as you do."

"I see," he said quietly.

"And as well as clothes for myself and Tibby and Nicky, I will need money to cover the expense of the wedding reception."

He folded his arms again. "That does not concern you."

"It does," she argued, frustrated. "If this was a normal wedding, my family would pay for the wedding and the reception. It's traditional: the bride's family pays."

"Yes, but you are a widow without close family. Besides, my aunt will have a fit if anyone—you or I—tried to reimburse her. It is her pleasure, her gift to us." The stubborn line to his jaw was back again.

"There is no *us*."

"Isn't there?" he said. "It looks very much like there is to me. It is the whole point of this marriage."

She frowned, wondering if he really did mean that. And why he kept referring to it as a marriage, when really, it was just a wedding. "But—"

"No, you are quite right, at the moment we are two separate entities," he said angrily. "*This* is us." And he kissed her. Thoroughly. And very possessively.

She emerged from the embrace flustered but determined not to show it. She could handle it—him.

"Stop it—you will not distract me from my purpose. If you won't help me sell my jewels, I'll find someone who will."

He glared at her for a long moment. "You're an infuriatingly stubborn woman," he said at last. "Very well, hand the blasted things over. It will take some time to effect the sale, so in the meantime have all your accounts sent to me at this address—and yes, I'll keep a separate account for you if you insist—and take this for pin money."

She tucked the banknotes he passed her into her reticule and gave him the jewels. The pearls, too. They would fetch a very good price, she knew. A woman making a paper marriage for political reasons with a man she had known less than two weeks could not afford to be sentimental.

He saw the pearls among them and his face darkened. He carefully separated them from the tangle of jewelry she'd given him and dumped them back in her lap.

"I might agree to sell some of your precious trinkets, but not these," he growled. "There is a limit."

"Didn't you listen to a thing I said?" she began.

"I listened to everything," he said shortly. "And I'll sell these other blasted bits and bobs, since you insist—though it goes very much against the grain. But the pearls your father gave you for your sixteenth birthday are not for sale. They are for your daughter, or your granddaughter. You will not sacrifice everything, dammit!"

He stalked out of the room, leaving her with a lap full of pearls and a lump in her throat.

*I*n the morning they woke to soft, steady drizzle. The weather would not affect the shoppers, but the plans to take Nicky and Jim for a riding lesson in the park had to be postponed. However, as a visit to the Tower of London to see the wild beasts, followed by an excursion to Astley's Amphitheatre was to take its place, the boys were not too cast down.

Lady Gosforth had sent for Giselle, her own mantua maker, to come and measure up Callie and Tibby, and to choose designs for the wedding dress and other dresses.

Giselle, an elegant, acidic-looking Frenchwoman, had flung up her hands in horror. "*Mais* milady, *ce n'est pas possible*—such short notice!"

Lady Gosforth raised an eyebrow. "Not even for a royal wedding, Giselle—the 'secret' royal wedding of Princess Caroline of Zindaria?" She made a careless gesture. "In that case we will have to call on Madame—"

Giselle visibly melted. "A *royal* wedding? *Non, non.* I speak without thinking," Giselle said hastily, her sharp black eyes assessing Callie swiftly. "I have just recall that I 'ave a cancellation. I 'ave assistants to take care of other matters." She snapped her fingers and the assistant leapt forward with the tape measure. "I will devote myself to the princess."

Callie and Tibby were caught up in a whirlwind of designs and choices. Callie had to be firm, refusing to order the number of dresses Giselle and Lady Gosforth assured her was necessary.

Giselle soon regretted her sudden cancellation, as the princess seemed regrettably uninterested in the latest kick of fashion.

"They are too heavily ornamented," Callie insisted. "Look, this design looks more like a wedding cake than a dress."

But after some discussion, they finally were able to agree on the design for her wedding dress. It was to be was made of café au lait satin, very simply cut with a little lace at the sleeves and neck. Giselle became passionate about a border of frilled and plaited white and coffee satin around the hem, neck, and entirely covering the short sleeves, but Callie put her foot down. She agreed to a plaited border, but no frills.

"I don't want to look dowdy and unfashionable," she told them, "but my dresses will be of my own choosing. And not frilly. I am not a frilly person."

Giselle gave a sniff that indicated she entirely agreed. It was not a compliment. Royalty, the sniff gave them to understand, was not what it used to be.

They visited silk warehouses with Giselle, where they selected dozens of lengths of fabric to be made up. She and Tibby tried them out, holding up swathe after swathe of colored material—silk and satin for Callie, Tibby stubbornly maintaining she needed bombazine, cotton, and wool.

They preened like young girls over all the colors, and Callie bullied Tibby into a blue silk dress for her wedding, saying, "It brings out the color of your eyes, Tibby," and then unguardedly, "Oh, Ethan will love that on you!"

Poor Tibby blushed furiously and put the blue silk aside. Callie ordered it secretly.

She felt dreadful about her slip. Tibby had a *tendre* for the big Irishman, she knew, but they both knew there was no possibility of a match between two such different people with such different backgrounds. It had been careless and cruel of her to suggest there could be anything between them.

Callie ordered dresses in bright, brilliant colors; morning dresses in rose and green and peach. She ordered a walking dress of green and gold cambric and another in sky blue; an emerald pelisse with scarlet and white trimmings; a blue spencer with white satin frogging that quite wrung her heart, it was so beautiful.

Her favorite of all her new purchases was a scarlet cloak in fine wool with a hood and black silk velvet trim, to replace the cloak she'd left on the ship. She held the fabric up against her and examined it in the looking glass, and heard, *You look like a delicious bonbon wrapped in that red thingummy* . . .

She flushed at the memory and was about to choose a green fabric instead, but changed her mind. She'd never worn scarlet before. Why let his words stop her? Besides, she liked feeling like a bonbon.

They bought stockings in silk and cotton; ordered new corsets and purchased chemises, petticoats, drawers, and nightgowns.

"You aren't going to buy those!" Lady Gosforth exclaimed at one point.

"Yes, why not?" Callie had selected several cotton nightgowns and one of flannel. "They will last well and be warm."

Lady Gosforth was so shocked she could not speak for a full minute. "One doesn't buy a nightgown for warmth and durability! Not at your age, and not when you are about to become a bride!"

"I do," Callie said firmly and bought the nightgowns she'd chosen.

Lady Gosforth gave a sniff that outdid Giselle's in scorn for the state of royalty today, but Callie didn't care.

She wanted to splurge on the sort of clothes she'd craved, but was also aware of the need to conserve them and to have as flexible a wardrobe as possible. She was having fun. And she was answerable to no one. It was a heady feeling.

*T*he night before her wedding, Callie woke in the middle of the night to the sound of rain falling, pattering steadily on the window panes and gurgling down the gutters.

It wasn't the rain that had woken her. It was dreams. Dreams of kisses. Disturbing kisses that woke her in the night, hot and with her nightgown twisted around her.

It was very hard to take a kiss calmly and politely, especially the way Gabriel did it.

She wished he kissed like Rupert.

No, she didn't.

She didn't know what she wanted.

Yes, she did. But it wasn't going to happen. This was going to be a paper marriage, a maneuver, a chess strategy. As soon as Count Anton was defeated, it would be over. They would go their different ways, married but with separate lives.

Would Count Anton ever be defeated?

She slipped out of bed. She should not be dwelling on gloomy things. Just because it was night and raining didn't mean she had to be dreary, too. She pushed her feet into the too-big slippers she still had from Mrs. Barrow and shuffled to the window. Drawing back the curtains, she looked out.

The rain had softened from its initial heavy downpour. Now it continued in a steady drizzle, making constantly changing rivulets down the windowpane, trickles of water meeting and joining, then splitting again. Like people.

Gabriel would go his own way one day, too. Pure disinterested gallantry would only stretch so far.

The lights of the gas streetlamps glowed through the rain like fuzzy golden haloes glowing in the darkness. The rain dripped from the eaves, picking up the light of the gas lamps like a string of golden pearls.

She glanced at her pearls, sitting on the dressing table where she'd dropped them, and picked them up. They were so long she used to wear them wrapped around her neck several times. Such pure, perfectly graded spheres. She ran them through her fingers, admiring the luster and sheen and feel of them, and remembering.

The first time she'd worn them had been at her sixteenth birthday party. She'd worn them a few days later, at her wedding to the handsome, golden prince, the embodiment of all her lonely dreams.

She hadn't worn her pearls for years. Not since the day she'd visited Rupert in the woods.

But they were beautiful. She recalled Gabriel's words, *The pearls your father gave you for your sixteenth birthday are not for sale. They are for your daughter, or your grand-daughter.*

He was right, she decided. It was not Papa's fault, nor the pearls, that Rupert had not loved her. She would keep them for her future granddaughter. And in the meantime she would wear them again, starting with her wedding to-morrow, a gesture of faith in the future.

Fifteen

*C*allie took a deep breath and stepped inside the church. And stopped, horrified.

The church was full. Not standing-room-only full, but more than a hundred people full. Mostly sitting on the groom's side of the church.

It was supposed to be a small, private ceremony.

Now she had more than a hundred witnesses for what she was about to do. She'd been feeling sick with nerves all morning. Now she started to shake.

The music of the organ swelled. A ripple of anticipation went through the congregation and a hundred faces turned toward her.

She wanted to bolt.

"Come on, Mama." Her son tugged her hand. Her little boy in his formal suit looked so handsome and earnest and determined. Nicky was giving the bride away.

Tibby, her bridesmaid in blue, stepped forward. "Callie, what's the matter?" she whispered.

"I can't do this, not with all these people there," Callie whispered back.

"Why not? It is the same thing, whether there is one or a hundred people watching," Nicky said in a reasonable voice.

Callie had to laugh. Men started young at this. Being rational when the problem was emotional. It settled her. In just such a patient voice he'd explained to her that west was where the sun set. When they were standing in the sea at midnight.

"My wise, wonderful son," she said and bent and kissed him on the forehead. He bore it manfully, then tucked her hand firmly in the crook of his arm and led her down the aisle.

He was happy for her to marry Gabriel, he'd told her when she'd first broached the matter with him. He'd thought about it for several minutes and then declared that Mr. Renfrew would make a very good stepfather.

His words had shocked her. She'd taken pains to explain that it didn't mean anything, that it was just a formality, just a way of stopping Count Anton's petition. Like a chess maneuver.

Nicky was very good at chess, she was certain he understood what she was telling him. He nodded seriously all through her careful explanation, and he thought about it for a few moments afterward. And then his intense little face had lit up, and he'd made his decision: he approved.

So here she was, marrying Gabriel Renfrew. He stood at the altar waiting for her, tall and solemn and unbelievably handsome, devouring her with his eyes; the sort of man who could steal a girl's heart if she wasn't careful.

Callie was determined to be careful.

She looked at the faces of the congregation as she passed.

On the groom's side of the church the only person she recognized was Mr. Nash Renfrew, who stood there with a tall, unsmiling man. He stared at her with coldly assessing Renfrew eyes; Gabriel's estranged brother the earl, no doubt.

She was curious about the few who were sitting on the bride's side, and as she reached their pews they turned to look at her. She felt a lump in her throat as she saw their faces. Mr. Ramsey, Mr. Ripton, and Mr. Delaney stood together, the groom's best friends, claiming the bride as part of their family. In the pew behind them stood Mr. and Mrs. Barrow, dressed in their Sunday best, Mrs. Barrow in a magnificent straw hat lavishly trimmed with flowers. She beamed at Callie and burst into tears. Barrow produced a handkerchief and handed it to her, and Mrs. Barrow leaned against him and sighed gustily at the bride. How wonderful it must be to have a marriage like that, to love for a lifetime.

A woman in a magnificent purple turban turned: it was Lady Gosforth, clutching a wisp of lace to her eye and beaming at Callie. She looked as proud and as happy as if she were Callie's own mother.

Sitting with her was a group of other ladies, Lady Gosforth's circle of intimate friends. She recognized their faces. She'd met them once or twice in the last few days. She couldn't even remember their names.

And yet, here they were, these ladies, pillars of the *ton*, come to see her married, sitting on her side of the church, and smiling, moist-eyed, at the bride as if she weren't some stranger with no family, but one of their own.

Callie managed a misty smile back. Her eyes blurred with tears. Such kindness . . . Such kindness . . .

And then they were at the end of the aisle and he stood there, Gabriel Renfrew, hand outstretched, watching her, waiting to claim her hand.

His gaze caressed her, then he looked at her son and gave him a small nod of approval. Nicky's chest puffed out proudly as he bowed and stepped back.

More tears prickled at her lashes. Gabriel would make a very good stepfather. But it could not to be. Her future, eventually, was back in Zindaria, as mother to the prince. He had property and friends and family here.

Behind him stood his brother Harry, his best man, looking somber. He had the Renfrew eyes, too, except his were gray, like the earl's. Harry caught Nicky's eye and winked. Callie felt a rush of gratitude at the easy acceptance these men had given Nicky.

Gabriel took her trembling hand in his and they stepped forward to be married. His hand was warm and a little damp. She glanced at him. Surely he was not nervous, too?

"Dearly beloved, we are gathered together . . ."

Her thoughts drifted.

"First, it was ordained for the procreation of children . . ."

Children. There would be no children of this union. A paper marriage. Paper children.

"Secondly, it was ordained for a remedy against sin, and to avoid fornication . . ."

She stared at the hand that held hers so firmly, his large thumb rubbing back and forth across her skin.

She heard Gabriel saying his vows, ". . . To have and to hold . . . to love and to cherish . . ."

She didn't want to listen. Paper vows, false promises.

And then it was her turn to repeat after the minister: "I, Caroline Serena Louise, take thee, Gabriel Edward Fitzpaine Renfrew, to my wedded husband, to have and to hold from this day forward, for better for worse, for richer for poorer, in sickness and in health, to"—mumble—"cherish, and to"—mumble—"till death us do part, according to God's holy ordinance; and thereto I give thee my troth."

The minister looked at her and frowned. She'd mumbled the love and obey bits so they were quite unintelligible.

She gave Gabriel a rueful glance. His lips were tight. She'd warned him she wasn't going to promise to love and obey him. She took her promises seriously. Even paper vows.

Fulfilling a promise to love a husband had broken her heart once; she wasn't going to do it again. Especially not for a chess-maneuver wedding.

It wasn't her fault that a hundred people were there to see her embarrass her new husband. She hadn't intended anyone except Gabriel and the minister to hear. She hoped they hadn't; she'd spoken all her vows in a soft voice.

The minister looked a silent query at Gabriel.

He gave a terse shake of his head, and the minister gave a small shrug and continued. He finished the ceremony quickly. Callie was so relieved she almost missed "You may kiss the bride."

Gabriel turned toward her and for the longest moment stared at her with an odd, intense expression. Then he lifted her clear off her feet and kissed her full on the mouth in front of everyone. It was a proud, possessive kiss, a public claiming, a promise.

It shook her, to have him kiss her like that, so unguardedly, with passion, in a church, in front of a hundred witnesses.

It was supposed to be a paper wedding.

Wasn't it?

After the wedding, in a move that surprised the groom as well as the bride, everyone present was invited back to Alverleigh House for a wedding breakfast—even though it was already early evening. Everyone except the bride, the groom, and the groom's best man, his brother Harry, had known about it. It turned out that Lady Gosforth, the earl of Alverleigh, and his brother Nash Renfrew had organized the whole day. Between them they'd managed to entice some of the most influential people in London to the wedding.

Nash had explained to Callie why: the more important people who could put pressure on the government to deny Count Anton's claim, the better.

The day had been full of surprises and Callie was resigned to it. There had been a complete takeover of her small, private ceremony and there was nothing she could do. Besides, it was all for Nicky's benefit, so who could argue or resist such wonderful kindness?

Several times she caught herself wishing it could all be real. She stomped on those thoughts.

Gabe and Harry were furious with the earl for taking over and hosting the reception. "Typical high-handed arrogance," Gabe fumed to Nash. "Tell him I won't be patronized by him and I'm damned if I'll dance to his tune."

"It's a peace offering, Gabriel," Nash told him. "An apology for past wrongs."

"I don't need his—"

"It's a public declaration of support for your wife. Everyone in the church will be there to meet the princess."

Gabe shut his mouth and glared at Nash. Damned slippery diplomat. He'd said the one thing that could stop Gabe from snubbing the earl publicly.

He glanced at Harry, who shrugged. "No choice, Gabe. You know it. Outflanked and outgunned." He turned to Nash and said, "But that doesn't mean that I have to go."

Gabe grabbed him hard by the elbow. "Oh yes, you do, dammit, Harry. If I have to swallow my pride, so do you."

Harry made to pull away, but then he met Gabe's eye, sighed, and accepted his fate.

*I*t was quite late by the time the last of the wedding guests left Alverleigh House. The servants had cleared up and melted discreetly away. Now there just remained Gabe's friends, his brothers, and Aunt Maude. Miss Tibthorpe and Ethan had taken the little boys back to Aunt

Maude's sometime earlier. Gabe looked at his bride. She was looking distinctly sleepy. He rose and held out his hand to her. "Shall we depart, my dear?"

"No, Gabriel," his aunt interrupted. "You two are staying here. You have the house to yourselves; the servants have been given the evening off, but will be back by morning. Marcus has lent you the house for the week—in fact for as long as you need it."

"What?" Gabe looked around for the earl. Apart from a formal greeting and a stiff thank you for his support of his wife, Gabe had barely exchanged a word with his oldest brother.

Nash said, "He's already gone. He's like Father was; hates town, prefers to be at Alverleigh. But he made arrangements for you to stay. And I do think it's an excellent idea. Give it out that you two have gone on your honeymoon."

"What do you mean give it out," said Aunt Maude. "They *are* on their honeymoon."

"I meant instead of traveling out of town," Nash corrected himself smoothly. "The princess will not want to leave her son."

"No," Callie said. "I won't leave Nicky behind."

"Nonsense, you need a few days alone with your new husband," Aunt Maude declared. "This is perfect. You are just around the corner from your son and he's perfectly safe with me: Miss Tibthorpe and Mr. Delaney are with him constantly. Besides, there is no place for a child on a honeymoon. Children usually come afterward."

"But—"

But there was no stopping his aunt in full flight. "I've had all of Callie's things removed to the rose bedroom upstairs, left at the top of the stairs, my dear. The entire house has been redecorated since you were here last, so there can be no unpleasant associations for you, Gabriel. Your things are here, too. Accept it graciously, my boy, and we shall be off." She surged to her feet, kissed him on the cheek, embraced Callie warmly, and swept out.

Gabe swallowed his objections. More than anything else he wanted to be alone with his reluctant bride and begin the tantalizing process of seducing her, but he could see from her face that she was uncomfortable about being alone with him. The slightest excuse and she'd be back at his aunt's and there was no possibility of seduction in that situation. He just wished it didn't have to be at Alverleigh House, the home of his lonely early years.

Still, he could make happier memories . . .

He and Callie walked to the front hall hand in hand, and farewelled their well-wishers. He grasped her hand firmly. He wouldn't put it past her to run after them and jump in the carriage. She was trembling again.

Just before he left Nash told Gabe, "I shall notify the officials concerned that the princess is now an English citizen. That should clog up the works nicely. Oh, and I let fall a few hints this evening that you were off to Brighton on your honeymoon, and the child was going with you. Thought a red herring or two would help draw any interested parties away, at least until Aunt Maude's party."

Gabe nodded. It was good strategy. He held out his hand to his brother. "I want to thank you for everything you've done for my wife. You're a good man, Nash, and I owe you an apology for—"

"Nonsense." Nash wrung his hand. "It was all our parents' making, and it's behind us now. I just wish you would give Marcus a chance—"

"Don't push it, brother. I'll try to put the past behind me, but there's Harry to think of."

Nash nodded. "I know."

Harry had left Alverleigh House early. Gabe knew exactly why. It was the scene of one of Harry's biggest humiliations.

But this was no time to dwell on the past. He had a future to build, with a woman who wanted no part of him.

Or thought she didn't.

C allie found the rose bedroom. It was a pretty, spacious room, painted in shades of cream and rose. A large, oval looking glass hung over the mantelpiece. Satin drapes in striped dark rose and cream lined the large windows and thick Persian rugs carpeted the floor. A fire had been lit and the bed turned down in readiness.

Her new clothes had been unpacked and hung in the wardrobe and the rest of her things were in a chest of drawers.

Callie sat down on the bed. It was wonderfully soft, with a thick feather mattress. She leaned back, heard something crackle, and looked down. It was a tissue-wrapped parcel. The note said simply, "With love from Tibby."

Intrigued, Callie picked it up. It was light and squishy.

She removed the ribbon and unwrapped the parcel. It was something in white silk. She lifted it and her eyes widened. It was a nightgown, but nothing like any nightgown Callie had ever worn. It was beautiful, with delicate embroidery around the neck, but so fine and sheer she could see her fingers faintly through the fabric.

Tibby had given her this? Sensible, spinsterly *Tibby*? She couldn't believe it.

She smiled and refolded the nightgown. It was not at all practical, but still, it was a lovely gift. And it must have cost her a fortune. She set it aside and found herself yawning. She was so tired.

There was a bell pull hanging beside the bed, so she pulled it and waited. After a few minutes she pulled it again. Still nothing.

Suddenly Callie recalled Lady Gosforth's statement

that the servants had all been dismissed for the night. That did not really mean all, surely? Not the maids as well.

She needed a maid to get her out of her wedding dress. It was fastened down the back with dozens of tiny mother-of-pearl buttons, and though she might be able to manage them at a pinch, underneath the dress she wore a specially made corset that was laced tightly at the back. She could never get that undone by herself.

She opened the door and stepped out into the corridor. "Excuse me," she called.

"Yes?" said a deep voice behind her.

Callie almost leapt out of her skin. "Gabriel, you startled me."

He looked amused. "Who else did you expect?"

"A maidservant?" she said hopefully.

He shook his head. "Need help to get out of that dress, I expect."

She nodded, and he said, "Come on then." And before she realized what he was about, he guided her back into the bedchamber, twirled her around, and started undoing her buttons.

She jumped away and faced him. "Wh—what are you doing?"

"Undoing your buttons. There is no maid and you won't get a wink of sleep in that dress."

"But you're a man."

He gave one of those slow, crooked smiles that had such a disturbing effect on her. "I know." He turned her around again and said, "Don't be missish, they're only buttons, and I am your husband."

He was right. It might only be a paper marriage, but she was a mature woman and she could be rational about this. As he'd said, they were only buttons.

There was no such thing as "only buttons" she decided two minutes later. She could feel every movement he made as his long fingers undid tiny button after tiny button.

There was no sound in the room, only the crackling of the fire and the sound of his breathing. She could almost feel his breath on the nape of her neck, though that was silly. He wasn't standing that close.

She glanced across at the beautiful looking glass that hung over the fireplace. She could see him in profile, frowning with concentration over the buttons, his face part in shadow, part in light.

His fingertips brushed her skin and she shivered.

"Are you cold?"

"A little," she prevaricated. The shiver had nothing to do with cold and everything to do with . . . him. His touch.

"Then let us stand closer to the fire."

They moved, and now she could see him in the looking glass even more clearly, as he bent to the task of the fiddly buttons.

He worked his way downward, and she felt the dress coming away at the back. She clutched it to her breasts to keep it up.

"Shall I lift it over your head or would you prefer to step out of it?"

"Neither, thank you. I will do that later. If you could just unfasten the hook and the laces now . . ."

She saw his mouth quirk in the slow smile she found so irresistible, but he said nothing and set to work on the corset.

"I don't know why you women do this do yourselves," he muttered. "It must be deuced uncomfortable."

"It's not," she assured him. "It was made for me, especially to wear with evening dresses, my wedding dress in particular."

"You did look beautiful in it," he said and met her gaze in the mirror. She realized then that he'd known all along she'd been watching him.

"You look even more beautiful out of it," he murmured and parted it. Without taking his eyes off hers in the mirror, he drew one long finger slowly down her spine, from the nape of her neck to the small of her back. Even though she was still wearing her chemise she arched against his finger as if it were flesh against flesh.

She quickly stepped away and turned to face him, clutching her sagging wedding dress and corset to her like a shield. "Thank you for your help," she told him. "I shall manage on my own now."

She couldn't see the expression in his eyes, they were in shadow. For a moment she thought he wasn't going to move, but then he simply bowed and said, "I shall leave you alone then."

The door shut behind him and she let out a huge sigh of relief. At least she told herself it was relief. She felt a bit . . . hollow.

She dropped her dress and corset, stepped out of them, then picked them up and draped the dress carefully over a chair. She stretched and gave her ribs a brisk rub. The corset wasn't uncomfortable but it was tight, and it was lovely to be free of the constriction.

There was some lukewarm water in a jug on a small table and she used it to give herself a quick rub over with a washcloth and soap in front of the fire. She would have preferred a bath, but with no servants in the house, that wasn't possible.

She looked through the chest of drawers for her nightgown. She'd bought several on her shopping expeditions, but none of them were there. She went through the drawers twice. No, whoever had packed her things had forgotten nightgowns.

She would have to sleep in her chemise, she decided. Her eye fell on the silk nightgown Tibby had given her. It was scandalously thin, but the bed was soft and warm and, after all, one should use a gift in the spirit in which it was given. She slipped out of her chemise and into the nightgown. It slithered softly down her body, like a cool flow of water.

It felt lovely. She glanced at her reflection in the looking glass. Heavens. She looked virtually naked. She could see the smudge of darkness at the apex of her thighs. She stared again. It looked like her breasts were slightly different sizes. Surely not. She squinted and yes, they were, not by much, but definitely there was a difference. She looked down at them. How had she never known that? Or had it just happened recently?

She'd never really looked at herself naked in a mirror. In the palace the only looking glasses in her apartments were in the dressing room, and there she'd always had at least one maid with her, dressing her and undressing her. And although she could have stared at her reflection if she'd wanted, it was an embarrassing thing to do when someone was watching.

Now she was alone and free to look, and look she did, turning herself all around, twisting her head to see herself from behind. She was a bit fat, she decided, especially her backside. It didn't look so big in dresses, though. Maybe it was the nightgown. Experimentally she lifted the nightgown and looked at the reflection of her naked buttocks. Definitely fat, she thought. Certainly not "beautiful" as he'd said. She sighed. Gallant compliment number eighty-seven.

Suddenly there was a knock on the door and she leapt in fright, dropping the nightgown back guiltily and covered herself with her arms.

"Who is it?"

"It's Gabriel, of course," said a familiar, deep voice.

Of course. There was no one else in the house. "What do you want?" she called.

To her horror, the door opened. She snatched up her dress from the chair and used it to cover herself decently. "What do you think you are doing?" she demanded breathlessly.

"Coming to bed," he said. He'd removed his coat and

waistcoat and his neck cloth lay untied around his neck. The top of his shirt was open.

"What? Here?"

"Yes, here." He walked across to the large wardrobe on the other side of the room and opened a door, saying, "My clothes are here, haven't you noticed?"

She hadn't. "But my clothes are here," she told him.

"That's probably why there are two wardrobes and two chests of drawers," he suggested. He sat down on a low chair and proceeded to remove his shoes and stockings.

"You mean both of us are to sleep here?"

"Exactly." He stood up and then didn't move.

"No," she told him, wondering what he was doing. He was staring not quite at her, but at something over her shoulder.

He smiled. "Simply beautiful," he murmured.

She glanced over her shoulder but all she could see was the fire and the looking glass. Then she realized. The looking glass! He could see her back view in the looking glass. In the transparent nightgown.

"Stop that!"

"I can't," he said simply.

She started to turn and then realized that either way she was exposed, so she edged her way to the bed and with some difficulty slipped between the covers. Pulling them up to her chin she ordered him to leave.

"Can't," he said. "We need to make this marriage legal."

"It is legal. You said Nash arranged the license."

"Yes, all that part is legal and aboveboard, but now we have to consummate it."

"Consummate? But you said—"

"Yes?" His eyebrow rose quizzically.

"You said it was a paper marriage. A strategy. A—a chess maneuver."

He raised both eyebrows. "You want to play chess? Now?"

"You know what I mean."

"I know." The faintly teasing look faded. "It is what I said it would be, but the count is going to try everything, I'm certain, and this is one loophole he will be sure to check. If I slept in another room, and you were asked to swear later if you'd lain with me on your wedding night, would you be able to lie convincingly?"

She bit her lip, knowing he was right. She wasn't a convincing liar at all. "So we must consummate this marriage?" she whispered.

He sighed. "Not if you don't want to. If we sleep together then you can tell any judge or government official who is impertinent enough to inquire that, yes, we did sleep together. They will make the assumption."

Callie thought it over. She could do that. But they would have to share a bed. She swallowed.

The only person who'd ever shared her bed was her son and that was only since they'd fled Zindaria. Rupert had never stayed with her after his monthly marital visits. He preferred to sleep in his own apartments.

She surveyed the bed. It was big, more than big enough for two people.

"All right," she said grudgingly. "But only to ensure the legality of this marriage. And only if you promise me you will not pounce on me."

He gave her a shocked look. "Pounce? I never pounce. I have far more sophistication than that." He pulled his shirt off, then started to undo the buttons at his waist.

"What are you doing?" She felt as tense as a violin string.

"Getting undressed. I'm not sleeping in my trousers."

"Are you wearing drawers?" she demanded.

"Yes."

"Then leave them on," she ordered. She lay down and squeezed her eyes tight shut. She could get through this. It was a few hours, no more. It was just sleeping, nothing else. And it would make Nicky safe. All she had to do was keep herself safe from her husband. And the only way to do that was to keep him at a distance.

She could hear him removing his trousers. She sneaked a peek and saw him padding around the room in nothing but a pair of light cotton drawers, blowing out candles and turning out lamps.

He bent and put some more coal on the fire. Firelight turned his hard-muscled body to bronze and gold and ebony. He was lean and hard and beautiful.

All she had to do was keep him at a distance.

The bed creaked as he slipped into bed beside her.

The fire hissed softly. Flames caused shadows to dance on the ceiling. Callie lay on her back, stiff as a board, her arms crossed over her chest, wishing she was wearing the thick pink flannel nightgown Mrs. Barrow had lent her that first night.

"It was a very nice wedding, wasn't it?" he said conversationally.

"Yes. Good night," she said tightly. She didn't want to talk to him, not like this, sharing a bed with the fire dancing. It was too intimate.

"You looked a bit upset at the number of people in attendance at the service."

"Yes, I was. But Nash explained afterward. I don't know why nobody told me before. But now is not the time to discuss things. I would like to sleep, please. Good night."

"Yes, good night. And sweet dreams, Mrs. Renfrew."

Callie's eyes flew open. Mrs. Renfrew. Nobody had called her that before. At the wedding breakfast everyone had addressed her as Princess. Mrs. Renfrew. She liked the sound of it. It was ordinary. Normal. Nice.

She closed her eyes and tried to sleep. Sleep. She almost snorted aloud. It was like lying down in a tiger's cage for a nap.

After a moment he said, "I thought Miss Tibthorpe looked unexpectedly pretty in that blue dress, don't you?"

"Yes. Yes, she did." Callie was pleased with the comment. She'd talked Tibby into accepting that color and it really suited her. She lay there thinking about Tibby. "You know, before I saw her again—before I returned to England I mean—I thought she was quite old. But when we met after nine years, I realize she must have been the same age then, when she was teaching me, that I am now. I thought she was old, or at least middle-aged, and yet, she must only be about five-and-thirty now." She broke off, realizing she was chatting when she was supposed to be keeping him at a distance, physically and metaphorically. "I am going to sleep now," she announced in a definite voice.

She lay there listening to him breathe, listening to the low sounds of the fire, to the distant rumble of some vehicle rattling over cobblestones, to a dog barking.

He wriggled to get more comfortable and she felt something brush against her.

"Mind your hands!" she snapped.

"Why?" His voice was pure, mellow, wine-dark provocation.

"I don't want them wandering." She could see his head on the pillow, turned toward her, watching her. His eyes gleamed in the firelight.

"Don't worry," he said with a smile that would have melted her bones had she not been so determined to resist. "My hands may wander . . . but they never get lost."

She swallowed.

"I always know exactly where they are . . ."

She squeezed her eyes shut and wished that ears could shut at will, too.

"And they always find their way home in the end," he finished in a velvet tone.

She shivered.

"You're cold," he said.

"No, I'm n—what are you doing?" It came out more as a squeak than an indignant protest.

"Warming you." He'd turned on his side and flipped her on hers facing away from him. She tried to struggle but his arms simply wrapped around her and she found herself clamped to him, all down the length of her body, her back against his chest, her limbs tucked between his and her bottom pressed against she wasn't even going to think what.

"I'm not cold."

"You were shivering, and no wonder, in that altogether delightful garment you're not quite wearing. Did you wear it for me?"

"No. I only wore it because there was nothing else." And she was shivering because he was in her bed and making her feel things. Things she didn't want to feel.

"Mm-hmm," he said as if didn't believe a word. "That's a good description for a garment like that, 'nothing else.' Not quite nude, not quite clothed. Not that I have any objection to it, far from it. What I saw of it was stunning. You'll have to show it to me properly one day."

"I won't."

"It feels like silk. Is it silk? They say silk should be so fine it could pass through a wedding ring. Do you think it would pass through your wedding ring? You could slip it off and see. It wouldn't make any difference to me."

"Stop it. I have no intention of taking it off. You said this marriage was to be—" She couldn't think of the word. "—like chess!" she hissed.

"Fine game, chess," he murmured in her ear. His breath was warm on her skin.

"Let me go." She tried to push him away.

"Relax, sweetheart," he told her. "I'm not going to do anything. But you were lying there like a corpse all laid out with your arms crossed over your chest, and shivering, and you won't get a wink of sleep like that."

"Do you think I'll sleep like this?" she demanded.

"Perhaps not, but it will be much more comfortable than lying like a corpse." He squeezed her. "Isn't that nice?"

"No," she lied. "I am very uncomfortable."

It was a mistake, for he used it as an excuse to wriggle closer and pull her more firmly into the curve of his body. "Now go to sleep."

She lay there stiffly, crossly, knowing she'd never sleep, not with him in the bed making her all hot and tingly and aching and unsettled.

If this was how he started a marriage, she would have no chance at all of protecting her heart from him. He was that sort of man. She doubted any woman could resist him.

But it wasn't serious for him. He lived in the moment—he'd said that once, told her it was a soldier's habit, to seize the moment and live it to the full while there was life in you.

She couldn't live like that. Not anymore. She didn't take things lightly, like he did.

He'd found her on a cliff top and with no more thought than you'd give to rescuing a stray cat, picked her and Nicky up, took them home, protected them, and even married her, all without hesitation, and apparently without the endless worry that came with every decision she'd ever made.

So here he was, and here she was in bed with him, his powerful arms wrapped around her, his heat soaking into her. And as usual, he was seizing the moment—and her—and she was fretting about imaginary consequences.

He desired her—the hard, blunt evidence of that was pressing insistently against her body—and she knew he could simply take her if he wanted. He was very strong and they were alone, and legally he had the right. And of course he would want a reward for all his trouble. He deserved it.

Yet he'd made no attempt to take her, or even press her to change her mind. He was a man of his word. She respected that, even if right now, she was finding his rectitude irritating and inconvenient.

He'd made no secret of what he wanted from her all along. He'd been quite open and blatant, from the very first day when he'd suggested she become his mistress.

Probably once he bedded her, he'd lose interest. That was what she wanted. It was.

She moistened her lips, thinking about it. Ever since she'd met him she hadn't been able to stop wondering what it might be like with him. It meant nothing, she reminded herself. It was simply a matter of normal feminine curiosity.

The hard relaxed power of his big body lying against her was so tempting. She would love to explore it. She was aware of every single place they touched, and where skin touched skin and where skin and skin were separated by the merest whisper of silk.

His breathing was deep and even, but he wasn't asleep, she was sure. He was too aroused to sleep. So was she.

They'd made a paper marriage, a chess maneuver: he'd walk away one day. As soon as she and Nicky were safe from Count Anton, his commitment would be over. Then she'd be alone.

For the rest of her life.

If she didn't do this now, she would always wonder what she had missed.

Rupert had always been very predictable. In the early days she'd enjoyed it, but once she'd realized what a fool she'd made of herself it had become more of a ritual, not unpleasant, but without the warmth she'd imagined had accompanied the act in the first part of her marriage.

With Gabriel it wouldn't be a ritual. He wasn't at all predictable, not to her. Even when he'd just been flirting he'd aroused her with the wicked, exciting images he'd planted in her mind. Even his kisses brought her to the brink. He was warm, exciting . . . terrifying.

If she let him take her, the only consequences would be to her heart. She was barren. Something must have happened to her when Nicky was born, because despite Rupert's regular monthly visits, she'd never quickened since. Not that she'd mind if Gabriel gave her a child. She would love it and love having a small part of him.

Oh God, even considering this was playing with fire. But if she didn't, she would spend the rest of her life regretting it. So, yes, she was going to let him take her.

But how? She couldn't just ask.

She gave a small experimental wiggle, moving her backside against his aroused male member. He tensed. That was promising. She wiggled again.

"Keep still, won't you?" he muttered, tightening his grip on her.

For answer she wriggled some more, rubbing her bottom provocatively back and forth against his arousal. She kept her eyes closed, pretending to be half asleep and unaware of her actions.

"If you don't keep still, I won't be responsible for the consequences," he growled.

She wiggled again and waited.

"You're doing this deliberately, aren't you?" he murmured.

She didn't answer.

Without warning he flipped her over in the bed and looked her full in the face. "I gave you my word. If you've changed your mind, you need to say so."

She couldn't bring herself to say it. Not directly. Not out loud. After a moment she said, "You say I'm a really bad liar."

He frowned at the apparent irrelevance of the remark. "Yes, you are."

"So what if I messed it up—with the judge or the government man or whoever it is who might ask?"

"Messed up what?"

"The—the chess maneuver. Saying we'd consummated the marriage when we hadn't."

His eyes bored into her. "What are you saying?"

She stared at a point over his shoulder, took a deep breath and said, "I think perhaps we should consummate it."

One dark brow rose. "For the sake of the chess maneuver?"

"Yes." She was on firmer ground here. It was just a matter of legalities, not anything that she needed, or that made her ache and yearn. She was simply offering to do her duty. Dispassionately.

"Because you wouldn't want to lie."

"That's right."

"So, Princess, are you saying you wish to consummate this marriage?" he asked softly.

She swallowed and nodded. "Yes, please. If you don't mind."

"Oh, I don't mind."

She closed her eyes and waited. Nothing happened. He didn't move a single muscle. She knew; she was achingly aware of every one of them.

She opened her eyes and found him watching her with an enigmatic expression. "Well?" she demanded.

He smiled that slow, crooked smile of his that turned her bones to honey. "You start."

Sixteen

"Me?" she croaked. "Start?"

Gabe smiled. "Yes, you start." He rolled over and lay back, put his hands behind his head, and prepared to think of England. A man could die happy.

She raised herself on one elbow and stared at him, disconcerted. "But what do I do?"

"Whatever you like." She looked so lovely, so disconcerted. She'd said she wanted more control, he was going to make sure she got it.

She sat up and looked down at him. It took every shred of self-control he had to remain still. That nightgown was no nightgown, it was an instrument of masculine torture, revealing . . . almost, and concealing . . . not quite. A tissue-thin draping over full, creamy breasts, a silken veil revealing berry-dark nipples tight and uplifted, pouting for his caress.

It was more erotic than total nudity. Or perhaps it was simply that the woman in the nightgown excited him more than any woman ever had. He'd even had wild erotic fantasies about her in that enormous pink flannel tent Mrs.

Barrow had lent her. Thank God someone, some angel, had given her this silken invitation to madness, this covering that caressed her curves even as it both concealed and flaunted.

God, but she was beautiful, even with her sweet, earnest face scrunched with frustration as she stared down at him.

"But the man always starts," she insisted.

"Not always," he told her. "Besides, I'm tired." He stretched, keeping his hands behind his head, his fingers locked. He didn't trust himself not to reach out to her otherwise, and it was important she take the initiative.

She'd obviously never taken it before. And he was damned if he'd let their first time be for legal reasons. Or some sort of ridiculous sacrifice on her part.

She was deceiving herself, pretending she wasn't as aroused as he was. She didn't have to admit it in so many words—he understood that kind of reticence—but he wanted her to *know* it.

She'd started this thing, teasing him that way, long after he'd warned her. Now he was going to drive her mad with desire, the way she'd driven him mad since the night they'd first met.

Then he was going to give her—and himself—the night of their lives. Hopefully the first one of many. This was his woman. He intended to grow old with her, or die trying.

"Too tired?" She lifted the covers back and peered at his drawers where his cock was doing its damnedest to get to her. "Liar!" she exclaimed. "Stop teasing!"

"Why? You're teasing me."

"I am not," she denied indignantly.

His eyes dropped to her breasts in their silken wrapping. Her hands instantly came up to hide her nakedness, and he wanted to groan, but almost at once her eyes grew thoughtful and wandered to his own naked chest.

She put out one hand and ran it across his chest, stroking

lightly with her fingertips, exploring and watching his face to see his reaction. She touched his nipple. It tightened under her touch. She rubbed it gently, then started on both of them. He groaned and arched under her hand, fighting for control.

She stroked his chest thoughtfully with one hand, the other scratching lightly around and around his nipple. Her gaze dropped to where a faint line of dark hair led down his stomach and into his drawers and he braced himself, but she made no move in that direction. Dammit.

"You're like a living statue," she murmured, running her hands appreciatively over him, caressing each swell and ripple of muscle. "I thought so when I was putting that ointment on you. Perfectly proportioned and so hard and firm, yet warm." Her breasts brushed against him lightly as she moved.

"Very hard," he gasped. "Very warm." He wasn't going to be able to take much more of this. Who was supposed to be driving whom mad? he wondered.

She glanced again at the bulge in his drawers and chewed thoughtfully on her lip. He groaned aloud. "That mouth of yours is going to kill me one day."

"Is it?" She looked pleased and bent to kiss his mouth lightly. He seized the opportunity hungrily, his mouth claiming hers, tasting, enticing, possessing.

She drew back, her eyes, in the firelight, looking dark and smoky with desire. Her gaze wandered again to his drawers. "Would you mind if I—"

"No! Go ahead," he ground out and braced himself as she reached for the buttons that fastened them.

She undid them one by one, then slowly, almost cautiously pulled them down, the cotton fabric dragging across the sensitive tip of his erection. He arched his back, then waited, eyes closed, fists clenched, waiting for her to touch him.

Nothing.

He opened his eyes and looked. She was looking at him, examining his manhood curiously, more like a virgin than a married woman and a mother.

"Well, go on, you've seen one of these before," he grated.

"I haven't actually," she said. "Not on an adult, anyway. Rupert never removed his nightshirt. Not for me." Her face dimmed fractionally as she said that, but he was too far gone to hold a conversation.

"I felt it, of course, but never with my hands. Would you mind—"

"No. Go ahead." He didn't want to hear about Rupert.

She touched him, tentatively at first, just stroking the length of him lightly with her fingertip. He felt the shock clear through to the soles of his feet. Then she wrapped her palm around him and squeezed gently. He almost exploded.

And that was as much as he could take of letting her take the initiative. He seized her around the waist and in two seconds he had that silk thing off her and her spread out, naked, beneath him.

"I . . . can't . . . wait!" he managed to say, slipping his fingers between her cleft as he spoke. She was hot and slick and ready for him and he entered her blindly, surging into her without finesse.

Her sheath was tight, tighter than he'd expected. Dimly he was aware of her clinging to him, moving against him, but he was beyond all control, his body driven by the primitive beast deep within him as he thrust with blind, possessive compulsion: his woman, his wife. Once, twice, and then he shattered.

He wasn't sure how long it was before he came to himself again, but with the return of consciousness came guilt and self-recrimination. The more he thought about it the more mortified he was.

The plan had been to seduce her, entice her; to drive her wild with desire.

And what had he said earlier about never pouncing? Of being more sophisticated than that? He groaned.

He'd done worse than pounce on her. He hadn't even laid a finger on her until he'd parted her, and then he hadn't waited for any sign from her other than that she was wet. He'd ridden her blindly, selfishly to his own climax, oblivious of anything except his own need.

The best he could hope for was that she'd be furious. The worst, that she'd hate him.

He opened his eyes to find her watching him. "I'm sorry," he said.

She didn't reply. He couldn't read her expression because her eyes were in shadow. "I'm sorry," he said again. "I don't know what to say. I haven't—I've never—not since I was a young man—"

Callie was still too stunned by what had happened to speak. She'd put her nightgown back on after he'd finished. Now she pulled the covers up over her. It was getting a little chilly.

So, now she knew what it was like to lie with Gabriel Renfrew. She wasn't quite sure what she thought about it, but she knew she'd never forget it. She still felt restless and hollow and a bit cross, but also, deep within her, she was amazed.

To be desired so powerfully that a man like Gabriel, who prided himself on his self-control, had lost all sense of himself. She'd barely touched him and he'd exploded. It was amazing.

It made her feel . . . powerful. Not particularly satisfied, but powerful.

She, Callie, had done that to him, had caused this strong, disciplined man to fall on her with ravenous desire. He was still staring intensely at her now.

"I will make it up to you," he said, reaching for her.

She recoiled slightly. "But it's done. The marriage has been consummated."

"It hasn't," he insisted. "You didn't—you weren't *consumed*. I was too quick. I didn't make it good for you." He reached for her.

She fended him off. "You want to do it *again*? Now?"

"Yes. It will be better, I promise you."

"No. It's late. I'm tired." She lay down with the bedclothes pulled tight around her. She wanted to believe him. She needed to protect herself. She didn't want to relive that sensation of being taken partway up a mountain and then dumped, not twice in one night.

"Trust me. This time will be for you, I promise." He pulled the covers back.

"No!" she said crossly, pulling them up. "I know we made vows today, but if you remember I didn't promise to obey you, and this is why."

There was a short silence, then he said, "But I still need to fulfill my vows to you."

"We've consumm—"

"Not that. I vowed to cherish you. And now I *need* to cherish you." His voice was deep and sincere and his eyes compelled her to believe him.

She eyed him mistrustfully. "You ask a great deal."

"I know," he said softly.

Right now, she could walk away from this business, heart intact—almost intact, she amended. But she hadn't expected this, his willingness to stay, to make it good for her—even after he'd fulfilled his own needs—as if her feelings were as important as his.

He claimed he wanted to *cherish* her. If he truly did . . . how could she resist?

She said weakly, "It's just a paper marriage, a—a chess maneuver."

"Then let us play chess," he said instantly, sensing her imminent capitulation. "Black knight to white queen." And he kissed her.

He captured her mouth with his, molding it and pushing her lips apart to gain entry. His tongue moved in a slow rhythm that her whole body responded instinctively to. Hot shivers rippled through her, pooling in the aching inner core of her.

She ran her hands over him. His body was hard and hot and she loved the feel of it, the feel of him. She tasted his skin, salty and musky, loving the male taste of him.

He caressed her breasts through the fabric of her night-gown, a delicious silken abrasion that made her arch and shudder with pleasure. Her skin felt tight and tender and amazingly sensitive. She shivered and pressed herself against him.

There was an intensity to the way he was caressing her, she dimly realized, as if he were learning her, discovering what pleased her.

Everything he did pleased her.

He kissed a line down from her jaw and she flexed like a cat under him, reveling in the sensations of his mouth on her skin. His mouth closed hotly over first one nipple, then the other, playing with it, sucking and biting her gently through the silk, and she moaned and writhed rest-lessly as exquisite sensation burned through her in waves of pleasure.

Her hands raked his body, kneading, testing, demanding more, exploring the small nubs of his flat male nipples, the smooth bands of hard muscle across his belly, and the line of dark hair arrowing from his belly down to his groin. Last time she had touched him there he'd nearly exploded. She wondered if she could do it to him again.

He reached down and caressed the smooth skin of her thighs, and she forgot her intended destination as they fell apart, tautening and trembling with expectation and need. He drew the nightgown up and up, the fabric dragging against the rawness of her hot, fevered skin.

And then it was off and his hand was between her legs, stroking, circling, teasing, squeezing. She arched and shuddered and her legs splayed and jerked, out of her control, and she clawed at him, wanting something, anything, but not knowing what. His mouth closed over hers and his eyes locked with hers as his fingers stroked and stroked and stroked, and sent her spiraling over the edge.

She lay gasping, half on top of him, still feeling the small aftershocks of sensation deep within her. She looked down at him. He was still hard and wanting and unsatisfied.

She reached down and took him in her hand, stroking and exploring him the way he had explored her. He shuddered and stiffened, gritting his teeth and bracing his legs, as if resisting.

With an instinct as old as Eve, she ran her hand up and down the length of him, caressing the sensitive tip, running her fingers over the tiny bead of liquid, smoothing it over him. She marveled at the hot, satiny feel of him and her palm tightened around him. He groaned.

She paused, not sure what to do. She wanted him inside her now, she was hot and achy again but he wasn't moving, just watching her, letting her play with him, even though his body was racked and trembling with barely controlled need. For a moment she didn't understand why. He wanted her and she wanted him, so why didn't he . . . ?

And then she knew. He was making up for last time.

"You could ride me," he told her, his voice harsh with need. "It gives you the control."

"Ride you?" She was intrigued. She straddled his body and then, a little awkwardly, positioned herself over him and guided him into her. She felt the smooth, hot length of him pushing into her and stopped. He groaned and gritted his teeth, but didn't move. She moved again, lowering herself until he was fully within her. It felt amazing. She leaned forward with her hands on the bed on either side of him, and moved experimentally. He moaned and thrust upward and sensation spiraled though her. She moved with him, flexing her inner muscles, feeling the whole length of him.

She moved again and he thrust and then, suddenly—there was no other word for it, she started to ride him—she, who'd never ridden any animal in her life—rode her husband, rode him as he thrust and bucked beneath her, moving within her. His palms caressed her breasts as she moved, faster and faster, with small, high cries of exhilaration.

And at the last minute he slipped his hand to where they were joined and caressed her and suddenly she was flying, flying and shattering into a thousand pieces around him. With a thin, high cry she collapsed onto his heaving chest, oblivious of anything.

Gabe held her against him, gasping for breath, unwilling to let her go, barely able to think past the thought that he'd just made her his wife in fact as well as in law. His arms tightened around her and he kissed the top of her head where she lay sprawled and sated on top of him. He pulled the covers over them so she wouldn't get cold.

He'd claimed her: now all he had to do was keep her.

Gabe woke some hours later to the sound of water dripping, slow and relentless. The rain had stopped. But that wasn't what had wakened him. He listened. It was some time in the still hours before dawn, when London was almost quiet. All he could hear was the last of the rainwater dripping steadily.

He reached out for her, but she wasn't there. He sat up and saw her, curled in the window embrasure, wrapped in her red shawl, her knees tucked up under her chin, staring out into the gray, miserable night.

He knew that look, the look of someone on the outside, looking in. Or in this case looking out, wanting something she didn't have, something out there. Yearning for it. Not wanting what she had: him.

Gabe felt suddenly cold. She had to love him, she had to. He would make her, force her to love him.

As if love could ever be forced, he thought desperately. But what else could he do? He had to try.

She'd liked what they'd done in bed, he was sure of that, he would bed her and bed her and love her until she cared.

She hadn't wanted to marry him. He'd had to work hard to convince her. And now it was their first night together and she was already regretting it?

He thought—hoped—he'd recovered from the disaster of his loss of control. Obviously not.

Unless it was not the bedding at all. He was sure she'd felt at least some of what he had that second time. If he knew anything about women he knew when he'd satisfied them and when he hadn't. He would have bet his life that this time he'd made it good for her. It had been more than good for him.

But she'd already left him, left his bed. She was sitting there, alone in the cold, hunched into a ball of misery, looking out into the chill of the night as if there was something out there she wanted, and wanted more than anything she had in here.

A cold stone lodged in his chest. All he brought to this marriage was the ability to protect her son: such a slender thread to catch her with. He'd hoped, he'd banked on his bedroom skills to hold her, as least for long enough to try and make her love him.

He wasn't going to lose her. He had to make her love him.

As easily cage the moon as make someone love you.

But he could perhaps reach her another way. Maybe she was worrying about her son. She was a wonderful mother. If she was given a choice between her son and her husband, Gabe knew what she'd choose: her son, the opposite of what his own mother had chosen.

Gabriel, always the loser to love.

But he was also a fighter and he wasn't going to give up. This small, beautiful, scrunched-up piece of misery at the window held his heart in her hands, whether she knew it or not, and he wasn't going to let her give it back.

He slid out of bed and came up behind her. The look on her face wrung his heart. "What is it?" he asked.

She gave him a bleak look. "We shouldn't have done that."

"Why not?" The words came out roughly.

The question hung in the air. Her mouth trembled, but she just shook her head.

"We can try again," he said urgently. "If it wasn't any good—"

"It was wonderful," she said in such a small, sad voice it took him a moment to register what he'd said.

"Then—?"

"I don't want to talk about it."

He stared at her, frustrated. If he didn't know what it was, he couldn't fix it. She was cold. He fetched an eiderdown and tucked it around her, hesitated, and then gathered her against him. She made no objection, thank God, because he didn't know if he could let her go.

He held her in his arms, tucked against his chest, warming her with his body, supporting her. She stared out of the window, and a tear rolled slowly down her cheek.

Gabe felt desperate. How could he make her trust him enough to talk to him? "Whatever it is, I will make it right. Just say . . ." There was nothing he wouldn't do for her.

She shook her head. The tears came again, rolling silently down her cheeks.

"Was it something I did? Or didn't do?"

Her face crumpled. "No," she said brokenly and turned to him in distress. She hugged him convulsively. "It's not your fault at all. What you did—what we did together was utterly . . . I've never . . . It was just . . . perfect."

Her eyes filled with tears and she dashed them away. "I'm sorry; I don't know what the matter is with me. I felt—I feel wonderful and cherished, I really do."

She felt wonderful and cherished, Gabe thought bleakly. That's why she looked so miserable.

What was a man supposed to do with that?

How could he teach her to want him the way he wanted her?

"Come back to bed and let me cherish you some more," he said hoarsely. He had no idea what to do, other than to love her. All he could think of was that he needed to wipe that desolate look off her face. If he could make her body sing with passion, and keep it singing, then maybe . . .

He kissed her, and she kissed him back. It was a start, he told himself. She kissed as if she meant it.

He carried her back to bed and made love to her for the third time, very slowly and thoroughly, cherishing her with every fiber of his body and soul. She returned kiss for kiss, and caress for tender caress with a kind of desperate earnestness that almost broke his heart.

She was trying too hard. He knew what that meant.

Their eyes locked as he brought her to a slow, intense climax, the pressure building relentlessly until she thrashed and shuddered and collapsed bonelessly against him as he shattered also and drowned in her eyes.

She fell asleep with her cheek against the bare skin of his chest, cradled against his heart. He held her to him, unwilling to let her go, even for a moment.

He was going to lose her. He could see it in her eyes.

Oh God, what was he going to do?

Gabe awoke much later to find the day well advanced. It was still wet and gray and chilly.

She slept curled like a cat against him, her lashes long and dark and silky against her satin-pale skin. He watched her sleeping, her mouth fallen a little open, her breathing deep and regular.

He leaned over and kissed her lightly, and though she stirred a little she didn't wake. He nuzzled the hollow between her jaw and her shoulder and inhaled deeply. If he lived to be a hundred, he'd never forget the scent of her.

He slipped out of bed and, naked, padded across the thick carpets to the fire, which was almost out. He fed it with chips of wood and then coal until it was blazing again.

He turned to return to bed and found her sitting up on one elbow, watching him. He crossed the room, feeling a little self-conscious with her eyes on him. She inspected him with frank interest, a small smile—he hoped of appreciation—playing about her lips.

He slipped back into bed with her and kissed her.

"Good morning," she murmured and reached for him again. Her palm curled possessively around his hardened flesh, and the most adorable mouth in the world curved as she registered the evidence of his desire.

"Good morning indeed," he murmured, feeling a surge of new hope. "And it's about to get even better . . ."

*A*fterward he rang the bell and ordered hot water for himself and her, which she amended to a bath. He ordered breakfast to follow.

Then, with a self-consciousness that amused him, she excused herself to take her bath in her dressing room and sent him off to his, to dress and shave.

For a moment, Gabe considered the possibility of assisting her with her bath, but decided against it. Despite her years of marriage, she wasn't used to sensual delights, and he didn't want to throw his entire battery at her at once. It was going to be a long, slow siege. He could wait another day, he thought. Perhaps tomorrow.

Callie sat in the bath, soaping herself and thinking

about the extraordinary few moments of utter despair she'd experienced in the middle of the night. Strange that it had occurred just hours after she'd experienced the most intense moment of bliss in her life.

Not really strange, she realized. The bliss had caused the despair. Last night in Gabriel's arms, he'd shown her what she'd missed all her married life, and worse—showed her what she could have if this wretched marriage was real instead of merely legal.

She hadn't been able to talk to him about it then—not when she was feeling so raw and vulnerable. All her defenses . . . he'd destroyed them making love to her as he had. She hadn't known it was possible to feel like that.

She wanted her marriage to be real, wanted to have this man for herself and love him with everything she had in her.

He was everything she'd ever dreamed of: kind and strong and loving, a man to be cherished and loved, not used and discarded. She wanted him forever, not just for a day or a week or a month.

But no matter how she looked at it, she couldn't see how it could work. A marriage was more than just feelings, it was a living, day-to-day partnership. His life was here. Hers, eventually, as soon as Count Anton was dealt with, had to be back in Zindaria.

Zindaria was Nicky's future, his heritage. What sort of a mother would she be if she traded her son's glorious future for her own selfish happiness?

Gabriel's whole family was in England: his brothers, his aunt, the many others who'd come to the wedding. His friends were here, too, and they were close, more so than many brothers.

Callie knew the importance of friends and family, she who had so few of either. She had a few distant cousins she'd never met scattered across Europe, and almost no friends in Zindaria. A princess lived a very isolated life. How could she ask him to exchange his full, exciting life for her lonely, routine existence in a foreign land.

He had family, friends, a home, land, and responsibilities. He belonged. What man would give all that up for her? None. So she should face that and move on from there.

She scrubbed at her skin briskly and tried to count her blessings. She'd made Nicky a little bit safer by her marriage. And she had a wonderful husband, albeit for a limited time. She could mope around feeling sorry for herself, waiting for the day he would walk away, or she could make the most of what she had now. Seize the joy while it was hers to enjoy.

She soaped herself meditatively, aware of her body in a new way, soaping her breasts with their tender, aching tips, and recalling the way he'd suckled on them, lavishing her with pleasure. And the pleasurable soreness between her thighs, aching in places she'd never known could ache.

The last time she'd felt like this about her body was when she'd been carrying Nicky. She remembered being fascinated with its female power and its mystery—this seemingly ordinary body of hers that was actually creating a baby, a living miracle.

Last night her body had amazed her again. She'd never imagined the pleasure it was capable of feeling—that she could shatter in a thousand shards of ecstasy and afterward feel like she was floating in a bubble.

And she'd never in her life imagined it could bring a strong, disciplined man like Gabriel Renfrew to his knees with uncontrollable lust. And it had. Three times in the night. Four, if you counted this morning. She smiled to herself. Again.

She hadn't been able to stop smiling all morning. She felt like her body: female, powerful, and mysterious.

She suddenly didn't care that it was temporary, that one

day they would live hundreds of miles apart, still legally married, but living separate lives. What good did it do to dwell on that dismal prospect? She'd made the marriage to save her son. That alone was worth any heartbreak to come.

She hadn't understood Gabriel's motives for marrying her, had wondered what he would get from the marriage, and now she knew: *her.* He desired her. Uncontrollably. Her body tingled and ached with the knowledge. And her heart exulted in it.

It was as though somehow, something inside her had burst in the night and drained away, and now she was . . . different.

She suddenly felt lighter, freer, as if the rain in the night had washed her as clean as it had washed the air. Like a clean slate. Her slate, to write and rewrite on as she wished.

She was going to take that man and love him while she could. And if—when he walked away, as they'd arranged to do, she would know that she had loved, and loved well. And that would be enough.

She dried herself and donned a fresh chemise, then rang for a maidservant to come and lace her stays. While she waited for the maid she brushed her hair.

She was no longer frightened of losing her heart to him. It was too late for that. Her heart had been lost some time in the hours before dawn. Perhaps when he'd put himself so entirely in her hands, so generously. He'd taken her to the top of the mountain and shown her how to fly . . .

Or perhaps it happened when he'd simply held her in her misery, wrapping her in warmth and wanting to fix it. Or when he'd kissed her tears away, making her feel like something precious and lovely and not at all foolish.

Or maybe it was when he'd carried her back to bed and made love to her for the third time, so tenderly it almost broke her heart, so that she fell asleep feeling utterly cherished.

Whenever it was, her heart was well and truly lost to him.

She would accept these moments of happiness, but she still had enough of her old defenses left to know it would be easier in the end if she kept her feelings to herself.

As Gabriel escorted her downstairs for breakfast the hall clock chimed four times.

"Four!" she exclaimed. "That cannot be right."

He checked it against his fob watch. "It is."

"But where did the time go? I told Nicky I'd see him in the morning."

He gave her a slow, reminiscent smile. "Nicky will manage. It was time well spent, if you ask me."

She blushed and smiled. She couldn't stop looking at him. It felt like her whole body was smiling.

"I'm ravenous," she said as they entered the breakfast parlor.

He stopped dead. "Me, too," he said, his eyes devouring her. "Shall we go back upstairs?" His eyes were dancing, but he was also quite serious, she saw.

No." She tried to hide how his words had pleased her, but smiles kept breaking out. She felt so wonderful, so feminine, so . . . *desired.* "I want my breakfast."

"Yes, you need to keep your strength up for tonight," he agreed.

After breakfast—he'd ordered bacon and eggs and hot chocolate and crumpets and coffee and she ate almost all of it—they walked around to Lady Gosforth's.

It was just a few moments' walk. The rain had started again, but it was not heavy and they shared an umbrella. Their bodies bumped pleasurably as they walked. Sometimes the bumping was deliberate; Callie could not stop touching him. They were both in high spirits, jumping puddles like children and laughing at nothing.

Callie told herself it had to stop. It was one thing to acknowledge to herself she had feelings for him, it was quite another to be acting like a giddy girl in love. Even if she was.

It was a certain way to heartbreak, that she knew from experience. Tomorrow, she decided. Tomorrow she'd be sensible.

They reached Lady Gosforth's after five o'clock. The butler, Sprotton, unbent so far as to give them an almost fatherly smile as they entered. "You will find Prince Nikolai in the nursery, madam," he told Callie as he took the wet umbrella and handed it to a footman.

When Gabriel inquired after his brother and aunt, Sprotton surprised them both by saying, "Your aunt is Out at present, but everyone else is in the nursery, sir. All of them, sir: Mr. Morant, Mr. Delaney, Mr. Ripton, Mr. Ramsey, also Mr. Nash Renfrew."

"In the nursery?" Gabriel said in surprise.

Sprotton gave an enigmatic smile. "It was the continuing Inclement Weather, sir. I recalled other Inclement Days when you were a boy, sir, and it gave me a Notion, which I venture to suggest has Proven Successful."

Gabriel led the way to the old nursery, which was on the third floor. "I haven't been up here in years," he told Callie. "I wonder what this notion of Sprotton's was. He seemed pretty pleased with himself."

As they entered the nursery the sounds of vigorous masculine debate suddenly stopped. Callie smiled, understanding immediately what had drawn them all up to the nursery. Five men and two boys lay sprawled on the floor in various poses, completely absorbed, while Tibby sat by the fire placidly sewing, an indulgent look on her face, as if she were supervising a room full of boys. As perhaps she was, Callie thought in amusement.

At their entrance all the men had scrambled to their feet, looking faintly sheepish, and bowed to Callie. Ethan hauled Jim to his feet.

Nicky carefully made his way across the floor and greeted his mother with a kiss.

"You said you would come to see us this morning, Mama. What have you been doing all day?" he asked.

Nicky's mother glanced at her husband. A tiny smile quivered on her lips. "Playing chess," she said serenely.

"Best chess I ever had in my life," Gabriel murmured in her ear. She repressed a giggle.

"Who won?" Nicky asked.

"It was a draw," Gabriel told him, squatting down to pat Juno, who was temporarily tied to a table leg lest she do any damage to the arrangements.

Callie shook her head. "No, I won."

"Now that's a surprise," Gabriel said softly. "I was certain I had."

Nicky looked at them both, then shrugged, uninterested. "Mama, I am having a splendid time here and we are at a crucial point, so if you don't mind . . ."

"No, of course not, darling," Callie said. "Tibby and I will go downstairs and have a comfortable coze, and you can all get back to your toys."

"They're not toys, Mama," Nicky told her, deeply shocked. "They're *soldiers*."

Callie glanced at the nursery floor, upon which which had been laid out a huge and very elaborate battlefield made up of hundreds of model soldiers, and at the five grown men who stood politely by, concealing their impatience to get back to the battle only slightly more successfully than her son and Jim.

"Of course they're not toys," she agreed.

As she and Tibby left, she heard her husband saying, "The blue company on the left flank is in the wrong spot . . ."

*T*he following two days were spent much as the first. Each night they made love, sometimes slow, hot, and intense, sometimes ravenous and explosive, sometimes sweet and achingly tender. He seemed insatiable, and to Callie's surprise, so was she. A look, the merest brush of his skin against hers and their eyes would meet, and the heat and urgency returned.

They spent the nights making love until the quiet hours of the night, sleeping a few hours at a time, only to wake again and make love again. It was like a drug; she could not get enough of it, of him. And when they were not sleeping or making love, they talked.

They talked of Callie's years with Tibby, of her life in Zindaria, and how she'd always felt out of her depth as a princess. They talked of Gabriel's early years in Alverleigh house, and of coming to the Grange and meeting Harry. They'd fought, just as Jim and Nicky had.

As Gabriel described the boyhood adventures he had with Harry, Callie came to understand the deep bond between the two men, both excluded from their family. They even talked about Gabriel's war, and he told her a little of how it felt to be one of the few who came home . . .

And as they talked they became closer and closer, and she worried about how it would be when it came time to part. She thrust it from her mind. She was happy now, so she would live now and let the future take care of itself.

The days assumed a rhythm of their own: they rose late in the day after making love far into the night and again in the morning. They bathed, ate, and then walked around to Mount Street and Lady Gosforth's house. They would stay there until evening. Callie would go upstairs to join the two boys and Tibby. Invariably Ethan and one or two of the other men—usually Harry—were there, too. Callie would spend the last part of the afternoon with them, then the two boys would eat their supper.

They read the boys an episode of a bedtime story— Callie was amused to see that Ethan was always present for the story—and then Callie would put Nicky to bed and kiss him good night, while Tibby did the same to Jim.

The two boys shared a room that opened onto two adjoining bedchambers. Ethan slept in one and Harry in the other. Nicky was well protected at all times; Gabriel had seen to that.

Once her son was asleep, she would come downstairs and they would all dine together. Then Tibby and Ethan would return upstairs, Lady Gosforth would prevail on whichever of the young men was present to escort her to some social engagement, and Callie and Gabriel would walk back around the corner to Alverleigh House and make love.

Callie passed through the following days in a happy daze, until suddenly it was Tuesday night, the night of Lady Gosforth's small party to celebrate their wedding.

Callie dressed with care, choosing her favorite of the new evening dresses, a short-sleeved emerald satin underdress, trimmed around the hem with a border of lace, and topped with a long robe of gossamer net, trimmed with matching lace, silver satin knots, and scarlet beading. With it she wore a dainty pair of scarlet Turkish slippers, a buff-colored Grecian scarf with scarlet embroidery and tassels, long, white lace gloves, and her mother's tiara.

"How do I look?" she asked Gabriel when he came to escort her downstairs.

"Beautiful as always," he said.

Her brow puckered slightly. She didn't want any more gallant compliments from him. "I know I'm not beautiful," she said. "I don't need extravagant compliments, Gabriel. I'd be happy if you just said I look nice."

"So you want me to lie."

"No, just to tell me the truth."

"I am telling you the truth." He cupped her jaw in his hand and said quietly, "To me you are as beautiful as the moon. Your skin is like silk, your eyes are the most glorious color, and you have the most luscious mouth in the world."

She blinked. The most luscious mouth? Could he really think that? She could not help but smile. "Oh."

"Yes, oh. So don't tell me what I think, my beautiful wife." He leaned forward then stopped, saying, "I won't kiss you now, because if I start I won't be able to stop, and we have to get to that party."

He took a velvet oblong box from his pocket. "I thought you might wear your mother's tiara, so I got you these to go with it." He passed her the case.

She opened it and said nothing for a long moment. She was stunned. "Diamonds. But—"

"Yes, I know they should be paste, to match," he said, his eyes dancing. He lifted the necklace from the box and turned her to fasten the necklace. "But I didn't have time. Now, let's have a look." He turned her toward the looking glass. "Perfect."

She stared at her reflection. Diamonds? It was the sort of gift a man gave his wife. His true, until-death-us-do-part wife. "It's beautiful," she whispered.

"Like its owner. Now don't sell these ones, all right?"

"No, I would *never*—" she began, horrified, and then saw he was teasing. "Thank you, Gabriel. I will treasure it always." She stood on tiptoe and kissed him.

He wrapped his arm around her and kissed her back, a deep, possessive kiss that made her want to melt.

"Now, come on," he said after a while. "The sooner this wretched party is over—and we can go to bed—the better."

"Is that a promise?"

"A vow."

Then that's when she would tell him, Callie decided. For the last two days she'd tried to decide whether to tell him how she felt or not. Gabriel had made her feel things she'd never felt before. He understood her, he cared for her, she was sure.

But how much? That was the question. She had to know, to try, at least. Nothing ventured, nothing gained.

Tonight after the party, when they made love, she would tell him.

Seventeen

"You know when we first talked about this, I didn't understand your amusement when your aunt said it would be a small and meager affair," Callie murmured to Gabriel. They'd been standing with Lady Gosforth at the foot of the staircase for nearly an hour, greeting the guests who flowed in a never-ending stream through the front door. Luckily Callie was used to it: Zindarian state receptions were not dissimilar.

"But it is, my dear, positively *shabby*," Gabriel retorted imitating his aunt's fruity tones.

She giggled. Lady Gosforth's "few intimates for a bite beforehand" had turned out to be dinner for twenty couples. The "small private party, a positively meager affair" meant as many of the *ton* as could be squashed into the large house in Mount Street.

Callie was in a wonderful mood. Gabriel had flirted with her all through dinner and she was feeling light-headed and excited and breathless. She couldn't wait for the night to be over, for the moment when they were finally alone. She kept planning it in her mind . . .

"Princess Caroline," a fussily dressed elderly man bowed low over her hand, reminding Callie to concentrate on the matter in hand. With an effort she recalled his name. He'd come to her wedding—Sir Oswald Merri-something. "How do you do, Sir Oswald," she said.

"I'm well, thank you, my dear." The old gentleman beamed at her in a fatherly manner. "No need to ask the blushin' bride how she does—you're bloomin', my dear, positively bloomin'! You're a lucky devil, Renfrew!"

"Thank you, Sir Oswald, and thank you for coming," Gabriel said and, after Callie had promised him a dance, the old gentleman moved on.

After another half hour, the press of guests had slowed to a trickle and Lady Gosforth sent them off. "Have some fun. Go and dance, my dears."

A small string orchestra played in the ballroom and as if by some prearranged signal, as Callie and Gabriel entered the room, they struck up a waltz. "Shall we, my dear?" Gabriel asked her and without waiting for a reply, he swept her into the dance. The dance floor had cleared as people stood back to watch the bridal couple take the floor.

Callie circled and circled in Gabriel's arms. The surroundings were nothing but a blur of color and movement, all she could see was Gabriel. With one hand on his shoulder and the other clasped in his big, warm hand, she twirled and twirled, gazing into his blue, blue eyes as her feet in their scarlet dancing slippers floated on air.

Their first waltz, she thought.

"But not our last," he said, reading her mind.

She didn't want to think about the future. Right now, she was happier than she'd ever thought possible.

"So, you're the little foreign widow who managed to hurry Gabriel Renfrew to the altar," a sultry voice behind Callie said.

Callie turned, not much liking being called a little foreign widow. Looking down at her was a statuesque blonde whose dress of gold satin seemed to have been molded to her body. She was very beautiful.

"I beg your pardon?" said Callie. "Have we met?"

The blonde held out three languid fingers. "Lady Anthea Soffington-Greene." She scrutinized Callie with an air of faint, dismissive amusement. Callie bristled.

"Gabriel's marriage has thrown the ladies of the *ton* into mourning," Lady Anthea drawled. "Not me, however." She glanced at Callie's gown, smirked, and smoothed her own gold satin over her hips. Her dress was cut extremely low; her large, full breasts were almost wholly visible, rather like two large blue-veined cheeses, Callie thought.

She reminded her of the Valkyrie.

Lady Anthea added, "A small thing like a hasty wedding won't change what's between Gabriel and me." She smiled knowingly.

Callie's fists curled in their lace gloves. She wanted to scratch the woman's eyes out. "My husband is taken," she said fiercely, looking the woman in the eye. "However, his brothers are free." She glanced across the room to where Harry stood, tall and handsome, surrounded by women and flirting shamelessly. He didn't dance, she noticed, perhaps because he was embarrassed by his limp.

Not one of the women was an unmarried girl, she realized with shock. They were all young, glamorous matrons. They could be hunting Harry for one reason only.

Lady Anthea tittered. "You mean Harry the Crippled Bastard?"

Callie stiffened. "If you are referring to my brother-in-law, Mr. Harry Morant, how dare you refer to him as a cripple in my presence! And I'll have you know he was born in wedlock!"

Lady Anthea arched an eyebrow and said in a suggestive tone, "So the wind sits in that quarter, does it? Harry is a handsome devil, I grant you, but Gabriel is more my kind of meat. The thumbs say it all."

Callie saw red. Gabriel's thumbs were hers! "My husband is not on your menu, Lady Anthea! If you need servicing, I suggest you approach Mr. Morant. He's kind to animals, I know. He may even take pity on an underdressed bitch in heat!"

Lady Anthea, her eyes glittering with rage, drew herself up with a hiss. Callie braced herself, ready for battle, but Gabriel came up behind her and slid his arm around her waist.

"Lady Anthea, is it not?" he said smoothly. "How do you do? You must excuse us, my wife is needed elsewhere." And before Callie could say a word he steered her firmly away.

"Gabriel, do you know that woman?" Callie demanded.

"Yes, I know her, but *not*, my love, in the biblical sense," he said as he led her out onto the terrace. He turned her around to face him, his face alive with amusement. "And here I was elbowing my way through the crowd in the rudest way because I thought you might need defending from one of the most poisonous harpies in the *ton*."

Callie scowled suspiciously at him. "You think she's a poisonous harpy?"

"I know she is."

His words pleased her, but she wasn't finished yet. "She's quite beautiful."

He nodded. "Very beautiful, yes, she is. For an underdressed bitch in heat." His eyes were dancing.

She narrowed hers at him. He hadn't needed to add on the *very*. "She talked about your *thumbs*," she accused.

He smiled and cupped her cheek with his palm. "She may have seen my thumbs, but I promise you that's all she's seen of me. I wouldn't touch that woman with a barge pole, let alone with, er, anything else."

"Never?"

"Never. Never in the past and certainly not in the future. Besides, my body is wholly and exclusively dedicated to you—or had you forgotten those vows I made in church the other day?"

Mollified, she relaxed. His arm slid around her waist and the hand cupping her cheek moved to the back of her head. One long, strong finger stroked the nape of her neck, sending delicious shivers down her spine. "She was horrid about Harry," she told him.

His face hardened. "I'm not surprised. She's a vicious creature. Harry was once hopeles—" He broke off. "But that's in the past and besides, it's Harry's tale to tell, or not. Would you care for some supper?"

"In a minute," she said. She wasn't quite finished. "Lady Anthea told me all the ladies were in mourning since you got married."

He gave a smug smile. "Well, of course they are. I'm a very charming fellow. Quite good-looking, too, I'm told."

"Not as handsome as your brothers," she said dampeningly.

"Yes, but they all feel sorry for me now, knowing I'm firmly under the thumb of a shrew."

"A shrew?" she said indignantly.

"Yes, but a very beautiful one, and she wears me out so that I am not the least use to any other women."

Strangely pleased by his words, she kissed him.

After a very satisfying interlude, he murmured, "Besides, she's a very jealous creature and all the other ladies will be too frightened to cross her."

"Jealous? I am not jealous!" She stared at him shocked. "And nobody is ever frightened of me."

"Tell that to Lady Anthea," he said and kissed her again.

After that Callie was walking on air as well as dancing on it. She'd never enjoyed a party more. Gabriel didn't precisely hover, but he was never more than a few paces away and she was aware of his eyes on her throughout the evening.

Rupert used to watch her, too, waiting for her to make some gaffe, or drop something, or say the wrong thing. She was never comfortable with Rupert watching. This was different.

Gabriel watched to make sure she was having a good time. When her glass was empty, he would appear to have it filled. If she hovered between groups of people, not sure who to talk to next, he would appear and introduce her to someone. Or if she was being bored to death, Gabriel would come to rescue her.

Nash, Luke, and Rafe danced with her, and they and Harry were all very attentive, making sure she had whatever she needed, that she wasn't bored or feeling lonely in this crowd of people she didn't know. It was wonderful to have such tall, handsome men watching out for her. Callie had never felt so cared for at a party before. She was not on trial. Her only job was to enjoy herself.

She smiled and nodded at the most recent bore, a hunting-mad lord whose name she had forgotten. He'd pontificated for ten minutes now about the delights of hunting and the various horses he owned and all their interesting foibles and she hadn't been able to escape. He was impervious to hints and excuses. At last, she thought as she saw her husband threading his way toward them. Rescue was at hand.

"But there," said Lord Hunting-Mad, "I've been goin' on about my own mounts when really what I'd like to hear about are yours, Princess. I hear the horses of Zindaria are something quite special." He nodded genially as Gabriel arrived and said, "How do, Renfrew. The princess here was about to tell me about her favorite mount."

Gabriel, his eyes dancing, said suavely, "Really? Do tell, Princess."

She looked him straight in the eye and said, "I ride often, of course, and find it a most stimulating form of exercise. But not horses. Never horses." And with a sweet smile at his lordship, she sailed away, leaving Gabriel choking on his champagne.

"Not horses?" she heard Lord Hunting-Mad demand. "What the devil does the gel ride then?"

Callie paused to hear what her husband would say, knowing full well the only creature she ever rode was himself.

"Camels," Gabriel said when he had recovered his composure. "She's very fond of riding camels."

Lord Hunting-Mad turned and peered at Callie in astonishment. "*Camels*? Well, bless my soul, how dashed peculiar!"

Callie was still laughing when Gabriel caught up with her. "Minx," he said. "I think the Lady Anthea victory has gone to your head."

No, thought Callie, it was Gabriel Renfrew who'd gone to her head. She was bubbling, as though she had champagne in her blood.

She pretended to consider him, scanning him from head to toe in a thoughtful manner. "You are rather like a camel," she began and then froze as a movement over his shoulder caught her eye. Her fingers bit into his arms.

"Count Anton!"

As she spoke, the count spotted her from across the room. He bowed elegantly, enjoying her discomfiture.

Callie clenched her fists. "How dare he come to our wedding party!"

"My fault, I'm afraid," Nash said, coming up behind them. "I notified the Foreign Office and the Zindarian Embassy of your marriage straight away. I should have guessed that the count would find some way to gain entrance to this party."

"I don't want him here. Can't we throw him out?" she asked Gabe.

"Not without making a scene and mortifying Aunt Maude," Nash said quickly, seeing that Gabriel looked quite willing to do just that. "The count is the guest of the Austrian ambassador. He escorted the ambassador's wife here, Princess Esterhazy, a very influential leader of the *ton*—she's one of the patronesses of Almacks. If you tossed the count out, she would be mortally offended and take it out on Aunt Maudie."

Callie scowled. "Then I will tell him to leave—very politely—and you don't need to look so worried Nash, I am the soul of politeness—"

"Lady Anthea will vouch for that," Gabe murmured.

Callie looked daggers at him. "Count Anton is no joking matter."

"No, I know," Gabriel said soothingly. "But remember, he can do nothing to you here. We've stopped his legal move to have Nicky handed over and he's surrounded by some of the most influential people in England. And I'm here, and Harry and Rafe and Luke and Ethan and Nash." He gestured to where Harry and Rafe had positioned themselves on either side of the count—not obviously, but with clear intent to protect. Ethan, as Callie knew, was upstairs with Tibby and the boys.

Gabriel slid an arm around her waist. "We won't let him touch you, so there's no need to be afraid."

"I am not afraid of that snake," Callie declared, and suddenly realized she meant it. She wasn't afraid of him anymore. Not since that moment when Gabriel had handed her the sword stick. And then offered to kill him for her.

She took a deep breath and said with dignity, "I merely wish not to have my party spoiled by his vile presence."

She stalked across the room toward the count.

Harry stepped out in front of her. "Time for supper, is it? I shall escort you." He offered her his arm.

Callie blinked at him in surprise. "No, thank you, Harry, I have eaten," she told him and made to step around him.

Again he stepped in front of her, blocking her way. "Then will you dance?"

She stared at him. "But you haven't danced a single dance all evening."

"Yes, well, I feel like dancing now," he said coolly. "A dance with my lovely sister-in-law. To celebrate the wedding. You can't deny me that."

"Harry, are you perhaps trying to stop me from talking to the count?"

He gave her an opaque look. "Why would I do that?"

"I have no idea. Oh look, here comes Lady Gosforth with a young lady for you to dance with." His head snapped around and she took advantage of his momentary distraction to skip around him and make a beeline for the count.

"Princess Caroline," the count purred as she reached him. He gave a perfectly correct bow that somehow managed to be insolent. "I am informed that you have found someone to marry you. A younger son, I am told, and of paltry fortune." He smiled.

She was aware of Gabriel at her back. And Harry and Rafe and Luke and Nash. She was deeply moved by their immediate and unquestioning support.

She gave the count a cold look and said simply, "That is correct, you may felicitate me before you leave."

He arched an incredulous eyebrow, as if surprised by her daring. "May I? I believe the so-called felicity remains to be seen."

"Which do you doubt? My happiness or that you are leaving? There is no doubt of either," Callie said serenely. She had no doubt in the world of her happiness now. She looked at the count and said clearly, "Good-bye."

He flushed a little, aware that people were craning to hear the conversation. It was obvious from her attitude as she faced him that something was going on, not to mention the five men standing protectively at her back.

His lip curled. "Look at you in your fine feathers, flaunting that stupid tiara with its paste jewels—it's pathetic! What would all your elegant friends say if they knew it was a worthless piece of—"

Her hands flew to her tiara. "How did you—" she broke off.

"Know?" He sneered. "From Rupert of course. He used to laugh about it—we all did."

Gabriel stepped forward. "Then he was a fool. You all were. This tiara, like the woman wearing it, is unique and priceless."

"Priceless," Count Anton scoffed.

"Don't you think a younger son with a paltry fortune would check up on that sort of thing before he married its owner?" Gabriel said in a hard voice.

Callie looked at him in shock.

The smile died on Count Anton's face. He looked from Gabriel to the tiara, to Callie and back to Gabriel.

Gabe rested his hands on Callie's shoulders. "She might tell people the diamonds are paste and that it's worthless, but I am not so easily gulled. You may take it from me, this tiara is priceless."

The count glared at him.

"Now," Gabriel said softly, "my wife asked you to leave. Good-bye."

Balked, aware of the eyes on them, the count had no alternative but to go with as much grace as he could muster. He gave them a supercilious smile. "I will go then, since you behave so boorishly, but you'll find soon enough that Count Anton is not so easily defeated."

They watched him go. "I don't like the look of that smile," Gabriel said.

"I don't like the look of anything about him at all," said Harry. "Little golden weasel." They all laughed.

He heard them, too, turning back to fling them a glance filled with vitriol.

*L*ater in the evening when they were alone for a moment, Callie said to Gabriel, "I didn't lie to you about the tiara, it really is paste."

"I know," he said.

"But—then, why did you say it was priceless?"

"Because your mother's tiara is priceless to you. And if it is to you, it is to me. Now, would you like a drink? It's been quite an eventful evening. I think another champagne is called for."

Callie stared at him. He had no idea how much his words meant to her. And that he simply took it for granted that he would support her. "Gabriel," she said as he was about to go off and fetch her a drink.

"Yes?"

She kissed him. "I cannot wait for this party to end."

He looked surprised. "Aren't you enjoying yourself?"

"Oh, yes, I am. It's been wonderful. It's just that I am so looking forward to . . . um . . ." She blushed.

His eyes danced. "Chess?" he said gently.

"Yes." And telling him she loved him.

*I*t could not be said that the rest of the evening dragged, but Callie was glad when finally people started to leave. It was very late. The party had been a great success. She stood with Lady Gosforth thanking and farewelling people; she smiled and smiled and wished them gone.

Finally it was over. "I'll just pop up and look in on Nicky," Callie told Gabriel. "I won't be long."

He nodded. He was used to the routine. She checked on

her son last thing every night. She hurried up the stairs to the third floor and tiptoed into Nicky's room, so as not to wake him.

The room was empty. Callie stared disbelievingly at the sight of the two beds with the covers pulled back, the window open, and her son gone. She felt the sheets. Cold.

She flew to the adjoining rooms—first to Harry's, then to Ethan's. No sign of Nicky. She ran across to Tibby's room and found her and Ethan poring over a book. "Where is Nicky?" she gasped.

"In bed, asleep," Tibby said. "Why?"

"He's not there. Neither of the boys are. And their beds are cold."

"But they must be," Tibby said, shocked. "I checked both boys at about eleven. They were sound asleep."

Callie looked at the clock. It was now after two.

She ran back to the boys' room and screamed "Nick-yyyy!" out of the window. But there was no response. Her son had disappeared.

*A*t the sound of her scream, Gabe hurtled up the stairs two at a time. Harry and the others followed.

"What is it?" But the cold, empty beds and Callie's distress said it all. He peered out through the open window and found a dangling rope hanging from the roof.

Harry, who was standing beside the wardrobe, heard a faint sound. He unlocked the door and a bundle fell out. It was Jim, bound and gagged and wrapped in a quilt. Harry quickly freed him.

"They took Nicky!" Jim gasped the moment he could spit out the gag. "We was asleep and by the time I was awake I couldn't say nuffink." His sharp face crumpled as he looked at Callie. "I'm sorry, ma'am, real sorry. I let you down—"

Callie shook her head. She was beyond words, Gabriel saw.

"Who were they, Jim, did you get a look?"

"Two men. Foreigners. They tied up both of us, then one passed Nicky through the window to the other, and then I got shoved in the wardrobe."

Gabe glanced at the rope. "They must have taken him across the rooftops. But why?"

Callie moaned. Gabe grabbed her by the shoulders. "Listen to me! If they've taken Nicky, they must mean to keep him alive!"

She stared at him blankly. "Why?"

"I don't know, but it would have been easier to slit both boys' throats while they lay sleeping. They didn't, so they want Nicky alive."

Faint color stole back into her cheeks.

Gabe hoped to hell he was right. He turned back to Jim. "How long ago was it?"

Jim shook his head, his face scrunched with distress. "I dunno, sir."

"Tibby checked the boys around eleven," Ethan said. "So, sometime in the last three hours."

"I took the dog downstairs to do his business afterward," Tibby confessed, almost in tears. "And then Ethan came looking for me, and I left the dog shut out in the garden. If I'd only—"

"Never mind," Gabe interrupted her. "The count, Nash, where was he staying?"

"Not sure. With the Esterhazys, I think."

"Right, we'll start there. Ethan, get the horses saddled. Harry, lend me a pair of riding boots." The others hurried off to obey his orders. Gabe followed, then halted when he saw her; Callie stood huddled against the wall, frozen-looking and tragic.

Gabe couldn't bear it. She'd married him for one reason only: because he'd sworn to protect her child. He'd failed her.

Gabe seized her hands. "I'm sorry," he said urgently, "but I will find him, I promise you."

She gave him a frozen look.

"I *promise* you," Gabe said, and with a last desperate gesture he kissed her hard on the mouth and went into Harry's room, stripping off his evening trousers and coat almost before he was in the door.

She followed. "What are you doing?"

"Changing into my riding buckskins—or rather, Harry's. Can't ride in evening clothes—no flexibility—and mine would take too long to fetch." Harry handed him a pair of riding boots and he pulled them on. "Good thing we're the same size."

He raced down the stairs, shouting at Sprotton. "Are the horses here yet, dammit?"

"Any moment, sir." Sprotton snapped his fingers and a footman ran out into the street to look.

Ethan, Rafe, Nash, Luke, and Harry were all in riding clothes, she saw. "What are you all doing?"

"Going after them, of course."

"I'm coming, too," Callie said.

"You can't," Gabe said brusquely. "You'll slow us down."

She stared at him, agonized, knowing he was right. But how could she bear to wait, helpless, not knowing?

"I'll take her," Harry said to Gabe. "We'll follow in the curricle."

Callie flung him a grateful look and looked at Gabriel. "Please. I will go mad, otherwise."

He sighed. "All right. Sprotton, tell the stables we need the curricle and the grays, at once." He snapped his fingers and a footman went running.

"It'll be cold in the curricle. You must take my cloak," Lady Gosforth said. "Sprotton, fetch my fur cloak."

"Immediately, my lady," said Sprotton, and a maid went running off to fetch it.

Gabe turned to Harry and said in a low, urgent voice. "Look after her for me, brother. She is my *life*!"

Harry nodded. "I know."

Callie blinked. Had he said "wife," or "life"? But he was gone, Ethan, Rafe, Luke, and Nash with him, galloping down the street.

Shaken, she managed to gather her thoughts together. She drew Lady Gosforth aside. "Do you have a pistol I could borrow? I'm going to kill that man."

"Who, my nephew?" Lady Gosforth exclaimed, shocked.

"No, of course not! I *love* your nephew. It's Count Anton I'm going to kill."

Lady Gosforth's face cleared. "Well, in that case, by Jove, I do. Sprotton, fetch me my pistol. And make sure it's loaded."

"At once, my lady," Sprotton said, and a footman went running.

The footman and two maids arrived at the same time, the footman with a case containing a tiny muff pistol, one maid carrying an enormous sable cloak and the other carrying a small bag. "Just a change of clothes and a few other necessities," the girl told Callie, passing it to a footman to put in the curricle.

"Good thinking, that gel," declared Lady Gosforth approvingly.

The curricle and grays arrived at the front door. Callie kissed Lady Gosforth and said, "Take care of Tibby and Jim for me. And thank you for everything." Harry helped her up and in moments they were off, following Gabe to the Esterhazy residence.

G abe spurred his horse along the road, followed by Rafe, Luke, Nash, and Ethan. His face was grim. He was furious with himself. He should have taken more care, should have thought that kidnappers might come across the roof in the night. He'd been so busy trying to seduce the mother, he'd forgotten that his marriage was all about the child.

She'd asked just one thing of him: protect her boy.

He'd failed her. He'd failed Nicky. And he'd failed himself.

There was no chance she would ever love him now. Her couldn't blame her.

He thought of Nicky, in the hands of that smiling devil. He was gripped with cold rage, at himself, as well as Count Anton. Nicky was such a gallant little boy, so bright and full of pluck, it made Gabe sick to think of him in the hands of the count.

Where was that devil taking him? And for what purpose?

He could think of at least one reason why Nicky had been taken alive; if there was no body, you could not prove murder.

On the other hand without a body, the count could not inherit for at least seven years. Gabe kept telling himself that.

Arriving at the Austrian ambassador's, they pounded on the door until someone came to open it. Gabe pushed his way inside. "Where is Count Anton?" he demanded.

Servants came running to eject them, but confronted with five tall, angry gentleman men they hesitated.

"Count Anton—where is he?" Gabe growled.

"What is the meaning of this intrusion?" The ambassador, Prince Esterhazy himself, came down the stairs, dressed in a gorgeously embroidered dressing robe. He was accompanied by a number of guards. Recognizing Gabe, he frowned and waved the guards back.

"By what right do you come shouting and brawling into my house, Renfrew?" His cold glance took in the others. When he saw Nash his brows rose even higher.

"A matter of the utmost urgency. Where is Count Anton?" Gabe demanded.

The ambassador glared at Gabe. "If it's any business of yours, he left. He was called away suddenly. But—"

"Called away? Where to?"

"Zindaria. But—"

"To his yacht?" asked Nash. He turned to Gabe. "We've been having it watched. It was moored at Dover two days ago." He turned back to the ambassador. "So was he going to his yacht in Dover?"

"I expect so," the ambassador said impatiently. "I shall complain to your government about this invasion—"

"Do that," said Gabe as he left. "And then explain why your houseguest kidnapped a seven-year-old child—the crown prince of Zindaria—from his bed in the middle of the night!"

"What do you mean, kidnapped a child? He can't possibly—" the ambassador began, but Gabe did not stay to listen. By the time the ambassador had finished his sentence Gabe was thundering down the road, riding as though the devil were after him.

But the devil was ahead. With a seven-year-old child in his power.

*T*he curricle pulled up outside the Esterhazy residence. Harry jumped down, peered at some marks on the pavement under the gas lamp, then swung himself back up into the curricle and snapped the reins.

"Where are we going now?" Callie asked.

"Dover."

"How do you know that's where they're going?"

He jerked his head at the pavement. "Rafe left a note in chalk. He always used to do that when we were in the army. Only time it fails is when it rains." He gave her a quick grin. "Good thing the weather has cleared up, isn't it?"

She nodded. "You think Nicky's going to die, don't you?"

"No!" He looked shocked. "What the hell are you thinking those kind of thoughts for? Stop it at once. Gabe will get him back."

"Do you really believe that?"

"Yes," he said simply. "Once Gabe sets his mind to something, there's no stopping him."

Harry put his arm around her to steady her as they swung sharply around the corner. "It will be better if you hold onto my arm from now on," he told her. "I'm going as fast as I can and if we hit a bump, you'll go flying unless you're anchored."

She slipped an arm through his and hung on. His solid warmth was comforting.

"You meant it, didn't you?" Harry asked after a time.

"Meant what?"

"What you said to Aunt Maude back there. That you love my brother."

"Of course I meant it."

"Even though he didn't protect Nicky?"

She turned a shocked face toward him. "It wasn't his fault. It was mine. I was the one who goaded Count Anton to—"

"Nonsense," Harry cut her off bluntly. "That job took a lot of planning. He had his plan in place long before you said a word to him. It wasn't you at all. But it was Gabe's job to protect Nicky and he botched it. And yet you still say you love him?"

Callie was shocked by his simplistic view of things. "Is that what you think Gabriel expects? That if he fails, I would stop loving him?"

"Of course."

"Well, I won't. What sort of a love is it that treats everything as a test? If he—if he fails, I will need him more than—" her voice broke.

Harry covered her hand with his and patted her. "Don't worry," he said gruffly. "He'll bring Nicky back to you."

"Yes, yes, I know he will," she said, trying to stay positive. She stared out into the black night and prayed for her son and the man she loved to be returned to her safe and sound.

She needed quite desperately to hold them in her arms and know they were safe. Both of them.

T he lights of London were behind Gabe now. The notorious Black Heath lay a short distance ahead. Footpads, highwaymen, all kinds of criminals lurked on the wild heathland, picking off coaches and lone travelers.

Gabe was some miles ahead of the others, thanks to Trojan's speed, stamina, and great heart. The others had been forced to make do with whatever horses were in Lady Gosforth's stables.

But even Trojan was tiring. Gabe would have to get a fresh horse soon, perhaps at Rochester, on the other side of the heath. There was a livery stable there, he recalled.

He pressed on. He had to catch up with them before the count reached the yacht. Once the yacht cast off, it was anyone's guess where he'd take Nicky. He couldn't believe the count had gone to all this trouble to return Nicky to Zindaria. All kinds of possibilities chased through Gabe's mind. The boy could be sold into slavery, put on the galleys, tossed overboard . . .

But the count would need a body before he could inherit the throne. Whatever he planned, it had to look natural. Was that his plan, return Nicky to Zindaria, let a few people see him, and then . . . another dose of poisoned milk? Dreadful as it seemed, the thought was almost reassuring. It would give Gabe more time to reach them.

He reached Black Heath but didn't slacken his pace. It was a fine, bright night and the road ahead was clear. The areas with scrubby vegetation were the danger spots. His pistols were primed and ready. If there were footpads, he would be ready for them.

Trojan was blowing hard, so Gabe slowed his pace to a fast trot. He glimpsed a movement up ahead. Gabe narrowed his eyes but the moon chose that moment to slip behind clouds. He pulled out a pistol and continued on his way, keeping a wary eye out.

He heard it before he saw it, one horse, coming fast, heading directly toward him. He pulled Trojan up to the side of the road, cocked his pistol, and waited.

The horse came closer and closer. Gabe frowned. He could hardly see the rider. He must be lying down along the horse's neck. Tricky devils, highwaymen.

The horse was almost upon him. Gabe lifted his pistol just as the moon came out. The moonlight glinted on its barrel.

"Mr. Renfrew, don't shoot!" a thin, high voice screamed. "It's me, Nicky. I escaped!"

Eighteen

"Nicky! Thank God!" Gabe was so relieved he simply leaned over, lifted the boy out of the saddle, and wrapped him in a big hug. Nicky hugged him back.

"Are you all right?" Gabe demanded. "How did you get away? I can't believe it!" He hugged the boy again. "Thank God."

Nicky grinned up at him. "I escaped."

"All by yourself?" He laughed and ruffled the boy's hair. "How did you manage that? No, wait." Gabe squinted into the darkness. "Is anyone following you?"

"Probably," Nicky said. "It will depend on how long it takes Count Anton to discover which way I went."

Gave laughed again at the frank triumph in the boy's voice, and the relish with which he repeated the word "escaped."

"Good lad! Come on then, let's get back. Tell me on the way. The others are behind us."

"Where's Mama?"

"Following in the curricle with Harry."

They turned and cantered back the way Gabe had just come. Trojan was tired, but gallant as ever.

When they met up with Rafe, Ethan, Luke, and Nash they all whooped with delight. They pelted Nicky with questions as they rode back to the inn, and Nicky happily answered them.

Gabe grinned, enjoying the boy's triumph. The rock in his chest had eased considerably now that the boy was safe. He was just waiting for the moment when he could put Nicky back in his mother's arms.

The way he felt, Count Anton could send an army after him. It would make no difference. Nicky was safe and they were going to keep him that way.

They found the inn and woke the landlord who, seeing the flash of gold coins, was only too happy to provide hospitality to a bunch of gentlemen. He chivvied his wife out of bed to see to the provision of food, rousted out a sleepy stable boy to care for the horses, and hurried back in to see to the drinks.

Luke and Ethan kept watch on the road outside.

"So, Nicky," Gabe said when they were inside. "Tell me again from the beginning and leave no detail out." There were aspects of the story that hadn't made sense to him, but he'd only got it in snatches. "The men who took you from your room, did they carry you over the rooftops?"

"No, they tied me up like a sack of potatoes, and they lowered me down in the back alley with ropes. I could see, but because of the gag, I couldn't yell out or anything."

Gabe nodded. "You were very brave. What happened next?"

"There was a carriage waiting, and they put me in that. It was dirty and smelled of onions. Then we went somewhere and the count came and he, he—" The little boy's lip trembled, but he mastered himself and went on. "He had a bottle of something nasty and he made me drink from it."

Gabriel swore under his breath.

"I thought it was poison, like he used on my puppy," Nicky continued. "And I fought, but there was nothing I could do. He forced it into my mouth, but I didn't swallow it. And then he lifted me into the curricle so I let it dribble down my front. He never saw. But I must have swallowed some, because I don't remember anything after that until I woke up and we were out in the country somewhere and my hands and feet weren't tied anymore, but I was still wrapped in the quilt. I felt sleepy and a bit sick, so I just lay on the seat and didn't move, not even when we stopped and the count checked me."

"They stopped to change horses, and the count went inside, and that's when I climbed out of the curricle. One of the soldiers saw me, but he only bowed and said how pleased he was I was free and coming home."

"He *what*?"

Nicky shrugged. "He wanted me to go into the inn to eat something, but I told him I needed to make water first. Well, I did."

"And he just let you go? By yourself?" Gabe exchanged glances with Nash and Rafe.

Nicky nodded. "Yes, and he went into the inn so I made water, and afterward I found the horses all saddled and waiting, so I untied them all. I kept one for me and set the others loose. I got on mine—it was a bit difficult without you to boost me, sir, but I managed and I rode at the other horses so that they ran off, and then I rode away."

Gabe frowned. "The soldier knew who you were?"

Nicky nodded. "Yes, he called me Prince Nikolai. But he didn't see me stealing the horse. I think he would have stopped me then."

Gabe was puzzled. The soldier ought have stopped Nicky as soon as he saw he was free. It didn't make sense. To go to all that trouble to kidnap the boy and then just let him walk away. It was crazy!

Nicky grinned. "Nobody expected me to be able to ride.

I heard the count yelling and swearing and screaming at everyone."

Gabe laughed at Nicky's expression. Far from being cowed by his adventure, he was positively crowing at his victory. And why not? He'd rescued himself in the best possible way.

But it was a very strange story. And Gabe was determined to get to the bottom of it.

The sound of horses outside drew his attention. He heard Rafe whistle and tensed, with a different sort of tension.

"Brace yourself, Nicky," he said, "Your mother is here." A moment later a small whirlwind in a large fur cloak flew in the door.

"Nicky, oh Nicky!" Callie exclaimed and hugged her son convulsively. She checked him all over. "Are you all right, my darling? They didn't hurt you?"

"No, Mama. I am perfectly splendid!"

She paused. "Perfectly splendid?" She stared at him, then shook her head. She gave a shaky laugh, wiped a tear away, and repeated, "Perfectly splendid?" She laughed again and hugged him. "How can you be perfectly splendid?"

"I am, Mama. I foiled Count Anton all by myself!"

"You did? But I thought—" She threw a puzzled glance at Gabe then turned back to her son and hugged him again. She drew him to a settee, saying, "Tell me all about it."

She'd turned away from him. Gabe had expected it, but it didn't make it any easier. He watched the joyful reunion between mother and son. She was like a bear or a wolf in defense of her cub. She would have killed for him.

He'd promised to protect her child and he'd failed. So she turned her back on him. Perhaps, if he'd rescued the boy in some heroic fashion . . . but Nicky had done it all by himself.

And Gabe couldn't regret that—he was proud of the lad, as proud as if Nicky were his own son. The boy had shown courage, initiative, and endurance. He'd dealt with a thoroughly nasty situation with a marvelously cool head. And he wasn't an experienced rider. To tackle a long ride in the dark, alone and on an unknown horse, was a feat to celebrate.

Harry had come in behind her. He and Gabe watched Nicky telling his mother about his adventure, then exchanged glances. Gabe couldn't stand to see the pity in his brother's eyes. Harry knew how Gabe felt about her. There was a narrow balcony that ran the length of the inn, and Gabe took himself out onto it to watch for Count Anton. He wouldn't be caught off guard again.

Count Anton would be desperate now, with witnesses to his perfidy. He had nothing left to lose. And desperate men did desperate things.

A shrill whistle from below came a few minutes later. He interrupted Nicky's story. "They're coming," he said. He couldn't quite look her in the eye. "Go out on the balcony, please. If there is a fight, I need you both to be out of harm's way."

She didn't look very happy about it, but she nodded and moved outside, taking Nicky. She wrapped them both in the large fur cloak, just as Ethan, Luke, Rafe, and Nash arrived and took up a defensive stance.

A few minutes later Count Anton, accompanied by half a dozen men in uniform, stormed into the inn.

"Where is the prince?" Count Anton scanned the room.

"Safe," Gabe told him.

The count sneered. "Give him up. He belongs to us. You are outnumbered."

"I think not," Gabe snarled. He'd lost almost everything he'd cared about tonight and this man was the cause of it.

The count glanced at the sword Gabe was wearing. "We shall see if you can fight like gentlemen." He gave an order and the soldiers drew their swords. Gabe and the others did likewise.

"Stop this at once!" Callie stepped into the room. Nicky followed.

Instantly the soldiers bowed. "Princess Caroline," their captain said. "You are safe."

"Get back outside," Gabe told her furiously. "Dammit, woman, will you learn to follow orders for once in your life!"

"Do not use that tone of voice with the princess, swine!" the captain of the soldiers roared.

"I will use any damned tone I like if it will keep her safe! Now for the last time, Callie, get out of here. This is going to get ugly!"

"I won't have any more fighting," she ordered. "I don't want you hurt! I don't want anyone hurt." She looked at Count Anton. "Except him."

She pulled out the pistol and pointed it at Count Anton.

With a roar of exasperation, Gabe snatched the pistol from her. "If anyone is going to kill that devil, it will be me," he told her furiously. "Now get outside before one of these idiots hurts you."

She gave him an angry look and stepped back, pushing Nicky behind her. But she still didn't go outside. Gabe glared at her.

"Princess, did this thug hurt you?" the captain of the soldiers demanded.

She frowned at him. "Of course he didn't. You are Captain Kordovski, are you not? I cannot believe that a captain of the Royal Zindarian Guard is involved in such filthy business as this."

"What filthy business, Highness? We have come to rescue you." The captain glared at Gabe.

Gabe glared back. "Will you stop bandying words with this bandit and get back outside!" he told her.

She ignored Gabe and gave the captain a puzzled look. "Rescue me from whom?"

The captain looked at Gabe and then back at Callie. "I

thought—is that thug not the enemy who stole you away?" he said doubtfully and looked to the count as if for confirmation.

"Enough of this nonsense," the count said and lunged at Gabe with his sword.

"Callie, Nicky, get the hell outside! The rest of you, stay back," Gabe warned as he parried the count's thrust. Count Anton was a skilled swordsman with a stylish manner, but Gabe had been fighting for his life for eight years: there was no comparison.

Gabe thrust and at the same time twisted his blade. It slashed into Count Anton's left shoulder and blood blossomed through his coat. He snarled and thrust wildly back at Gabe and with a flick of the wrist, Gabe sent the count's blade spinning out of his hand and across the floor. Harry clamped a boot on it and the fight was over.

The count stood panting, staring at Gabe with flat malevolence. "Kill them all!" he ordered the guards.

"Sheathe your swords," Captain Kordovski ordered, and the guards sheathed their swords.

The count swore viciously.

"That's enough," Gabe snapped. "Were it not for the presence of this lady and her child I would butcher you where you stand. As it is I'll be glad to see you dance at the end of a rope."

"You can't touch me," the count snarled.

"Nash, you're the diplomat, what say you? Surely a member of a foreign royal family cannot be immune from prosecution for arson, kidnapping, and attempted murder?"

"What are you talking about?" Captain Kordovski demanded belligerently. "Arson? What arson? And as for kidnapping—you are a fine one to talk, you, who stole our prince and princess from us. And as for attempted murder, we are all witness to the fact that it was a fair fight."

"What are *you* talking about?" Callie stepped forward. "Nobody stole me. But he—" She pointed at Count Anton, who sat nursing his wound. "He stole my son from his bed last night as he slept."

"His agents did," Captain Kordovski corrected her. "He organized the rescue attempt to save the prince from the fiend who was holding him prisoner." He glared at Gabe.

Suddenly it was clear to Gabe. The count's so-called agents—he'd wager the original plan had been for them to assassinate Nicky. Planned for the night of the party, when everyone would be distracted and the count himself would be downstairs innocently hobnobbing with the highest born collection of witnesses in the land.

Then Captain Kordovski and his Royal Guards arrived on the scene and the assassination had to be turned into a rescue attempt.

"Stop calling him a fiend!" Callie snapped. "He is my husband. My beloved husband."

Gabe blinked. What had she just called him? *Beloved?*

"And he wasn't holding anyone prisoner, or hidden away. Nicky was peacefully asleep, and Gabriel was downstairs dancing with me at the party to celebrate our wedding."

Captain Kordovski's jaw dropped. "What? I don't understand."

"Neither do I," Callie said.

Neither did Gabe. Had she really called him her beloved husband? And if so, did she mean it, or was it just to calm that captain fellow?

"I do," an unexpected voice said. Nicky stepped forward and pointed at the count. "*He* told you we were prisoners of Mr. Renfrew, didn't he? And *he* told you that Mr. Renfrew was responsible for us fleeing Zindaria."

"Fleeing?" Captain Kordovski repeated. "You were stolen."

"No, Mama and I fled because *he*"—he pointed again at the count—"was trying to kill me and nobody would believe Mama." Nicky looked at Captain Kordovski. "That's why you didn't stop me back then, isn't it? You weren't holding me prisoner, you thought you were rescuing me."

Captain Kordovski nodded, a grim look in his eye.

Nicky grinned. "And because *he*"—he stabbed his finger at the count for the third time, this one with glee—"didn't know I could ride I was able to steal a horse and get away."

The count glowered at the small boy. "You should have been drowned at birth, a twisted little weakling like you," he snarled.

"Weakling enough to outwit you," Nicky crowed, undaunted.

And Callie saw . . . In that tiny spilt second as Nicky crowed, she saw the expression on the count's face change. She saw his hand move . . .

"No!"

She wasn't close enough. Gabe was between her and Nicky, and Ethan was too far to reach. She was too far away. She caught the glint of the pistol rising, pointing straight at Nicky's heart, and she knew . . . she knew . . .

"No!"

Afterward she wasn't sure whether she'd screamed or not. It must have been only for that one spilt second that he aimed the pistol but it seemed an eternity, a nightmare that went on and on and on.

She couldn't reach. She couldn't . . .

But Ethan—Ethan saw and launched himself through the air, throwing himself between the count's gun and her son. Gabe was behind Ethan. She couldn't see . . . She couldn't see . . .

"Nicky!"

The sound of the pistol shot cut across her scream, breaking it off, causing her to catch her breath in horror. And then, before she could see, before she could even react, another shot slammed into the stillness . . .

He was before her. Gabe was before her . . . What . . . what . . .

In Gabe's hand was a pistol, cold and gray, lethal, aiming straight before him.

And now she could see. The count sagged where he stood. A bloodred bloom was spreading over his waistcoat. His eyes were wide, astounded, as if he'd been caught unawares . . . His hand lifted and then fell. His gun clattered to the floor . . .

There'd been two shots. Two!

"Nicky," Callie screamed again and tried to shove Gabe aside. He caught her as he'd catch a child and held her.

"Let me . . ."

"Ethan," Gabe said urgently and set her aside. She grabbed Nicky, hauled him to her, hugged as if she'd never let him go.

"Did he hit you? Oh God, Nicky, did he hit you?"

"Mama, no . . . Mama, Mr. Delaney . . ."

She stared down at Nicky, unable to believe he was really unhurt. But there was nothing. No blood. No hurt.

Mr. Delaney . . .

Finally she dared look at the other players in this horror.

The count's still form lay crumpled over the gun, his eyes staring lifelessly up at the ceiling.

Count Anton was dead. *Dead.* It was over at last. Nicky was alive and Count Anton was dead. And Gabriel was alive.

And Ethan . . .

"Damn, I wasn't fast enough," Gabe was saying, pushing his friend into an armchair and examining his arm in concern. "Damned hero . . ."

"Just winged me in the shoulder, sir," Ethan gasped. "Nothin' serious."

"Mr. Delaney, you saved my son's life," Callie managed, even now unable to believe the nightmare was past.

"How can I ever thank you?" Somehow she forced herself to let Nicky go.

Averting her gaze from the count's lifeless form, she stepped forward and tried to see the damage. "Here . . . here, let me help you." She pulled out a tiny lace handkerchief and began to mop up blood. It was completely ineffectual. The blood oozed from between her fingers.

"I'll be fine, ma'am," Ethan said, looking an entreaty up at Gabe.

"He'll be fine," Gabe reiterated, gently moving her aside. "It's not even hit muscle by the look of things. Winged is what he's been. What we need is a pad." He cast a look of distaste at the floor, at the count. "Callie, my dear, fetch the landlord. We need to get rid of this offal and we need some clean rags."

"I need to help Eth—" she started.

"You need to take care of your son," he told her. "You need to hug him and get him out of here while we clean up. This is no place for you and the child. I'll take care of Ethan. You hug Nicky—and Nicky, you hug your mother."

She gave Nicky a hug then released him. "Gabriel, this blood was shed because of me and my child, so give me your handkerchief and let me do what I must," she told him.

Reading the determination in her eyes, he handed her his handkerchief. She knelt and pressed it to Ethan's wound. "I'm not the least bit bothered by blood," she informed Gabriel.

"So I see," Gabriel stood back, a faint smile on his face. "That will teach you to be a hero," he told Ethan.

The landlord, having heard the shots, burst into the room.

"Ah, landlord, some brandy, please, and a quantity of clean linen," Callie ordered over her shoulder.

"Were that a gunshot? In my inn?" the man demanded. He saw the count's body on the floor and recoiled. "Is he— is that—?"

"Yes, there is a dead body, but don't worry, Captain Kordovski will remove it, won't you, Captain?"

"Y-yes, of course, Princess." Captain Kordovski was still in shock at the count's blatant attempt on the crown prince's life.

The landlord's eyes bulged. *"Princess?"*

"Yes?" Callie responded. "Landlord, the brandy? The clean linen? Make haste, if you please. There is a man bleeding here!"

"Yes, Yer Royal 'Ighness." The landlord bowed deeply and hurried off.

*L*ater Captain Kordovski explained. The day after Princess Caroline and Prince Nikolai had disappeared Count Zabor—no, uncle Otto was not dead—had officially frozen all of Count Anton's property and assets pending an inquiry into the prince and princess's disappearance. He'd accused Count Anton of murder, but Count Anton had claimed their disappearance had nothing to do with him, and that the princess and her son had been stolen by enemies of Zindaria.

"But you weren't stolen, were you, Princess?" Captain Kordovski finished. "Not by this man or any other."

"No," she told him. "Mr. Renfrew never stole me, nobody did. But he has saved me and my son, over and over, and I married him of my own free will."

Every generous word was like a knife in Gabe's heart. He hadn't saved anyone. And he'd blackmailed her into marrying him under the guise of protecting her son. And then failed to do it.

Captain Kordovski continued, "Count Anton left Zindaria, insisting he could find the prince and princess. He vowed to get them back, safe and sound."

"I suppose it was that or become a pauper and a pariah in his own country," Nash interjected.

"Yes, that is true," the captain agreed. "But now I think maybe Count Zabor did not trust him, for he sent myself and the Royal Guards after Count Anton to ensure the safety of the prince and princess." He glanced at the princess and said stiffly, "He knew I would die before I let harm come to either of them."

Callie nodded. "I know that, Captain. I wouldn't have come into this room otherwise." She gave Gabe a speaking look.

"Were you at Tibby's cottage?" Ethan said in a cold voice.

Captain Kordovski raised a brow. "Where do you mean?"

"At Lulworth. Little white cottage, covered in roses."

Captain Kordovski shook his head. "No, we only met up with the count in London two days ago. It took us several days to discover he'd sailed to England, but we traced him through embassy connections, and from there to the home of the Austrian ambassador, Prince Esterhazy."

Ethan grunted.

Gabe nodded. It was as he thought. The captain's arrival had saved Nicky. Nothing else. Nobody else.

"We shall convey the count's body back to Zindaria," Captain Kordovski told Callie. "It is the correct thing to do. No matter what he has done, he belongs in Zindaria."

Callie nodded. "Yes, you are right."

"And you, Princess, you belong in Zindaria, too, you and Prince Nikolai." Captain Kordovski hesitated, then said, "You are much beloved in Zindaria, Princess."

"Me? You mean Nicky."

He shook his head. "They don't know Prince Nikolai—he has never made any public appearances."

Callie nodded. Rupert was ashamed of Nicky's limp.

Captain Kordovski continued. "I am sure they will come to love Prince Nikolai, but you, Princess—you are very special to us. Zindaria has never had a princess so much loved by the people."

"Me?" Callie was amazed.

"The whole country is in mourning at your loss."

"For me?" Callie couldn't believe it. "But it was Rupert they loved. I saw it whenever I went out in public with him. The people always cheered and waved and some threw flowers."

Captain Kordovski shook his head. "It was for you, Princess, only for you. Prince Rupert was greatly respected, but he was never loved, not like you. And that is why we need you, as well as Prince Nikolai, back in Zindaria."

All the Royal Guards bowed and clicked their heels and gave her speaking looks to show their agreement.

Callie smiled mistily at them all. She'd had no idea. She still could not quite believe it, but one thing was clear, she had no choice. She had to go back. "Thank you. We will return soon, I promise." She did not look at Gabe.

The stone in Gabe's chest turned to lead. She was leaving him.

*T*hey returned to London a lot more slowly than they'd left. Partly that was due to the inferior quality of the horses they'd hired, but also everyone was tired. It was just on dawn.

To Callie's great disappointment, Harry drove her and Nicky back in the curricle. She had thought, hoped, that Gabriel would have, but he'd been withdrawn and kept himself away from her, organizing horses and men and paying the innkeeper. And ordering his brother to drive them home.

"Will you really return to Zindaria?" Harry asked her after a while. Nicky was asleep, his head in Callie's lap, both of them wrapped in the fur cloak.

"I have to," she said. "Nicky is the crown prince. His future is there."

"And what of Gabe?"

She sighed. "I don't know. I don't know what he wants anymore."

"What do you mean?"

"He barely even looked at me just now. All that time in that horrid little inn, he didn't so much as touch me or even come near me."

Harry frowned. "But you know why. I told you before."

She was bewildered. "No, I don't know why!"

"He failed you. He expects you to be disappointed in him."

"But why? Nicky is safe. It's all all right now."

"Yes, but Gabe lost him in the first place, and then he didn't rescue him."

Callie stared at him in disbelief. "You can't possibly mean that! That's ridiculous. As if I would hold that against him. I don't care how Nicky was rescued, I only care that he's safe." She smoothed her hand over her son's sleeping body as she spoke. "Not that it would have made any difference to how I feel about Gabriel anyway. As I said, love is not a series of tests."

"You really do love him, don't you?"

"Yes, of course. And why do you keep asking me that? Is it so hard to believe? Gabriel is a very lovable man." She sighed. "He's a wonderful man." And she didn't know how she was ever going to be able to live without him.

Harry gave her a searching look. "I used to think you were using my brother for your own ends."

"I was. I am," she said guiltily. Love was an end, wasn't it?

His face softened. "Yes, but you do love him. It makes all the difference. I don't want to see him get hurt. Women can do terrible things to a man."

"Men can do them to women, too," she said.

"Maybe, but Gabe's not one to lay himself open to a woman—he's always been careful. He's kept himself protected, ever since he was a boy and his bitch of a mother dumped him."

"His mother dumped him?"

He nodded. "Used him as a pawn in the games she played with our father. Kept him locked upstairs in that house you've been staying in, hidden away, as if he didn't exist. Seven years he was up there and never once saw his father or the other brothers, or their country home, not for Christmas or Easter or anything. And he was legitimate."

He paused to negotiate a narrow passage between a stationary wagon and a pile of boxes. "The old lady, Great-aunt Gert took him away and his mother didn't care in the least. Never even visited him. He never saw her again."

Callie was horrified. It was worse than being orphaned.

"He told me about Great-aunt Gert. She sounds like a wonderful lady."

Harry snorted. "She was all right, but she was nobody's idea of a mother, either. Treated both of us like the dogs she bred. Tough, strict, and very demanding. A right old tartar she was; fair, but not the sort to give a little boy a hug."

"So who gave Gabriel hugs?" Callie asked, her heart moved by the thought of the little boy whose mother didn't want him.

"Nobody," Harry said.

"You must both have been very lonely," she said, stroking her son's hair as he slept.

"I was all right. Mrs. Barrow took me in as her own, but though she was fond of Gabe, she never dared to treat him as her own. Great-aunt Gert wouldn't have had it. 'Twas all right for the cook to cuddle an orphaned bastard like me occasionally, but mollycoddle a legitimate son of the house of Renfrew? Not in her lifetime."

"Then I shall just have to make up for all the hugs he missed out on," Callie said. "If he'll let me, that is." She watched dawn rising over London. She and Nicky would have to return to Zindaria soon. She hoped it wouldn't be alone.

But she didn't feel at all sure of that.

First she had to tell her husband that she loved him.

Then she had to find out if he loved her at all.

And then if he would give up everything he had for her.

It was too much to ask, she knew. But she had no choice.

And at the very least, she was going to have one more night with him. One more night of love.

*T*he household was still awake when they got back. Nobody had been able to sleep for worrying. Everyone piled into the drawing room and once again, Nicky described his kidnapping and escape, and everyone exclaimed and expressed amazement and horror in equal amounts.

Callie sat wearily, watching her son in his hour of glory. She'd had no sleep and was exhausted and, despite her relief and joy in her son's triumph, she was also dispirited. Gabriel hadn't said a word to her. He hadn't even looked at her since she'd promised the captain she would return to Zindaria.

He'd positioned himself at the far side of the room, saying nothing, just watching. Whenever she looked at him he was looking elsewhere, at Nicky, at Rafe or Nash—anywhere except at her. She could see part of his face in the looking glass hung on the far wall. She shifted her position until she could see his whole face and his expression.

He was watching her, she saw. If she turned her head, he looked away, but the moment she turned away from him he was watching her again.

He watched her sadly, hungrily, as if gazing at something he couldn't have, some fond memory.

Callie sighed. Harry was right. Gabriel seemed to believe her love was conditional on his having prevented Nicky's kidnapping. The dear, foolish man. She would put him right on that. Right after she told him she loved him.

Nothing ventured, nothing gained.

"Come along, Nicky," she said, rising. "It's time you went to bed. Time we all got some sleep."

Nicky's face fell. "But, Mama, it's morning. The sun is up."

"No argument, my love. You've had a big adventure but even heroes need some sleep."

"Yes, Mama," the hero of the hour said dolefully.

G abe took himself out onto the terrace with a brandy. Everyone else had gone off to bed. He was too depressed to sleep.

A few moments later he jumped as his wife's soft arms slid around his waist. She hugged him hard. "Thank you," she said.

"I didn't do anything," he muttered. "Nicky rescued himself. I merely bumped into him on the road."

"On the contrary, you taught him how to ride, and thus gave him the means to effect his own escape, which is a thousand times better than being rescued—or have you not noticed that my son is currently standing ten feet tall?" She hugged him again.

"It's my fault he was kidnapped in the first place."

"How interesting you should say so. I thought it was all my fault, but Harry put me right. And I am very sure Tibby and Ethan have been blaming themselves, and Lady Gosforth, too, no doubt, so we could all have a competition for the blame. Or we can all simply rejoice that we have my son back."

"It was my responsibility."

"It was our responsibility. But we thought we were defending Nicky by legal means—who would have guessed that the count would send his men over the rooftops in the middle of a party?"

"I should have."

"I see, well, if you prefer kicking yourself and being

gloomy to kissing me, I will just have to find someone else to kiss."

"What?" Gabe's head jerked around.

"I have been needing to be kissed and hugged for several hours now, and if you're not interested—"

"You mean—?"

The most adorable mouth in the world pouted. "Gabriel Renfrew, what do you think I mean?"

He wasn't going to question his luck. He snatched her up and kissed her, hard and possessively. With some difficulty, for her skirt was quite narrow, she wrapped her legs around him and kissed him back, holding on tight to him with every part of her, pressing her softness against him and covering his face with moist, enthusiastic, passionate kisses.

"Take me to bed, Gabriel. I need you to take me to bed."

Gabe could hardly believe it. He'd been given a second chance. He wasn't going to waste it.

He carried her upstairs to the bedchamber he'd been allotted when they first arrived. His aunt Maude had arranged for their things to be brought back from his brother's house and placed there. She knew that Callie would not be willing to be parted from her son again.

Gabe had not expected to sleep there, or if he did, he knew he would sleep there alone. He hadn't dreamed he would get another night with her.

Nineteen

*H*e drew the curtains so that the morning light came through them in a faint golden glow and removed her clothes slowly, one by one, kissing each inch of skin as he bared it.

She removed his clothes much less slowly, pushing his coat impatiently down his arms, unbuttoning his waistcoat with quick, nimble fingers and dragging his shirt off over his head.

"Slow down," he murmured. "We have all day."

"And more," she said.

"Yes, and all night," he agreed, planting kisses across the upper slopes of her breasts. He caressed her breasts, cupping them with his hands, feeling the firm thrust of two hard little nubs even through the layers of fabric. He kissed them, nipping them gently through the fabric with his teeth.

"Now turn, my love, and let me deal with these laces and free these poor, imprisoned beauties."

She turned, presenting him with the lovely line of her nape. He kissed it and loosened her hair, tossing pins aside impatiently and nuzzling her neck, enjoying the taste of her skin and the perfume of her silky hair as it fell, surrounding him.

He unlaced her corset with practiced skill, and she gave a big sigh of pleasure as it opened. He tossed it aside and slipped his hands around her and caressed her breasts through her fine cambric chemise.

"Oh, that feels lovely," she said with a shiver. "Somehow whenever it's you who takes off my corset, I seem to get a little dizzy."

"Ah, that's my special technique," he growled against the skin of her neck.

"So much nicer than when a maid does it." She gave an appreciative sigh, turned in the circle of his arms, wrapped her arms around his neck and kissed him full on the mouth.

He would gladly unlace her corsets for the rest of his life. But he didn't dare suggest such a thing. One night, one day at a time. He had to win her trust back. He'd let her down badly, he couldn't press her for anything more than what she was offering right now.

His blood hammered through his veins as he kissed her and held her, relishing her sweet, unique taste, the warmth and generosity of her.

Her fingers tangled in his hair, her eyes half closed as she leaned into him, her warm, soft body pressing against him, her hips moving with slow, erotic rhythm as her tongue moved with his.

He cupped her head in his hand and controlled the kiss, angling his head to fit her seamlessly, mouth to mouth, one breath, stroking the tender skin on the underside of her jaw.

He couldn't give her up. He had to know. "Tell me about Zindaria," he murmured.

She stiffened. It was the wrong thing to say. His lips covered hers before she could respond, reminding her of what he could give her, knowing that it would not be enough, but he was desperate. He could not, would not let her go.

He slid his hands down her body in a fevered need to have her naked. With one movement he lifted the chemise over her head. And stared.

"Drawers?" She hadn't worn any before. These were pink. With lace. He'd never seen pink drawers before.

"They're very fashionable," she told him, blushing.

"They're very inconvenient," he said.

"What's sauce for the goose . . ." she said and rubbed her palm over the front flap of his buckskin breeches. She smiled, apparently pleased with his response.

He groaned. As her fingers fumbled with the fastening of his breeches his plans for a slow seduction flew out the window. Reluctantly he let her go. "You deal with those things and I'll see to the boots and breeches," he gasped.

She had the damned pink drawers off in one swift action. She stood there, watching him, a small feminine smile on her face as he dragged off the boots and breeches almost in one movement.

She was beautiful. He needed to be inside her.

He lifted her onto the bed. She fell back, pulling him with her. Her legs opened to him naturally and he settled himself between her thighs, savoring the satiny feel of her skin against his, the firm give of her flesh.

He suckled her breasts until she was moaning and thrashing with need. "Now," she told him, "now!"

"Soon," he murmured. He slid his fingers into the sweet triangle of dark hair, feeling her dark liquid heat, smelling the aroused female scent of her, knowing with fierce masculine triumph that she wanted him as much as he wanted her.

He caressed her to peak after peak of shuddering pleasure until she was boneless and whimpering with pleasure, stroking his body with soft, feverish hands, and kissing any part of him she could find.

Then and only then he entered her, groaning at the sweet,

hot fit of her. She moaned in response, clutching him to her, gasping, "Yes, yes, yes," as he thrust and thrust in a wild, hard rhythm that drove them higher and higher until at last they spiraled over the edge into ecstasy and nothingness.

He held her then, as together they floated.

After a long time, she said, "I really wanted to be the one to shoot the count. Why did you stop me?"

"It would have eaten at you later," he told her. "You've never killed a man. You don't know."

She turned against him and, propping her chin on his chest, contemplated his face. "I imagine you've had to kill a lot of men," she said softly. "Does it eat at you?"

"Not anymore," he told her. "But the first one did for a long time. And for you, with your soft heart, it would have been much worse."

She hugged him and kissed his chest. "Tell me."

He shook his head. "There's nothing to tell. He was a soldier, about the same age as me."

"And how old were you?"

"Nineteen." To this day Gabe would never forget the look in the other boy's face when he realized he was dying, actually dying. He wouldn't wish that on anyone, especially not her. Not even for a man she hated.

She said nothing, just hugged him tightly. Eventually she said, "It's hard to believe there's nothing to worry about anymore. It's all over."

"Yes." Nothing to worry about? Gabe didn't agree.

"You know I must return with Nicky to Zindaria, now."

Yes, Gabe realized that.

"And I will ask Jim to come, to be Nicky's companion, to be like a brother to him, because it is important my son have a friend to whom he is just Nicky, not 'the prince.' And because Jim needs a family."

Gabe nodded.

"And I am going to ask Tibby to come with me, too, to be my secretary."

Still Gabe said nothing.

"And—and I thought perhaps Ethan would come, for a while, at least. There are some very fast horses in Zindaria . . . and perhaps he and Tibby . . ."

He shook his head. "I doubt it."

She sighed, then gave him an anxious look. "But more than anything I need to know . . . what are your plans, Gabriel?"

"I'm not sure." For once Gabe wasn't sure what she was thinking. He had to know.

"I thought you were going to work with Harry on your horse-breeding project," she said.

"Harry doesn't need me for that. It was always his idea, his project. It's his dream. And Ethan's."

"And what about the Grange? It's your home. There are people there dependent on you."

He shook his head. "I spent eight years away, and they managed perfectly well without me. In any case, Harry will probably manage the Grange, at least until he gets his own place."

He added, "I was always restless there. I didn't know what I wanted."

"And do you know what you want now?"

"I do." He waited for her to ask what it was.

She waited, looking at him expectantly. He couldn't speak. He had to know, first, what he was up against.

The silence stretched.

She slipped out of bed and, naked, padded to the chest of drawers and pulled out her red shawl. She wrapped herself in it, covering herself, just barely.

He sat up in the bed. "What are you doing?"

"There is something I have to say to you, Gabriel," she told him. "And I can't say it like this. Not when I'm naked. Or touching you."

She was an utterly enticing sight but Gabe watched her with a cold feeling of dread. She looked to his eyes very much like a woman on the verge of a difficult decision. She was going to give him his marching orders.

If she thought she was going to thank him for his most inadequate protection services and dismiss him, she had another think coming.

He deserved to be dismissed, he knew. She'd married him for protection and he'd failed her. And now Count Anton was dead, she didn't need Gabe anymore, not even as a convenient husband.

He watched her pacing back and forward in that damned red shawl, inadequately covered, deliciously revealed, her bottom peeping out with every step she took.

She might miss him in the bedroom, he supposed, but men would be queuing up to be her lover. She was too sensual, too obviously delectable not to have them fighting for her favors.

Over his dead body.

All Gabe had were his legal rights as a husband and by God, if that's what it took, he'd resort to that.

She paced restlessly back and forth beside the bed, her brow furrowed, chewing her lip, driving him wild, even as she drove him to the edge of despair.

She turned and said in a rush, "The thing is, Gabriel, you made a commitment in front of witnesses and God and I don't think it's right that you want to wriggle out of it. I know you have a family here in England, and a home, and friends—very good friends. There are hundreds of people here who love you but—"

Gabe felt a sudden surge of hope. Was she heading where he thought she was? "How many hundred?"

"Don't tease me, I'm serious. I know you have a whole world full of people in England who care about you, and in Zindaria you would only have—" she broke off.

"In Zindaria I would only have—?" he prompted.

"Me."

"You?"

She nodded. "I haven't said this to you and I should have. I was going to tell you the night of the party but—"

"I know," he said ruefully. He'd failed her.

"Yes, and with so much happening and then you were being so strange—"

"I was being strange?"

"Yes, very. You wouldn't even talk to me or look at me or touch me and it was terrible, just terrible. So there just didn't seem to be the right moment."

"Is there ever a right moment?"

"Yes, I have to say it now, otherwise I will regret it all my life. I may—never mind." She closed her eyes and told him, "I love you, Gabriel Renfrew, and I want you and need you to stay on as my husband, my real husband, and go to Zindaria with me, and grow old with me."

There was a long silence. Gabriel felt as though he'd been hit by a falling tree. If a falling tree could make you want to shout and sing and dance.

He slipped out of bed and moved until he was close enough to smell her, close enough to see each individual eyelash fanned out across her pale satiny cheek, but not close enough to touch her. If he touched her, he wouldn't trust himself to be able to speak. And the words needed to be said.

"Why are you saying all this with your eyes closed?" he asked gently.

"Because I'm a coward." Her eyes were still shut tight.

"No, you're not."

"I am. I'm scared to look, scared to ask. In case it's no."

"Open your eyes."

She cautiously opened them, bracing herself for whatever he might say.

He smiled, crookedly, and said the words he'd had locked in his heart for so long. "I fell in love with you the first time I met you, when you were standing on a cliff top, wet, tired, angry, frightened, and beautiful. I've fallen more in love with you every day I've known you, and I can't imagine that ever changing."

Her eyes shimmered with tears. "Oh, Gabriel, is that really true?"

"It is, my dearest love." He cupped her face in his hands. "I have a house, a family, friends, and fortune in England, it's true, but everything I want is right here in my hands. Everything. You are my home, my family, my purpose, and my heart." And then he kissed her.

"Provocative, tantalizing, and
wonderfully witty romantic fiction."
—*Heartstring Reviews*

Look for the next book in the
Devil Riders series by Anne Gracie

His Captive Lady

Now available from Berkley Sensation!

Enter the rich world of
historical romance
with Berkley Books.

Lynn Kurland

Patricia Potter

Betina Krahn

Jodi Thomas

Anne Gracie

Love is timeless.
penguin.com